Prisoner of War

Prisoner of War

Shane Lee

XULON ELITE

Xulon Press Elite
2301 Lucien Way #415
Maitland, FL 32751
407.339.4217
www.xulonpress.com

© 2022 by Shane Lee

All rights reserved solely by the author. The author guarantees all contents are original and do not infringe upon the legal rights of any other person or work. No part of this book may be reproduced in any form without the permission of the author. The views expressed in this book are not necessarily those of the publisher.

Due to the changing nature of the Internet, if there are any web addresses, links, or URLs included in this manuscript, these may have been altered and may no longer be accessible. The views and opinions shared in this book belong solely to the author and do not necessarily reflect those of the publisher. The publisher, therefore, disclaims responsibility for the views or opinions expressed within the work.

Paperback ISBN-13: 978-1-66285-995-3
Ebook ISBN-13: 978-1-66285-996-0

Acknowledgments

I would like to thank the following people for making this book possible.

To Dr Patrick Kee, dedicated physician, loving grandfather of my children and an author in his own right, who sent me details of the short story competition that kicked off this whole project. Thank you. None of this would have even started without you.

To Randy Surles and Laura Graves, my editors who took one look at my first draft and gently but firmly steered me away from the train wreck this book would otherwise have become. To be clear, they never got a chance to see anything after that, so while whatever works in this book is a credit to them, whatever *doesn't* is likely where I stubbornly decided to ignore their advice.

Thank you for your professional insights, and even more for your tough love and honesty.

To Manfred Hertenberger, my neighbor and friend who just happened to be a native German speaker and kindly reviewed the language for me. Any German that works linguistically in the story is a credit to him. Anything that doesn't is something I didn't check with him. Thank for your help in this. In such matters, a single person who cares is more valuable than the entire internet.

To Pastor Paul Choo, who gave me crucial advice at a critical time which could be best summarized as, "Just get on with it." Thank you for your simple and brutally direct support.

Lastly, to my dear wife Sharon. At one point, I swore I would *not* put her in the acknowledgements section of this book, so frustrated and angry was I. She just smiled benignly and carried on. Thank you for bearing the brunt of my self-pity through all this. Thank you that you are *not* like me and can live life on life's terms without too much drama. Thank you for loving me all this time. I love you.

This book is dedicated to alcoholics and
addicts all over the world who are still looking for
their Higher Power.

It *could* be the God you've been running from all along.
Stop fighting and let Him find you.

Prologue

1930—Berlin

He smashed his fist into his wife's head, and she crumpled to the floor.

This time, she did not get up.

Swaying unsteadily, he took another swig of the bottle.

That will show her, he thought darkly to himself.

A stifled whimper from the kitchen told him his son was probably watching, but he was too tired to chase the boy.

Probably hiding again. Such a coward.

His mother is to blame. Yes, it's all her fault he's such a coward. She always hides him or tells him to run. Or gets in my way when I'm trying to whip him.

Can't she see she's spoiling him? How is he going to be a man when all he learns is to run and hide?

He finished the bottle's contents and placed it heavily on a stack of bills marked "Unpaid" and "Final Notice". The wall lamp flickered, and a glint of light caught his attention, drawing his eye to a precious glass-covered frame. He picked it up and looked at the photo inside.

It showed four young men in full German Army uniform standing proudly in front of a Bergmann MG 15nA light machine gun. Each had signed their names under themselves. Haunted, bleary eyes drifted to the words "Karlsen Wagner".

Above them, a younger version of himself looked at him almost mockingly.

He glared back at it with hatred.

"I'm sorry, my brothers, for my failure," he whispered. "Better to have died than surrendered that day."

Tears of regret and shame sprang to his eyes, and he stifled a sob.

Unable to tolerate the crushing darkness in his chest, he reflexively reached for the bottle and found it empty. Cursing angrily, he smashed it into the wall and kicked his fallen wife in frustration.

When she didn't respond, he stood back and readied himself to kick her harder until she did.

A frightened yell and a blur of movement distracted him, and he spun round in time to see the back of a frying pan moving toward his face at great speed.

He turned instinctively, and it bounced harmlessly off his shoulder.

Blinking, he stared in amazement as his ten-year-old son stood protectively in front of his mother, holding the frying pan like a weapon. His teeth were chattering, and his blond hair was plastered over his forehead with sweat. Startlingly blue eyes were opened wide in confusion, anger, and fear. His tiny hands grasped the pan's handle so tightly that they were white and shaking.

Karlsen swatted the pan aside and slapped the boy angrily.

The pan dropped, and the boy started crying.

Then Karlsen's rage at being attacked was quickly overtaken by his shame at the sight of his son cowering before him.

"Pick up that pan and fight me," he said through gritted teeth.

His son shook his head vigorously, which only deepened Karlsen's disgust.

He picked up the pan and held the handle toward his son. Under his fierce glare, the boy tentatively took the pan with trembling hands.

"Now, try and hit me," Karlsen said.

His son didn't move.

"HIT MEEEEEEE!" screamed Karlsen suddenly, and the boy jumped and swung the pan.

Karlsen effortlessly blocked the blow with one hand and struck out with the other, leaving his son on the floor in a daze.

"Get up," Karlsen snarled, "GET UP!"

The boy stood up shakily and picked up the pan.

"You hit like a girl," Karlsen shouted, "Hit hard like a man!"

His son swung again, and once more, Karlsen blocked the blow and struck him.

The boy went down and stayed down, whimpering.

Incensed now at the display of weakness, Karlsen loomed over his son and screamed, "Are you giving up? Are you a coward? Fight!"

He kicked his wife and shouted at his son, "Fight!"

He kicked her again and shouted, "Fight!"

As he aimed another kick, his son screamed and swung the pan at him in utter terror and anger.

Again, Karlsen batted off the weapon and struck back, but this time, his son did not fall.

The boy swung wildly and desperately, eyes wide with horror and face twisted in anguish. Karlsen slapped and jabbed him in between the attacks, provoking him to more vicious action until, in a complete frenzy, the boy got lucky and smashed the pan on his father's head.

Karlsen lashed out instinctively and punched his son full force in the face. The boy collapsed on the floor, almost senseless, blood pouring from his nose.

Karlsen sat down on the floor with a grunt, rubbing his head where the pan hit him. A strange pride welled up inside him, mixed with regret that he struck his son so hard.

The boy stirred weakly on the floor and sat up slowly. He looked at his father with uncertain eyes.

"Come here," commanded Karlsen.

The boy hesitated.

"I'm not going to hit you," Karlsen said irritably, "Come here."

His son slowly crawled over to him.

Karlsen took out his handkerchief, put it over the boy's nose, and pinched it firmly to stop the bleeding.

Then, with one hand pressing the cloth and the other holding his son in an awkward embrace, he said, "I'm sorry I hit you, but I am your father. I have to teach you how to be a man."

"Yeb, Farber," came the muffled reply below him.

"Real men fight and never give up. Only cowards surrender. Better to die than surrender," said Karlsen as his eyes drifted back to the photograph.

"Yeb, farber," his son said.

They sat in silence for a while.

"Farber?" the boy said.

"Yes, Hans?" said Karlsen gently.

"I thing marber is deb."

Chapter 1

1937—Berlin

Hans punched the old man in the face.

Hard.

The man fell heavily with a grunt, blood streaming from his broken nose.

His old German Army field cap had flown off, and an ID tag flew out from under his beer-stained shirt and dangled against his chest.

Through bleary eyes, the old man looked up at the tall teenager standing over him, fists balled up at his side, ready to strike again. His young face was fixed in a grimace of pure hatred.

"Don't you ever talk about the *Führer* like that again!" Hans shouted down at the old man.

When he made no response except to wipe the blood from his nose and tuck his tag back inside his shirt, Hans stepped back, drew his Hitler Youth knife, and brandished it at him.

There was a sharp intake of breath from his friends who were watching, but no one moved to stop their leader.

"Veteran or not, I'll gut you like the traitorous pig you are," Hans snarled.

There was still no response from the old man.

Finally, a tentative hand touched Hans's shoulder and pulled him back.

"Come now, *Stammführer*, let's not waste our time on this coward," a soothing voice said.

Hans flinched in frustration.

It was Erich, his Hitler Youth Company second-in-command, and best friend.

"He calls himself a soldier, but I bet he pissed his pants and ran off and as soon as he saw any fighting in the Great War," said Erich, glancing anxiously at the old man on the floor while gently pushing Hans away.

Hans resisted for a moment, then let himself be led away.

"You're lucky I didn't call the Gestapo on you, coward," Hans hissed at the old man as he walked away.

The boys of Caesar Company, 2nd Battalion, of the *Hitlerjugend* left the town square where the old soldier had confronted them and marched back to camp.

"You really should learn to control your temper, Hans," said Erich reproachfully when they got back to camp.

Hans replied hotly, "Why? He was spouting all kinds of defeatist talk, trying to sow doubts in our minds."

"He didn't actually say anything. He only asked questions," said Erich reasonably.

"He asked who Adolf Hitler thought he was and if he knew what he was doing, as though the *Führer* was an idiot," shouted Hans.

Erich stayed silent as he often did when Hans was worked up.

Hans fumed, "From the time he became Chancellor, Adolf Hitler has been the only one who has sought to reverse the humiliation and exploitation of our people.

The only one willing to fight for us, while everyone else surrendered and cowered before the other great powers."

"*I* am willing to fight for us," said Erich calmly.

Hans was about to respond with something rude when he saw the old scar on Erich's chin and paused.

Unbidden, the memory of how they met came to his mind ....

Hans had just turned eleven. His father was in another drunken rage, and with his mother no longer around to protect him, Hans had simply fled, with his father hot on his heels.

Erich, a complete stranger then, had called to Hans and tried to hide him in his own house, but Karlsen Wagner opened the door and yanked Erich out. Erich yelled for Hans to run, but Hans refused to leave him at his father's mercy.

So he fought.

When his father released Erich to turn on him, Erich refused to run too.

So for five long minutes, both did their best against the raging Karlsen Wagner, each boy afraid of the big man but even more afraid to leave the other to face him alone.

In the end, there was only ever going to be one outcome. His father caught him with a sharp backhand that left him dazed while a roundhouse to the temple knocked Erich out.

He still remembered the crunching sound Eric's chin made when it hit the floor ….

Still looking at his friend's scar, Hans said in a softer tone, "Yes, Erich, I know."

There was an embarrassed silence as both boys looked on the floor for a bit, then Erich spied a newspaper on the common room table.

"Look here," he said to Hans, picking up the paper.

"Italy joins Germany and Japan in the Anti-Comintern Pact" ran the headlines.

Erich scanned the article while Hans broke out into a triumphant smile.

"You see?" he said. "Now we have the Italians on our side. No one would dare look down on us now. The *Führer* knows what he's doing."

"It might come to war," said Erich seriously, still reading the article.

Hans hesitated at his friend's comment. Then his expression hardened as he said, "Well, no one wants war, but if it comes to it, we will be ready, and we will win against the others."

"The Americans won it for them last time. What if they come again?" asked Erich.

"Let them come," snarled Hans with sudden anger. "This time, they will find Germany defended by men of courage and conviction, unlike the cowards of the Great War like that old soldier. I really should have reported him to the Gestapo."

"I think that old soldier *was* Gestapo," said Erich softly.

"And we will… whu… What?" spluttered Hans as Erich's comment threw his train of thought.

Erich repeated, "I think that old soldier was Gestapo. His tag flew clear of his shirt when you hit him, and I saw the eagle with outstretched wings instead of the plain *Erkennungsmarke*."

Hans groaned, "You mean I just punched a Gestapo Officer in the nose, and you didn't stop me?"

"I didn't *know* he was Gestapo *until* you hit him," protested Erich.

Hans put his head in his hands and groaned again.

"I *told* you you should learn to control your temper," said Erich smugly, then ducked, laughing as Hans threw a mock punch at his head.

Hans said defensively, "Well, at least if I go to prison, it won't be for disloyalty or disrespect to Hitler."

"No, I guess not," Erich sighed. "With all that's happening, they can't afford to throw fine young men like us into prison for vigorously defending the *Führer's* honor, can they?"

And he looked meaningfully at the newspaper on the table.

Chapter 2

11th December 1941—Kriegsakademie grounds

"The *Führer* has declared war on the United States," cried the Officer Cadet as he ran into the barracks, clutching a newspaper.

His classmates, the graduating cohort of Officer Cadets, dropped shoe polish, brushes, boots, and other assorted items as they swarmed their fellow cadet. All thoughts of preparation for their impending parade forgotten.

Someone roughly ripped the newspaper from his hands and spread it on the table while everyone else crowded around.

For a few seconds, the room was silent as each person tried to read whatever portion of the paper he could see. Then a loud cacophony erupted as everyone started voicing their opinion on the news.

"It's about time…."

"Now we shall see what they are made of…."

"Can we fight them at the same time as the Soviets…?"

The loud chatter in the room was cut off abruptly when their *Stabsfeldwebel* burst into their barracks, his face a thundercloud.

Even though, in a matter of hours, they would be commissioned as full officers and outrank their fiery Sergeant Major, no one in their right mind dared to do anything other than pay full attention to the man as he stormed into their barracks.

"Cadets, much as we are all excited by today's news, might I remind you your graduation ceremony is *today*, and there is much left to do," he snarled.

Muted heads nodded in embarrassment.

But even their *Stabsfeldwebel* could not hide his own excitement as he continued scolding them, "There will be plenty of time to deal with the Americans later. But right now, you have less than three hours to prepare for your parade."

"After that, you become young *Offiziere*. I will salute you, bow down and lick your boots," he said sarcastically.

Then his voice rose to a shout, "But if I can't see my bald head in the shine of your boots before that, none of you will survive long enough to graduate, never mind fight the Americans!"

Good-natured grumbling broke out as the cadets chorused, "Yes, *Stabsfeldwebel*!"

Three hours later, after surviving an intense, last-minute inspection by their Sergeant Major, they marched out on parade and graduated as officers in the German Army.

As the best performing cadets from their cohort, Hans and Erich, were invited to the Conference Room to serve drinks to the senior officers after the parade.

After a few polite words from the assorted Majors and Generals, they found themselves largely ignored by everyone else.

As the party progressed, it also became apparent the senior officers needed no help with getting their own drinks. So, Hans and Erich decided to be unobtrusive and stationed themselves outside by the doorway.

Inside, the senior officers celebrated the events of the last few days.

They clinked their glasses and cheered about the stunning attack by the Japanese at Pearl Harbor. They hailed German victories against the Soviet Union.

But mostly, they toasted Hitler's declaration of war on the Americans.

A vigorous discussion broke out in the conference room, which Hans and Erich could not help overhearing. Voices were talking loudly, and some were slightly slurred.

Confident sneers and taunts like, "It's about time we ended this farce," and "now we can shoot Americans and not pretend we thought they were Jews," were thrown about, bringing roars of laughter from the celebrants.

Alone in the room, however, was one single voice of dissent.

Beginning with a few derisive remarks in response to the triumphal babble, after one particularly nasty comment about Jewish children, the owner of that voice clearly had enough and slammed his glass down on a table so hard that it shattered.

Tension filled the room as he spoke angrily to his now-silent companions.

"The Japanese were wrong to attack the Americans at Pearl Harbor. Instead, they have provoked a fight they cannot win and dragged us into it," he said.

"But they achieved complete tactical surprise and they destroyed the American fleet there," protested someone in a high-pitched nasal voice.

The first voice shot back quickly, "They sank a few battleships and some destroyers, and completely missed their aircraft carriers."

The room was silent. Hans moved closer to the door so he could hear better.

"The fleet is not destroyed. Not even crippled. Not until the carriers are taken out. Yamamoto would have sacrificed his entire raiding force to sink the carriers in that attack," the speaker concluded.

The nasal voice spoke testily, "But see here, Wolfgang, they sank eight battleships! *Eight*! The Americans have lost a third of all their battleships, *including* those we will face in the Atlantic! Surely, they can't come back from that. How can they control the Pacific now?"

"Idiot," came the contemptuous reply. "Do you not see? Their carriers are still at large! Do battleships matter now? Did eight of them make a difference at Pearl Harbor against carrier-based aircraft? The very success you gloat over can be repeated against them. Against *us*!"

"You go too far, my friend," a deep voice broke in. "It is one thing to fear the Americans on behalf of the Japanese with their tin can fighting machines; it is another matter entirely when they face us. They will fall. Like all of Europe has fallen to us. They cannot prevail against the might of the entire *Wehrmacht*."

First Voice replied sarcastically, "Like Britain could not prevail against us? Like the Soviet Union?"

"They will fall," said Deep Voice with confidence.

"They *would* if we didn't have to fight the Americans," said First Voice bitterly.

"Be careful what you say, Generalleutnant. You tread dangerously close to treason here," Deep Voice said ominously.

First Voice said defiantly, "I show no disloyalty to the Party, the country, or my own command. Man for man, I challenge you to find any army in the world that can match the quality of our soldiers."

His tone softened as he continued, "Sadly, it is not a matter of the strength of arms, nor the skill and courage of our soldiers."

He paused thoughtfully, "It is not even about the *number* of soldiers anymore. Look at what we did to France and Poland! We crushed them even though we were outnumbered.

"War is about how much fighting power you can bring to bear, when you want it, where you want it…. and logistics."

The anticlimactic conclusion caught everyone, including Hans, by surprise.

Another voice joined in, "Logistics? Is that what you fear?

"My friend, you are right to think about such things. But it is here, perhaps even more than anywhere else, that we have the advantage! We are practically on home ground. Our supply lines are secure since we control the whole continent now, while they have to cross the Atlantic Ocean to reach Britain just to get at us.

"And by next year, there will be German guns waiting for them *on* the British Isles. Our factories…"

"…are no match for theirs," First Voice cut him off.

"They have more raw materials and more production facilities that cannot be bombed, whereas ours already have been. What use are secure supply lines when the very sources of the supplies are destroyed?

"It is not the American soldier I fear or even their war machines, but their fuel, munitions, and spare parts that we will run short of!"

First Voice was getting louder now.

"How do our soldiers shoot when they have no bullets? How do our tanks flank the enemy when they have no fuel? How do our planes fight when there are no spare parts to keep them flying?"

Nasal Voice broke in angrily, "But what the Americans have been sending over so far...."

"...is only a fraction of what they can bring to bear, you fool!" First Voice snorted.

"Up till now, their President faced a divided nation. They had no stomach for another fight, not so soon after the Great War, so their leaders had to be surreptitious about sending aid to their allies. They would never have gone to war unless someone attacked them first!" First Voice was shouting now.

"And now, with this foolhardy attack by the Japanese, their entire nation has just united behind their President for the first time in a generation. Now, the resources of the whole country can be openly devoted to making war, and their people will cheer about it.

"And we put ourselves in the firing line by declaring war on them!" yelled First Voice.

Hans was holding his breath now, and it seemed, so was everyone else in the room.

Such open talk, especially around high-ranking officers, could only lead to one thing. So, when he heard the distinct clack-clack of boots heralding the arrival of three Gestapo Officers, he was not particularly surprised.

The first two were Oberleutnants—Junior officers in pristine uniforms with erect bearings. Their expressions were stern and no-nonsense as they walked in time with each other with the arrogance of those who were untouchable. They marched past Hans and Erich without even looking at them and entered the room.

In the few moments before they stepped in, First Voice was the only one speaking. In hushed, haunted tones, as though he knew he had said too much already, he articulated his last regret.

Wistfully, he said, "It didn't need to come to this. The Americans and Soviets hate each other with a passion that is almost holy. They were already squaring up to fight each other until we got in the way.

"If we had just left them alone, they would have destroyed themselves without costing us a single German life. But then we had to attack one, and now the other...."

The two SS Officers stepped in, and seconds later, they came out with a one-star general between them.

As they marched off with their captive, a shorter, older man ambled by.

His rank insignia marked him as an SS Senior Leader, the equivalent of an American or British Colonel. Evidently, he had been present to supervise the arrest of the Army General.

He walked with his hands behind his back at a slower, almost leisurely pace.

Hans and Erich drew themselves to full attention as he approached and saluted smartly, eyes staring straight ahead into the distance.

The SS Officer walked past Erich first, and it was Erich's frightened gasp that first gave Hans a warning that something was amiss.

His eyes went wild as he strained to see what was going on on the side while maintaining his forward gaze.

He didn't need to.

The SS Officer stood right in front of him and said, "Hello Hans, you have done well, I see."

Still in full salute, Hans's eyes rolled crazily as he strove to look for a name tag or any indication of who the SS Officer was, while maintaining the required steady gaze to the horizon.

Unable to find any clue about his identity, Hans's mouth answered with an automatic, "Thank you, Oberst..." and ended lamely there.

Then a flash of recognition shot through him, and he almost fainted.

An old man in Great War uniform on the floor, bleeding from a broken nose.

The SS Officer caught on to Hans's distress and grinned, tapping his nose meaningfully, "Yes, I see you remember now, Hans Wagner."

Hans started trembling.

The SS Officer let him squirm for a bit more before he said, "Much as it hurt me then, I was impressed by your steadfast loyalty to the *Führer*. You are here now because of that incident."

Hans fought to stop his jaw from dropping at the revelation.

He *had* wondered about the unusually high intake of Officer Cadets from his Hitler Youth Company. Now he knew why.

Then, the SS Officer turned to leave and said, "I am Oberst Richter of the SS. I expect you to do well, Hans. Do not disappoint me."

Hans gulped and managed a soft, "Yes, Oberst Richter."

As he walked away, Oberst Richter turned one last time, rubbed his nose, and said, "And one last thing, Leutnant."

Hans replied, "Yes, Oberst Richter?"

The SS Officer said, "You really should learn to control your temper."

Erich sniggered, and Hans rolled his eyes.

CHAPTER 3

23rd July 1943—Hamburg

Hans lifted his glass and said solemnly, "To the best man."

And downed his shot.

Erich giggled and punched him on the arm.

"Idiot," he said, "*You're* the best man," he said.

"I know," belched Hans contentedly, "That's what I meant."

Erich laughed and downed his drink while Hans poured himself another shot. When Erich finished, he refilled his cup.

"Seriously though," said Hans, lifting his glass solemnly again, "To my best friend."

Erich looked like he was going to crack a joke about that, then changed his mind and said, "And to mine."

They clinked glasses and downed their drinks, belched at the same time, then burst out laughing together.

The *Bierbar* they were drinking in was near the central district of Hamburg and a moderately lively one. So, no one paid attention to the two young *Wehrmacht* officers sharing a celebratory drink late into the night.

"Erich," Hans began, "You've been my best friend and comrade since you saved me from that beating from my father...."

"You mean I *joined* you in that beating from your father," interrupted Erich. "Neither of us were of a size to stop him, even together."

Hans said, "Shut up. I'm trying to give my best man's speech here."

Erich smiled and theatrically motioned for him to continue.

When Hans was satisfied, he said, "As I was saying, you've been my best friend since we were eleven.

"We've been beaten by my father together, been to school together, joined the army together, finished Officer School together...

"We are like brothers. We know everything there is to know about each other."

Erich beamed happily.

Hans hiccupped and said with increasing volume, "So how is it then, as soon as I turn my back on you, you manage to meet a girl, fall in love, propose, get her to agree, and arrange a wedding, within the space of few months, in the middle of a bloody war?"

"I didn't plan for any of this," protested Erich. "Marianne and I met at the station, started talking, had a meal, and it just happened...".

"I don't know how you did it," said Hans, shaking his head in mock disgust.

"As I said, we met at the station, started talking..." began Erich.

Hans cut him off irritably, "No, no, not that. I can understand if she's pretty enough, you'd want to marry her quickly.

"What I meant is—how did you manage to plan your wedding *and* get both of us on special leave *at the same time*?"

Erich gave a sly smile and said, "Ah, the mysteries of the Manpower Division and the officers who run it from within."

Hans snorted, "The officers sitting in the offices...."

"...who determine the comings and goings of the lowly, sweaty riflemen, and where they shall be deployed to be sweaty," said Erich in a booming tone.

Hans laughed and said, "So you drag me out from France to Berlin on a special assignment—*without telling me*, then get me to go on special leave—*which I did not ask for*, just so that I can be your best man for your wedding tomorrow—*which I did not know about*."

Erich said with a self-satisfied grin, "Exactly. And the wedding is today. It's well past midnight."

"You could have told me earlier instead of on the train yesterday. I would have gotten you a gift," complained Hans.

Without any hint of irony, Erich said reassuringly, "Your presence is present enough, Hans. And I thank you for agreeing to be my best man."

Hans muttered, "If I didn't, you'd have me deployed to the Eastern Front." But he was pleased by Erich's comment.

He downed his drink again, then looked at his glass and groaned, "I think I drank too much. How am I going to be ready for the wedding?"

Erich laughed, "Don't be a baby. It's in the afternoon. You'll have plenty of time to sober up."

"Easy for you to say. You just have to stand there and not fall over. I have to make a speech," retorted Hans.

Erich smiled, "And a fine one it will be, I am sure.

"However, I do not have to 'just stand there and not fall over'. Don't forget I have other duties as well?"

And he made an "O" shape with one hand and extended a finger through the circle with the other.

Hans was so stunned by such a crude gesture from his customarily reserved friend that, for a moment, he just stared in surprise.

Erich caught his shocked look and stared back, puzzled. Then he looked at his hands, finger of one hand still inside the circle of the other, then back at Hans.

Blushing furiously, Erich said, "Wait, I meant putting the ring on Marianne, not... uh... you know...."

Hans laughed so hard he choked on his drink. Then Erich started laughing too. Soon, the two were howling with laughter, tears rolling down their cheeks.

After a long moment, they finally ran out of breath and stopped.

But the sound of laughter seemed to carry on.

Hans held his breath and was sure it wasn't him. Looking at Erich, he saw that his friend was spluttering now instead of laughing. Why did the wailing noise still carry on?

Hans started to feel uneasy as a vague recognition stirred inside of him. Erich also stopped laughing and cocked his head to make sense of the sound.

Suddenly, it hit them like a lightning bolt, just as someone cried, "Air raid!"

They looked at each other in alarm as panic erupted in the bar. Some people started moving deeper into the building, while others made for the exit.

With the leadership instinct drilled into him in the *Kriegsakademie*, Hans climbed on his chair and drew himself up to full height.

"Quiet!" he bellowed, and the room fell eerily silent against the background wail of the air raid sirens.

Pointing to the bartender, he shouted, "Bartender, do you have a cellar or basement?"

The man nodded hastily and pointed to the back door.

Hans ordered, "Everyone, move quickly and quietly to the basement. Women and children first. No shouting. Keep order. Go now!"

The first bombs landed just as the last of the customers were safely underground. Distant explosions sounded in a pulsing rhythm, getting ominously closer and closer.

"Come on," Hans said impatiently to his friend as he moved down the stairs. But Erich seemed distracted and took out his compass.

He looked toward the sounds of the explosions, then at his compass again.

"They're bombing the city itself, not just the harbor," Erich said.

Hans just stared at him like he was mad. What difference did that make to any….

"Marianne," said Erich simply, and he moved to the exit.

Hans grabbed his arm and said, "Don't go. It's too dangerous!"

Erich turned and gave him a look that made Hans stop in his tracks.

The same look he gave Hans all those years ago when Hans yelled for him to run. But Erich had stayed on, his little face set in a serious expression, and joined Hans in the fight of his life against the raging Karlsen Wagner.

And Erich had the same look of determination now, and Hans knew better than to try and stop him.

Sighing in resignation, Hans said, "Alright," and he shut the door to the basement and followed Erich out of the *Bierbar*.

"But you'd better know the way to her place in the dark!" he shouted after his friend, then followed him at a dead run as bombs exploded around the city.

Erich sprinted down the street toward a church with a tall spire dominating the end of the road. The lights were out, but the bell was furiously tolling, joining in sounding the alarm.

They reached the junction, and Erich turned unerringly to the right, with Hans close at his heels. Then he turned left into a side street and ran straight toward a house with a green door.

Banging furiously on it, he shouted for Marianne. The door opened seconds later, and a small, pretty woman in nightclothes opened the door.

"Erich," she cried in relief and embraced him. Erich hugged her tightly as the woman's father quickly ushered them into the house and down to the cellar.

They sat in pitch darkness for the next half an hour with Marianne and her family. Erich held on tightly to his fiancée while hasty introductions were made.

Hans quickly warmed to the girl and her family, who kept their spirits up by telling family stories and teasing Marianne and Erich even as explosions rocked their home city.

They welcomed Hans like a lost son, and whatever reservations he had about his best friend getting married evaporated.

When at last, the bombs stopped, they slowly crawled up the stairs to the living room. The windows had all been blown in, but their house and street had been spared from direct hits.

However, when they opened the door, a scene like one out of a nightmare greeted them.

It seemed the entire city was in flames. In some sectors, tornadoes of flame and smoke spiraled in the air with screaming bodies caught up in them.

Just beyond their street, an inferno raged so hotly the asphalt melted, and the cars on them sank.

Hans looked around grimly and said, "We have to help them."

Erich said, "I'm coming."

Marianne said, "I'm coming too."

Erich opened his mouth to protest, but a slim hand went to his face and touched his lips shut, Marianne's expression stern and identical to Erich's own just before he left the *Bierbar* to look for her.

He sighed and said, "Alright, but if there's any risk at all, you get back, understood?"

Marianne stuck her tongue out at him and said, "It can't be more dangerous than getting married to you, can it?"

Erich laughed, and the three of them walked down the street to start helping the shell-shocked residents of Hamburg.

Long through the night, they labored. Pulling people out of the rubble, helping whatever firemen they came across, bringing water to the wounded, and holding the hands of the dying.

They worked until dawn, but it was only by mid-morning that most of the fires had been brought under control.

The church with the tall spire acted as an impromptu rallying point for that area of the city. Lost and dazed citizens looking for loved ones made their way there. The wounded were gathered in the main hall, and any who had any skills worked hard to take care of them. Grocers with food and drink brought what they could and selflessly shared them with those in need.

The church priest, a tiny man with a surprisingly loud voice, stood in the center of the chaos, directing those in need and those who came to help with calm and efficiency.

He greeted Marianne warmly, then shook hands solemnly with Hans and Erich before directing them to help move the wounded.

It was only later in the afternoon that they finally got to rest. The four of them sat on the church's steps, drinking ash-tasting water drawn from the church well.

"Thank you all for your help today," began the priest, "but I'm sorry about your wedding, Erich."

"What are you sorry about?" asked Erich.

"Well, that with all this," said the priest, waving his hand at the destruction around them, "we can't go ahead with it."

"Why not?" asked Erich impishly, and Marianne's eyes went wide, and she squealed in delight.

"Why, because... uh...," floundered the priest.

Erich said, "It's only a quarter past four now. We'd start fifteen minutes later than planned. Weddings always start late, don't they?

The priest looked thoughtful, then said with a grin, "Yes, yes, I don't see why we can't do the wedding after all. Since when did being a little late stop anyone from getting married?"

Chapter 4

24th July 1943—Hamburg

Word quickly spread, and the crowd began to buzz excitedly.

Someone came with a bucket of water for Erich and Marianne to wash themselves down. One woman took off her cardigan, reversed it so the white interior showed, and placed it on Marianne's shoulders.

A little girl shyly handed her a bunch of flowers picked from the church graveyard while a young woman quickly braided chamomile flowers together to form a wreath which she placed on Marianne's head.

Hans took out his Hitler Youth knife, passed it to Eric, and said gruffly, "Here, take this. It'll look good on you."

Erich's eyes widened, "Are you sure? I know how important this is to you."

Hans waved him off, "I'm just *lending* it to you for the wedding, then I'll take it back. We can't have you getting married in military uniform without a single weapon on your person, can we?"

Erich smiled in appreciation and quickly attached it to his belt.

In minutes, Erich and Marianne were standing on the church's steps, hand in hand, and everyone who could stand gathered around.

The priest stood on a box on top of the steps at the landing.

He took out his bible, opened it, looked around, and began, "Dearly beloved, we are gathered here together to witness…."

Many in the crowd started weeping before he finished the first sentence. Shell-shocked, distressed, grieving, or fearing for loved ones, emotions ran high amongst the spectators.

Marianne was crying freely. Erich tried his best to keep a stoic expression, but tears flowed down his cheeks.

Hans, taking the traditional role of best man seriously, stood at his side and scowled fiercely at anyone in the crowd who got too near the couple. But even he could not stop his eyes from becoming moist nor keep his lower lip from trembling.

Then it was time for the couple to exchange rings, and the priest asked, "May I have the rings, please?"

Hans nearly had a heart attack patting himself down frantically and finding nothing on his person. Giggles burst out in the crowd before he realized, in all the confusion, that Erich never had the chance to pass them to him for safe-keeping.

Grinning at his friend's consternation, Erich made a great show of putting his hand in his pocket and pretending to be amazed as he drew out a tiny box and showed it to Hans, who was close to stripping off his uniform to look for it.

Hans growled at his friend and settled back to his position with as much dignity as he could muster. The priest blessed the rings and handed them to the couple to exchange them.

Then, covered in dust, disheveled, hair singed but eyes bright, they put rings on each other and exchanged vows.

Hans found himself sniffing furiously and, after a quick wipe of his nose on his sleeve, turned round to look at the crowd.

There wasn't a dry eye to be found.

Amid the carnage the people of Hamburg had endured, the sight of a dashing young officer and his brave and beautiful bride defying the circumstances to get married in a bombed-out city was more than anyone could bear. It was a ray of hope they so desperately needed.

As he watched his friend, Hans's heart swelled with pride for him. Not just for who he had grown up to be, not just for marrying such a wonderful girl as Marianne, but for the inspiration he now gave to the people by his defiant celebration of life.

Before he knew it, the priest pronounced the couple man and wife. Marianne pulled Erich in and kissed him deeply before the priest gave them permission. Hearty cheers and loud whistles rang out in the crowd as Erich, still locked in the kiss, turned a deeper and deeper red. Suddenly he broke free and, in a swift movement, lifted his wife into his arms.

Then he turned round in confusion as, while he obviously felt it was the manly thing to carry his new wife, in this case, there was nowhere to carry her *to*. No waiting carriage, no nearby house.

Seeing his predicament, the priest raised his voice and said, "Everybody inside the church to celebrate!"

The crowd surged forward and pressed the newlyweds inside, and the atmosphere took on a decidedly festive air. Singing and dancing broke out even before they went in.

Through the press of bodies around him, Erich caught Hans's eye and mouthed: *Get some wine*.

Hans grinned, gave him a mock salute then strolled off. He knew it would be hard to find any alcohol in the devastated city, but at least he knew where to look first: Up the hill, all the way on the straight road, to the *Bierbar* he and Erich had their modest, two-person stag party the night before.

As luck would have it, the bar was undamaged except for the smashed windows, and the bartender recognized the man who prevented a stampede when the air-raid sirens went off.

Gratefully, he presented Hans with two bottles of his finest wine, firmly declining any offer of payment for it.

"You saved many of my customers last night," he said. "In a time like this, we must find whatever joy we can. So please take these as my wedding gift to your friend."

As though in response, the church bell started tolling.

Hans looked down the road and smiled.

A little late to sound in celebration, he thought critically. But then, the wedding was so spontaneous that maybe no one had thought to ring the bell until now.

Never mind, he shrugged to himself. *Better late than never*.

Then his smile froze on his face as his eyes perceived something amiss.

In the distance, beyond the lofty church spire, he could see several dots in the air.

Dots that grew larger and larger as they disappeared behind the spire on one side and reappeared on the other.

As Hans tried to process the sight, the joyous tone of the church bells suddenly took on a frantic, urgent quality. His mind rebelled at what his senses were telling him. And for precious seconds, he couldn't move.

It was only when a trail of smaller dots emerged from the first ones that, at last, he conceded to the dreadful reality in front of him.

"Air raid!" he screamed at the top of his lungs, just as the first bombs exploded in the city's western sector.

"Into the *Bierbar*, get to the basement. Hurry!" he called out to whoever was around.

The bartender had already flung open his doors and cleared the path to his basement for the bystanders. But, unlike last night, when the crowd was merely alarmed, this time, the people panicked. It was all Hans could do to stop them from trampling on one another.

Then a trail of bombs landed in their sector of the city.

One by one, they fell and exploded with the regularity of a metronome.

In horror, Hans watched helplessly as the line of fireballs puffed remorselessly toward the church until the last and final one landed directly on the nave and detonated with terrific force.

Chapter 5

"Erich!" Hans screamed as the church was engulfed in flames.

The bartender appeared at the door and yelled for Hans to come in, but Hans ignored him and ran down the hill toward the burning church.

Amazingly, the tall spire was still standing, but practically everything else was in flames or collapsed.

As he approached, Hans called for his friend frantically, looking for an entrance to the building. One side of the church was burning, but the main entrance was clear of flames.

Hans dashed inside and was confronted with a scene from his worst nightmares.

The bomb had crashed through the roof and exploded in the nave. Everyone there would have died instantly.

Hans quickly searched through the area, finding more body parts than bodies, none of them in German Army uniform.

Then, near the front, he found the priest, head buried under a large stone. Next to him, a pale left hand with a ring on its fourth finger protruded from the rubble.

Marianne!

He started to pull the rubble away from around the hand, but as he removed enough debris to loosen it, the hand dropped to the floor, completely severed from the rest of the body.

Hans recoiled in shock and gagged to stop himself from retching.

Taking a deep breath, he was just about to start digging again when a flickering glint caught his eye.

Beyond the nave, where a passage led to another room, a beam of sunlight reflected off an inch of shiny metal. Hans raced to it and picked it up.

It was the broken tip of a knife.

Dread filled his heart as he looked around the room knowing it was only a matter of time before he found ….

"Erich!" Hans shouted as he spotted his friend lying in the corner of the room.

He raced to him and stopped in horror.

His friend was pinned under a pillar that had collapsed across him. His legs were sticking out from one side of the pillar but weren't moving. On the other side, Erich lay with his head limp and staring at the sky.

His right held Hans's Hitler Youth knife, blade broken as he used it to try and free himself. The fingernails on his left hand were bloody from clawing at the massive weight on him. His face was pale and completely covered in dust, and a trickle of blood oozed from his mouth.

At the sound of Hans's voice, his eyes flickered, and he looked groggily at his friend.

Hans called out urgently, "Erich! Hang on. I'm going to get you out."

He launched himself on one end of the pillar and heaved with all his might, but it didn't budge.

Looking around desperately, he found a likely piece of rubble and wedged it under the pillar, fighting the rising panic within him.

Even if he managed to lift it, would Erich be able to crawl out? Or perhaps he could roll it off him. But which way? Over his head? That would kill him instantly. Over his legs? They would be crushed. But they might already be paralyzed. With the entire weight of the pillar clean across his spine, there was a good chance it was already broken. Or maybe he should get help. Surely, firefighters must be on their way....

"Hans, where's Marianne?" Erich called out weakly.

Hans avoided his gaze as he busied himself, looking for tools.

"I haven't found her yet," he lied.

But he heard Erich sigh and slump even deeper beneath the pillar.

Somehow, Erich could always tell when he was lying.

Ignoring the tears that started spilling from his cheeks, Hans grabbed a piece of rubble, shoved it under the pillar, and tried to push it.

"Hans," Erich's voice cut through his scattered thoughts, "I'm done for. You can't help me."

"No!" cried Hans, trying to lift the pillar again. "I'll get you out. I'll get help."

Erich smiled at his words, then he coughed weakly, and more blood oozed from his mouth.

"They're coming back. Go, save yourself," he said in a fading voice.

"I'm not leaving you," said Hans furiously.

Then he stopped and stared.

Something was wrong.

Something was so out of place that it took him until now to register the sheer awfulness of it.

Beyond the apparent injuries to his friend, there was one more thing that made him look strange.

Hans's gaze went to his friend's face, then to his feet, then to his face again. And when he estimated the distance between them, Erich had to be at least one foot taller than he actually was.

A widening pool of blood seeping from his friend confirmed his growing dread.

Erich had been bisected by the pillar.

Hans couldn't help it.

He scrambled away, got on his hands and knees, and vomited. His stomach heaved and emptied its contents until there was nothing left. Then it heaved again, and he retched loudly.

Shaking with spasms, it took him nearly a minute to recover enough to crawl back to his friend. But sometime in the midst of his retching, Erich died.

His brown eyes were staring sightlessly into the sky. His dust-covered face was completely neutral and relaxed. His hand had released its grip on the broken knife and dropped it.

Hans stared at his friend as a pit of unimaginable darkness began to form in his stomach. It swelled from deep inside him, growing exponentially as wave after wave of anger and regret started to wash over him.

He started shaking again, this time with rage and outrage.

Erich's last words to him had been for him to save himself.

And his last words to Erich were an oath.

An oath which he broke as soon as he made it when he turned away just as his friend died.

With tears streaming down his cheeks, Hans choked and gasped for breath. He looked at the sky above for answers, but there were none. Anger welled up inside him slowly and inexorably until it built up like a volcano.

Rising on his knees with his arms outstretched to the uncaring heavens, Hans gulped down a deep breath and screamed.

The air raid siren started wailing at precisely the same time, blending in with his scream such that the two sounds were indistinguishable.

Prisoner of War

Hans screamed and screamed until he was spent.

Then he collapsed exhausted, his rage replaced with cold anger that was even more terrifying. Gently, he closed his friend's eyes. Then he picked up his Hitler Youth knife and held it tightly.

He got slowly to his feet and walked out of the building as the bombs started falling.

Like a wraith rising from the depths, he emerged from the church door and climbed the small hill to the graveyard where moss-covered tombstones marked ancient resting places of unknown people.

From his vantage point, he saw Hamburg in flames again as bombs rained down. Overhead, a B17 Flying Fortress flew low, trailing smoke. Underneath each wing was a white star emblazoned in a blue circle—the distinctive insignia of the USA Air Force.

The Americans.

Hans's grip on the broken knife grew so hard that his hand went white. At that moment, his heart burning with hatred, he swore that when the Americans came, he would be there.

And there would be hell to pay.

Chapter 6

17th December 1944—Ardennes Region

Hans stared in amazement as the German soldier came running toward him.

He had no helmet, no rifle, his arms were pumping wildly, and his eyes were wide with fear.

Ignoring the shouts of Hans's lead squad, the soldier just ran past them, intent on fleeing whatever lay behind him.

Hans whacked him with his rifle butt as the soldier sought to pass him. The man flew a few feet and slumped on the floor, dazed. The platoon stretcher-bearer automatically moved to aid the fallen soldier, but with a sharp gesture, Hans waved him off angrily.

"Save your strength for real soldiers, not cowards," he snarled at the medic, who wilted under the displeasure of his platoon commander.

Looking down in disgust at the semi-conscious soldier, Hans spat and motioned for his platoon to move on.

Seconds later, his lead squad came under fire from the Americans the first soldier had been fleeing. They hit the ground, spread out, and returned fire with practiced smoothness until Hans brought the second squad to support them.

He turned to order the third squad to flank the enemy, but his platoon sergeant was already on the move. With a short wave of acknowledgment, Sergeant Klein and the third squad leader took their men and disappeared into the woods to the right.

A minute later, gunfire sounded from the enemy flank, and as the Americans turned to face the new threat, Hans yelled, "Grenades!"

Four stick grenades sailed in the air toward the American position. As they exploded, he shouted, "Charge!"

Squad One and Two of Platoon Two surged forward with Hans in the center, firing and shouting.

Attacked from two sides, then dazed by the grenades, the Americans stood no chance. Hans didn't care whether they intended to surrender or not, and he was not about to give them the opportunity. Firing savagely, he overran the enemy position and shot anything that moved.

In seconds, the fight was over. Sergeant Klein quickly brought up Squad Three, secured the area, then reported, "No casualties for us, eleven enemies killed, and they had two prisoners."

Hans looked at the two men to which Sergeant Klein pointed.

Like the fleeing soldier, they had no helmets, no weapons, and were a sorry-looking pair. As Hans's men cut them loose from their bonds, he was filled with an urge to punch them in their faces.

How could they drive the enemy back to the sea when German soldiers ran and surrendered at will?

Gritting his teeth, he ordered, "Make them gather and carry weapons and ammunition from the fallen. They follow us as the last men until we link up with the company.

"So, if we get surprised in the rear, at least they can do something useful for once and die to give the rest of us some warning. Now get them out of my sight!"

Fifteen minutes later, they linked up with the rest of their company.

Hauptmann Hauser, the Company Commander, gathered his platoon leaders to give orders.

"Anton Company, listen up. Things are moving quickly, so I'll be brief," he said briskly, pulling out his large map.

"As you know, the British and American are thinly spread along their respective sectors," he said, pointing to the map.

"The *Führer* has planned a major counter-offensive against the weak points of the Allied lines in the Ardennes. The American units based there are either resting or inexperienced and using the area as a training ground," said Hauptmann Hauser.

Hans snorted in outrage at the contempt the enemy showed.

Hauptmann Hauser continued, "They will face our heavy Panzer divisions, reinforced with SS Divisions. The weather is bad, so they have no air cover. It is a foregone conclusion that they will be crushed."

"Our final objective is Antwerp. Once we get there, we split the British and Americans in half, then we destroy them one at a time and drive them back to the sea," said Hauptmann Hauser.

"Who first then?" asked Leutnant Jung fiercely, the young Platoon One Commander and the newest addition to the company.

"The British," said Hans immediately.

Everyone stared at him, knowing his particular dislike of the Americans.

Leutnant Jung asked, "How come?"

Hans gave an evil smile and said, "Because this is war. And in war, it must always be business first before pleasure."

Amused chuckles sounded around the group before Hauptmann Hauser impatiently drew them back to the matter at hand.

"Before we get to that pleasure, we still have a counter-offensive to launch," he reminded them.

"Our battalion has been tasked with supporting the initial assault on Bastogne. To help us keep up with the main assault, we have a company of Panzers attached to back us up, so we don't get left behind," explained the Anton Company Commander.

The three Platoon Commanders nodded approvingly. The might of German tanks was legendary.

Oberleutnant Stein, the Platoon Three Commander, rumbled in his deep voice, "With a company of Panzers in the mix, it would be difficult to tell who is backing up who. The tanks could probably do the job all by themselves."

"Agreed," said Hauptmann Hauser, "but after the tricks they pulled at Normandy, we don't want to take any chances. So, if we attack, we attack with overwhelming force, cause maximum damage and take minimal losses ourselves."

"No more surprises," he finished firmly.

Everyone nodded in agreement.

Pointing to the hill in front of them, Hauptmann Hauser said, "Major Schmidt's plan for the battalion is as follows: Berta Company is dug in there, as the anchor point of our battalion, as a shield against localized counter-attacks.

"The rest of us will attack west. Caesar Company in the northern pincer with two Panzer platoons, us in the southern pincer with one Panzer platoon. Anyone who slips in between us will be ground up against Hauptmann Brandt, and good luck to them."

Amused chuckles broke out once more. The Berta Company Commander was a master of defense. Nothing could dislodge him once his men were dug in.

"Orders," said Hauptmann Hauser crisply, and his officers straightened up sharply.

Looking at Hans and Stein, he said, "The tanks will advance in the middle. Platoon Two on their right, Platoon Three on their left."

"Platoon One behind the tanks with me, acting as tactical reserve," he said to the crestfallen Jung.

"Dismissed."

Hans clapped Jung on the shoulder as their dispersed. "Cheer up," he said lightly, "There'll be plenty of Americans to kill later."

"It's not that," said Jung uncomfortably. "It's just that I don't think Hauptmann Brandt trusts me yet, being the newest officer in the company."

"And the youngest too," teased Stein, "You're practically a child."

Jung laughed good-naturedly, "I suppose I am, fresh out of the *Kriegsakademie*. But I was voted Most Sporting Cadet by my classmates."

"When you next meet the enemy, just think of how you can be the most sporting to them, then do the exact opposite," quipped Hans, and they all laughed and headed back to their respective platoons.

As Hans walked back, he was met by Erwin, one of his two Platoon Messengers.

Hans smiled when he saw him sprinting in at great speed.

A new addition to Platoon Two, Erwin was the youngest in the whole company and certainly looked it. He instantly became the Platoon's mascot because he looked so out of place amongst men barely a year older than him. Hans wasn't even sure if his voice had broken yet.

But he was fast. And he liked to run, making him a perfect fit as Platoon Messenger.

Erwin saluted as he came whizzing in, screeching to a stop a respectful distance from Hans.

"Oberleutnant, Sergeant Klein reports the men are ready and asks if there was anything else you wanted him to do," said Erwin breathlessly.

"No need," said Hans, "I'm already heading back. You go to Company HQ and standby to receive the order to march."

Erwin saluted smartly, then dashed off.

When Hans made it back to his platoon, Sergeant Klein wordlessly led him around the men for a quick final inspection and a few words of encouragement.

All was in order, and Hans was quietly grateful for a Platoon Sergeant like Klein. Not just good in a fight, but a solid Non-Commissioned Officer who could practically read his mind and get the men ready before he even issued orders.

Then they were done, and there was nothing left to do except wait for Erwin to return with orders to get moving.

"You think we will win?" asked Sergeant Klein.

Hans looked at him sharply. From anyone else, except for the new ones like Erwin, he would mark the question as defeatist, possibly treasonous.

But he had come to respect the laconic Sergeant, who had repeatedly proved himself to be no coward.

"This battle? Of course, we will. We have the tanks with us," said Hans, even though he knew that wasn't what his Platoon Sergeant was asking.

Sergeant Klein didn't need to say anything.

Hans sighed and carried on, "Yes, I think we will win. This battle and then many others before the final victory."

His Platoon Sergeant grunted noncommittally.

Hans looked at him and said, "When the *Führer* took power all those years back, I followed him wholeheartedly because, at last, here was someone willing to fight for our honor, pride, and dignity as a people.

"But it was only when war broke out that I saw—not only was he passionate about our nation, he was a brilliant strategist and military mind.

"See how quickly we overran all of Europe? We chased the mighty British Expeditionary Force before they could even get started. Their soldiers had to be rescued by their fishermen at Dunkirk!"

Sergeant Klein muttered, "But now the Americans...."

Hans's face darkened at the mention of the Americans.

Unconsciously, his hand closed over the hilt of the Hitler Youth knife in his breast pocket.

"Yes, I know the Americans swung the tide in the Great War," Hans said coldly, "and like blundering, spoilt children, they think to come here again and do the same.

"But this time, it'll be different."

Taking out his Hitler Youth knife, Hans drew it from its leather sheath and started to caress the weapon.

Sergeant Klein looked at the blade curiously and said, "Broken."

Hans held the grip firmly, remembering his days growing up in the *Hitlerjugend* after his father died.

"So I never forget," he said harshly.

His finger touched the cold, broken steel blade, and the image of his friend's broken body again flashed in his mind.

"The Americans are only now mobilizing for war, whereas the *Führer* has been preparing our country for years. I can see that now."

His thumb pressed over the pommel where he had etched a star within a circle and then viciously crossed it out.

"And this time, they will find a people ready, brave, and angry at their attempts to be our masters again. They will fail."

Sergeant Klein inclined his head toward where they were about to attack and said, "That they're here at all though...."

Hans cut him off angrily, "...is part of the greater plan of the *Führer*.

"We were going to fight the Americans anyway. We always were. Perhaps it's easier to bring them here instead of chasing them to their own country."

With satisfaction, Hans said, "Now they have to suffer the torpedoes of our U-boats even to reach the British Isles. Then they have to cross the English Channel just to get here.

"This way, we bring them to our doorstep and can destroy them at our convenience..."

Just then, Erwin returned from Company HQ at a full sprint and relayed orders to attack.

"... as we are about to do now," finished Hans grimly.

Chapter 7

The Panzer fired once, and the American machine-gun nest was no more.

Hans led his men in an extended line beyond the four tanks that were leading the attack against a small village.

The many contingencies he had planned turned out to be unnecessary.

The tanks engaged anything remotely resembling a machine gun or bazooka position and ignored the rest. Nothing else could stop them. Small arms fire bounced off. Even grenades only irritated the occupants and drew their ire and attention, usually with fatal results.

The men of Platoon Two kept low in a disciplined formation as they moved up. Any fire they drew was instantly pounced on by the nearest three men, who would pin down the enemy with return fire until a small group could flank them and finish them off.

Thus, with ruthless efficiency, Anton Company marched up to their objective with the Panzer Platoon.

When the Americans broke and ran, Hauptmann Hauser released Leutnant Jung to give chase.

The young Platoon One leader, his face shining with delight, led his men in a charge that gave the Americans no time to regroup. His three squads streamed through the gaps between the tanks and fell upon the hapless enemy with glee.

Leutnant Jung's enthusiasm was infectious, and Platoon One charged at their foes with something more akin to a fierce joy than battle frenzy or blood lust.

Hans was careful to make sure his men kept pace with Jung on Platoon one's right flank.

This was to ensure that, in his eagerness, Jung didn't inadvertently over-extend himself and find his platoon surrounded. On the left side, Hans knew Stein was doing the same thing.

The most senior of the three Platoon Commanders, Oberleutnant Stein was a solid and dependable officer, even if he wasn't particularly inspiring.

To his right, shouts of warning from his second squad alerted him to a significant force of Americans seeking to flank them from the side. But they unwittingly moved straight into Hauptmann Brandt's defensive kill zone with predictable results.

Heavy machine gunfire erupted from the hill as Berta Company opened up. Men screamed, then fell silent as the American flanking force died.

Looking forward, Hans found that their attack had more or less concluded. The village was theirs. Any Americans remaining in the vicinity were dead, wounded, or captured.

Sergeant Klein came over and reported no casualties after a battle for the second time that day.

His manner remained gruff and practical, but there was no mistaking the confidence in his tone.

"Good fight," he noted with satisfaction, "The tanks really make a difference."

Then he took off his helmet and scratched his head.

"I was getting worried about all this... the Americans joining the war and the Allies landing on the continent...." Sergeant Klein admitted ruefully, "But with how we're winning now, with the Panzers spearheading our efforts, I believe we can push them back to the sea in the end."

Looking at Hans, Sergeant Klein said, "I think your faith in the *Führer* is justified after all."

How could it not *be?* Hans thought.

As Sergeant Klein left him to organize the men, Hans closed his eyes and drifted back to that fateful day so many years ago.

Hans stifled a sob.

At thirteen years of age, he was far too old to be seen crying like a baby.

More, he was still in his Hitler Youth uniform and would rather die than show weakness and bring disgrace to the *Hitlerjugend*. But with how his father looked in the hospital bed now....

A flustered nurse had shown up at his training school and whisked him directly to the hospital, so he didn't even have time to change. That afternoon, his platoon of boys had completed six months of probation and passed their grueling courage tests with flying colors.

When they had changed and cleaned up, they were presented with the coveted Hitler Youth Daggers.

As a platoon leader for his group, Hans was last to receive his, to the tumultuous applause of his mates. Finally, he and the boys he led were fully accepted.

They spent the rest of the afternoon preparing for that evening's parade.

Uniforms were starched and pressed. Boots were polished till they gleamed. Torches were prepared.

And most importantly for the boys, their newly-earned daggers were carefully secured to their belts, placed to show them off at the best possible angle.

One moment, Hans's heart was bursting with pride, and in the next, it pounded in fear and dread as he saw the nurse approach him with an unmistakable look on her face. She took him by the hand and ushered him into a waiting car that took them to the hospital.

Along the way, she spoke quickly and quietly to him. Something about his father and "his stomach ulcer" and "can't stop the bleeding" and "shouldn't have been drinking so much."

Hans didn't understand most of it, but he had seen the same expression three years ago when his mother was taken to hospital for a "fall" and "concussion."

There were a lot of medical words and earnest explanations, but it always ended with, "there was nothing more we could do."

Fifteen minutes later, she ushered him into a ward with gray walls. In the background, a radio crackled and blared as an excited announcer reported the appointment of Adolf Hitler as Chancellor.

Outside, the sun had set fully, and the night was upon the city. Acrid smoke filled the air as the crowds gathered and lit torches.

In the very last bed in a corner, Karlsen Wagner lay with a photograph clutched tightly in his hand. Hans had almost cried out aloud when he saw him.

Instead, he bit his lip to stop from making any noise and fought to hold back tears at the wretched sight of his father. He was shockingly pale, and his face had a horrible waxy sheen.

When he heard Hans approach, he turned weakly to the side to face his son.

"Did you pass," he croaked weakly.

Hans nodded silently, showing him his brand-new Hitler Youth knife. His father smiled tightly and said, "Good, good. I knew you could do it. No son of mine is a coward."

Looking out of the window toward the sounds of the crowd, he continued, "You hear that? Such joy and celebration in the streets of Berlin."

Hans nodded again.

"And indeed, there should be," his father said.

Then with sudden strength, he sat up and rasped, "Berlin is sacred. It has never been taken. Even when the Americans joined in the Great War. Even when our cowardly leaders surrendered."

He coughed suddenly, and flecks of blood appeared on his mouth. Hans started forward in alarm and gripped his father's arm. It was ice cold.

Waving toward the noise of the cheering crowds outside, his father then looked at his bedside table and smiled, "But now the city will be safe forever."

Hans followed his father's eyes to the newspaper on the table. It was dated 30th January 1933, and the headlines proclaimed the imminent appointment of Adolf Hitler as Chancellor of Germany.

Karlsen said, "So the doctors tell me I'm dying."

Hans couldn't help but gasp in distress, his eyes brimming.

"I'm not afraid," wheezed his father. "I've lived beyond my time, far longer than I should have."

His eyes drifted to the photograph of four soldiers standing by a machine gun.

"I've done what I could to make up for their sacrifice," he said, eyes still on the photograph. "Not enough, but I'm glad to have lived to see this day."

On the radio, the announcer's voice chattered excitedly as he reported the events at the Reich Chancellery, his tone taking on a frantic quality.

"I've raised a fine son, strong and brave," Karlsen said, looking at Hans. "My only regret is that I won't live to see you become a man."

His eyes closed briefly, then another bout of coughing seized him.

Then they opened as the radio announcer's voice crescendoed and rose practically to a shriek, "I think I see the *Führer*—yes, it is the *Führer*! There he stands with his ministers, Adolf Hitler.... the unknown soldier of the

World War, the unyielding warrior, the standard-bearer of freedom...!"

Outside, a call sounded out, and a thousand boots stamped down in unison as brown-shirted members of the Nazi Party came to attention. Then, at a command, they started marching down the streets of Berlin in celebration amidst a sea of torches.

The rhythmic pounding of the goose-step was hypnotic.

Soon, almost inevitably, the cries and wild cheers of the crowd morphed and settled in time with the crashing sounds of marching feet.

Sieg Heil! Sieg Heil! Sieg Heil!

Tears streaming down his cheeks, Hans said, "Father...."

His father shook his head and pointed to the window, "*He* is your father now."

Sieg Heil! Sieg Heil! Sieg Heil!

Looking straight at Hans, he raised his right hand weakly and said, "Heil Hitler."

Now, crying uncontrollably, Hans gulped and returned the salute, "Heil Hitler."

And Karlsen Wagner died.

Chapter 8

2nd March 1945—Eastern France

"*In Deckung!*" roared Hans to his men as the familiar whistle of mortar shells in flight grew louder and louder.

The men of Platoon Two ducked in their trenches seconds before the first round hit the ground more than three hundred meters in front of them and exploded harmlessly.

Harmlessly for them, but not so for the men below.

Platoon One was deployed at the base of the hill Anton Company defended and the target of the mortar barrage.

Once sure his position was not under attack, Hans risked peeping over the parapet of his trench to watch the bombardment.

It was modest by American standards, probably just one mortar section firing.

And not too accurately either, noted Hans critically, as many shells fell short of their targets.

But mortar fire didn't need to kill anyone at all to be effective. If well-timed, it just needed to shock the defenders enough so they would be unable to gather themselves to fight off the inevitable ground attack that followed.

So he still feared for Leutnant Jung and his men far down the slope from his position.

Barbed wire three layers thick ran across the entire stretch of open ground in front of Platoon One's positions. But at two points, small gaps were left to encourage charging attackers to funnel into killing zones which the defenders had covered with their heavy weapons.

The defenses looked good. The men were spread out evenly, and there were no weak points. However, against a determined attack by the enemy, they would struggle to hold their position.

And, as Hans counted the number of troops massing just out of range of the mortar bombardment, a determined attack looked to be exactly what the Americans were planning.

Hans looked around at his position and mentally reviewed Anton Company's deployment.

He and his men were midway up the hill, more than three hundred meters behind Leutnant Jung's men at the bottom. Far enough that mortar fire on Platoon One would not affect them, but also too far for them to influence the battle below when it came to close fighting.

Platoon Three and the Company HQ were deployed even further back, right on top of the hill. If anything, they would be even more disconnected than Hans from the imminent battle below.

Earlier, Hans had argued their deployment with the Company Commander, pointing out that his platoon could better support Platoon One with covering fire if they were closer.

And, if they at least posed a threat of counter-attack, it would make the Americans think twice and divert forces to account for that.

Hauptmann Hauser had only given him a tired look and said, "Oberleutnant, your sentiment to help your fellow soldiers is admirable, but there are larger forces at play here of which we know little.

"Our orders are to hold this hill as long as possible, with no specific instructions on when or if we can withdraw."

"So we are to be sacrificed then," Hans said flatly.

His company commander had paused thoughtfully at his remark but shaken his head in the end.

"No, not yet," he said. "We are not bodies being thrown against the Americans to slow them down so others can escape.

"In time, perhaps. But at the moment, we are a blocking force to enable a counter-attack by the rest of the battalion. If that is successful, this position can be reinforced as the center of gravity for the entire Regiment.

"Otherwise…"

Hans scowled as his Commander left his last sentence hanging.

Otherwise, we regroup and fall back further and further east again, Hans thought moodily.

Already they were in the eastern parts of France. How far more were they going to retreat before the German Army rallied and threw the Western Allies back to the sea?

Hauptmann Hauser then said briskly, "Anyway, you have your orders, which are to hold your position until otherwise ordered.

"The Americans are much less wasteful with the lives of their soldiers compared to the Red Army. Before they attack, they will pound us with artillery first rather than charge straight in. I will not risk two-thirds of my force coming under bombardment at the same time."

Hans had bristled in frustration but kept his face impassive as he saluted and returned to his platoon to give orders to dig in.

So now, here he was, watching Platoon One come under bombardment and unable to do anything for what would happen next.

A sudden silence filled the air as the mortar bombardment finished and was immediately broken by a loud whistle. Shouts and cries sounded in response as the Americans attacked.

Hans estimated at least a full company heading toward Platoon One's trenches. And the return fire was practically non-existent.

It seemed the mortars had done their work, and the defenders were sufficiently subdued so that the Americans crossed the space between the two forces with little trouble.

Hans shook his head in frustration. He knew it would be a close fight at best. And this looked to be anything but the best.

Tapping Erwin on the helmet, he quickly said, "Advise Hauptmann Hauser that Platoon One is under attack and will be hard-pressed. I request permission to reinforce or counter-attack should the need arise."

Erwin nodded once, scrambled out of the trench, and started running uphill.

Then Hans turned to look at Sergeant Klein in the trench behind and gave a curt hand signal.

The Platoon Sergeant turned pale but moved swiftly. He whistled sharply to the left and right and pointed toward Hans. The Squad One and Two leaders climbed out of their trenches and sprinted to the Command trench as fast as they could, jumping in before any Americans could spot them.

Satisfied they made it safely, Sergeant Klein took a deep breath, then climbed out and led Squad Three down the hill to the left of Platoon One's position, below the line of sight of the attacking Americans.

Hans nodded approvingly as his third squad disappeared from view, then looked at the two Squad Leaders in the trench with him, breathless from their sprint across open ground.

He clapped them reassuringly on the shoulders, then looked anxiously down the slope where the Americans were now less than one hundred meters from Platoon One.

Why was Platoon One not shooting back? Hans fretted.

The attackers had already made it across the open ground unopposed.

The first Americans reached the line of barbed wire and dived down in front of it. Then, drawing out pliers, they started cutting the obstacles while the rest of their mates instinctively ran toward the gaps in the barbed wire....

....and bogged down in the mud from the recent rains.

Leutnant Jung had evidently blocked off the hard-packed ground with wire defenses and left open the most unpleasant, sodden terrain for the attackers to get through.

The American charge slowed to a walking pace as soldiers cursed and struggled through mud that came up to their shins. But there was no one to take advantage of the bottlenecks that had developed.

A squad of American soldiers actually made it through the gaps and then stopped, amazed by the complete lack of opposition.

Assault drills dictated half the attackers shot at the defenders to pin them down while the rest moved forward. But with no defenders even in sight, let alone shooting, it didn't seem to make sense to fire at empty trenches.

Hans was just as confused.

What was Jung playing at? Had the mortar fire been more effective than he thought? Was the young Leutnant dead?

The defender's main advantage was that attackers had to be subject to withering fire from dug-in troops as they approached. But at close range, that advantage was all but negated.

Surely, Jung would engage when the Americans clustered together and tried to pass through the gaps, but there was still no movement from Platoon One.

More Americans came through until an entire platoon was either inside the barbed wire or slogging slowly through the gaps. Baffled by the absence of fire, the soldiers slowed and looked around uncertainly.

It was only when an officer started shouting for them to form up and advance that three stick hand grenades suddenly sailed through the air from the German trenches.

Screams of "grenade!" erupted as soldiers ran away from them in all directions.

At the same instant, seemingly heedless of the impending detonations of their own grenades, the Platoon One soldiers suddenly popped up from their trenches and opened fire on their attackers.

Many Americans running from the grenades never made it as bullets ripped through them.

Those that ran toward the trenches were cut down at practically point-blank range. Those who ran sideways crashed into their comrades who were fleeing *their* grenades and collectively became easier targets for German rifles.

Those that ran backward fared worst of all.

Blocked by the barbed wire, they angled toward the gaps where more soldiers were pouring through, adding to the confusion.

Platoon One machine guns, already trained and aiming toward the gaps, then opened up, pouring deadly fire into the mass of bodies crowding the gaps.

A dozen Americans were down in seconds.

With their attack formation completely disrupted, surviving squad leaders had no opportunity to exercise any control over the remnants of their squads.

The front-most ranks were either dead or dying. Those in the middle cowered in the ground, waiting for the grenade explosions that never came while German troops fired freely.

Dummies! Hans thought triumphantly, *Jung, you clever bastard!*

The rear-most ranks of Americans were unable to shoot for fear of hitting their own men, and the reinforcements trying to come through the gaps were mowed down by murderous machine gun fire.

When it became apparent the grenades were duds, the Americans within the barbed wire finally dared to pop up and shoot at the trenches as they retreated backward. Their firing was wild and disorganized against the deeply dug-in Germans, who picked them off one by one.

Finally, someone must have decided there were insufficient friendlies in front to warrant restraint, and the back ranks of the Americans started firing in earnest from behind the barbed wire.

At that range, the defenders still had the advantage. But more and more attackers massed behind the barbed wire and started shooting, pinning the Germans down.

Suddenly there was a thunderous explosion as, unseen by anyone in Platoon One, the Americans managed to place and detonate a Bangalore torpedo, destroying the barbed wire chain and last obstacle to Platoon One's positions.

Then the battle started in earnest.

Chapter 9

With no more barrier to infantry between the two forces, it was now a straightforward assault against a fortified position.

The Americans fanned out in a line and started advancing.

Slowly but surely, they made their way up the hill, edging closer and closer to the German trenches.

Hans looked impatiently behind him to see if Erwin had returned with permission to move. If he was to reinforce Jung, it had to be very soon. Any later, and he would be reinforcing dead men.

But Leutnant Jung, it seemed, still had a few tricks up his sleeve.

A volley of dummy grenades flew against the attackers and caused the attacking line to dive for cover, giving the defenders precious seconds to aim and pick off targets again. When the Americans realized they had been tricked a second time, they angrily resumed their attack.

The next volley of grenades was, of course, very real. And many were caught off-guard who, frustrated by the dummy grenades, had refused to take cover. The explosions hit them, and the ranks of the attackers thinned further.

After that, the line was too close for any more organized tactics and it was down to each pair in each trench to deal with the foes directly in front of them.

Hans fretted as he saw the Americans closing in. They were taking heavy losses, but not enough. And once the Americans got within the range where they could safely throw their grenades uphill, it was basically a matter of numbers.

And the Americans had many more.

There were still no orders, but Hans had seen enough.

With a bark, he got the attention of the two squad leaders and told them to prepare to counter-attack. Nodding nervously, they were just about to climb out to gather their men when a body came crashing down into the trench from behind.

Erwin, breathless from his sprint down from Company HQ, gasped out, "Orders are to hold position, Oberleutnant. No reinforcement, no counter-attack."

Hans could have screamed in frustration.

He cursed his decision to send a request for permission. If he didn't, he could have attacked and claimed it was a necessary initiative, and there was no time to seek clarification from higher up.

Now he was foiled by his obedience to protocol, bound by explicit orders, and Platoon One would be destroyed.

He looked back to the battle below, and it had entered the ugly phase.

The Americans reached the first trench, and fierce hand-to-hand fighting took place. Amazingly, the two Germans in it managed to fight them off and survive. But as they returned to firing positions, a grenade flew in and detonated, killing both men instantly.

The next trench was under attack and only saved when the platoon machine gun switched aim and mowed down the nearest attackers.

Then the machine gun fell silent as it was overrun.

Seconds later, the second trench was taken.

A movement to the right caught Hans's eye, and he gasped in horror as at least a squad of American soldiers came in from the right, flanking the front trenches entirely and attacking from the side.

He quickly estimated the distance and angle and yelled at his right machine gun crew to open fire. Having spotted the flanking attack at the same time, the crew was already shooting before Hans finished his orders.

Three Americans fell in the first burst, then another, then another. The rest beat a hasty retreat.

Hans heaved a sigh of relief as the flanking attack evaporated, then turned as his left machine gun opened fire.

Having heard their counterparts on the right side start shooting, the left machine gun crew evidently took it as permission to engage. A stream of bullets flew directly over Platoon One's position into American ranks, and men fell one after another, screaming.

While it seemed like insanity to fire into Platoon One's position, the remaining defenders were still in trenches and less exposed. And there were many, many more Americans to hit than Germans.

The American attack faltered and stalled. They did not have the strength left to overrun Platoon One *and* follow on with an assault on a fresh position far above them.

There was a long piercing whistle, a short series of shouts, and the Americans retreated.

Hans sent another messenger down to Platoon One's position to find out their status, and the report was bleak: Fully one-third of the men had been killed, and the remaining were exhausted, many with wounds.

Among the dead was the talismanic Leutnant Jung, who had died leading a localized counter-attack and charging the Americans when it looked like they were breaking through the center.

The move was so unexpected the Americans hesitated, thinking fresh forces were attacking them. That delay was enough for Hans's machine guns to come into play and halt the attack, saving the rest of Platoon One.

But at the cost of yet another young, promising German, Hans raged as he fought back tears.

He called Erwin and spoke, "Advise the Company Commander I am moving down to reinforce Platoon One. After the battering they received, the next attack will finish them."

But just as Erwin prepared to carry the message, the Company HQ messenger arrived and jumped in the trench.

"Orders from Hauptmann Hauser: Platoon Two to hold position and not reinforce Platoon One," said the messenger.

"What?" said Hans in shock.

The orders were a death sentence for the remaining men of Platoon One.

Incensed, Hans climbed out of his trench and stormed up the hill toward the Company HQ with the messenger and Erwin in tow.

When he reached the top of the hill, he burst into the Command tent and shouted, "Hauptmann Hauser, I request you reconsider your orders not to reinforce Platoon One!"

The Company Commander looked up from the map he was studying and turned around in annoyance.

"My orders stand, Hans. You are to remain in your position and *not* reinforce Platoon One," he said crisply.

Hans went red in the face and forced himself to speak calmly, "But they are severely depleted after the battle. They have lost half their fighting power, and

Leutnant Jung is dead. Another determined attack by the Americans will finish them off entirely!"

Hauptmann Hauser replied, "I am well aware of Platoon One's situation, but my orders are to hold this hill at all costs. Otherwise, the attack by the rest of the battalion will be at risk. I will not risk fresh troops defending ground we cannot hold with certainty."

"Then at least let them withdraw to my position, or even up here, rather than let them be exposed to further attack. So they can rest and recuperate to fight again tomorrow," said Hans desperately.

"There might not be a tomorrow if the battalion attack fails," said his commander grimly. "And if Platoon One is not there, there is nothing for the Americans to attack."

Hans's mouth opened in horror as he slowly understood what his commander was saying. In a hoarse whisper, he said, "You *want* the Americans to attack. Platoon One is *bait*!"

Exasperated now, Hauptmann Hauser said impatiently, "The battalion's attack must succeed, or we all die. To ensure that success, we must not only hold this hill but divert as much enemy attention to us as possible, away from the rest of the battalion."

Hans opened his mouth to object but shut it when he saw the glint in his Commander's eye.

"The forces at the base of the hill are a threat to the Americans they cannot ignore," Hauptmann Hauser said more softly now, as though he were reflecting on it.

"If there were none, they'd just put a scouting party to keep an eye on you, leaving the rest of their forces free to repel the battalion attack. As it is, they are forced to divert soldiers to clear Platoon One's position," he finished.

Still struggling to control his emotions, Hans said tightly, "But if I reinforce Platoon One, we can force them to divert more men to an attack. We might even hold...."

"Fool!" shouted Hauptmann Hauser suddenly, "*Yours* is the anchor of this hill's defense. *Yours* is the position in which the Americans will not get through. Why do you think I put my best platoon there?" he continued angrily.

Hans ignored the implied compliment, then nodded reluctantly in agreement at his commander's assessment. With a narrow front and steep slopes on either side, any force attacking Platoon Two would have no option to flank, and could only attack straight ahead into a meat grinder.

"All this will be undone if you abandon the best defensive position of this entire area and stupidly put yourself under their next artillery barrage. And it *will* be artillery this time, not just mortars. After that, we would not just lose two platoons but the entire hill," said the Company Commander angrily.

Hans tried one last gambit.

"Can we at least resupply them?" he asked.

If some of his men, led by himself, tasked with bringing ammunition and grenades to Platoon One, lingered and just happened to be there where the next attack took place, it would hardly be sensible for them to run back up with their backs to the enemy, would it? And since they were there, they might as well occupy the trenches and fight.

Hauptmann Hauser shook his head, "You know we are short on supplies. The entire Army is short on supplies."

"We are low on food, low on ammunition. We don't even have any *Panzerfäuste* left in this company," he fumed, referring to the single-shot recoilless anti-tank weapon that German infantry used against tanks. "No, I will not risk more bullets and grenades unused and lost to the Americans when they are overrun."

Hans, infuriated by his Commander's use of "when" and not "if" Platoon One was overrun, raised his voice and said hotly, "Leutnant Jung was using dummy grenades in that attack. If they were throwing sticks at the Americans then, what do you think they have left now?"

"ENOUGH!" roared Hauptmann Hauser, slamming his fist on the table with a loud bang.

There was silence in the tent while Hans and his commander glared at each other in frustration.

Finally, Hauptmann Hauser said coldly, "You have your orders, Oberleutnant, do not defy me, or I will have you relieved of command."

Then he turned his back on Hans and went back to reading the map.

Hans saluted stiffly, turned on his heel, and stalked out of the tent without saying a word. Erwin fell in step behind him like a shadow.

"Orders, Oberleutnant?" he asked tentatively.

"Gather the platoon leaders," Hans said tersely and walked down the hill in measured steps while Erwin sprinted ahead to pass the message.

When Hans reached his platoon, the Squad One and Two Leaders and Sergeant Klein were assembled and waiting for orders.

"We are not to reinforce Platoon One," Hans said.

Looks of shock and disappointment turned to pity as his commanders looked down toward the remnants of Platoon One, trying to rebuild some of their defenses.

Hans continued tonelessly, "We are to hold position until otherwise ordered. Just like Platoon One has been ordered to hold position until otherwise ordered."

The rest were silent as they digested the implications those orders had on Platoon One's fate.

It was Sergeant Klein that broke the silence.

"What now, Oberleutnant?" he asked. "Squad Three is still out there. I left them in a nice ditch down on the left. Out of sight and good cover, even against artillery. Shall I bring them back?"

Hans considered for a while, then sighed, "Yes, bring them back. If we are forbidden to reinforce, we are certainly forbidden to counter-attack."

Sergeant Klein threw a quick salute, climbed out of the trench, and left.

The Squad One and Two Leaders stayed behind, awaiting further orders from their Platoon Commander, but Hans had fallen silent, deep in thought, ignoring the stares from his Squad Leaders.

Even when Erwin looked over inquiringly at the unnatural silence, he still said nothing.

Then the American howitzers started to fire.

Chapter 10

"My father fought in the Great War scarcely twenty years ago. He was the gunner in a four-man machine gun crew. He was a good soldier," said Hans calmly, sitting on the tiny field chair in his trench, elbow resting on his knees, hands open, fingers pressed together.

WHUUMP!

The first shell landed with bone-jarring impact, and everyone but Hans ducked. This wasn't the loud, ringing explosions of the earlier mortar fire but a deep, mournful wave of force that shook the very ground they sat on.

Hans carried on talking as though nothing had happened, "They were the best. Because of them, his company defeated all who came against them."

WHUUMP! WHUUMP!

Two more shells fell—closer this time. The men clenched their teeth tightly as if to stop them from falling out from the force that rattled them.

Hans paused a bit until the ringing in his ears subsided.

He continued, "Then the Americans joined the war and turned the tide. The cowards in charge ordered our forces to surrender. So my father obeyed orders and laid down the machine gun."

WHUUMP!

A shell detonated frighteningly close, and Erwin started crying.

Hans smiled sympathetically at him and then resumed his story, "But his company refused to surrender and took the fight to the Americans. Even his crew abandoned the machine gun he put down and attacked with their personal weapons."

WHUUMP!

Another shell landed. Just as close as the previous one.

Some of the men crouched and whimpered, trying to press themselves as close to the floor as possible.

"Without his machine gun in the fight, his company was repelled and overcome," said Hans, his voice bleak.

WHUUMP!

This one seemed further away, up the hill, instead of down at the base.

When Hans spoke again, his voice wavered with emotion, "When the Americans broke through, they butchered everyone behind him, including the *next* company that was preparing to surrender."

WHUUMP! WHUUMP!

The men stopped whimpering and cowering, shocked at the story their Platoon Commander was telling them.

Tears fell from his eyes as he said, "Because he surrendered, his friends died, his company died, even the next company died."

WHUUMP!

"My father taught me it was better to die than surrender," said Hans fiercely, suddenly looking up.

WHUUMP! WHUUMP!

The men ignored the explosions, utterly spellbound now by Hans's story.

Piercing blue eyes flashed with fire as Hans looked around at his command as though seeing them for the first time.

Through gritted teeth, he said, "Our fellow soldiers down there have bled already, defending our country, defending *us*."

Pointing toward where the remnants of Platoon One prepared for a final battle, he raised his voice and said, "And now, they are being asked to die where they are?"

WHUUMP!

"Enough!" cried Hans.

WHUUMP!

"I'll be damned if I sit here and do nothing while our brothers are butchered once more," he snarled.

WHUUMP! WHUUMP!

"I'll be damned if I let another German soldier die while we idly sit here, cowering in our holes," he called out, shaking his fist to the sky.

WHUUMP! WHUUMP!

"And I'll be damned to hell if I let the Americans set foot on German soil again while I still have breath in me!" Hans shouted.

WHUUMP! WHUUMP! WHUUMP!

Went the last shells as the artillery barrage ended.

"Platoon Two!"

His sharp command was like a slap in the face for all his men. Heads popped up all around from their trenches.

Hans climbed out of his trench, rose to full height, and bellowed,

"CHAAAARGE!"

As one, the men of Platoon Two leaped out of their trenches and joined Hans as he ran down to the battlefield.

Any doubts about the wisdom of this reckless move were silenced by one look at their leader.

Towering at six and a half feet, his eyes ablaze with anger, Hans was the very image of an avenging angel of death. His men drew on his rage and ran hard to keep up with him, their own faces now set in masks of grim determination.

When they closed the distance to one hundred meters, they shouted their battle cries and fell upon the Americans just as they began their assault on Platoon One's positions.

The American front platoon had no chance.

Launching a volley of smoke grenades at Platoon One's position, they had crept in, hoping to close in on the German trenches before the smoke cleared and the defenders could see them.

But the same smoke that hid them also blinded them.

So, when at last the first soldiers emerged from their own smokescreen, they were met with a volley of fire from the defenders who had survived the artillery barrage.

Pinned down, they waited until more troops had massed until there were sufficient numbers to take the trenches the hard way—a full-blooded frontal assault.

When at last enough men were gathered, the whistle was blown, and commands to attack were shouted and echoed down the entire front line.

The timing of that order was fatal.

Just as the Americans left their cover and rose to attack, they beheld the surreal sight of a line of German soldiers running toward them in a shallow wedge formation more suited to a medieval charge than a modern battle.

At the point of the wedge was a blond giant with death in his eyes, roaring defiance against all who would stand against him. On either side of him, soldiers with stern faces and hard eyes ran with him, screaming vengeance upon those who would attack their comrades.

Confusion reigned in American ranks as the soldiers, distracted from their assault by the onrushing German platoon, faced a deadly dilemma: Continue their attack and rush the trenches but risk being overrun within seconds? Or hold and engage the German reinforcements.

Half the men did the first, and the other half did the second, with disastrous results.

The ones who continued their assault suddenly found themselves doing so with far too few men to succeed and were cut down by the fire from the trenches at close range.

The ones who stayed down to fire at Platoon Two were unable to safely do so by their comrades rushing forward to carry on the attack. As a result, the momentum of the entire American assaulting force faltered, then stalled, just as Hans and his men came in range and started shooting.

Desperate American commanders, trying to take control, shouted to their men to hold their positions and prepared to engage freshly reinforced German trenches.

Except that when Hans reached Platoon One's trenches, instead of jumping into the nearest one to reinforce it, he simply ran over it and carried on directly into American ranks as though he intended to annihilate the entire force by himself.

Caught off guard by this unexpected move, the front row of Americans were first to feel his fury as, caught up in a berserker rage now, Hans plowed through the opposition like a force of nature.

Reaching the first soldier, he reversed his rifle and swung it upwards, the butt catching the unfortunate man on the chin. He crumpled to the ground without a sound.

The next soldier had his nose smashed in by a brutal thrust of Hans's rifle butt to his face. The third went down with a bayonet thrust to the abdomen, and the fourth died as Hans shot him at point-blank range.

Two American soldiers backed off and aimed at the fearsome German Officer tearing through their ranks like an angry bear but were shot down by the Platoon One soldiers in the nearest trench.

Then the rest of Platoon Two arrived and joined the fight.

The momentum of their charge took them deep into the ranks of the American assaulting platoon. They crashed in with a ferocity that shocked the would-be attackers who, caught in the midst of shifting targets, found that the range of a rifle was no use when your opponent was already close enough to punch you.

Vicious hand-to-hand fighting erupted as Platoon Two attacked with bayonets, rifle butts, and boots. The momentum was clearly with the enraged Germans, and the American front ranks fell in less than a minute.

An American machine gun crew, late into the battle, emerged from the smokescreen to a scene of utter chaos. They hastily deployed and started firing into the German line, pinning them down and buying precious seconds for their comrades to regroup and rally.

For a moment, it looked like they would turn the tide. Once coordinated, superior American numbers would overwhelm the German forces attacking them.

But the machine gun fire was cut short abruptly as Sergeant Klein and Squad Three appeared from their right and quickly overran them. They kicked the bodies clear, seized the machine gun, turned it toward American lines, and started firing.

The remaining attackers broke and ran.

Even though the Americans still outnumbered the Germans, an unknown force's attack from the flank shattered whatever resistance they were attempting to mount.

Stalled attack turned to rout within seconds. The fleeing Americans retreated into their smokescreen just as their reserve platoon came up to reinforce the attack, adding to the chaos.

The second American platoon, seeing men with guns moving toward them through the smoke, opened fire in panic, rightly assuming there was a German counter-attack but not realizing their own men were between them.

The retreating Americans, hearing fire from behind, turned and shot back, thinking the Germans had outflanked them and were attacking in the rear, with tragic results.

The opening exchanges cost the Americans as many men as Hans and his platoon had accounted for so far before screaming American commanders could restore order and stop their losses from friendly fire.

Shouting desperately at their men, they issued orders to shoot only if they could identify the enemy,

The attacking Germans, however, had no such restrictions.

Quickly, they formed a line and plunged into the smoke in pursuit. With poor visibility, the fighting was close and brutal. Often it came down to who saw who first.

But the Germans had the advantage of being free to shoot without hesitation. In contrast, the Americans had to pause for a second to identify any figure they saw ahead of them, often fatally.

The smoke forced the attacking Germans to slow down to a walk, and the battle shifted to a new and deadly phase. Their rage had abated somewhat but was now replaced by a cold fury that was no less destructive than their furious initial charge.

They walked forward coolly, firing with calm and deadly precision. Most of them quickly exhausted the two magazines they started with. Even the lucky ones who had a precious third magazine ran out of bullets within a minute of entering the smoke.

Their giant leader was first to run out. So he drew his pistol and fired until that too clicked empty. He threw it savagely at the next opponent, then picked up an

American rifle from the floor and started shooting with that instead.

His men followed his example, dropping their weapons and picking up American ones when they ran out. They started using those until they too were spent. Then they'd either pick up another rifle or snatch spare magazines from the ground.

With the momentum firmly on their side and the Americans in disarray, Platoon Two went about the grisly task of systematically destroying the two American platoons that, mere moments ago, were on the verge of destroying their friends in Platoon One.

Chapter 11

It was only when they stepped out of the other end of the smokescreen that Platoon Two met with significant resistance.

One of the American junior commanders had gathered a few soldiers behind a rock and started shooting. One German went down, then another, and at last, Hans paused, concern for his men overriding his rage.

Shouting for his men to get down, he looked around to see if he had the forces to rush the Americans at the rock.

Then he quickly realized why the Americans at the rock were making a stand: Behind them lay what looked to be the entire company supply area, virtually undefended.

Part of him was angry. Were the Americans so arrogant? So sure of their strength that they placed their supply camp this close to the front?

But another part of him rejoiced. To destroy it would deny the entire enemy company the ability to fight until they were resupplied.

To capture it would be a prize of even greater worth, replenishing their own exhausted stocks of ammunition and rations.

He did a quick headcount and frowned.

He *did* have enough men to overcome the Americans at the rock, but it would be at a bloody cost. An attack would lose him at least as many men as they had to overcome.

Hans looked longingly at the supplies lying just a few meters beyond the Americans at the rock, then shook his head in disgust.

No more German blood would be spilled this day if he could help it.

The enemy attack had been beaten back. It was time to call it quits and pull out before the rest of the Americans rallied and turned the tables on his small force.

Scurrying back into the smokescreen, he called out for his men to start withdrawing back to the trenches. With luck, they could even make it back to his original position midway up the hill before the Americans even knew they were gone.

It was at that moment that a strong wind blew and completely dispersed the smokescreen. Having just turned to retreat, Hans and his men were caught in mid-step when their cover completely disappeared.

They froze in horror as they suddenly realized they could see each other clearly, and what that meant: The Americans could now see them too.

They all dived to the ground just as bullets whizzed through the air at them. Hans cursed in frustration as he shouted to his men to turnabout again to face the Americans.

He knew he had pushed his luck too far, and now there would be a price to pay.

Completely exposed now, there was no way they could make it back to their trenches unharmed with the Americans at the rock free to pick them off at leisure.

There was nothing for it now except to prepare to assault that position.

Hans ordered the squad on his right to lay down cover fire while he barked at the one on his left to form up and prepare to rush the Americans at the rock. But just as he prepared to charge, machine-gun fire erupted on his left.

American machine-gun fire.

Hans's heart went cold at the sound until he realized it was Sergent Klein and Squad Three. They had lugged the captured machine gun with them and finally caught up with the rest of the platoon.

Seeing his comrades under attack, Sergeant Klein had deployed the gun and started shooting without waiting for orders. The Americans at the rock, confused and dismayed, stopped firing and took cover.

Hans pumped his fist in delight as he saw the opportunity to charge the rock while the Americans were pinned down. Getting up to one knee, he raised his hand and took a deep breath to give the order to attack.

But the words died on his lips as suddenly, dozens of American troops appeared from behind the supply depot and rushed toward them, firing wildly. Hans dropped back prone on the ground a split second before a stray bullet whizzed through where he had been.

His men needed no orders. Instinctively they knew the charge for the rock was aborted, and instead, they were now fighting for their lives.

Hans looked around wildly. How could there be so many? Even the combined remnants of the two platoons they just broken through could not be so numerous.

With a sinking feeling, Hans knew there was only one logical conclusion. This was the rest of the American company rushing back to defend their supply depot.

Evidently, the American commander had rightly judged how critical this position was and diverted his entire force from whatever they were doing to come back to defend their base.

And the best way to defend a base was to kill those attacking it, Hans thought sourly to himself as he fired and felled yet another soldier.

But the Americans were attacking in a haphazard fashion, not in their usual organized lines. Had they been more coordinated, the battle would have been over by now. As it was, their runs were stuttered and their fire chaotic, as though distracted by something else.

Still, Hans thought to himself, they have numbers enough that it wouldn't matter to him and his men once they were dead.

By now, the men of Platoon Two had almost exhausted their supply of ammunition for their borrowed guns. Burrowed deeply into the ground, they fired sparingly, trying to nurse their dwindling supply of bullets.

However, in a situation where the only way they could hold off such superior numbers was the profligate use of every weapon they had, their disciplined firing only allowed the Americans to close in all the more.

Sergeant Klein's machine gun swung to the right and delivered a withering hail of bullets, covering the desperate men of Platoon Two with enfilade fire and holding off the Americans for a few more seconds.

Seconds in which Hans contemplated the unthinkable.

Because it didn't matter how bravely or cleverly his men fought—once they ran out of bullets, they were finished.

The only way they could escape was to flee with complete abandon, under cover of Sergeant Klein's machine gun, at the expense of Sergeant Klein and his crew, or be mowed down as they ran.

Hans wondered if there was time to get a message to his Platoon Sergeant. Perhaps just one volunteer could stay behind and fire the machine gun until he was overrun... but he knew Sergeant Klein would be the one to stay back and order everyone else to run.

Hans could have screamed in frustration, but in the end, there was no third option: He would either lose Sergent Klein and Squad Three or the entire platoon.

Taking one last regretful look in the direction of Sergent Klein, he took a deep breath and prepared to issue orders for a hasty retreat.

And, for the second time in less than ten minutes, his order died on his lips as two things happened simultaneously.

In front of him, the Americans had finally gotten their act together and formed an organized firing line facing his men.

The second thing that happened was heard rather than seen.

There were a series of clicks and clacks, followed by German oaths and curses as most of his men ran out of ammunition simultaneously. Just then, Sergeant Klein's machine gun jammed and fell silent as its operators worked frantically to clear the jam.

It was suddenly very quiet on the German side of the battlefield, and as his men cast anxious glances toward Hans, the Americans realized what the silence meant and charged.

It was too late to run, thought Hans desperately. He waited too long. If they tried to flee now, with the Americans already attacking, they would be cut down as they ran.

They could surrend…. *NO!* Hans thought fiercely as the word filtered through his mind.

They would never, *ever* surrender and be subject to humiliation again.

So if a last stand was what it came to, then a last stand it would be.

With that thought in mind, he picked up his rifle, fixed his bayonet to it, and started to rise. But his certainty faltered when he saw his men look at him with wide, frightened eyes.

He was willing to die for his country, his men, and the *Führer* in a final act of defiance, futile as it seemed. But could he ask his men to die with him in such a manner?

He wavered in the act of standing up as time seemed to slow down to a crawl.

He saw the onrushing Americans getting closer, faces twisted in fear and anger.

Hans raised his rifle and squeezed the trigger.

The gun clicked empty.

The nearest American closed in at a jog, raised his rifle, and aimed it at Hans.

At this range, he could not miss, and Hans knew he was a dead man.

Shouting in defiance, he pointed his empty rifle at the American soldier and frantically squeezed the trigger again.

BANG!

The American dropped dead.

Hans blinked in surprise.

Then he heard more bangs. And more American soldiers dropped.

Then a volley of fire erupted from behind and beside him, and yet more Americans fell to the floor, screaming.

Sergeant Klein cleared his jammed machine gun and started firing again, and the American attack collapsed entirely.

Hans spun round and saw German soldiers armed with American guns filling the gaps between his men. Behind them, more German soldiers ran down the line, pausing at each Platoon Two soldier.

One of them reached him and quickly handed him two magazines full of bullets, then scooted off to replenish more soldiers.

Instinctively, Hans took them and reloaded his weapon while his mind reeled to comprehend this unexpected turn of events.

A body plonked itself heavily beside him and gasped, "Sorry we took so long, Oberleutnant, but there were many bodies to plunder, and we didn't want to leave anything behind."

Hans stared at the vaguely familiar face until he recognized it, and everything clicked in place.

Platoon One!

They had come out of their trenches to follow on with the attack but paused to loot the fallen Americans, many of whom barely fired a shot before they died.

"I've got my last squad picking the field clean behind but thought you might need some help in a hurry, so the rest of us came up first," said the man Hans now recognized as Sergeant Sammer, the Platoon One Platoon Sergeant.

Hans nodded in appreciation, then saw four men hauling bags full of magazines running up to his lines and start distributing the ammunition.

"What are your orders?" asked Sergeant Sammer.

Hans looked across the field and considered. The battlefield was eerily calm. The American attack on his position had evaporated. The men at the rock were either dead or had run out of ammunition.

So all the Americans had on their side would be the remnants of their first two platoons and their third platoon, less whoever they lost in the assault they had just repelled.

Against them, Hans had most of Platoon Two, plus the remnants of Platoon One. All were replenished and had ammunition to fight.

But to attack now was madness. If they failed, there would be absolutely nothing left between the Americans and Platoon Three and the Company HQ on the hill.

Prudence dictated a fighting retreat to the rear. Hans was confident they could do this. The Americans were demoralized and in disarray. They would not pursue a force of equal size with conviction.

But even if they got back safely, they would leave behind an enemy force intact with their supplies.

Then what? Wait in Platoon One's position for the next assault? Pull back to his position midway up the hill to prepare to be pounded by artillery? For how long? To what end?

All around him, the reassuring clicks of rifles being reloaded sounded like drums calling to battle.

Alright then, one last push, one last fight, this had to end now. If they didn't take the enemy now, the enemy would take them later.

"We advance and take the supply depot," Hans said firmly.

Sergeant Sammer grunted in acknowledgment and moved off to the right to oversee the soldiers there, leaving Hans to bark orders to the men on his left.

Then he rose from cover and trotted forward quickly, eyes darting everywhere. The men of Platoon Two and One joined him in a staggered line, ready to drop to the ground as soon as they were fired upon.

They reached the rock position without incident, and the prize of the American company's supplies loomed in front like a mound of treasure.

All they had to do was cross the open ground between them to reach it.

Making sure his men were in formation, Hans signaled, and they walked forward slowly, keeping as low as they could, hardly daring to breathe as they walked into the enemy base.

Chapter 12

He felt it before he heard or even saw it.

A deep rumble in the ground like the beginnings of an earthquake that resonated in one's bones. Except it was far too regular for a natural occurrence and too painfully familiar to Hans.

"Sherman!" one of the men screamed as his entire command dived for cover.

Hans ducked as the tank shell whooshed over his head and hit the ground, exploding into the rightmost edge of his ragged line.

Bodies flew, and men screamed as shrapnel ripped through unprotected flesh.

Then the tank lurched forward, and suddenly it was among them, hull machine gun blazing as it rolled through their ranks.

Hans cried out in anguish and despair.

A tank!

What was tank doing here?

By all reports, this was a rifle company. So the nearest tanks should have been miles away. But it didn't matter now.

Even a single tank was more firepower than his entire force could match, let alone when the American soldiers rallied.

A few of his men fired on the tank.

They might as well have fired on a mountain.

Bullets bounced off the thick armor harmlessly as the tank rolled on completely unhindered.

The sound of bullets ricocheting off the armor suddenly took on a faster tempo and deeper tone as a heavy machine gun engaged the tank.

Sergeant Klein!

Could American firepower punch through American armor?

He never found out.

The tank commander, evidently judging the machine gun to be a threat worthy of his attention, slew his vehicle's main gun to the right.

"*Nooooooo!*" screamed Hans.

The tank fired, and the machine gun fell silent.

For a second, the entire battlefield was once again eerily quiet.

Then the silence was broken by a bloodcurdling scream that ripped through the air as Hans rose in fury and charged at the tank, firing wildly as he did so.

Someone in the tank spotted him, and the vehicle moved like a giant insect to face him. The main turret swiveled left to point at him, while below it, the tank's main body turned right to bring its hull machine gun to bear.

When the swiveling turret aligned with the turning body of the Sherman, the tank would face Hans with all its firepower, and he would be dead.

A split second before the tank's machine gun faced him, Hans dived to the ground, firing his last rounds as he did so.

The tank exploded in a flash of light and heat.

Hans stared in amazement at the flaming ruins of the American tank, then at his rifle, then back again at the tank.

He didn't know how he did it, but the tank was dead. He raised his fist and shouted a loud cry of victory. The supply depot was theirs!

As if on cue, two more tanks emerged from the tree line and started firing.

Hans, fist still in the air, was astounded by their appearance. How much more unlucky could he get?

But before he could react, two streaks of smoke lanced across to each tank and impacted with force. One burst into flames an instant later, while the other rolled on for a second before another streak of smoke hit it, and it too erupted into a conflagration.

Furious gunfire erupted from beyond the supply depot, and men shouted and screamed. Frantic American soldiers lined up facing to his right, engaging some unseen enemy.

The rest of the battalion! Hans thought excitedly.

With Americans busy with other German forces, Hans found his unit inadvertently in a perfect flanking position. And he was not one to allow such an opportunity to slip by.

"Charge!" he roared, and the men of Platoon One and Two rose to attack across the supply depot.

Prisoner of War

The battle ended within seconds.

The remaining American forces, primarily composed of the company's last platoon, had expected to merely be the reserve for a simple assault on a beaten German position.

Instead, they were attacked by the soldiers they were meant to overrun. The tank platoon attached to them was destroyed in minutes, just as another force of Germans attacked them from the side. As they oriented to face that threat, the charge in the flanks by Hans and his men was the last straw.

Calls of "Cease fire!" in English were heard as the Americans threw their weapons and stood up with hands raised in the air.

The first two nearest Hans were shot down in quick succession before he knew it.

Spinning to around to face his men, he shouted out sharply for them to stop shooting.

Sullen faces told him the story, and his heart burned with the same anger.

He would happily see the Americans all dead now for what they had done, but to shoot now after they surrendered might incite the rest to start fighting again, causing more German casualties needlessly.

The squad leaders of the other German force were also having the same problem as here and there, American soldiers with their arms in the air were shot down, almost randomly.

There were shouts in German, none too urgent, to cease fire. Rude noises were heard in reply, then a gunshot rang out as a last American soldier went down, and someone laughed coarsely in a distinctly guttural voice.

With that one final act of brutality, the battle ended.

Hans paused for a long moment to catch his breath and blink through sweat and tears as he looked around.

To almost the last man, his command was either sitting or kneeling in exhaustion as the adrenaline that kept them going drained away. Elation at a victory was quickly swept away as fatigue came back with full force.

But before the lassitude settled over his men, Sergeant Sammer was there, rousing them and setting tasks for each man to get them moving again.

Some were sent to form a defensive perimeter, while others set about the gruesome task of recovering the dead and wounded from the battlefield.

As with all good platoon sergeants, he did it in such a manner that, though he was the Platoon One Sergeant, the men of Platoon Two took to his instruction without objection and got on with their respective jobs.

In the midst of this, Sergeant Sammer caught Hans's eye and said, "You go ahead. I'll deal with this lot here."

Hans nodded gratefully, sent Erwin to report the battle to Company HQ and ask for new orders, then set off to link up with the other German forces that had appeared to save the day.

He recognized enough faces to know it was Berta Company that attacked the Americans. This must have been part of the grand battalion mission for which Anton Company had to hold the hill at all costs.

Relatively fresh and unbloodied, the Berta men moved quickly to take the surviving Americans prisoner and soon had them in a line on their knees with both hands tied behind their backs.

Hans walked past the line, trying to ignore the pitiful state of the men on their knees until he spotted the Berta Company Commander.

Hauptmann Adolf Brandt, besides sharing the same first name as their esteemed leader, was also tall, blond and blue-eyed—the perfect Aryan ideal as espoused by Hitler.

Hans had only met him once—at a small inaugural event for officers when their current Battalion Commander first arrived to take charge—and had instantly disliked him.

Hans noted Brandt always included his first name when introducing himself and fed on the awe and respect most people accorded to him when he did so. Coupled with his appearance, he carried himself with a confidence that didn't border on arrogance—it embraced it.

His handsome features seemed to be set in a perpetual sneer, and his tone was one of constant disdain.

Even when he spoke to the newly installed Battalion Commander, Major Wolfgang Schmidt, any deference he offered to his superior was grudging and condescending.

But when Hans was introduced to him by his Anton Company Commander, Hauptmann Brandt did a double-take. He hid it well, but a slight widening of the eyes told Hans more clearly than words that he was not used to having another Aryan around to share his glory.

Hans didn't know if he was more handsome than Brandt or not, and didn't care, but he was undoubtedly taller, and that, he was sure, was why the Berta Company Commander took an instant dislike to him too.

The term frosty as a description of the greeting he received would have been a gross understatement. Hauptmann Brandt's words were polite and proper, but his eyes would have killed Hans there and then if they could.

By contrast, their new Battalion Commander at least was a more pleasant person. Relatively short and stocky without being fat, he had dark, graying hair and seemed a bit older than a Battalion Commander should be.

Though he held a glass of wine throughout the event, he hardly drank from it, and his sharp brown eyes looked everywhere, missing nothing.

When Hans was introduced to him, Major Schmidt had spoken warmly and encouragingly to him without being too friendly, and Hans had been quietly impressed by the man's manner.

Shaking himself from his reverie, Hans mentally prepared himself to face the Berta Company Commander to report in and link up. Pushing aside his feelings toward the man, he braced himself to ignore the likely baiting and contempt he expected to receive from Brandt.

Instead, he focused on delivering a concise battle report to the senior German commander on the field until orders from his own Company Commander were received.

As Hans approached, Hauptmann Brandt drew his pistol and shot the first prisoner in the head.

Chapter 13

Hans froze as the prisoner toppled over and slumped to the ground, dead.

Nearby soldiers cast a few anxious glances in the direction of the shot but quickly returned to work at hand when Hauptmann Brandt broke out in a harsh, guttural laugh.

The same one Hans heard minutes ago.

Then, before his disbelieving eyes, the Berta Company Commander took one step smartly to his left, stood in front of the next kneeling prisoner, and shot him in the head without preamble.

The man collapsed backward, shocked eyes staring sightlessly into the sky.

Hans was aghast.

Mistakenly shooting surrendering soldiers in the heat of battle was one thing. But this—executing soldiers on their knees after they had surrendered….

"Hauptmann Brandt," called Hans loudly and ran forward.

"Yes?" came the reply as the Berta Company Commander turned left to face Hans. His pistol, pointing forward at waist height, turned with his body and now pointed at Hans.

Hans balked as he suddenly found himself in front of a loaded hand gun.

He looked into Brandt's eyes and quailed under his stare like a mouse mesmerized by the gaze of a snake.

So cold, so merciless, and equally deadly.

His mouth went dry, and he found he had no words to say. He hadn't thought about how to confront a superior officer about….

BANG!

Another prisoner went down as Hauptmann Brandt, hearing nothing from Hans that required his attention, casually turned back and shot the third man.

Hans jumped at the gunshot and rushed forward, putting himself between the next man and Hauptmann Brandt.

Then, standing at full attention and throwing his smartest salute, he said loudly, "Oberleutnant Hans Wagner, Platoon Two, Anton Company, reporting contact with the Americans."

He knew what he said bordered on idiotic. Berta Company had been in the same battle and probably had a better sense of what had happened, but he was desperate to distract the Berta Company Commander from killing any more soldiers.

"Oh, really?" said Hauptmann Brandt sarcastically and made a show of looking around the battlefield as though seeing the scene for the first time.

Then his eyes narrowed and zoomed in on the prisoner Hans was blocking.

Brandt moved to step around him, but Hans, right arm still in parade-style salute, stepped to the side and blocked him again.

Hans said in a rush, "Yes, Hauptmann. An American company attacked Anton Company's Platoon One at the base of our hill. We reinforced them, then counter-attacked and drove them back to their supply depot here. We were trying to overrun them when three enemy tanks appeared and engaged us. If it weren't for the timely arrival of Berta Company, we would have…. *HAUPTMANN BRANDT, WHAT ARE YOU DOING?!*"

His last words were a shriek as Brandt suddenly stepped to the side, angled his pistol, and fired behind Hans.

The bullet took the man in the chest, and he slumped backward, gurgling as blood bubbled from his mouth.

No longer pretending to be making a report, Hans dropped his salute and crouched in front of the dying prisoner, right hand outstretched toward the Company Commander as though to hold him off.

Hauptmann Brandt slowly cocked his weapon, clearly intent on finishing the job.

"Hauptmann Brandt, do not do this," said Hans desperately.

"They are the enemy. It is our duty to destroy all enemies of the Fatherland," came the chilling reply.

Hans pleaded, "They are prisoners of war, our prisoners. It is our duty to protect them from harm."

Brandt grimaced, "They are enemy combatants who just killed our soldiers. My soldiers, and *your* soldiers."

Hans tried again, "I would kill them myself in battle, but they have surrendered now. This is... summary execution! This is wrong!"

"Do you think we have the resources or men to keep them under guard and feed them? We don't even have enough food and water for ourselves! Do you have any better ideas? Do you want to let them go? They will join the next American unit they come across, recuperate and rearm, then they will come back to kill us!" said Brandt, getting angry.

Hans raised his voice, "This is murder!"

"No, *this* is murder," yelled Hauptmann Brandt as he pointed to where Hans's men were collecting their dead.

He continued in low, harsh tones, "This continent was already ours. *Ours*. By right and by might. And now these Americans come from afar to invade our lands, kill our soldiers.... you think they will stop here? Do you think they will stop when they cross the Rhine and march into the Fatherland? *Nein*, my dear, foolish, Oberleutnant, this young American here you degrade yourself by squatting in front of, should he live, will not stop until Berlin is a smoking pile of ruins!"

At the mention of his beloved city in ruins, Hans choked back a sob as he knew the Hauptmann was right.

Brandt, satisfied that Hans had fallen silent, motioned at him with his pistol. "Step aside so I can shoot this dog, Oberleutnant," he said contemptuously, "I am merely following Hitler's orders."

Hans stiffened at the mention of his beloved leader's name in the same sentence as cold-blooded murder. He would not stand for such effrontery. And while he had doubts about what to do with the prisoners, he was at least sure of one thing....

"The *Führer* would never give such a dishonorable order," Hans said through clenched teeth as he slowly rose and defiantly locked eyes with Hauptmann Brandt.

The senior man stared back in amazement as Hans rose to his feet.

"He has already given such an order, you fool," hissed Hauptmann Brandt.

Hans, his face an angry mask, took a step forward, but Brandt was ready for that and pointed his pistol at his head.

Prisoner of War

"Step aside, or I will shoot you where you stand, Oberleutnant," he said.

Hans flinched and turned pale but held his ground. Only when Brandt cocked the pistol did he reluctantly move aside.

Without taking his eyes off Hans, Hauptmann Brandt suddenly pointed his pistol at the wounded soldier and shot him in the head with no more emotion than one putting a wounded animal out of its misery.

Hans cried out in rage only to find the pistol pointed at his head again, behind which a cold, menacing voice said, "Back off, Oberleutnant, I won't say this again."

Shaking in anger, Hans took a step back, then another, and another as Hauptmann Brandt followed him a few paces until he was nearly in the middle of the line of prisoners.

Satisfied Hans was far enough, the Berta Company Commander turned around and strolled back to the end of the line where the next live American waited.

Mein Gott, thought Hans, *he's not going to stop until he kills them all!*

And there was no one around who could stop him.

All the nearby men were from Berta Company, and none showed any sign of outrage or even discomfort at what their commander was doing.

His own commander was all the way on top of the hill. By the time Hans got a message to him, Hauptmann Brandt would have murdered all the prisoners.

The men of his own company were too far away. But even if they weren't, *he* was Anton Company's senior officer in the field.

Hans started to shiver as he realized there was no other choice.

He would have to arrest a senior German Officer at gunpoint to make him desist, or else Hans would have to…. shoot him if necessary? Would he really kill a higher-ranking officer to save men who, minutes ago, were trying to kill him?

Hauptmann Brandt closed in on his next victim and pointed his gun.

There was no time left.

"Hauptmann!" barked Hans sharply as he strode forward and unbuttoned the holster on his side to draw his pistol.

Only to find the leather pouch tragically empty.

His heart sank as he remembered the battle in the woods and how he had lost his weapon there.

Brandt's attention had flickered to Hans when he called out, and he had seen enough to surmise Hans's intentions correctly.

"Lost something, Oberleutnant?" he said innocently, with triumph in his eyes.

He turned to face Hans, pistol at the hip and turning with his body so that it too was pointing at him. Hans started trembling with rage and fear.

Brandt then turned his body and pistol to the next prisoner. Hans lunged forward but stopped as Brandt turned back to him again and laughed that guttural laugh.

Then abruptly, he stopped laughing, and his eyes went cold.

Still facing Hans, he slowly pointed his pistol to the right, in the direction of the next prisoner, as though daring Hans to attack him.

Hans paused and calculated his next move. A feint to the left. A surge to the right. Seize the gun, knock Brandt out if he had to.

Brandt opened his mouth and eyes wide in mock fear as he aimed at the next prisoner, clearly anticipating, even welcoming, an attack from Hans.

Hans snarled and tensed to leap.

"What's going on here?" cut in another voice sharply.

With a deftness that stunned Hans, in one fluid motion, Hauptmann Brandt holstered his pistol, spun round, executed a crisp salute, and replied smoothly, "Merely a misunderstanding, Major Schmidt. Some of the prisoners here were trying to escape. Regrettably, we had no choice but to shoot them."

The Battalion Commander cast an eye over the dead bodies, still with their hands tied behind their backs, and replied evenly, "I see."

"It seems you managed to shoot them in a straight line, too," said the Major. His voice was soft, but there was an edge to it.

Hauptmann Brandt replied without batting an eyelid, "Due to the swift action of alert German soldiers, Major."

"And the misunderstanding with Oberleutnant Wagner here?" asked Major Schmidt. Hans was surprised that the Major remembered who he was, having met him only once.

"Wagner here thought we were executing the Americans out of hand when, in fact, we were shooting them as they sought to escape," said the Hauptmann, his face completely impassive, betraying no doubt nor fear of being challenged.

The man was a snake! Hans fumed, appalled at Brandt's audacity.

His face reddening with anger, Hans looked at his Battalion Commander in anticipation of being asked to speak.

If Major Schmidt noted Brandt's omission of his rank when referring to Hans, the Major ignored it. Instead, he turned to Hans and asked, "Well, what say you, Oberleutnant? Is that what happened?"

The bastard murdered four men in cold blood is what happened, thought Hans as he angrily opened his mouth to retort.

But the Major cut him off before he could speak, "Remember that in the absence of any more senior witnesses, in the case of a dispute of accounts, it is your word against that of a senior officer."

"And in such cases, the word of the senior officer will overrule that of a junior officer," finished Major Schmidt.

He emphasized the last sentence carefully, as though giving a lecture in the *Kriegsakademie*, all the while looking at Hans with a strangely intent expression.

His mouth still open, Hans froze uncertainly while Hauptmann Brandt gloated in triumph.

"Furthermore, if an officer is uncertain about the accuracy of his report, he is not required to say anything until he is certain," said Major Schmidt, still looking at Hans with a peculiar expression.

Hans snapped his mouth shut and glared at Hauptmann Brandt.

The tension in the silence that followed was palpable until Major Schmidt finally said to both men, "Very well, I note Oberleutnant Wagner has not disputed Hauptmann Brandt's version of events and I, therefore, regard this matter as closed."

"Brandt, carry on with securing the area and supplies," said Major Schmidt. His omission to mention his rank was not lost to either man, and Hauptmann Brandt went red in the face at the implied insult.

He saluted sullenly and stalked off.

"Hans, come with me," said Major Schmidt, and Hans hurried forward to walk in step with the Battalion Commander.

Chapter 14

"Tell me what happened," Major Schmidt asked in a low voice as they walked.

Hans, confused, hesitated then said, "But Major, just now... what you said about the senior officer's word overruling the junior officer's...."

The Major stopped and looked around. "Do you see anyone else here?" he asked pointedly.

Hans shook his head.

"Then tell me what happened," he snapped. "Now, you are merely reporting to me what you saw. There is no officer more senior than you here to dispute your account."

Hans nodded in understanding, then said, "He shot them, Major. While they were on their knees with their hands up."

Major Schmidt's face turned grim, and he said, "I thought as much."

He started walking again, much slower this time, as though deep in thought. Hans followed him at the side and tried to keep a respectful silence but could bear it no longer.

"Are we going to let him get away with it, Major?" asked Hans in frustration. "He murdered them in cold blood! Can you not hold him to account for it?"

Then he shut his mouth, wondering if he had gone too far.

Major Schmidt did not seem to mind the outburst.

Instead, he sighed and said, "I cannot do anything at this time. If I had arrived sooner and seen it for myself, I would have him in chains and shipped to Berlin for a court martial. But as it is, there is no one to dispute his version of events."

Looking at Hans, he continued, "If you had disputed his account, it would be your word against his. His would prevail, and I would have to ship *you* to Berlin for a court martial. But since you said nothing, he has no reason to press for charges to be made against you."

The Major's expression then turned dark, and he said, "But there will be a reckoning. I promise you that."

Hans was taken aback by the sinister tone.

Seeing the look on Hans's face, Major Schmidt seemed to read his mind.

Softening his tone, he said, "No, I don't mean assassination or suicide missions. That would no better than what he just did."

"But there will be plenty of opportunities for Hauptmann Brandt to serve his country bravely and, if need be, give his life for it," he concluded with conviction.

Then he muttered, almost as though he was talking to himself, "And if I can't facilitate that, the Americans will. God knows there will be enough opportunity for all of us to die for our country in the next few months. I only pray that, in all this mess, someone above makes sure justice is done."

Hans nodded somberly.

Changing the subject, Major Schmidt said, "Tell me what happened on your side of the battle."

Hans nodded and said, "Anton Company was tasked to hold the hill at all costs. Accordingly, Hauptmann Hauser deployed Platoon One at the bottom, my platoon in the middle, and Company HQ with Platoon Three on the top.

"Platoon One was attacked with mortars, followed by an infantry assault. They withstood that attack but at great cost. The Americans then pounded them with heavy artillery and prepared another infantry assault—one that would have finished them for sure."

Hans paused bitterly as he remembered his shock at receiving orders not to reinforce Platoon One.

He said, "After the artillery, I led my men down the hill to reinforce Platoon One. But as we had the momentum, we carried on and counter-attacked and drove the Americans back until we reached here.

"When I found it was their supply depot, I prepared to push through and capture it, but then the tanks showed up."

Hans's expression turned sheepish at this point.

"It was then I realized my entire force was not enough against the tanks...."

"And yet you decided to charge the first tank anyway," finished the Major for him.

Hans was startled. Was the Major so close to the fighting that he saw that?

"Yes, I charged the tank because...uh...um....," Hans fumbled to explain.

"The tank attacked and destroyed your machine gun position commanded by Sergeant Klein," finished the Major for him again.

Hans fell silent, deep in thought, as he wondered how Major Schmidt knew.

He had obviously been close enough to the battle to see what had happened.

Unusual for a Battalion Commander. Not only that, despite taking over the battalion in wartime and having only met junior staff once, he knew the names of his men down to the level of Platoon Sergeant at least.

There was more to Major Schmidt than met the eye.

Realizing the Major was waiting for him to finish his account, Hans said, "Uh... yes. I charged the tank. It was a futile gesture, and truthfully, I should have died. But at the last moment, someone took out that tank with a *Panzerfaust*. A very good shot. Clean and precise."

"Thank you," said the Major modestly.

Hans stared hard at the man. Was the Major saying he fired the anti-tank weapon himself?

"You made it a lot easier with your suicidal charge. He had to stop and turn the turret, and so the gun barrel moved out of the way of my shot," Major Schmidt explained.

Hans looked at him a bit longer, then shook his head ruefully. There was undoubtedly *much* more to Major Schmidt than met the eye.

"Thank you for the save, Major," Hans said at last. "You and the rest of the battalion arrived in the nick of time."

"Not really," said Major Schmidt, scratching his chin. "We weren't there to save you. This was our primary objective all along."

Hans nodded in understanding. The grand plan Hauptmann Hauser had been talking about.

Major Schmidt explained, "The Americans are planning for a big push forward with a tank division. In preparation for that, they set up depots as near the front as possible to keep their supply lines short.

"Anton Company was deployed on the hill to look like a simple blocking force—there only to deny them the high ground while the rest of the battalion retreated. The Americans would feel safe enough to set up a depot here, confident they could hold it with only an infantry company."

Hans nodded thoughtfully. That made sense. An attacker needed a three-to-one numerical advantage to succeed. Anton Company could not hope to overcome the depot defenders if they were of equal strength.

"But why us?" Hans blurted, "Why not Berta Company? Hauptmann Brandt is the best at defense, is he not?"

Major Schmidt nodded, "Yes, he is. I was preparing him to dig in on the next hill with Anton poised to strike from here, but the Americans deployed further south than we expected. So there was no time for both companies to switch places."

Hans nodded.

The Major continued, "In the meantime, with American attention on your company and unable to track us unless they took the hill, the rest of the battalion would flank the defenders and hit them from the north."

Hans thought the plan through and shook his head, "Still a gamble, Major. Even without their tanks, the Americans are fresher and better supplied."

Major Schmidt nodded thoughtfully, "Yes, a gamble. Assuming they'd keep one platoon facing your company on the hill, it'd still be two of our companies against two of their platoons. We'd have the required numbers to win on paper, but it would be a close fight and one we could not afford to lose."

Looking at the hill in the distance, he continued, "So your company commander deployed your platoons in such a fashion. With your platoon holding the strongest defensive point as the anchor for the entire hill, Platoon Three denying the high ground to scouting parties so they would not spot the rest of the battalion moving. And Platoon One...."

"Deployed so close that they could not ignore it and therefore had to commit men and resources to attack," said Hans bitterly, continuing Major Schmidt's line of reasoning for him.

It all made sense now. With Platoon One seemingly isolated, the Americans could realistically expect to destroy them with one company, especially with artillery support.

"And when they did so, the rest of the battalion could attack them from the flank, with a better chance of defeating them and capturing the depot, with minimal casualties and minimal damage to the supplies," said Major Schmidt, finishing the explanation for Hans.

Then, pointing to the burnt-out tank that almost killed Hans, Major Schmidt said, "The last problem was, as you saw, reports of their Armored Division already on the move with lead elements expected here soon.

"So we stripped your company of all your anti-tank weapons and gave them to Caesar Company, which functioned as a blocking force. They had their hands full with the American tank company that arrived.

"Fortunately, the Americans expected a nice, quiet resupply at a safe depot and weren't ready for a fight. The three that spilled over here were the last of the company that Caesar Company ambushed at close range."

Hans nodded numbly as he recalled his near-miss with death.

Suddenly exhausted beyond belief, his shoulders slumped, and he almost stumbled as he walked. The Major caught him with a surprisingly firm grip and pulled him upright.

"Hans," he said gently, "Your unexpected counter-attack destroyed one American platoon, disabled another, and distracted the last one sufficiently so that, when

Berta Company attacked, it was against a confused and disorganized force. They succeeded with hardly any casualties.

"Caesar Company was also able to engage the tanks without needing to reinforce Berta Company. Saving us all from being overrun by American Shermans."

Major Schmidt clapped him on the shoulder with a smile, "You have saved many German lives today."

Hans pondered his Battalion Commander's words and began to smile in satisfaction. Haunted by the deaths of so many today, at least he could take comfort in the fact that his actions prevented many, many more.

Soon, they reached the collection of tents that formed the Battalion HQ.

Major Schmidt stopped outside his tent and said, "And Hans, I know your counter-attack wasn't part of the plan because I gave Hauptmann Hauser orders to hold only and not attack."

Hans winced in embarrassment.

The Major continued sternly, "Even if your madcap charge *did* save the day, you do know you were very, very lucky. Please do not do that again in the future. I cannot afford to lose my best company commander to heroic but rash antics."

"Begging your pardon, Major, but I am only the Platoon Two Commander, not Company Commander," said Hans, correcting his battalion commander.

Major Schmidt gave him a sad look, then turned around and entered his tent without saying another word.

It was only then that Hans noticed Erwin, his platoon messenger, standing by the tent, his face ashen and in tears.

Then Hans turned to look and his breath caught in his throat as he saw in the distance, on the very top of the hill he had been defending, the smoking ruins of Platoon Three and Anton Company HQ.

Chapter 15

"They're dead, Oberleutnant, all dead," cried Erwin. "I ran up to report about our battle, but when I reached the top, no one was left alive. It was just craters and body parts!"

He babbled on, "So I ran back as fast as I could. I couldn't find you, but the Major here spotted me and called me over, so I reported to him, and he told me to wait here."

Hans nodded mutely as he tried to process what Erwin was telling him.

"We're going to lose the war, aren't we?" said Erwin miserably, sniffing now.

Startled out of his thoughts by the young soldier's question, Hans was about to reprimand Erwin for defeatist talk when he saw the despair on his young face.

Taking a shaky breath to calm himself, he put his hand on Erwin's shoulder.

"No, we're not," said Hans gruffly.

"We might lose a fight, a battle, even our lives, but we will not lose the war," he said firmly.

Erwin looked unconvinced.

Hans sighed and reminded himself Erwin was barely a teenager when the war began.

"Remember the start of the war? How we marched across Europe and conquered all of it in weeks?" asked Hans.

Erwin began, "But now the Americans...."

"The Americans are children," said Hans, cutting him off.

"All this," he gestured vaguely around him, "and even this," he said, pointing to the smoking ruins of his company HQ, "are regrettable losses, but all part of a bigger plan.

"Remember the victories in the beginning. The *Führer* led us then, and he leads us now. He will not let us down. Once he gets a handle on the Americans, we will rally and throw them back to sea with all the others. You wait and see."

But a sliver of doubt gnawed at him when he said that. Children the Americans might be, but there were a lot of them, and with very big guns.

"We just have to be brave and face the enemy, not run, nor surrender," said Hans.

Erwin sniffed once more and said, "Thank you for your patience, Oberleutnant. I will not doubt again."

Hans nodded slowly, then put his hand on Erwin's shoulder.

"You have done all you could. Go rejoin the platoon, help out where you can, then get something to eat," Hans said gently to his distraught messenger.

Erwin sniffed and nodded, managed a salute, then went off to find his platoon mates, leaving Hans alone with his thoughts.

Shaking his head in disbelief, and despite his encouragement to Erwin, Hans felt himself sinking into deep despair.

Platoon Three and the entire Company HQ—gone, just like that. Like they never existed.

He was never particularly fond of Hauptmann Hauser. But he was a decent enough company commander and, with the new insight Major Schmidt had just given him, a competent one despite Hans's initial misgivings on his plan to defend the hill.

More, he functioned as someone above him who had to take responsibility. Someone Hans could blame when things went wrong. And he represented a position Hans could fall back to, often literally, with the additional men and resources at his command.

Now…. what?

Had Major Schmidt implied he was now Anton Company's commander?

Did he want to be?

A platoon he could command.

There weren't that many men to manage, and he knew them well.

His men, likewise, trusted him and followed him unquestioningly into battle.

However, as a Company Commander, he would have to send men into battles he might never see, let alone lead. Be responsible for the deaths of compatriots he might not even know the names of, with no one else to blame but himself if things went wrong.

If he had been the one to order Platoon One to dig in and die in place….

Hans shuddered at the thought. There had to be another way.

Just then, Major Schmidt stepped out of his tent.

Hans quickly stepped up and said, "Major Schmidt, I have just been updated by my platoon messenger about the destruction of Platoon Three and Company HQ."

"Yes," replied the Major. "Anton Company needs a Company Commander now. I am offering you the job. Do you accept?"

Hans hesitated, shuffling his feet.

Then he said, "I will do my best to get the rest of Anton Company ready for Hauptmann Hauser's replacement."

Major Schmidt paused, gave him a curious look, and asked, "And who might that be?"

Taken aback by the unexpected question, Hans floundered, "I don't know...Perhaps one of the battalion operations staff?"

The Major shook his head and said, "My Communications Officer has been taken to Regiment to replace personnel lost there. My Adjunct is effectively managing the entire battalion supply trains on his own. My Combat Clerk functions now as my Adjunct and delivers my orders unless I can do so myself. So unless you want the Battalion Physician to take over Anton Company, I have no other officers to spare."

"But surely the Regiment has...." Hans began in protest.

Major Schmidt cut him off crossly, "There is no one else. With Hauptmann Hauser dead, Platoon One and Three Commanders dead, you are the senior ranking officer in the company.

"You are the *only* officer in the company. By default, you are in command of this company until relieved."

When he paused for breath, Hans could see the lines of agony and fatigue etched on his face. It wasn't just Hans reeling from the shock of the loss of an entire platoon to American artillery. Major Schmidt also felt the pain at the decimation of one of his companies.

Major Schmidt said in a tired voice, "It is my preference you take command of Anton Company. The men know you and you, them.

"But I will not force a command appointment on an unwilling officer. I cannot afford an unstable leader in a time like this."

Hans brightened at the prospect of an alternative until Major Schmidt elaborated, "If you do not take command of Anton Company, I will consolidate its men into a single platoon and add it to Berta Company under the command of Hauptmann Brandt."

Hans froze in horror.

He looked back at the field where his men, exhausted from the battle, were struggling just to gather their dead and wounded.

The men of Berta Company, fresher and with far fewer casualties, were busy plundering the supply depot of anything that could be used, ostensibly for the rest of the battalion.

But Hans did not doubt that, with no one to stand up for them, the distribution of precious resources would be grossly uneven for his men.

As a new platoon in Berta Company, things would be even worse. He would inevitably be in charge of it, and under the direct command of someone who had drawn a gun on him barely a few minutes ago.

Hans shook his head in frustration.

The men of Anton Company would be sent on the very next suicide mission just because of him, and that would be their end. Never mind the problem of supplies and resources.

But if he were officially the Anton Company Commander, he would be of equal appointment, if not rank. He would be answerable to the Battalion Commander rather than the murderous Brandt. He could better look out for his men.

Still looking at where his men dragged the dead and wounded together, he answered Major Schmidt softly, "I will take command of Anton Company, Major."

The Major, following his gaze back to his men, nodded knowingly.

Then he said gently, "Hans, all that's left of Anton Company are those who survived this battle. Your platoon, the remnants of Platoon One, and perhaps a few who survived at Platoon Three's position. Effectively, Anton Company is a reinforced platoon at most. There isn't much more to command than what you are already doing."

Hans nodded glumly in agreement.

Major Schmidt stared at him for a while, then, satisfied that Hans had accepted the assignment, moved on to the next matter.

He started walking toward the supply depot and nodded for Hans to follow.

As they walked, he spoke speculatively, almost to himself, but there was no missing the tone of urgency underlying his voice.

"We have to change," he said. "We have to do things differently."

"Until now, this war has been a slugfest. The Americans hurl themselves at us in full frontal infantry attacks. We are dug in. They are inexperienced. We give ground, but only at great cost to them in lives. Man for man, we are more than a match for them," said the Major defiantly.

Hans nodded in agreement. In every engagement he had been involved with, in any confrontation between similar-sized forces, all things equal, the Germans would prevail against the Americans.

But things were not always equal, he thought sourly to himself, looking at the American rifle in his hand and despairing at the shocking shortages of even the most essential things needed to fight a war. How could one shoot at the enemy with no bullets?

Major Schmidt continued, "But things are different now. It is not man against man, soldier against soldier anymore. With their heavy weaponry now in place, they can bring firepower to bear that we cannot match, no matter the skill of the bravest German soldier."

He looked meaningfully at the smoldering hulk of the M40 Sherman tank across the field.

"We cannot sit in prepared defensive positions and wait for them to bleed themselves dry against us in costly infantry assaults. They no longer need to. A dug-in position is now an invitation for their howitzers to practice on stationary targets until our men are smashed to bits," said the Major, pointing to the top of the hill where smoke still trailed from the remnants of Platoon Three.

"We cannot afford a situation where we can be attacked, but we cannot strike back," Major Schmidt concluded.

"No," he said softly, "we have to do things differently."

They reached the first stack of crates of the American supply depot.

Then, looking at Hans, Major Schmidt asked, "How long would it take a Panzer Company to attack an American artillery position five kilometers away?"

Hans frowned. What was the Major really asking?

At a road speed of forty kilometers per hour, it would take a tank less than ten minutes to travel the distance. Factoring in giving orders, organizing the troops….

"Thirty minutes?" replied Hans uncertainly.

"Yes, If they just tried to roll up to the target at full speed, in the open, with no other considerations," said Major Schmidt.

"But they would be subject to enemy fire and traps, have no contingency, no plan for how to maneuver when they get there, no plan for refueling and rearming. And this is assuming the tanks were ready to roll, to begin with," continued the Major while Hans nodded in bemusement.

"Upon receiving orders, the tank company commander would have to formulate his own plan, including the route of march, expected resistance in the form of ambushes, traps, or obstacles, and how to overcome them.

"He also needs to know the terrain at the objective or risk his tanks being stranded in the open, subject to fire while unable to move clear.

"To that end, scouts might be dispatched and given time to report back. The commander then has to disseminate the plan to the platoon commanders, who have to disseminate it to their own men.

"Moreover, the tanks have to be fueled, armed, and checked for roadworthiness before they move. Then, as they move, they either move with dismounted infantry screening ahead of them or risk being ambushed."

"It would take them five hours," concluded Major Schmidt.

Turning to Hans, he suddenly asked, "How long would it take your company to attack the same target?"

Without hesitation, Hans replied, "One hour."

Major Schmidt nodded in approval.

Then he reached over one of the supply boxes and opened it, revealing stacks of neatly folded American uniforms.

"One hour," he said, looking solemnly at Hans.

Chapter 16

It took a while for Hans to register what Major Schmidt was saying. When he did, despair filled him as the prospect of getting a little rest after the battle faded in the face of a new mission.

Then, as he looked over to the dead and wounded of his company and at the smoking hilltop, a familiar, cold anger began within his stomach and filled him with energy.

Looking at Major Schmidt, he said grimly, "I understand. Give me one hour."

Major Schmidt patted the American uniforms in the boxes and said, "Take two. You need time for a costume change. And you'd still be faster than the Panzers anyway."

Then he snapped his fingers, and one of the Berta Company Platoon Commanders came running over. The

Major started rattling off instructions before the young officer even saluted.

"Inform Hauptmann Brandt that Berta Company is immediately responsible for retrieving the dead and wounded of Anton Company, including those on top of the hill. From the fallen Americans, gather all weapons and munitions and deposit them at the Anton Company staging area. Lastly, get hot food and water and clean towels for washing up. I want every able-bodied man from Anton Company freed from mop-up duties and assembled here in ten minutes," said the Major.

He paused a second to read the officer's face to ensure he understood, then dismissed him and turned to Hans.

"You got all that?" he asked Hans.

Hans nodded, "Yes, Major. Thank you."

Major Schmidt waved it off and said, "Don't thank me, that artillery position is as likely to shell me as anyone else if they get the chance. If we do this, I'd like to make sure you have as much of a head start as possible."

"In that case, would you like to brief me on the mission target now, Major?" asked Hans.

"Let's wait for Hauptmann Brandt to arrive, then I can update you both together," replied the Major.

Hans thought and said, "Ah, Major Schmidt, I don't think you sent for Hauptmann Brandt in your orders."

"Oh, he'll come soon," said Major Schmidt confidently.

Meanwhile, the Berta Platoon Commander started barking orders to his platoon first, and soon men were running this way and that. Bewildered Anton Company soldiers, dragging their dead and tending to their wounded, were shooed away from their tasks and sent toward where Hans and the Major waited.

A squad of Berta Company soldiers trotted to the woods between them and the hill, calling for Anton Company to assemble at the supply depot. Then they started systematically combing the area and salvaging weapons and munitions from the fallen soldiers with smooth efficiency.

Satisfied he had gotten things in motion, the Berta Platoon Commander then tromped off to look for his Company Commander with the expression of one walking to his execution.

Minutes later, a shriek of outrage was heard, and Hauptmann Brandt came storming up to where Major Schmidt and Hans waited for the men of Anton Company to assemble.

Barely able to muster a salute, he shook with anger as he said, "Why are my men being asked to act as servants for Anton Company after a battle? Can they not treat their own wounded? We have wounded to deal with too!"

Without flinching, Major Schmidt replied, "So glad you can join us, Hauptmann Brandt. Just in time for my briefing for the Anton Company Commander." He nodded toward Hans.

Brandt's mouth fell open in shock.

Major Schmidt ignored his reaction and commenced his briefing.

Unfolding his map and placing it on one of the supply crates, he pointed to a spot west of their position and said, "The artillery position that just obliterated Anton Company HQ and Platoon Three is here. Word is they are preparing to redeploy further forward so they can fire deeper into our Regiment positions.

"Any further east, and not only can they fire on our combat units, but they can also hit our supply trains and depots. This cannot be allowed to happen."

He paused for a moment to let the gravity of the situation sink in.

Hans and Brandt both nodded. They understood the disaster that would spell for the entire Regiment. Brave men might fight after a bombardment, but not without ammunition. And every company, even front-line ones like theirs, was running out.

"Therefore, I intend to immediately launch a company raid against the American artillery position that just pounded us here and eliminate that threat to us," said Major Schmidt.

Hauptmann Brandt protested, "But Major Schmidt, our standing orders from Regiment are to hold our position for as long as possible, not attack the Americans."

"Those are indeed our standing orders. However, it is my judgment that we cannot do so with the artillery free to engage us at leisure. And we certainly cannot hold if our supply bases are destroyed," said Major Schmidt.

He continued, "There is no time to report back to Regiment about this battle and await further orders. I am therefore interpreting my orders to hold our position differently from the traditional execution of a static defense.

"Instead of digging in and waiting to be bombarded by artillery, then overrun by infantry, I intend to attack enemy positions of importance, such as artillery batteries and supply depots, while keeping my units mobile and fluid, able to adapt and move as required."

Hans nodded in understanding. If they could deny the enemy their artillery support, plunder or at least destroy their supplies, the Allied advance would stall on their own, and their battalion would effectively still be in control of their sector of responsibility.

Major Schmidt said firmly, "We hold ground by destroying the enemy's means to take it from us."

Everyone around nodded in agreement.

"Anton Company will launch the raid. Therefore, they will concentrate on resting and rearming for the raid and are relieved of all other duties. Berta Company will provide local security, mop-up, and care for the wounded. One squad will also be dedicated service and support for Anton Company," finished the Major.

Hauptmann Brandt scowled at the last order but kept his mouth shut. Then, seeing there was nothing more for him, he saluted crisply and marched off, giving orders to the trail of Berta Company officers and sergeants that had followed him in.

Within seconds, they peeled off one by one, and a flurry of activity erupted wherever they went.

By now, the men of Anton Company had gathered in a loose circle. Most had heard the briefing, and the rest quickly filled in those that came late.

Some from Platoon One were shell-shocked and on the verge of a breakdown, having seen half their mates die in a single day. Others were staring at the ground listlessly at the prospect of going on a dangerous mission before they'd even finished mopping up the battle they had just fought.

All were exhausted.

Meanwhile, the lively bustle continued in the background as Berta Company went about their tasks like ants in a nest.

Like magic, barbed wire defenses appeared, and machine-gun strong points were erected. Hot food and water were brought to where Anton Company gathered. Men started working on the pile of American rifles they had salvaged and checked them for workability and function, while others busied themselves reloading the magazines with ammunition.

Standing in the middle of it all, like a magician in the center of a maelstrom he summoned, Hauptmann Brandt, with his hands behind his back, watched his men like a hawk. His face was set in a sneer, and every command he made was delivered in a contemptuous tone.

But it worked. He expected to be obeyed instantly and without hesitation, and his men did so.

Hans was grudgingly impressed. He disliked Hauptmann Brandt with good reason but reluctantly admitted he ran a tight and efficient company.

As Major Schmidt turned to leave, Hans called out, "What do I do, Major?"

His Battalion Commander paused and looked at him, his eyes searching. Obviously, Hans wasn't asking about the technical aspects of his orders. Those were straightforward enough. Gather his men. Get them dressed and armed for battle, and attack the artillery position as soon as possible.

No, it wasn't the physical details that bothered him, but the inner workings of every soldier in battle pushed to the limit and then asked to go on some more.

The Major nodded sympathetically, then pointed to the hill which Hans charged down less than one hour ago.

"You just led your platoon down that hill in an insane assault against a superior force and prevailed. How did you do that? *Why* did you do that?" he asked.

Hans stayed silent, his mind in turmoil.

"Now do the same with Anton Company," said Major Schmidt.

Then he looked meaningfully at Hans.

"*Your* company," he finished softly and walked off past Hans.

Chapter 17

Hans stared at the exhausted remnants of Anton Company.

Without thinking, he reached over his shirt pocket and pressed on the Hitler Youth knife inside it. Then, as always, the image of his friend lying dead in the ruins of the church flashed before his eyes and shook him.

But the solidity of the knife, its heaviness, brought him back and grounded him. Eyes flashing with fire now, Hans raised his head and looked at the men assembled before him.

"Anton Company," he began.

"You have fought well and bravely today. The enemy expected us to roll over and die, but we did not. Instead, we held against overwhelming force and prevailed. Defying the odds, not only have we fulfilled our mission, we have overturned the battle against the Americans," said Hans.

He looked at the bodies laid neatly in a row, and fought to hold back tears.

His voice shaking, Hans continued, "But at a terrible cost. Such terrible cost."

"I know you are all tired, exhausted. I know you want to curl up and close your eyes. So that the sleep might bring rest and reprieve from the demons that haunt us and let us mourn our dead," said Hans, looking in the distance.

Then his eyes hardened, and his voice took a bitter edge, "But it will not be so. Even now, the enemy artillery that did that," he pointed to the ruined hilltop, "and helped do that," he pointed to the bodies in a line, "is preparing to move and redeploy."

"And when they do, they will be able to do all this again, to more of our brothers," said Hans.

Looking at each man in the eye now slowly, he raised his voice, "Well, I say no more! No more will we sit in holes while they shell us at leisure. No more will we wait for them to attack when *they* are ready.

"By the blood of those who have died, we now have the opportunity to strike back. Let us not allow their sacrifice to be in vain.

"This time, *we* take the fight to *them*. We return with interest what they gave to us."

In a firm tone, he finished, "For the sake of those who have fallen, for the sake of those who *will* fall if we do not do this."

There was a long silence from the men.

Finally, Sergeant Sammer spoke up, "Oberleutnant, I can only speak for myself, but I'm sure the men feel the same way. We will follow you. Let's go make the Americans pay."

Hans nodded in acceptance of the support as the men rose with muttered agreements and stern faces.

Quickly, Hans got the men organized. He said, "Sergeant Sammer will function as Company First Sergeant."

"Who's the senior Squad Commander left in Platoon One?" he asked.

A hand shot up. "I am, Oberleutnant. Corporal Lang," said the Platoon One Third Squad leader.

Hans hesitated.

He knew of Corporal Lang's reputation. Enthusiastic, irrepressible, a bit of a loose cannon. But there was no one else. He wasn't just the senior Squad Leader left—he was the only one.

Sighing to himself, Hans said, "You are now Platoon Leader of Platoon One. Understood?"

"Yes, Oberleutnant," said Corporal Lang, saluting proudly.

"Platoon Two will remain as you are, under my direct command," Hans said.

His Squad Leaders nodded in acknowledgment.

"What about Platoon Three?" asked Sergeant Sammer quietly.

Hans was quiet for a while. Then he patted the shirt pocket over his heart and felt the Hitler Youth knife in it.

He said, "We carry them here, with us, along with all the other fallen."

Then his eyes blazed with anger, "And when we next fight, we unleash them on our enemies like the legions of hell."

Grunts of approval sounded all around as the men moved to get ready.

Preparations went on smoothly from there.

Sergeant Sammer ensured all the men washed up before fitting on the new American uniforms.

"If we're going to pretend to be American reinforcements, we have to look the part," he explained to Hans. "Anyone who sees us in brand new uniforms but with blood and mud on our faces will be suspicious."

Hans nodded in agreement. It took more time, but aside from the necessity of doing it to strengthen their disguise, it also refreshed the men visibly, as though cleaning the dirt and blood washed away some of their weariness at the same time.

The hot food helped tremendously, too, as Anton Company helped themselves to large portions from the sullen Berta Company soldiers tasked with serving and washing up after them.

American rifles were assigned. Each soldier checked and inspected his new weapon and ensured it was in good working order. Then they were gifted with as much ammunition as they wanted to carry.

Once cleaned, changed, fed, and armed, the soldiers stole whatever time they had left to snatch some sleep while Hans gathered the commanders to discuss and plan the raid.

It was a simple plan.

Effectively only a reinforced platoon rather than a full-strength company, they were a small enough force to slip in undetected. Armed to the teeth, unencumbered by heavy supplies, they would move quietly and quickly through the forest trails until they got to the artillery position.

They would form a single line, creep forward as far as they could until detected, and then charge in guns blazing to overrun the position. When they were done, everyone would evacuate and fall back to base before any American response.

Hans had just finished the plan and dispersed the Squad Leaders to brief their men when Major Schmidt walked up.

"Yes, Major Schmidt," said Hans, jumping up to attention, "we are just about ready."

"Fine," replied his Battalion Commander, "let's go then."

Hans raised an eyebrow in query.

"Yes, Hans," said the Major calmly as he checked and cocked his pistol, "I'm coming with you.

Chapter 18

Hans fretted as he led his force into the woods. Bad enough he had to lead a raid deep into enemy positions on short notice with a tired and understrength force; now, he had his Battalion Commander tagging along. Protests that it wasn't safe for him to come along were waved off by the Major himself.

"Pah," he had said irritably when Hans pointed out he couldn't guarantee his security, "I can take care of myself. Besides, I am the Battalion Commander, yes? I am with one of my companies, yes? That is safe enough."

The Major mused, "Besides, how safe do you think I will be if we do not neutralize this artillery? Once they find out we have taken their supply depot, the first thing they will bomb is the German force occupying it. The next thing will be that unit's Battalion HQ if they can find it.

"I am as safe with Anton Company as I am back there, a sitting duck and target practice for their artillery."

Hans had shrugged off the reply and carried on. As long as the Major could keep up and didn't hinder his men, he would leave him be.

Skirting parallel to the main road, they made their way through the dense forest rapidly and without detection. Soon they reach their target.

Hans stopped his men out of sight, then crawled forward to take a closer look.

He frowned as he reviewed the positions.

From their vantage point, only one gun was within easy reach. Three men were guarding it, but they did not seem to be expecting trouble. The rest of the artillery pieces were widely dispersed across the clearing and, as far as Hans could see, similarly guarded by three men each.

In the center was a cluster of tents where the commander was probably based. Hans assumed the rest of the men gathered there for orders and rest.

Standard tactics called for the attackers to deploy one squad to cover the main road where reinforcements were most likely to approach, while the rest fanned out in one line and charged the clearing.

However, from their position, they could only surprise the guards at one gun without loss before the rest were alerted at the first shot.

While Hans was confident they would overwhelm the Americans, he wasn't sure they could do so without loss. Even one casualty needed four men to carry him back, leaving Hans with four men less to fight if they encountered more enemies on the way back. And if there were more casualties, his available fighting force would diminish exponentially.

Hans pondered his plan as Major Schmidt appeared and wriggled into position next to Hans.

"How goes the.... ah," the Major's greeting was cut short when he popped his head up for a glance and arrived at the same conclusion as Hans.

"Widely dispersed positions, extra guards at each gun, alert for trouble... word must have reached them about the supply depot.... only the guards at one gun will be surprised. The rest will have a few seconds before we reach them. Not forgetting the men in the main cluster of tents.... it will be a straight fight, and we will take casualties," murmured Major Schmidt, echoing Hans's thoughts.

Hans replied in a whisper, "And if we redeploy to the right, we can surprise two, maybe three guns, but will be too far from the squad watching the road. We cannot support them against reinforcements, nor can they support us if the raid falters."

The Major nodded somberly.

Without a word, they both eased themselves back, then stooped low as they made their way back to the rest of the men.

Hans almost had a heart attack when two American soldiers suddenly materialized from behind a tree, rifles pointed at him. Only belatedly did he realize it was his own men guarding their positions.

Resisting the urge to scold them for scaring him like this, he quickly grasped they had done nothing out of the ordinary. It was simply the fact that they were in American uniforms that had shocked him so.

A wild idea formed in his head as he called for the company leaders to gather for a final briefing. The more he thought about it, the more plausible it seemed. By the time they all assembled, looking like nothing more than a squad of American soldiers, he knew his plan would work.

Grinning wolfishly, he started to brief the squad leaders.

"Does anyone have any cigarettes?" he began.

Corporal Lang guiltily raised his hand.

First Sergeant Allen, Battery Sergeant of Bravo Company, 2nd US Army Infantry Cannon Regiment, was worried.

He stood silently watching as his commander, Captain Barrett, pored over his map in the command tent and contemplated the unthinkable: Planning a fire mission on a friendly position they had lost contact with.

There were reports that the supply depot had been overrun shortly after their fire mission on a crucial hill in preparation for an infantry assault.

A fire mission that was, by all accounts, a success.

How had things turned so badly so quickly?

He fervently hoped it was just a misunderstanding. A cock-up in communications by some junior officer who would have his backside handed to him once the matter was resolved.

In the meantime, he had decided to beef up local security and added one extra man at each gun just in case stray German units wandered in.

He was just about to ask if Captain Barrett could request extra help from the nearby infantry company to strengthen their position when Private "Tiny" James popped his head in the tent flap and said, "Some infantry lieutenant here to see you."

Captain Barrett raised an eyebrow and muttered, "Must be the reinforcements," and motioned for his Battery Sergeant to see to the visitors as he went back to plotting his fire mission.

Exiting the command tent, First Sergeant Allen followed Tiny back to where a platoon of soldiers waited patiently.

He was impressed.

While he was posting extra men to guard their guns, his commander had evidently called for assistance, and they had arrived in good time.

Quickly identifying the Platoon Leader, a tall, blond first lieutenant, He saluted him and said, "Glad to see you, sir. All quiet here so far, but word is things have gone wrong at the forward supply depot, so we're all a bit twitchy."

The Platoon Leader returned the salute and said, "There are reports of a German force raiding deep into our lines, so we have been dispatched here to take care of the artillery position. I intend to deploy two squads immediately to the guns, and my third squad will set up with the rest of your men."

"Yes, yes," said First Sergeant Allen, relieved.

He quickly dispatched Tiny to lead the two squads around the compound. Tiny nodded and walked off briskly, motioning for the newcomers to follow him. When they reached the first gun, he called out to the three guards and waved. Then, four men peeled off from his group to join the guards.

Satisfied their deployment was underway, First Sergeant Allen turned back to the Platoon Leader and pointed as he spoke, "The ammo dump is there, behind the small mound, the command tent is there, and the rest of my men are in the tents nearby. Your men can set up there."

The Platoon Leader grunted in acknowledgment and, with a nod of his head, indicated to his Platoon Sergeant to organize the men. Then he took off his helmet, lit a cigarette, and offered one to First Sergeant Allen, who took it without thinking and accepted the light from the officer.

Puffing contently, he asked, "Where're your folks from, sir? I'm pretty good with accents. I reckon you're from the east."

The Platoon Leader nodded.

"New York? Boston?" probed the First Sergeant.

"Further east," said the lieutenant dryly.

First Sergeant Allen creased his brow in puzzlement. *Further east than Boston?*

Shaking his head, he changed the topic. "What did you do before all this then?" he said, waving his hand around as if to indicate the entire war.

"I was an officer in the German Army," the lieutenant said with a perfectly straight face.

First Sergeant Allen stared in shock at him for a moment, then burst out laughing, bending over and slapping his thigh.

"Hooo! Hey! You sure had me there, Lieutenant! The joke's on me. It is! That's a good one, sir, a really good one!" he whooped, wiping tears in his eyes.

Then he froze as he looked up to see the barrel of a pistol pointing right between his eyes.

"I wasn't joking," came a cold, menacing voice, utterly devoid of humor, as Oberleutnant Hans Wagner, Anton Company, 1st Battalion, cocked his pistol ominously.

And so, First Sergeant Allen realized at last that German forces were indeed raiding deep into American positions. His initial reaction of shock, then horror, gave way, incongruously, to a deep sense of hurt at the utter betrayal by someone who shared a cigarette with him.

He shook his head, a broken man.

Was nothing sacred anymore in this war?

Hans ignored the woebegone Battery Sergeant and waited impatiently as Sergeant Sammer trotted up to update him.

"All guns are under our control. Four of ours against three of theirs who weren't expecting anything like this... it was easy. No fights. All captured, tied, and dispersed into the woods as we planned," said Sammer. "It's just the men here at the tents, and their commander to deal with."

Hans nodded and then walked briskly toward the Command Tent.

He ducked in without a word, drew himself to attention, and saluted.

Captain Barrett, startled by the appearance of an American lieutenant, saluted back reflexively, then blanched as the junior officer dropped his saluting right hand and pointed a pistol at him with his left.

The commander's eyes went wide, then rolled down to where his own sidearm was holstered, impossibly far now from his right hand, still held at his forehead.

"My men have captured your guards at all six guns. They now surround this command tent and the rest of your men in their tents. Lay down your weapon and order your men to stand down now or you all die," said Hans curtly.

Captain Barrett stayed still, hand frozen in salute, but his eyes looked around wildly, desperately seeking any advantage, any opportunity that might prevent the capitulation of his entire command to the enemy without a fight.

"All of my men lost friends and comrades today when your battery killed half my company this morning," Hans growled. "I have *reluctantly* given orders not to do the same to you and your men unless you resist."

Gesturing to his men outside the tent, Hans said, "They are praying right now that you resist."

Captain Barrett remained still for a moment, then, with his left hand, slowly drew his pistol and placed it down on the table. Then he raised both hands.

"Well played, Lieutenant, well played," Captain Barrett said ruefully.

"I am not playing. I do this to save the lives of my fellow soldiers," hissed Hans.

Looking at the pistol he just laid down, Captain Barrett said sadly, "So do I."

Chapter 19

Hans was startled by the American Commander's identification with his own feelings, but the gun in his hand did not waver. He kept it pointed at Captain Barrett until he ordered his men to stand down.

The remaining Americans did not resist and were quickly secured.

Sergeant Sammer reported, "All enemies here accounted for, disarmed, and tied up without a shot fired. We've been very fortunate, Oberleutnant."

Hans nodded. Using the American uniforms, all he had hoped for was a few precious minutes of confusion to allow his men to get into position to attack swiftly.

Never in his wildest dreams did he imagine they could keep up the pretense until all their enemies were captured.

"Only because they were expecting someone, and that fool of a sergeant opened the door and let us in," mulled Hans. "But that means....."

"...the real reinforcing platoon can show up any minute," Sergeant Sammer finished the thought for him.

"We better hurry then," said Hans anxiously. "How goes destroying the guns?"

Sergeant Sammer looked worried, "We've smashed the scopes and are trying to remove the breech blocks, but none of us have succeeded so far. We're all infantry. Never seen heavy artillery up close, especially not American ones."

Hans cursed. The entire raid would have been pointless if they could not damage the guns beyond use. Once the Americans replaced the scopes, this battery would be fully operational again.

He stalked over to where First Sergeant Allen lay, all tied up, and pulled him out roughly by his shirt collar.

"How do you remove the breechblocks?" he demanded in English.

"You can't," replied the First Sergeant sullenly. "New design. Prevents easy sabotage but makes maintenance an absolute nightma... whulp!"

He was cut short as Hans suddenly seized him with one hand, pointed his pistol at his face, and screamed, "You lie! Tell me how to remove the breech locks, or I will shoot you now!"

"You can't! You can't!" shrieked First Sergeant Allen desperately, "I swear to God I'm telling the truth! They could be done on the older guns but not these!"

"Alright," said Hans in a quiet voice that was somehow even more chilling than his scream.

He slowly brought to pistol to the First Sergeant's mouth and pushed the barrel in.

Sergeant Sammer turned pale and said, "Oberleutnant?"

Hans ignored him and focused on the First Sergeant Allen.

He said in a deadly voice, "If your position was about to be overrun, surely you have the means to destroy your guns quickly, so we don't capture them intact, yes?"

First Sergeant Allen nodded, eyes wild and crossed, trying to look at the pistol barrel in his mouth. Then he mumbled something and tried to point with his head. Hans followed his gaze and his eyes fell on a crate, partially hidden behind some groundsheets.

He nodded to Sergeant Sammer, who hurried over to it and opened it.

"Thermite grenades," he announced. "These will do."

Hans pulled his pistol out of the First Sergeant's mouth, and the man slumped to the floor, weeping in relief.

Hans said tersely, "Two for each gun to seal and melt the breechblocks immediately. Then as many as you need for the ammo dump. We'll blow that when we're ready to leave. The Americans are bound to notice and come running."

Sergeant Sammer nodded and ran off, calling men to him to distribute the grenades, but left Erwin behind with Hans.

Hans directed Erwin to look for documents while he gathered the maps and stuffed them in a bag. Erwin found a satchel of papers and showed it to Hans.

"Are these any good?" he asked.

Hans scanned them eagerly but was soon disappointed. Requisition orders for food and routine items, a stamp with an ink pad, and some blank sheets with the US Army logo on them....

"Nothing much," said Hans, shaking his head, "But bring them anyway. You never know when they might come in useful."

Erwin nodded and stuffed everything in the satchel. Satisfied all documents and maps were safely gathered by his messenger, Hans left the tent and anxiously looked around.

The reinforcement platoon that was already en route could show up any second. And then things would get ugly very quickly.

The widely cleared area around their position afforded no cover or concealment back to the woods. The American platoon would see them, and his men would either have to face them and fight while moving sideways toward the woods or just run and risk being cut down.

The remnants of Platoon One were back in the woods, out of sight, with Major Schmidt. They were to cover the rest of the company as they retreated after destroying the guns and watch the road for any unwelcome guests. But they would be no match for a fresh and full-strength American platoon at close range.

Just then, Hans saw a figure running up the road toward him at a full sprint, and his heart sank: There was only one reason for someone coming up at that speed. Hans called his squad leaders to him before the runner even reached him.

It was one of the Platoon One men, and he was shouting as he came.

"The Americans are coming! Five minutes away at most. At least a platoon, if not two," he gasped.

Hans swore.

He could consider fighting one platoon, especially with their disguises and element of surprise. But two was too much for him to hope to overcome in an open battle.

Hans spun around and looked back anxiously at the artillery emplacement—four thin trails of smoke coming from the guns told him there were still two left to destroy, plus the ammo dump. If they left now, they could escape undetected and unscathed. But two guns and the ammo dump would be left intact to threaten the Regiment.

On the other hand, staying on to destroy the remaining targets almost guaranteed contact with the American reinforcements. Even if they survived the initial fighting, they would be running for their lives all the way back with the Americans in hot pursuit unless...

Seconds ticked by as Hans pursued another wild idea in his head.

Then suddenly, he had it.

It was dangerous, but with a little bit of luck and a dose of American naivety, it could work.

Snapping to the Platoon One soldier, he said, "Go back. Do not engage the Americans. I repeat, do not engage the Americans. Tell Corporal Lang if he does anything funny, I'll have his head. Stay hidden, stay very low, and prepare to run when we return. Go!"

The soldier ran back as fast as he could.

Turning to his Squad One leader, he said urgently, "Tell Sergeant Sammer to finish off the two guns and blow the ammo dump as soon as he can. He has three minutes. Go!"

And the man ran off in the direction of the ammo dump.

To his Squad Two leader, Hans said, "Get everybody else in an assault line facing the woods. Make sure no one is left behind. There are Germans in there attacking us. Get low and start shooting back when the ammo dump blows."

His Squad Two leader's face creased in confusion, then suddenly, his mouth opened in an "O" of understanding. With a grin, he saluted and ran off.

Hans watched as his men hastened to obey his orders. Within a minute, the fifth column of smoke rose from the artillery pieces while most of his men streamed in from the site and formed a line facing the woods.

As the sixth trail of smoke rose, the American lead section rounded the bend and came in sight. Hans crouched and yelled to his men, "Fire! Fire!" and prayed Platoon One and Major Schmidt had the sense to keep low.

Sporadic, half-hearted firing came from his men as they shot blindly into the woods. It wasn't entirely convincing, but Hans knew they were aware of their comrades in the woods. No want wanted to hit a friendly by accident.

Then Hans fired a few rounds off himself as the reinforcement's lead section ran up to him.

Before they could get their bearings, Hans shouted at them urgently in English, "German saboteurs in the woods! Secure the guns!"

Seeing an American Officer in the middle of battle, they nodded and ran off on a wild goose chase to secure weapons already destroyed.

Then, the rest of the platoon came running up with their Platoon Leader, a young-looking second lieutenant, in the front.

Hans didn't give him a chance to ask questions. He cried out, "German infiltrators in the woods, and...."

A thunderous detonation sounded as the artillery munitions blew up.

"... German infantry company attacking in the rear," cried Hans, improvising furiously. "Secure the site. We'll clear the woods."

The American Platoon Commander nodded nervously to his slightly senior counterpart and quickly shouted to his men to deploy, facing the back of the artillery position.

Hans smiled in satisfaction. Now the Americans were back-to-back with his men and looking the other way.

Sergeant Sammer darted back, gave a thumbs up to indicate the ammo dump was destroyed, joined his platoon's assault line, and started firing.

Hans nodded, then in his best American accent, he called out, "Platoon Two, Attack!"

Most of his men didn't understand his words, but his tone was familiar enough, and when they saw Hans stand and rush toward the wood, they gave ragged shouts of exhortation and started firing and running in their standard assault formations.

Hans cringed when some of the words shouted were German, but most had the sense to keep their shouting vague and inarticulate.

Fortunately, with unexploded shells cooking off and exploding at unpredictable intervals, there was enough noise and confusion to occupy the real Americans at the site, anxiously deploying as fast they could and shooting at anything that moved, real or imagined, to the rear of the position.

If the young American Platoon Leader had the presence of mind to watch behind him, he would have seen an American infantry platoon conducting a classic fire-and-movement maneuver attack into the woods.

An attack that stopped as soon as they reached the wood.

Then the entire force melted into the forest and disappeared as though they were never there at all.

The mood was buoyant when the raiding force returned.

Hans was giddy with exhaustion and exhilaration in equal measure. The mission had been successful far beyond what he had hoped. All objectives destroyed, the Americans in an uproar, without a single loss.

Major Schmidt clapped him on the shoulder in congratulations, then gathered all three Company Commanders to outline his plan for the battalion from now on.

He began, "Caesar Company will spread out across our entire front. Your role is to disrupt, delay and harass the Americans. Send small forces to key junctions and terrain. When the Americans appear, shoot and engage. When they rally to attack, disperse and evade. When they give up and organize to move, shoot and engage again."

The Caesar Company Commander nodded thoughtfully as Major Schmidt continued, "No point having any defensive strongholds. We waste our time and effort digging in to pin ourselves down for the Americans to attack.

"Instead, we cause maximum trouble for them, at minimum effort for ourselves. If one bullet causes half an hour delay each time, and one grenade puts their entire force on alert for six, we'd have done good work.

"Let them exhaust themselves having to be on the alert constantly. Do not stand up and fight to the death. Do not go toe to toe with them. There will be time for that later on once our forces regroup. But, for now, give them no rest, and give them no relief.

"Stay alive, and report back frequently so we can take advantage of their weaknesses as they tire."

Major Schmidt said to Hauptmann Brandt, "Two of your platoons are to secure and move the supplies here to the Regiment Supply depots. I cannot emphasize how critical these supplies are for our effort."

Brandt nodded in agreement.

"Your remaining platoon will be dedicated to supporting Anton Company. Including weapon maintenance, food and hygiene provisions, and local security. Anton Company is excused from all sentry and guard duties, trenching digging work, and patrols," said Major Schmidt.

The Berta Company Commander turned red in indignation, but he said nothing.

"I want Anton Company fresh and rested for their missions," said Major Schmidt. "They will to be the tip of the spear of this battalion. They will raid quickly and effectively deep behind enemy lines as they did today. They will have the flexibility to strike as the opportunity arises, disperse, and disengage if needed, only to strike again when the Americans are least expecting it. They need to be alert and think on their feet to do this. As such, they need to be fed and rested."

With that, he dismissed the Company Commanders.

Chapter 20

That night, safe within the security perimeter set up by Berta Company, Hans and his men had the rare luxury of sleeping through the night uninterrupted. The rest did them wonders, and they awoke surprisingly fit and ready to go.

Freed from the trudge of duties that wore infantry down in the field even if they weren't fighting, Anton Company was able to concentrate all their energy and efforts to prepare for their next mission.

This time, with better planning.

With his men still in their American uniforms, Hans received his orders and intelligence from Major Schmidt and was given a free hand on when and how to attack his next objective.

It was a company supply depot. Smaller than the first one they overran but holding mainly food and water rather than ammunition or fuel, and thus less heavily guarded.

They would strike as Berta Company prepared to move, distracting the Americans enough so that Berta's relocation would not be disrupted.

"You're going to try the American lieutenant trick again, aren't you," said Sergeant Sammer accusingly as Berta Company started moving.

"Yes, as a matter of fact, I am," said Hans brightly. "It worked the last time, didn't it?"

"You do have a good American accent, Oberleutnant," conceded Sammer grudgingly.

"Thank you," said Hans modestly and then explained, "I took night classes at the *Kriegsakademie.* Extra credits if we could fool a native English speaker."

Sammer nodded approvingly and went to ready Anton Company, while Hans went to the Battalion Command Tent, fished out the documents he captured from the American artillery base, and started writing.

Prisoner of War

Two hours later, Hans led his men unerringly to their target where, leaving his men hidden behind, he wriggled forward with Sergeant Sammer to have a better look.

"I make two groups of soldiers. One group just in fatigues and another in battle gear but not too alert," murmured Hans.

"The Staff Sergeant there is probably the Mess Sergeant, and the rest his cooks and helpers. The other group is probably a squad here to guard them," whispered Sergeant Sammer.

Hans nodded. About twenty men in all. His force was enough to overwhelm them in an open fight, but the specter of even a few casualties weighed heavily on this mission.

It would be a long walk back to carry any wounded they had.

He thought for a while, then made up his mind.

"I'm adding something to the plan," he said, turning to Sergeant Sammer, "but I will need your whiskey flask."

"What? How did you...." Sergeant Sammer began to protest but was cut short by a withering look from Hans.

Grumbling, he reached into his shirt pocket and handed the battered flask to his Platoon Commander.

"Thanks," grinned Hans, "I'll give it back to you, I promise."

Sergeant Sammer snorted in disgust.

As they made their way back to the men, Hans took a swig of whiskey from the flask, gargled with it, and carefully let the contents dribble down his chin and onto his shirt. Then he wiped his mouth and neck with his sleeves.

Five minutes later, the American private on sentry duty at the main trail leading to his supply depot blinked as he saw a platoon of soldiers marching up the road toward him.

Pointing his rifle at them, he called out in a nervous voice, "Halt! Who goes there?"

The column of soldiers, led by a tall, blond officer, walked on as though they didn't even hear him.

"Halt," called the sentry again, his pitch much higher this time. "Identify yourself!"

Still no response.

They simply walked on closer and closer until their leader, a first lieutenant by rank, loomed directly in front of him, oblivious to the rifle pointed at him.

"Is that how you address a superior officer, soldier?" he snarled.

The hapless sentry wilted under his gaze and quickly came to attention and snapped off a salute.

"Yes, sir! I mean, no sir!" he shouted.

The giant in front of him didn't reply. Instead, he just continued to stare at him with cold, merciless eyes until the private's saluting hand started to tremble.

Finally, the first lieutenant returned the salute casually and barked, "My men are hungry. Get your mess sergeant here and tell him to feed them immediately. We leave in half an hour. Sooner if possible."

The sentry fled back to the safety of the supply depot to find the Staff Sergeant in charge.

The men marched up at a steady pace until they were within the compound of the supply depot and unloaded their backpacks. Some noisily took out mess tins and canteens, while others settled down and started cleaning their weapons.

The Mess Sergeant, an older, portly Staff Sergeant, came out of the main tent with the sentry in tow with a bewildered expression on his face.

He demanded, "What is the meaning of this…. Sir?

The last word came out in a gasp as the tall, blond first lieutenant suddenly swung toward him angrily when he started speaking.

He stared steadily at the Mess Sergeant, eyes boring into him relentlessly until the older man saluted. Then he returned the salute and settled down.

"We are on a raid mission," the first lieutenant said curtly. "We were advised to stop by your position to resupply. My men need a hot meal now. Rations and water later before we go. Extra ammunition if you can spare any. We leave in twenty-five minutes."

"I, ah, know nothing of this, Lieutenant," said the Mess Sergeant uneasily, "Do you have any written orders?"

In a conspiratorial tone, he added, "There are rumors of Krauts running around impersonating our boys, you know. We can't be too careful."

A frosty stare was all his attempt at conversation earned him.

Slowly, the first lieutenant pulled out a paper and handed it to him.

The Mess Sergeant took the paper and wrinkled his brow as he tried to read it. It was on regulation paper with all the correct markings, but the main order seemed to be a vague requisition order for rations, amended in hand and signed by some senior officer.

"I don't know who Major Smith is," he frowned.

"Not my problem," snapped the first lieutenant.

"And I can't verify the order from this paper, I'm afraid. If you give me some time to check with my Company HQ..." began the Mess Sergeant.

"Then we will be late for our mission," cut in the first lieutenant.

"Very well, we will leave now, without food or help from your unit. If we fail, the Germans will come from that way," he finished, pointing to the road they just marched up.

Then he signaled to his Platoon Sergeant to get the men ready to move.

"Wait!" cried the Mess Sergeant nervously. "I suppose there's no harm in us preparing a meal while we wait for the orders to be verified? I'll get my men started, and then we can settle the paperwork later, sir."

The first lieutenant thought about this for a bit, then seemed to relax and said, "As you wish."

"But I'm sending a squad to clear your perimeter before we sit and eat. Your sentry just let us walk right in. What if we were Germans dressed in American uniform?" he said critically to the Mess Sergeant.

The Mess Sergeant couldn't think of anything to say, so he busied himself with shouting orders and getting his cooks and assistants moving while the visiting platoon's sergeant led a squad of men to the perimeter.

When there was nothing he could even pretend to do, he turned, at last, to face the first lieutenant again just as a gust of wind blew. He caught a whiff of whiskey, and his eyes widened in shock.

Had this officer been drinking on duty?

At that moment, Hans knew he had succeeded in his deception.

Caught up now in the scandal of an officer drinking on duty, just before a dangerous mission, the Mess Sergeant's train of thought would be firmly on this somewhat serious matter rather than the more deadly one of German infiltration.

Pushing his advantage, Hans belched contentedly, making sure the Mess Sergeant could smell his breath.

It worked.

The American's expression changed from shock to one of clear disapproval.

"Ah, sir, I didn't get your name or unit earlier," the Mess Sergeant said politely, clearly intending to remember it so he could report him.

"Lieutenant Wanger. We are Platoon Two from Alpha Company," said Hans easily.

"Major Schmidt is our Battalion Commander," he added and instantly cursed himself for his slip of the tongue.

The Mess Sergeant's ears pricked up.

"Schmidt? Isn't that a German name?" he asked.

Hans stalled by taking his flask out and taking a sip. Then he offered it to the Mess Sergeant, who refused reflexively at first. But Hans saw him lick his lips longingly, so he offered it again.

The Mess sergeant accepted it this time and took a tentative sip from the flask. An expression of bliss came over his face as he took another sip and sighed contentedly.

"He is German when we meet the Germans, *ja*?" said Hans, answering the question.

The Mess Sergeant raised an eyebrow in surprise.

Hans explained, "I am fluent in German. We all are. That is why we were chosen for this mission."

The Mess Sergeant mouthed an "ahh" in understanding and he nodded in approval.

"You should see me do my German Officer impersonation," said Hans, exaggerating his German accent to the full.

The Mess Sergeant stared at him, then chuckled, "Very good, sir, very good."

"Heil Hitler!" Hans barked suddenly.

The Mess Sergeant jumped in shock, and then he roared with laughter as the strange first lieutenant executed a crisp Nazi salute with a perfectly straight face.

Then he froze as he looked up to see the barrel of a pistol pointing right between his eyes.

"I wasn't joking," came a cold, menacing voice, utterly devoid of humor, as Hans cocked his pistol ominously.

"This is, as you Americans like to call it, a stick-up," he said grimly as Sergeant Sammer returned with the roving squad and gave him the thumbs-up: All sentries were subdued and out of action.

And so, the Mess Sergeant realized at last that he was the next victim of German forces raiding deep into American positions.

His initial reaction was one of shock, then horror. But as he looked at the whiskey flask in his hand, those feelings, incongruously, gave way to a deep sense of hurt at the utter betrayal by someone who shared a drink with him.

He shook his head, a broken man.

Was nothing left sacred anymore in this war?

The next day, Caesar Company scouts reported the Americans were getting nervous about an unknown

German raiding force deep behind their lines. As a result, movement and communications had slowed down dramatically as units beefed up security and introduced more rigorous checks and verification procedures.

Any unit without proper identification was treated with suspicion until they could be confirmed to be friendly and were therefore delayed for whatever purpose they had linked up.

Squabbles broke out, and tempers frayed. Combat units had to be on high alert continuously, sapping precious rest times their men would otherwise have had.

The result was tiredness, mistakes, short tempers, and significant degradation of the American forces facing the 1st Battalion.

Major Schmidt took all this in with grim satisfaction.

"Gentlemen, this is exactly what we want," he said to Hans and Hauptmann Brandt. "Confusion, suspicion, fear among the enemy will slow them down more than any material damage we can inflict on them."

Looking at Hans, he said, "Good job so far on your missions, but I think your days of strolling up to your targets and playing the friendly neighborhood Platoon

Leader are over. They'll check you out far more thoroughly from now on, and your accent isn't really that American."

Hans nodded glumly in agreement.

Chapter 21

5th March 1945—Eastern France

The next day, rested and refreshed, Hans and his men were ready for action again.

By pure coincidence, their route brought them within striking distance of where an American communications hub was thought to be, so Major Schmidt released Hans to raid that target.

They still had American uniforms, and Hans intended to maximize that advantage.

By now, he knew the Americans would be alert for German infiltrators in American uniforms walking up to an objective, befriending the guards, and capturing it once they got inside.

American soldiers *in battle*, however, were an entirely different matter.

With that in mind, he gathered his commanders and laid out his plan for them.

Their initial reaction was shock, followed by thoughtful contemplation, followed by a wicked gleam in their eyes when it dawned on them that perhaps this mad plan might work after all.

There was only one last detail to settle.

"Who is to command the firebase?" asked Hans out loud.

"I could, I suppose," said Sergeant Sammer, but Hans shook his head.

"I need you at the raid itself. We'll be spread out, and many things can go wrong."

"Then Corporal Lang," shrugged Sergeant Sammer, "He's the leader of what's left of Platoon One. He could command the firebase."

"Can we trust him?" asked Hans.

"I'm right here, you know, Oberleutnant," complained Corporal Lang from the side.

Sergeant Sammer grinned, "As far as I can throw him, Oberleutnant. He's a rascal and a clown. But he's indefatigable, and his unpredictability makes him good in a fight."

"Thank you, Sergeant Sammer," said Corporal Lang. Then he added, "I think."

Looking at the Corporal, Hans said earnestly, "This is a serious job, Lang. You have to balance attacking like a whole German platoon without killing any of us."

"I can do that," said Lang confidently.

"You also have to cover our withdrawal, and on short notice, you might have to pretend to be Americans," said Hans.

"I can do that too," said Lang.

Then, with a hint of pride, he added, "I've even been practicing swearing in English."

And proceeded to utter an oath so vile that Hans blanched.

"Alright, you'll have to do," sighed Hans. And he dismissed the commanders to get the rest of the men ready.

Two hours later, they reached their target area without incident and wordlessly deployed to their assigned positions as rehearsed—A single line stretched out facing their objective.

Hans pointed to a distinctive tree on their right and made sure everyone noted it. Then, Corporal Lang took his team beyond that tree and settled his men into firing positions.

Hans and Sergeant Sammer crept up to the edge of the tree line to scout the objective before commencing the attack.

"Some barbed wire, but mainly a sandbag wall for cover, guards at standard intervals, not expecting trouble," murmured Sergeant Sammer as he squinted at the base.

"But look," he suddenly said in an excited whisper, "Is that a two-star general walking toward that tent?"

Shielding his eyes, Hans peered carefully and muttered, "Two-star general indeed, so he must be a Division Commander at least, in a jacket but not in combat gear. No entourage or guards. He looks like he's familiar with the camp, so he is not a visitor. That must be the Command Tent he's walking into...."

"...meaning this is not just a Communications hub, it's the Division HQ," breathed Sergeant Sammer.

Both men fell silent at that point, pondering the same thing.

A Division HQ would be better defended than just a radio hub on its own, with a reaction force nearby on top of the existing guards. Of course, it would be a riskier attack than they had planned for. But the prize was far more significant.

An attack on the Division HQ would disrupt American operations across their entire area of operations for a few days at least. Longer if critical HQ staff were killed and could not easily be replaced.

"Orders, Oberleutnant?" asked Sergeant Sammer softly.

Hans thought of the men Anton Company had already lost. Hauptmann Hauser, Jung, Klein.... Could he take responsibility for losing more men in a high-risk raid?

Then more faces came to the fore. The numerous men of Platoon One, because he did not help them. His own Platoon Two men who fell as they counter-attacked.

Hans unconsciously reached for his Hitler Youth Knife and squeezed it hard.

To abandon the mission now was to allow the Americans to kill more Germans.

"No change to the plan," said Hans harshly. "We go in and kill everything that moves."

They went back to the men, then led them to the edge of the clearing. When all were ready, Hans started the attack by firing a three-round burst directly into the Command Tent. In response, Corporal Lang's team opened up, shooting into the base.

Hans got up and yelled in English, "Fall back! Fall back!"

At once, the men of Anton Company rose, turned and faced the woods, and started running backwards into the open ground toward the base.

Those deemed to have passable accents shouted a few words in English like "back" or "down" while the rest fired wildly to the right of the distinctive tree.

At the American base, the sergeant on duty cursed and yelled for his reserve guards to reinforce the perimeter where an attack was obviously taking place.

Hans spotted him and shouted, "Raiders in the forest, prepare to repel!"

Then to his men, he shouted, "Fall back to the base!"

And then prayed he was convincing enough.

Anton Company began a textbook fire-and-movement maneuver to the rear with practiced smoothness while American soldiers streamed to their defensive line and took up positions.

Most were blocked by the retreating American platoon that had apparently blundered into German raiders and was now falling back to join them.

Unable to fire without risking hitting the men in front, the defenders hunkered down and peered anxiously into the woods, seeking movement and targets.

Within seconds Hans and his men reached the wall of sandbags, jumped over them, and made a show of being relieved to have made it to safety.

With their front clear, the Americans started shooting wildly into the woods at anything that moved, real or imagined, adding to their confusion while Hans and his men got behind them.

Hans hesitated at his next order. Briefly, he considered, how different was this from Hauptmann Brandt's execution of prisoners? Shooting soldiers in the back?

Then the image of the Anton Company dead came to his mind. So numerous they needed help from Berta Company to gather them,

He hardened his heart and yelled, "Now!"

Raising his rifle, he shot the nearest American soldier in the back. The man yelped and slumped over his sandbag.

Then Hans shot the next and the next. On either side of him, his men opened fire on the American defenders.

Completely surprised by the attack by those they thought were friendlies, the Americans had no chance, and Anton Company butchered the entire defensive line in seconds.

Hans took a deep breath to settle the unexpected shaking in his hands while his men quickly looted the bodies for bullets and grenades.

He told himself this was no different from a flanking maneuver, where the object was to come to the enemy's side or rear and take them unawares.

He told himself that they would have done the same if the situation was reversed.

Steeling himself against the scene of slaughter before him, he ordered harshly, "Go, go!"

Breaking off into teams of three, his men fanned out throughout the base with simple instructions: Kill everyone they came across, retrieve what they could carry, destroy anything of value that they couldn't, and return in five minutes.

Hans led two men to the Command Tent. They fired wildly into it from the outside, then burst in. The two-star general was on the floor, clutching his left leg where a bullet had hit him. When he saw Hans, he tossed his pistol aside and raised his hands.

Hans froze in the act of aiming to shoot him.

Of all the scenarios he had prepared for, none of them included a Division Commander surrendering to him.

Now what?

In a raid, most of the damage inflicted on the enemy was within the first few minutes, where the attackers had the element of surprise.

But there was a certain point where to linger would yield only marginal gains while the risks increased exponentially as the enemy roused itself from the initial shock and fought back.

Hans was painfully aware that they had reached that juncture.

As though to emphasize that point, Sergeant Sammer popped his head into the command tent and said, "We're done. The men have cleared the entire area, including their radio hub, except for the ammunition store…."

A thunderous explosion sounded that shook the ground, then died down.

"Pardon me, *including* the ammunition store," Sergeant Sammer amended smoothly. "We're ready to go, Oberleutnant."

Then he noticed who was still alive in the room and surrendering to them, and his eyes widened.

"That's the Division Commander," he whispered.

"I know," Hans said impatiently, trying to gather his thoughts.

The raid was complete. The damage was done. The Division HQ had been wiped out. The Americans would respond quickly. It was time to leave.

Except he had a prize in front of him far beyond anything he'd expected to find.

The information a Division Commander could yield would be invaluable. Not to mention the impact on morale for both sides.

But he was wounded. They would have to take time to patch up him as they retreated, and he would certainly slow them down.

"Orders, Oberleutnant?" asked Sergeant Sammer impatiently.

Suddenly Hans made a decision. "Bind his wound quickly and get him ready to move. We take him with us," he snapped.

Sergeant Sammer's face fell. "He'll slow us down, Oberleutnant. Is this the time to take prizes?" he asked seriously.

"He's not a prize. There's no point raiding a Division HQ and leaving them with their Division Commander alive, is there?" snarled Hans, more angry with himself than Sammer.

He should have just thrown a grenade into the Command Tent and killed him as they attacked. But he had wanted to capture maps and documents intact, too, hence the more direct approach which led him to his quandary now.

Sergeant Sammer sighed and quickly ordered men to tend to the American general while others hurried to strip the tent of every document and map they could find.

Hans stepped outside to see what was going on.

His men were streaming back from all areas of the compound, and everywhere, trails of smoke could be seen rising to the sky. Even if no one had alerted other American forces, the smoke would give them away.

Sergeant Sammer emerged from the Command Tent with his men. Two with their arms full of maps and documents, another two supporting the American general as he limped out painfully.

Hans barked to Sergeant Sammer, "Get these maps and the prisoner back to base at all costs."

Then he commanded the rest of the men, "Defensive formation here until they reach the trees, then we run like hell."

His men exchanged worried glances and looked longingly to the safety of the trees. Still, they obeyed quickly, spreading out along the perimeter and settling in behind the sandbag wall facing into the camp.

Hans looked anxiously as Sergeant Sammer led his little group toward the trees. They took a painfully long time to reach even the halfway mark.

Overcome with impatience, Hans ordered the men with him to pull out and start heading back to the trees.

Just then, a shout of alarm rang out, and someone started shooting. Hans regretted his premature haste as he instinctively fired back.

Now his men were caught in the open instead of behind the sandbags.

Worse, there was a chance someone would spot...

"Hey, they've got the general!" someone shouted in English.

Hans swore.

Chapter 22

Hans couldn't believe how things turned so badly, so quickly.

His simple raid on a communications center turned into an attack on a Division HQ, which escalated into the kidnap of a two-star general. And they were caught red-handed. So now, the Americans were obliged to pursue.

And, if the Division Commander was popular and respected by his men, they would pursue with great vigor.

Barking commands to his men, Hans's raiding force began to retreat carefully toward the woods.

But unlike before, when they could do so rapidly, this time they were limited by the speed the wounded American general could walk. Sergeant Sammer was hurrying his group all he could, but they'd only just reached the tree line.

Only when they'd disappeared into the safety of the woods did Hans order a full retreat. His men broke and ran, but it was too late. The Americans had organized themselves and started to come after them from their base perimeter. At least a platoon strength of men poured over their wall.

More than a match for Hans's force.

Gritting his teeth, Hans delayed his retreat back to the woods and went to the ground, firing as he did so, determined to buy Sergeant Sammer as much time as possible.

Still in the open but hidden against the background of the forest, he managed to shoot two soldiers down before the rest paused and went prone, seeking out a dangerous enemy.

Precious seconds passed until Hans determined he could wait no longer.

He tossed his last grenade and then ran for the woods.

Angry shouts sounded as someone spotted Hans retreating, and their entire line got up and charged forward.

In his haste to get clear, Hans tripped and tumbled heavily. Then, still winded, he saw the lead American squad less than fifty meters away.

At that range, with the momentum of their charge, he knew he was finished.

To run now would invite being shot in the back.

Roaring in defiance, Hans rolled over, brought his rifle to bear on the nearest soldier, and fired.

The man went down, but the others ran forward.

Hans fired again and missed. He quickly fired again, and another soldier went down, grazed in the arm and cursing. Eight more to go. He fired again, missed, and knew this was it.

Suddenly one man went down, then another, then two, as gunfire erupted from the right. The rest of the Americans shouted in alarm and dived down. Hans looked around in bewilderment but saw nobody.

Then it dawned on him—the firebase team!

They had held their positions during the raid and now covered the retreat.

Needing no further encouragement, Hans got up and ran as fast as he could in a crouch while Corporal Lang and his men kept the assaulting force pinned down.

Far too quickly, though, Hans caught up with the rest of the raiding force, which in turn, had caught up with Sergeant Sammer and the prisoner.

One of the men carried the wounded general on his shoulder, but he trotted unsteadily, clearly exhausted.

The rest of the force surrounded them wordlessly as they moved at an agonizingly slow pace. The man carrying the general stopped, and another man took over.

Sergeant Sammer spotted Hans and said breathlessly, "He simply can't walk. We've taken to carrying him over the shoulder, but it's exhausting work. And even with everyone taking turns, the person carrying him can go no faster than a trot."

Hans was dismayed by the progress. By now, he'd hoped they were far enough into the woods so that a few men, scattered and sniping, would be able to delay the Americans while the rest made their way back to safety.

But at this rate, the Americans would soon catch sight of the main group and their prisoner and swarm them like bees.

Hans punched a tree in frustration.

Sergeant Sammer said, "They'll catch up. We can't take him with us."

Hans replied hotly, "We can't just let him go either. This is their Division Commander, and a damned good one too, from the beating his men have been giving us."

Sergeant Sammer just stared at the floor. They both knew what was coming.

In the distance, the gunfire from the firebase died down. Hans knew Lang and his firebase had broken contact with the Americans and were on their way back to join them.

They had minutes at most.

Hans punched the tree in frustration again.

If only their initial attack had killed the general. Or if only he had fought back. Then he would have been killed in action, fair and square. But now, as their prisoner...

He shook his head in frustration. To try to drag him along would endanger his entire company now. But to release him back to the Americans would jeopardize all German forces in his area of operations later.

There was only one other option.

Hans told himself this was different from what he stopped Hauptmann Brandt from doing scarcely weeks ago. That what Brandt did then was cold-blooded murder. Whereas this was... assassination. This would be for the greater good of his men and fellow soldiers. This was necessary. Even admirable.

He looked at Sergeant Sammer almost pleadingly. Sergeant Sammer saw the look in his eyes and quickly looked away, his expression pained.

Just then, Corporal Lang came sprinting back with his firebase team.

"They're right behind us," he said breathlessly.

Hans nodded in acknowledgment.

Tapping the man carrying the prisoner on the shoulder, Hans indicated for him to put his load down. The American general staggered and gasped but stayed on his feet.

Hans turned to Sergeant Sammer and said, "Leave the prisoner. Take the men and go. I'll deal with this."

Sergeant Sammer's eyes widened as Hans drew his pistol.

"Oberleutnant, are you sure?" he asked.

"Just go," Hans shouted with sudden force.

Calls and shouts in English grew louder as the Americans drew near. Sergeant Sammer looked anxiously at where they were coming from, then nodded and turned to get the men going.

Prisoner of War

Hans turned to face the prisoner and had a good look at him for the first time.

The general was of average height and had brown hair streaked with gray. Worry lines creased his face, and his nose was crooked—like it had been broken in a fight long ago. But he stood erect and straight.

When his eyes met Hans's, they were filled with fear. But underlying them was a sadness that seemed to come from beyond his own impending death.

Hans was startled when he realized the older man felt sorry for *him*.

Strong arms that could hold heavy weapons with rock-solid stability suddenly trembled to level a tiny pistol at the general's chest. Hans stared at his shaking hand, then back at the general.

"I'm sorry," he whispered in English.

The general drew himself to attention and replied with dignity, "I understand. Do what you must."

Hans cocked the pistol's hammer and started to apply pressure on the trigger.

He heard someone scream in English, "No, wait!"

There was a flash of light and a loud sound.

The general's expression changed from sorrow to surprise as he flew forward and slammed headfirst into Hans's chin. Hans's world exploded in light and pain, and then everything went black.

When he came to, the first thing he saw was Sergeant Sammer's face peering at his. His concerned expression changed to relief as Hans's vision slowly came back into focus.

"What happened?" Hans asked, sitting up and instantly regretting it as his head swam again.

"Some poor American soldier threw a grenade and credited himself with his highest-ranking kill—his own Division Commander. They were so shocked they stopped. Then they stopped to listen to their Platoon Leader scream at the soldier who threw it. And since they were stopped, they were easier to hit, so we shot them," said Sergeant Sammer with glee.

Hans sat up again, more slowly this time, and asked, "You drove off the entire American force?"

"Just the lead section," said Sergeant Sammer. "Someone wounded their Platoon Leader since he was shouting so much. Then, after they lost a few more men, they pulled back. So we came to find you. Pulled you out from under the general. Looks like he took most of the blast for you and saved your life."

"The rest of the men?" asked Hans.

Sergeant Sammer said, "Split up into three squads. One headed straight back to base with the documents and maps to get them safe and report what's happened. A second squad here to help carry you back. Honestly, Oberleutnant, I carried you the first leg to here, and I say if you can't walk, we'll have to stretcher you back, or we'll all collapse one by one trying to carry you."

"And the last squad?" asked Hans suspiciously.

Sergeant Sammer looked a little embarrassed as he said, "Uh, the last squad was made up of my former Platoon One boys, and they wanted to try something out since we were still in American uniforms and all.

"So they flanked the main American position, fired a few shots to get their attention, then turned around and attacked *away* from them, careful to let their uniforms show, shouting that the enemy was that way."

Hans pressed his hand to his face. He had no doubt it was Corporal Lang leading that madcap foray.

"They'll be fine, Oberleutnant," reassured Sammer. "With Lang's creativity, he'll probably lead the Americans in a circle and get them to attack their own friends in the rear. But in any case, I gave them strict orders to take no risks and disengage if there was any doubt."

Hans grunted appreciatively and surged to his feet. He swayed a little as a wave of dizziness washed over him, but after a minute more, he was sure he could make his way back to their base without the humiliation of being stretchered.

Looking back at where he thought he had been knocked out, he asked, "And the general?"

"Dead, as I said," replied Sergeant Sammer. "Grenade killed him outright. We took off his jacket and hid his body as best we could while retrieving you."

Seeing Hans's expression turn disapproving, he explained, "The lead squad was driven away before they could check the body. When the next lot arrives, until they find the body and identify it, they cannot be sure he's not still with us. So they have to be careful. No wild grenades, no indiscriminate fire, no reckless charges. They have to go slow."

"Alright," said Hans grudgingly. It was undignified for the general but not overtly disrespectful. If they had grenaded him in his Command Tent earlier, they would have just left his body parts where they fell.

Sergeant Sammer nodded and made to move, but Hans just stayed still, so he stopped and waited. There was just one last niggling issue that was unresolved and gnawed at his heart.

Finally, Sergeant Sammer sighed and broke the silence.

"You didn't do it, Oberleutnant," he said firmly. It was more a statement than a question. They both knew what he meant. Hans stayed silent for a long time.

"No, I didn't," said Hans at last, as he roused himself and got moving.

He left unsaid the thought that would haunt him from that day on.

But I would have.

Chapter 23

They made it back to the camp without incident. Sergeant Sammer did a quick check and found even Corporal Lang had made it back unscathed with his men. Then, satisfied everyone was accounted for, Hans went about the business of reporting to Major Schmidt.

Gathering everything of importance, Hans got Lang to help him bring all the documents they had collected and walked to the Battalion Command Tent.

Outside, Major Schmidt had just pulled up in a *Kübelwagen*.

Hans glanced at it curiously. The marking R01 on the door indicated this was the Regiment Commander's vehicle.

"Mine now," said Major Schmidt to Hans's unasked question. "The Regiment Commander was injured and has been withdrawn, so I asked to use his vehicle in the meantime. Could be useful later."

Hans grunted in agreement.

"Good raid?" Major Schmidt asked.

Hans nodded and proceeded to outline the events that took place.

"Division Commander, you say," Major Schmidt pondered.

"As far as I could tell," said Hans, shrugging. "He was a two-star general, and he seemed at home in the Command Tent when we attacked. We didn't have time to exchange pleasantries."

"Killed by an American grenade, explosion caught him in the back," said Major Schmidt.

Hans nodded.

"But no one else got hurt in that blast?" asked the Major.

Hans nodded.

Major Schmidt was quiet for a while. Then he said, "So the prisoner was well behind everybody else, his back to the Americans."

Hans grimaced and looked away.

There was only one scenario for that positioning to make sense. And he knew the Major knew.

Angrily Hans said, "He had it coming to him. They all do. If the grenade didn't kill him, maybe I would have."

Major Schmidt sighed. When he spoke, there was no accusation in his voice.

"Revenge is a dangerous thing, Hans. We spend our lives trying to force someone to drink the cup of our wrath and usually fail. But even when we succeed and make them drain it to the bitter dregs, we wonder why we feel so empty inside," said Major Schmidt.

Looking into the distance, he continued, "War is evil, Hans. Not just because people lose their lives, but because those who survive lose something else too.

"The Americans are human. That Division Commander was human. Even the *Führer* himself is human. Our people, the ones we protect, are most certainly human.

"But what if, in our eagerness to fight and kill, we ourselves become something *less* than human?"

He carried on somberly, "We fight now because someone is attacking us. So often, we think no further than immediate survival. But in the quieter moments, we know it is for something more.

"As soldiers, as officers, we have a duty to protect our men and our land and our people. If I could fulfill my obligation to do so without firing a single shot, I would gladly do so. If I could save our friends, comrades, women, and children without another battle, I would seize the opportunity with both hands.

"But for now, if this is the only way to save those to whom I owe a debt of honor, I will battle on. I will even kill Americans if I must. But only if I must."

"At least, that's what I'm fighting for," sighed the Major, "What about you?"

Hans kept quiet, but inside, his mind was a storm as, unspoken, he answered the Major's question. His hand went to his pocket and grasped his Hitler Youth knife. He pressed on the handle firmly as he recalled his father's last words to him. When Adolf Hitler became the only father he could have.

To win this war for the Führer and our dignity... Hans thought fiercely.

His fingers moved to the broken blade to finish his answer... a*nd make the Americans pay.*

His blue eyes flashed angrily at the Major, but he could not say anything.

Major Schmidt stayed silent for a while, then he shrugged and moved on.

Studying the map Hans had brought, he pursed his lips, then said, "Put this map up on the wall, Hans. Lang, get all the Berta and Caesar officers here for urgent orders. And someone make a copy of the positions and get it to Regiment HQ as soon as possible. Tell them we are moving in three hours. They will understand why."

Hans was vaguely puzzled by that last comment but dismissed it as yet another quirk of his commander.

Major Schmidt was so adept at anticipating orders that, as often as not, the battalion was already executing Regiment orders before they arrived. Sometimes, it seemed *he* told the Regiment Commander what to do rather than the other way around.

Hans dismissed his contemplations and went to set the map up while waiting for the other Company Commanders to arrive.

Absently, he looked at the map to see what was on it. It showed the sector they were operating in, and it didn't take him long to orientate himself on the map. He quickly located where they were, where the raid had taken place, and where the other units were.

He stopped.

Something wasn't right.

Something wasn't right at all...

Hans blinked hard and forced himself to concentrate on the diagrams in front of him. Blue markings showed Allied positions, and red ones presumably showed German ones. As expected, they were roughly divided to the right and left of the map.

The problem was *where* they were divided on the map.

Don't panic, he told himself. *This is only the best guess the Americans have of our positions. They do not have complete intelligence, so they estimate our strength, and they estimate far too lightly.*

But deep down, he knew this was a lie.

Overstating one's successes was for the masses. For the civilians who had no direct bearing on the fighting. They didn't need to know if things were going badly.

But for soldiers, it was always the other way round. They were trained to assume the worst and be prepared for it. As a result, any assessment of enemy forces that was known to be unreliable was always scaled *up* to avoid tactical blunders due to greater-than-expected resistance.

And if this was the American's *over*-estimation of German forces, something was terribly wrong indeed.

Hans stared at the map again, and rubbed his eyes to make sure he wasn't seeing things.

He found their current position again. Deep in the eastern part of France. They were scarcely a few miles away from the Fatherland itself. With all the retreats, Hans had assumed his battalion, and perhaps even the entire regiment was tasked with carefully giving ground to the enemy in the center while the flanks held firm.

This way, the enemy moved into a position where they faced enemies on three fronts. Naturally, the shape of German forces should have been concave toward Germany, with his own position representing the deepest Allied forces were allowed to penetrate.

Instead, the map showed the opposite.

A sea of blue markings covered the left side of the map. And on the right, a few red markings were scattered.

Far too few.

Focusing on his position again, he realized the rest of the German units were, in fact, mostly east of him. Their line was convex and bulging out toward the Allies, with his own regiment now the sole remaining one in France. All other red markings were placed firmly on German soil.

He started to feel sick. A wave of despair washed over him and threatened to overwhelm him. Were things that bad? Had he been wrong all along?

He trusted his battalion commander and his men. They had fought well, with much greater success and lower casualties than anyone in the war had any right to expect. And he assumed they were therefore tasked with the hardest part—luring the enemy in.

So, he thought bitterly, *it wasn't because we were the best that we were chosen as bait.*

They were indeed the best, but there was no bait.

It was simply that while they had held their line, their flanks repeatedly collapsed on both sides, forcing them to withdraw lest they themselves be cut off and surrounded.

It also explained how they ended up raiding an American Division HQ, usually situated well away from the front line, by mistake. The American position *was* well away from the front line. It was *his* battalion that was almost behind enemy lines.

The other officers filed in for orders quietly while Major Schmidt stood with arms folded, staring at the captured map on the wall. When all were assembled, he turned and faced his officers.

"We head east along the main road for three miles until we link up with the rest of the regiment," he began quietly. "There, we will dig in and hold the line against the Americans."

The tent was completely silent.

The orders themselves were unremarkable.

What was unusual was what Major Schmidt had *not* said.

They were two miles from the German border with France.

Their movement would take them into the Fatherland itself, where, as Hans now knew, the bulk of their forces had already retreated.

The officers looked at one another worriedly. Everyone was well aware of what those orders meant.

For the first time, Germany itself was threatened with invasion.

Hans took a deep breath. If ever there was a time for Major Schmidt to inspire the battalion, it was now.

Since becoming the Anton Company Commander, he had seen enough of his Battalion Commander in action to be confident of his ability to lift the men when they needed it the most.

He was always the odd one out among his peers.

Physically in good shape and not averse to crawling along in the mud with the troops if needed, Major Schmidt also had a seemingly encyclopedic knowledge of military lore and doctrine and a surprising familiarity with the opponents facing them.

His bold plan to convert Anton Company into a dedicated raiding force had been a stunning success overall and testament to his uncanny ability to adapt swiftly to changes.

Surely, he would have something up his sleeve this time, no matter what Regiment HQ ordered.

Instead, Major Schmidt said, "Caesar Company to lead off, Anton Company is rear guard. We leave in 2 hours."

He looked around the expectant room one more time.

"Dismissed," he said and walked out of the tent.

Hans dropped his jaw in shock, then slumped down in despair.

There was no inspirational speech after all.

No clever plan to outsmart the enemy.

From the Major's unusual reticence to elaborate further, he knew what those orders meant.

They were to retreat back to the German border itself....

.... but they would not be able to hold it.

Chapter 24

8th April 1945—Germany, West of the Elbe

When Caesar Company units reported an American supply column encamped due west of their position. Major Schmidt ordered Hans to attack it and then decided to come along himself.

To Hans's satisfaction, it turned out to be a fuel convoy. No need for elaborate ruses or dangerous gambles. All they had to do was burn everything.

His men, keeping in tight formation and taking torturous routes well away from American traffic, soon found themselves in an ideal ambush position less than fifty meters from the trucks without detection.

Armed to the teeth, with each man carrying several grenades, Hans deployed his small company quickly.

At his signal, the men threw a volley of grenades into the convoy. Two at each fuel truck and four at the trucks which carried the convoy guards.

The results were devastating.

Most of the fuel trucks exploded when the grenades detonated under them. The remaining ones were quickly destroyed when more grenades were thrown.

The front truck toppled over to the side, and, unfortunately for its occupants, it flipped toward the waiting Germans. They died to a hail of small arms fire before they could even get up.

The rear truck of guards fared even worse. A grenade landed inside it and detonated. The men inside never stood a chance.

The plan had been to attack with grenades and gunfire and then charge in to overrun the convoy.

But as Hans watched the carnage in front of him with a cold, calculating eye, he decided there was no need to expose his men to a stray bullet from anyone left alive.

The precious fuel trucks had been destroyed, and no organized force was left to pursue them.

With a terse, "Let's go," he led his men quickly back the way they came and retreated to Berta Company's location.

On the way, they passed near the assembly point the fuel trucks were heading to. Major Schmidt decided he needed to take a closer look despite the obvious risks.

Seeing that his battalion commander would not be dissuaded, Hans made the best of his situation. He took four men as security detail, then ordered Sergeant Sammer to take the rest of the raiding force back with special instructions to send the Major's vehicle to meet them in case they needed to retreat in a hurry.

Hans led his small group up a slope overlooking the assembly area, but Major Schmidt insisted he needed to get closer. So, Hans deployed his men on the high ground to cover them, then tramped unhappily behind Major Schmidt, who kept on going closer and closer until he finally found a spot where he could observe the Americans to his satisfaction.

For a few minutes, Hans fretted while Major Schmidt looked and counted and wrote in his notebook to his heart's content. Then they were spotted.

"Grenade!" cried Hans, and he dived forward.

Tackling his battalion commander with his whole body weight, they both fell to the ground just as the grenade exploded in a ditch less than ten meters away.

Ignoring the ringing noise in his ears, Hans rose and fired blindly downhill into the smoke as he grabbed his stunned commander by the arm and hauled him upwards.

Major Schmidt took a second longer to recover from the blast, then drew his pistol and fired precise shots at the oncoming enemy in tandem with Hans's random cover fire.

Step by step, they retreated carefully up the hill while Hans fumed at the danger Major Schmidt had put himself in.

Fortunately, it seemed the enemy was content to take potshots and throw grenades to drive the observers away rather than launch a determined assault up the hill against an unknown force.

Hans and Major Schmidt made their way back to the security detail, then beat a hasty retreat before the Americans figured out no one was left on the hill.

On the other side of the hill, they were relieved to see Major Schmidt's *Kübelwagen* with the now-familiar R01 marking waiting for them. Major Schmidt got in the front seat while the rest squeezed into the vehicle and headed back to base.

While Hans took the opportunity to relax and enjoy the ride back, Major Schmidt was unusually agitated. When they reached their base, he made straight for the Command Tent, took out a map, and pored over it. Then he took out his notebook and started scribbling furiously, muttering darkly to himself.

Curious, Hans went over closer to have a look and found himself gradually included in the conversation the Major was having with himself.

"... fringe elements from the US 30th Infantry who have been chasing us from Western France. 2nd Armored still here too... oh, hullo Hans..." said Major Schmidt as he wrote notes and compared them with the map.

Pointing to the map, he spoke as though Hans had been listening all along, "... there, elements of the 8th Armored Division. Not supposed to be here, but they are part of the same XVI Corps as the 30th Infantry, so perhaps not so surprising...."

Hans's eyes started to glaze over.

Just then, a messenger ran up to Major Schmidt, saluted, and handed him a note. He glanced at it, then absently passed it to Hans to read.

Hans unfolded the letter with curiosity and read the contents. His eyes widened, and his hands trembled when he realized who it was from.

The *Führer* himself had written this with his own hand!

On closer inspection, he was slightly disappointed to find this was only a copy. Of course, it was likely printed out and circulated widely across German forces, but still, it was a message from no less than Adolf Hitler.

"My brothers in arms..." it began. Hope sprang anew in Hans's heart as he read on eagerly.

Major Schmidt was still talking, "... but who were these? Never seen these markings or unit numbers before. Weapons new and undamaged. They looked fresh. Some were even clean-shaven. New recruits? Rested veterans? ...

"This changes everything, Hans. A war of attrition is not a viable option to win a war when you were fighting in your own country and outnumbered, but *verdammt*, at least we were doing *some* attrition...."

But Hans wasn't listening.

Prisoner of War

He was reading the letter in his hand, holding back tears.

Over the last few weeks, he hadn't just been fighting the Americans; he had been fighting despair. When they retreated onto German soil for the first time, his faith was shaken. When they were pushed back further and the enemy set foot on his homeland, it broke his heart.

But Hans shook off his anguish and fought with even greater ferocity than before. As if, by sheer force of will and effort, he would shift the world and make it spin the other way.

Battle after battle, he threw himself into the thick of the fighting, rallying his troops and wrestling his way through the opposition.

It was a frenzied, desperate attempt to quell the gnawing doubt that grew within him: The *Führer* wasn't in control, and they were really losing the war.

Until now.

The letter commended the men for their unflagging efforts and heroic stands. It conveyed sympathy for their plight and understanding for the despair they felt for their seeming losses. It promised a new beginning soon, a renewal of spirit and revival of their fortunes.

Finally, it exhorted the men to greater heights, to give their all, for the final victory was at hand.

Hans took a long shuddering breath. At long last, here was confirmation and assurance that all would be well, that all the sacrifices were not in vain, and that the reward for all they had done was soon in the coming.

Hans heaved a sigh of relief and gulped down a half sob just as Major Schmidt caught his eye and stopped mid-sentence.

"What?" the Major asked.

"Major, the letter," said Hans, holding the paper out to him.

"Yes, I read it," came the curt reply, "What of it?"

Hans stared at him in disbelief.

"Final victory is at hand. The *Führer* himself has promised it," said Hans.

Now it was Major Schmidt's turn to stare at him in disbelief.

"Have you not heard a word I've been saying?" asked the Major. "There are fresh forces arrayed against us. Not just the units that have been hounding us from France...."

"But the letter... what the *Führer* says..." insisted Hans.

Prisoner of War

Major Schmidt's eyes suddenly widened in understanding, and he whispered, "*Mein Gott*, you still believe in Hitler. You still believe we can win...."

"Don't *you*?" asked Hans incredulously.

With effort, his commander composed himself.

"Hans," he said gently, "Final victory might be at hand, but first, we have to survive the next few days to see it. We are outnumbered, out-gunned, and low on supplies."

When Hans said nothing, Major Schmidt continued in a low voice, "The American forces we just ran from were fresh and reinforced. We cannot hold here for long."

There was a painful silence.

When at last Hans spoke, it was through a forced smile that made him look sinister.

"Final victory is at hand," said Hans stubbornly. "The *Führer* has said so himself. He will lead us to victory once more."

His commander replied evenly, "If we want to share in his victories, we must share in his mistakes. If we want to share the spoils, we must share in the loss. If we unite ourselves with him to rise to glory, we must be prepared to go down with him in defeat.

"This is not a battle we can win."

Hans's jaw tightened, but he said nothing.

Saluting his commander, he turned around smartly and walked off.

He took a slow, steady walk back to his tent, outwardly calm. But inside, he was seething with rage. He had seen the look in Major Schmidt's eyes.

He did not believe! Hans had looked up to him all this time, and now when it mattered most, he had fallen short.

At any other time, to see his commander like this would have shattered Hans's confidence. But now, with his faith hanging by a thread, he lashed out in anger at anything that threatened what remained of his hope.

Hans took out his Hitler Youth knife and cradled it lovingly, hands caressing the beaked pommel of nickel-plated steel. Then, running his fingers over the plastic handle, he lingered when his index finger touched the black swastika on the diamond-shaped Hitler Youth emblem.

Lightly, he swept his fingers along the hunting-style blade until they reached the broken edge. As he turned the knife over to examine the other side, his eyes welled up when he read the words etched on the smooth surface of the blade.

Inscribed in a flowing script, it said "*Blut und Ehre*". Blood and Honor.

In the Hitler Youth, and later in the German Army, the words had been the driving force of his life. The one thing that kept him going when times were tough. An irresistible demand of obedience, an uncompromising code to live by. Yet a comfort and balm to his soul in times of uncertainty.

Clenching the knife tightly in his hand, Hans whispered fiercely to himself, "Even if no one else believes, I will go on."

Chapter 25

That night, the Americans retaliated.

Hans and his men were sleeping on a small knoll guarded by one of Berta Company's platoons. The rest of Berta Company deployed on the hill just next to them.

Used to getting a full night's sleep undisturbed, they were taken entirely by surprise when an American force attacked their position an hour before dawn.

The silence of the night was broken by grenades exploding, followed by heavy machine-gun fire.

Hans woke immediately and looked around frantically. Sergeant Sammer was at his side a moment later, hurriedly readying his weapon.

In the bright moonlight, Hans pointed to the sounds of battle and ordered, "Hasty defense, single line facing that way. Berta's platoon is there, so don't shoot unless I order. Prepare to reinforce their position."

Sammer nodded and ran off, leaving Hans to organize the men nearest him. Within seconds, all had their helmets on and rifles ready, peering into the darkness in front of them.

A minute later, there came the sounds of running as a line of soldiers emerged from the tree line and headed toward them. Only Erwin's good night vision saved them from the tragedy of friendly fire.

"Germans! They're Germans! It must be Berta's men retreating!" he cried.

Hans bellowed instantly, "Hold fire! Hold fire! Berta's platoon is coming back to us!"

The call was hastily echoed, and weapons that were a hair's breadth from being fired were put to safe. The Berta Company platoon came jogging toward them, the men turning around and firing blindly into the dark every few steps.

"What happened?" called Hans as the first man approached.

"American raid," came the breathless reply, then he ran past Hans and down the knoll on the other side.

"Where is your Platoon Leader?" Hans asked urgently to the next few men who closed in.

"Up ahead," said the nearest one to him, then he too ran past and down the hill.

Hans was dumbfounded. Their Platoon Leader was first to retreat?

Confusion reigned for a minute as the Berta platoon defending them mixed up with the men of Anton Company and then ran past them after their Platoon Leader.

"They're retreating back to Berta Company's position," said Erwin incredulously, staring behind them in the darkness.

Hans stared back in disbelief. Their guards had simply abandoned their positions with barely a shot fired and run off.

"Americans!" someone screamed.

Then all hell broke loose as the raiding force reached them.

The battle that followed was like a nightmare he could not wake up from.

Gunfire erupted from all sides, and grenades exploded randomly. In the first moments of confusion, there was simply no way he could exert any kind of command or control.

And, with only the moonlight to fight by, it was hard to identify an approaching figure until they were close enough to attack.

Then it was every man for himself in hand-to-hand fighting.

Hans fought with a controlled frenzy that bordered panic.

His world shrank to the few meters of near darkness in front of him. Every sense coiled and tensed to attack as soon as he was sure it was an enemy in front, frustrated he could not cut loose and fire freely for fear of hitting any lagging Berta soldiers.

Grimly, he considered giving the free-for-all order to his men. It was all well and good to avoid friendly fire at all costs, but they were being overrun, and Anton Company was fighting for their lives. Shooting another American soldier in the face, he looked around at the chaos.

It might be too late for that, he thought. *They're already among us.*

A flash of movement to his right caught his eye, and he spun around to see an American soldier approaching him from the side, rifle with bayonet pointing straight at him.

A cry from the ground sounded as a German soldier on the floor fired wildly at him. Distracted from Hans for that split second, the American simply pointed his rifle down at the new threat and stabbed forward.

Hans heard the sickening sound of steel entering flesh, and the German soldier sank back to the ground, gurgling. Hans quickly raised his rifle and fired two quick rounds into the American, and soldier jerked back. As he fell, his bayonet pulled free of its victim with a horrible sucking sound.

With that final convulsion, the battle ended.

As suddenly as they appeared, the American raiding force vanished.

Confused shouts in German sounded, but there were no muzzle flashes to give away American positions, so they simply could not see the retreating raiders. Only a few calls in English, getting softer and softer as they faded into the night, gave any indication that the Americans had even been there at all.

Catching his breath, Hans called for his commanders to gather when a weak voice sounded from his right. Looking down, he saw Erwin on the ground, pale face flecked with blood, a dark, expanding circle staining his shirt.

"No," Hans whispered in horror.

Quickly he knelt by his faithful Platoon Messenger to tend to his wound, but he knew it was too late. At the rate the circle of blood was expanding, the bayonet must have hit a major blood vessel, and Erwin was bleeding to death in front of him.

"Are they gone, Oberleutnant?" Erwin asked in a frightened voice.

"Yes, Erwin, they're gone," said Hans, his voice shaking.

"Did we win?" asked Erwin softly.

"Yes, Erwin, we won," said Hans.

"I'm glad, Oberleutnant. I was so frightened, I wanted to run away," said Erwin, sounding ashamed.

Hans, tears filling his eyes now, said, "But you didn't run. You were very brave."

"But I *do* like to run, Oberleutnant," Erwin joked incongruously.

Then suddenly, his eyes went wide, and he looked so very young, like a little boy.

"I think I'd like to sleep for a while now," he said, his voice going faint.

"Yes, you get some rest, Erwin. You did well tonight," said Hans, but Erwin was already dead.

With a hand trembling in rage and grief, Hans carefully closed Erwin's eyes just as Sergeant Sammer came up with the Squad leaders.

"One-third of the remaining men on all-round defense, one-third to gather our supplies and be ready to move, the rest to tend to the wounded—we'll deal with the dead later," Hans said to them, his voice unnaturally harsh as he fought to keep his voice steady.

They nodded in acknowledgment and ran off.

Then Hans ran down his company's knoll and climbed up Berta Company's hill shouting Brandt's name as he went. The men of Berta company, roused by the American raid on Anton's company's position, were on high alert, but no one dared challenge Hans as he stormed up their hill and made straight for the Command Tent in the center of their position.

Ripping open the tent flap, he screamed, "You cowardly, feckless *Schwein*! Your men abandoned their positions to leave us at the mercy of the Americans!"

Hauptmann Brandt, who looked like he was expecting him, said in a most reasonable tone, "I ordered the Platoon Leader to hold until his position was no longer tenable."

"What do you mean no longer tenable? They ran off after the first volley of fire!" shouted Hans.

"An assessment that must be made by the senior officer on the ground, and his decision respected by all," said Brandt coolly.

While Hans fumed in silence, Hauptmann Brandt continued, "Surely, you don't expect my men to die in place for your men while you sleep through the night, untroubled by lowly matters such as sentry duty and trench digging?"

Hans replied in outrage, "I expect your men to hold fast and not run from our enemies like cowards at the first shot!"

Hauptmann Brandt, incensed by the insult, shouted back bitterly, "We were not running from our enemies. We were running from wasting our lives defending *you*!"

Shaking with rage, Hans resisted the urge to punch Brandt and left the tent.

Striding down Berta's position and up to his own, he saw Sergeant Sammer was ready and waiting. The rising sun cast a weak light on the battle scene, giving bloody visual emphasis to his report.

"Seven killed, another eight seriously wounded and will need evacuating to the rear. They won't fight again for a while," said Sergeant Sammer.

Han nodded bleakly. With fifteen men out, Anton Company was truly down to the strength of a single platoon now. And they were lucky too. The American attack had been called off for no reason, just when they were in a position to exploit the collapse of German defenses.

It made no sense unless...

Berta Company's Command Tent suddenly exploded with terrific force, with the central tent pole spinning crazily as it flew straight up into the air. Before it landed, another explosion rocked the hill as their heavy machine gun position was destroyed.

More explosions sounded, followed by machine-gun fire as Berta Company came under attack.

Hans and Sergeant Sammer looked at the hill in complete shock, then at each other as the same word flashed in their minds at the same time.

Tanks!

Sammer started, "How on earth…."

Hans thought furiously as the battle began on the next hill, then suddenly, it all fell into place.

"So that was why the night raid on us stopped. It wasn't a raid at all but a reconnaissance-in-force. The infantry had fought their way up this hill just to get a good look at Berta's hill. Once they were certain of where our center of gravity lay, they reported back in time to unleash their tanks for a dawn attack," said Hans hurriedly.

Sergeant Sammer said darkly, "Well, lucky for us and too bad for them, isn't it?" He clearly shared the same outrage at the desertion of the Berta platoon that was supposed to guard them.

Hans fell silent as another battle raged, this one inside him.

Looking at the corpses of his men, now laid out neatly in a row in preparation for burial in a shallow mass grave, he felt a sense of satisfaction about this.

He had wished Hauptmann Brandt dead, and now he probably was.

That Berta's platoon's abandonment of their duty here enabled the Americans to attack them now was poetic justice. He should let them die where they stood for what they did. Except….

He looked at the line of bodies of his men, then shook his head in frustration. If he did nothing, there would be another line of bodies on Berta's hill.

A much longer one.

He called out to Sergeant Sammer and the other squad commanders within earshot, "Leave one squad to care for and guard the wounded. The rest of the company, with me. We're going to flank the Americans and hit them from the rear."

"Cancel that order," came a calm voice behind him.

Hans turned around and raised his eyebrows in surprise as Major Schmidt walked quickly up to him.

"Your orders are to gather your company and wounded, grab whatever you can carry, and return to the battalion supply depot. Anton Company is now tasked to guard our supply trains as we move them," Major Schmidt said curtly.

"But Berta Company..." began Hans in protest.

Major Schmidt cut him off, "... will have to deal with the American attack. Brandt is a master of static defense. They will give a good account of themselves."

Hans snapped his mouth shut, looking conflicted.

His Battalion Commander spoke again in a gentler tone, "This is not about anyone getting what they deserve. Your men have nothing that will bother the American tanks. So your attack will fail, and your lives wasted for no useful purpose."

Hans looked over to the hill, eyes distant.

Major Schmidt said, "That their tanks are here means our attacks have hurt them. Badly enough for them to detach a precious tank battalion from their main efforts to chase us around here. We must survive to continue. But if our supply trains are found and destroyed, then the rest of the battalion dies. Period."

At last, Hans nodded reluctantly.

"I understand, Major," he said softly and saluted.

Turning to his commanders, he said, "Let's go."

Chapter 26

30th April night—East of the Elbe

Hans scowled in disgust as he led his men back across the bridge spanning the river Elbe. What was left of 1st Battalion had regrouped after the American surprise attack and managed to get organized. But despite their best efforts, the Americans pushed them back until they reached the river Elbe.

Reluctantly, Major Schmidt led his men across the river and abandoned the western bank. The Americans arrived shortly after and but stopped on their side of the river, seemingly content to hold rather than force a crossing.

That was two weeks ago.

Hans had scouted the bridge every night for an opportunity to cross and wreak havoc on his enemies, but the western side of the bridge was too well guarded to sneak through.

He walked into Major Schmidt's tent to report and stopped dead in his tracks.

Most of the battalion officers were present, their faces drawn and pale. The major himself leaned against the table with his body weight supported on his arms, his head slumped in despair. Then, without looking at his junior officer, he said three words that brought Hans's world crashing down.

"Hitler is dead."

Hans froze.

His mind went blank for a full minute, and he could not think a coherent thought. Instead, a jumble of images and flashes of light filled his mind. A dying man in a hospital bed. The acrid smell of torches lit in celebration. The stamping of marching boots and the cheers. New hope that would not die like his father.

He started shaking, his face went bright red, and his breath came in short, sharp gasps.

"It cannot be," he said hoarsely.

There was no reaction from anyone.

"This is falsehood!" he said more loudly.

Still, no one moved.

"Enemy deception," he almost shouted.

Major Schmitt said nothing but handed him a piece of paper.

Hans took the paper with trembling hands and read it.

It was an official communique from High Command, complete with the appropriate seals and authentication marks.

It stated that Hitler had committed suicide in his bunker and was found dead along with Eva Braun on 30th April 1945. German forces were ordered to mourn their leader and carry on fighting.

Hans read and reread the letter with disbelief until the tears in his eyes prevented him from seeing anything more.

"Lies," he whispered to himself.

"Lies," he said to everyone in the command tent.

"Lies!" he shouted at Major Schmidt.

There was no response.

"How do we know this to be true?" Hans's tone was almost pleading now.

"Ask him," Major Schmidt replied quietly, without looking up.

With a start, Hans suddenly realized there was an outsider in the room.

It was a senior SS officer in formal uniform. Familiar. Oberst Richter.

Seized by the sudden panic all German soldiers had when they faced an SS officer, Hans hastily stood straight and mentally reviewed his last few words for any sign of disloyalty to Hitler. Then, he quickly checked himself and dismissed any worries that he had shown anything but complete faith in the *Führer*.

Sure of himself once more, he drew himself up to face Oberst Richter squarely and, for the second time that night, froze in shock.

All SS officers, especially those of such senior rank, were always immaculately dressed and groomed. They invariably carried an air of confidence in themselves and a universal disdain for all others.

Even a relatively junior officer of the SS could walk into the headquarters of any regular army unit and instill fear in its commander many ranks higher.

Oberst Richter was no different on the surface. His uniform was clean and pressed. His hair was cut short, and he stood straight and still.

But it was his eyes that terrified Hans.

Worse than the casual arrogance that was the hallmark of one who was effectively untouchable.... was the very absence of it.

Their eyes met, and Hans saw a haunted look he never dreamed he would ever encounter in an SS officer. A look that told him louder than words that the news was true.

"The *Führer's* SS Aide, Sturmbannführer Günsche, reported this to me," said Oberst Richter heavily. "I can vouchsafe the news."

Hans began, "How can *he* be sure...."

"He carried the gasoline to burn the bodies," said the SS Officer abruptly, cutting Hans off.

"Now, if you'll excuse me, I have other units to visit and share the news," said Oberst Richter sarcastically. With that, he walked out of the tent without another word.

The atmosphere was tense with dread as the imagery hung in the minds of all who were there.

"Orders." Major Schmidt suddenly snapped, breaking the tension in the room.

"With the death of the *Führer*, Admiral Karl Donitz is now in command of the Third Reich," he stated.

He continued with a heavy voice, "Our orders are as follows: All hostile activities to the west are to cease immediately. All wounded, incapacitated, and non-combatants are to be taken west to surrender to any Allied forces they encounter. All functioning combat units are to head east and fight the Red Army."

Hans, lost in thought, suddenly came back to life when the Major's words filtered through the fog in his brain.

"Stop fighting the Americans?" he said incredulously. "After all that has happened, you want us to stop fighting the Americans and surrender to them?"

His voice rose to a shout, "I'll be damned if I stop fighting the Americans! *They* are the enemy; *they* are the ones who brought our country to its knees; *they* are the ones who have been killing us all this time!"

"You arrogant, deluded, pig-headed, Aryan fool! The Americans only kill *us* because we are trying to kill *them*!" Major Schmidt shouted back.

Hans yelled, "And so we should! I have no quarrel with the Soviets! It is the Americans I want to fight!"

"ENOUGH!" roared Major Schmidt, slamming his fist so hard on his command table that it broke.

Hans fell into sullen silence.

Major Schmidt continued through gritted teeth, "What you want or do not want is not relevant here, Oberleutnant. These are our orders."

He paused and stared hard at Hans.

"*Your* orders," he finished.

In all the time they had known each other, the Major had never once pulled rank on Hans, relying instead on a mutual respect and common understanding that made them such a formidable pair.

But that common understanding, already strained when Hitler's letter of encouragement arrived just a few weeks ago, had broken on the news of his death, and then shattered to a million pieces by the orders they now received.

Hans looked as though the Major had slapped him.

Softening his tone, Major Schmidt carried on, as though speaking to himself now, "The war is lost. We *will* surrender. It is only a matter of whom we surrender to.

"The western allies are led by the Americans and British. Neither of them has had their homeland directly invaded by us. Neither has had mother or sister killed by German bullets on the ground. They might be merciful.

"The Soviets were our allies until we betrayed them, invaded their land and slaughtered their people. They are out for blood. There will be no mercy."

The room was silent.

The major continued, "There is nothing left to fight for except ourselves. We throw everything we have at the Soviets so that as many of our countrymen as possible will fall into American hands instead. So gather your men and pack up. We leave tonight.

"That is our only hope now," he finished quietly.

Hans looked straight at his commander as his world fell apart and hissed, "Is that all, *Major*?"

He spat the last word out.

His commander made no response and only looked past him with sad, empty eyes.

When no further orders were given, Hans saluted stiffly and returned to his company.

As he slowly walked back, a black despair began to grow in the pit of his stomach and threatened to overwhelm him. He fought it down furiously by stoking his anger and giving his hate full flight.

Word of Hitler's death soon reached every man in the battalion. And Hans was not surprised to find his company leaders gathered when he returned. Anxious faces looked at him in expectation.

He sat down and began speaking slowly.

"The *Führer* is dead. His life taken by his own hand," he paused here to let the news sink in.

Then he said, "Our orders are to stop fighting the Americans and turn east to fight the Red Army."

Shocked expressions turned thoughtful as the commanders digested the information and comprehended their new orders.

"We fight the Soviets to let more of our country fall into Western hands then," said Sammer, voicing what the others thought.

"No," said Hans harshly.

Sergeant Sammer's forehead creased in confusion, "But our orders…."

"… are illegal and dishonorable," said Hans firmly, "and I intend to disobey them."

Audible gasps sounded from his commanders.

Hans said, his eyes distant and burning, "The Americans are the enemy, and I will carry on the fight against them. Alone if I have to."

Looking at his men, he said, "Who is with me?"

Stunned silence was all the answer he got.

"Sammer?" he asked.

Sergeant Sammer just stared back.

"Lang?" Hans looked at the impish Corporal.

But Lang just looked at the floor.

Stung and hurt, Hans stood up slowly and said bitterly, "I see. After all we've been through, this is how you pay me back."

Sergeant Sammer, his face pale, rose and said, "Oberleutnant. For all you've done for us since you took charge of Anton Company, we are grateful, we thank you, and many of us owe you our lives."

Murmurs of assent broke out.

"Please do not do this," pleaded Sammer.

His face a stony mask, Hans said coldly, "I will do what I must. Even if everyone leaves me."

And then he walked off.

"It is *you* who are leaving us, Oberleutnant," said Sergeant Sammer, sadly.

Chapter 27

1st May—East of the Elbe.

In the morning, the battalion packed up and headed east without even trying to hide their movements from the Americans.

It had been a simple matter for Hans to slip away with the three men he had persuaded to come with him and stay behind near the river. He knew no one could spare the effort to look for deserters at such a time.

Besides, he told himself fiercely, *we are not deserting. We are carrying on the fight where it matters most. It is* they *who are deserting.*

On some level, he was dimly aware that his thinking didn't make sense, but somehow, it was as if his mind had operated in a fog since he heard the news of Hitler's death.

Throughout the war, he had clung to the belief that no matter how bad things seemed, the *Führer* would always prevail in the end. His father had promised him that. The *Führer* had delivered that throughout his youth and into the beginning of the war.

But now Hitler was dead.

His mind recoiled at the awful fact and instead grasped desperately at the next thing he was sure of—the Americans were the enemy. The Americans had to pay. So he fed the anger inside to shout down the deepening emptiness inside him.

As he watched the last men of the battalion depart, a brief thought crossed his mind—to give up his mad scheme and rejoin his friends and comrades who were leaving before his eyes.

Even though there were three men with him, Hans never felt so alone in his life as he did now.

He fought down the urge to call out and go running after the 1st Battalion and instead convinced himself he was doing the right thing. He had three men with him after all, did he not? He couldn't possibly be *that* wrong about matters, could he?

As the last of 1st Battalion disappeared from view, Hans led his tiny command to occupy the highest point overlooking the bridge, watching for the Americans to make their move.

They didn't have to wait long.

"Here they come," said Hans to his men as five tanks started to rumble across the bridge.

"They see us running with our tails between our legs and seek to take advantage," he muttered angrily as the three men looked nervously down to the bridge.

The tank platoon crossed, formed up, then turned south as though scouting along the river bank. When the last tank turned its back on Hans, he called to the men.

"Now, while their backs are turned to us, spread and out and prepare to attack!"

The three men looked at their rifles, then at the tanks, then back at Hans, and stared at him as though he was mad.

"Oberleutnant, we are *four* riflemen against five *tanks*," said one of them desperately.

Prisoner of War

Hans ignored him, stood and drew his breath to shout to charge…. and went down at the bottom of a heap of bodies as the three men jumped on him and pinned him down.

He struggled and thrashed, but they held him until the tanks were out of sight. Then, when he finally stopped struggling, the soldiers abandoned their erstwhile commander and jogged east toward where they last saw the 1st Battalion.

Hans cursed the men for their cowardice and, shouldering his rifle, went down to follow the tanks.

By the time he caught up, they seemed to have reached the limit of their scouting mission and were returning to the bridge.

He found a rock, braced himself, and fired at the lead tank. The bullets bounced off harmlessly as the tank's machine gun swiveled to face him.

Hans ducked as a shower of bullets shattered the rock he was hiding behind. Then, finding another position, he fired again, equally ineffectively as the first time. The tank dutifully returned fire but did not bother to pursue.

Hans raced to another position and fired until he ran out of ammunition.

And just like that, the prosecution of his personal war came to a grinding halt.

The tanks proceeded north peacefully until they reached the bridge and returned to their side of the river while Hans glared impotently at them.

Muttering in disgust, he gave up the attack and started walking east. Maybe he could catch up with his battalion, or at least with someone who had ammunition so he could resupply and carry on his fight.

Walking quickly, he soon met with two soldiers who seemed lost. Whether deserters or genuine stragglers, it didn't matter to Hans anymore. All he was concerned with was if he could get more ammunition.

As it was, while they still had their weapons, they had barely any ammunition. Even if Hans took it all, it would hardly be enough to do any meaningful fighting. Once it was clear he could get nothing of use from them, he tried to walk off on his own, but they begged to come with him.

Hans refused initially, then his stomach growled and reminded him he hadn't eaten since the day before. And he had completely forgotten to bring any food along with him. The two stragglers shared some of what they had with him and, as he accepted what they offered, took that as permission to follow along.

Grumbling to himself, Hans led them east at a brisk pace.

Within the hour, they caught up with another group of three soldiers, equally woe-begone as the first pair. They mumbled what units they were from, how they got left behind, and how it wasn't their fault. Hans didn't care.

On interrogation, Hans found that they too had little ammunition and little food. But as he tried to walk off, the pair who were following him hailed hearty welcomes to the newcomers, and before he knew it, Hans now had five men following him.

As they marched, they met up with more soldiers, a mix of small groups from decimated units and stragglers drifting behind the larger units that had swung east to fight the Soviets.

With barely any words, they seemed to sense purpose in Hans's stride and simply merged into his group without asking.

The only ones he turned away were a pair who tried to join them as they paused to rest in the afternoon.

Former guards at Ohrdruf Concentration Camp, they joined in with the other men and exchanged stories. One of them laughed about how they enticed sick prisoners to the courtyard with the promise of food so that it was easier to execute them. The other told them tales of Auschwitz, where, he boasted, there were just so many to kill, they couldn't spare the bullets. So, they lured them to the gas chambers, telling them they would get a shower, only to kill them there en masse as the sealed rooms filled with poison gas.

Disgusted at the stories, Hans had driven the pair off at gunpoint and told them he would shoot them if he saw them again.

With that, he and his band moved on.

As the sun began to set, Hans looked behind him and saw a string of nearly twenty men following in his wake. All were lost, exhausted and low on supplies. As he watched them, they looked back at him eagerly in hope and expectation.

Like it or not, he was now their leader.

Hans sighed in resignation and signaled for the party to make camp.

After setting up a basic perimeter, they started a fire and settled down to eat and rest. Throughout the night, more stragglers came and joined, attracted by the light of their camp. By morning, their numbers had doubled.

Hans reviewed their situation. They had adequate food and water for now. All the men were better rested and armed, but critically short of ammunition. He shook his head in frustration, but he knew he should not have been surprised. Even in his own battalion, no one ever had a satisfactory load of ammunition; what more rag-tag soldiers who were lost and wandering aimlessly.

There was nothing for it except to push on until they met organized German units who could take over command of the men and resupply him for his personal war.

After a cold breakfast, they formed up and started to march.

Chapter 28

2nd May 1945—Further east of the Elbe.

A little later, Hans and his band reached the next village.

As they approached, he hushed them and signaled for his company to fan out. This deep into their own country, they were unlikely to encounter enemies here. But the village, more a hamlet really, seemed completely abandoned.

They entered quietly and spread out to look around.

Behind a large house, Hans entered an open clearing. It looked like an outdoor garage, and inside were two trucks that looked in serviceable condition. Eagerly, Hans went forward to inspect them when he heard the ominous click of a weapon being cocked behind him.

"Put your hands up where I can see them. I'll brook no thievery in my own home," said a harsh voice in German.

Hans raised his hands carefully and slowly turned around.

An old man with an ancient rifle stood at the entrance of the house's back door. His weapon was pointed directly at Hans.

The hairs on the back of his neck stood up, but Hans kept his voice firm as he calmly said, "*Guten Tag, der Herr.* I am Oberleutnant Hans Wagner. An officer of the *Heer*, and I lead this company of men."

The old man replied, "I am Rolfe Bauer, a veteran of the Great War, and I own this land you are now trespassing."

Hans said, "We are not trespassing. We thought this hamlet was abandoned and sought to salvage whatever we could use for the defense of our country."

The old man barked a short, ugly laugh.

"You call rounding up civilian men at gunpoint to join the army "defense of our country"? They only left me behind because I was lame and wouldn't be able to keep up. And if my trucks weren't in the field then, they would have taken them too," said the old man bitterly.

"German Army units passed through here?" Hans asked excitedly. "When? Which units?"

"Don't know, don't care," said the old man sullenly.

They stared at each other for a while.

Hans began again, "Look, *Herr* Bauer, in times of war, the German Army has the authority to requisition any necessary material from civilian sources. We have need of your vehicles to get us to the front line...."

"No," came the firm reply.

"Berlin itself is under attack. Without reinforcements, it will fall. We need your trucks to get us there in time to make a difference," said Hans urgently.

"Over my dead body," growled the old man.

Hans stared angrily at him. Was he so blind? So selfish?

He assessed the old man again. His hands were shaky, and he was squinting hard to keep sight of his target. Maybe he couldn't see well enough. Maybe his arms were getting tired...

Hans tensed up and prepared to leap. He was confident he could rush the old man and avoid the shot. Or at least he could dive away, call for help, so his men would... what? Shoot him dead? So they could take his trucks?

While Hans was incensed by the old man's disloyalty and selfishness, this was a matter for the courts to deal with. He deserved a fine or even imprisonment.

But desperate as he was to get to Berlin, wrong as this old man was to refuse to help, short of attacking him, what could he do?

Hans shook his head in frustration.

He needed those trucks. And he could take the old man down if necessary. But to kill him for them? How much of a loyal defender of Germany would he be if he stole from and killed the very ones he was sworn to protect?

Finally, Hans sagged and said, "Old man, on my honor and yours as a fellow German, we really need those trucks, but if you are unwilling to let us have it, we will not...."

BANG!

A spray of blood spattered across Hans's face.

In shock, he blinked his eyes clear and saw the old man still pointing his gun at Hans, his expression one of total surprise, with a new hole in his forehead.

Then his eyes rolled, and he crumpled to the ground, dead.

Behind him was a figure in the shadows, holding a smoking pistol in its right hand, now pointed straight at Hans.

The figure stepped forward and came into the sunlight to reveal the handsome features of a blond man with blue eyes.

Hans gasped in disbelief as he recognized him.

"Hello Hans," said Hauptmann Adolf Brandt mockingly.

Hans's mind reeled in shock.

"How is this possible?" he whispered. "I saw you die when the American attacked."

Brandt corrected him, "You saw my Command Tent blow up. I was using the field latrine when their tanks attacked. Then my men held them off for a while, no thanks to you, but even they have limits.

"So while you and the rest fled across the Elbe, my company died, and I was trapped on the other side."

"It took me more than two weeks to find a way across the river without getting caught," said the former Berta Company Commander sourly.

Hans shook his head to clear it, still not believing what he saw.

Then his eyes fell on the body of the old man.

"You killed him," gasped Hans, looking at the corpse.

Brandt said, "I *saved* you."

Hans stared at him incredulously and said, "From what? From him?"

Brandt replied coolly, "He was pointing a gun at a German soldier and fellow officer."

Hans shouted, "He was a frightened old man defending his property. He had the right to refuse to give it to us."

"He was a traitor to the Fatherland, threatening to shoot an officer of the *Wehrmacht* making a lawful demand," snapped Brandt, pointing at the dead man with his pistol.

As soon as he did so, Hans whipped out his own pistol as fast as lightning and pointed it at Brandt.

Alerted by the gunshot, Hans's men came running. The first few that reached the scene gasped at the sight of the two officers facing off each other with pistols drawn.

"You murdered him," Hans snarled angrily.

More men came running, and soon a small confused crowd gathered to watch, completely uncertain what to do.

"So that's how it's going to be, is it, Oberleutnant?" sneered Brandt.

Raising his voice so the men could hear, he said, "I save you from getting shot by this rebel here, and you want to arrest me? For saving your life?"

Hans said firmly, "Yes."

Softly, Brandt said, "And if I resist?"

Hans cocked his pistol in response.

Brandt laughed his guttural laugh and said in mock incredulity, "You would *shoot* me? Execute me here like what you accuse me of doing?"

Hans said coldly, "If I have to."

"And then what?" hissed Brandt. "Take the trucks anyway? You set yourself up to be so high and mighty, so noble and righteous. You defend a dead man's right to refuse to help, then kill me for saving you, then take his trucks *anyway* because he was conveniently eliminated by me?"

Brandt taunted, "How different would that be from killing him yourself?"

Hans wavered.

Brandt spat, "You'd be worse than what you accuse me of being. A murderer *and* a hypocrite."

Then he lowered his pistol and holstered it, daring Hans to shoot him.

In a low voice, Brandt said, "I need.... *We* need to get to Berlin. And the only way we are going to do so in time to make any difference is to take those vehicles."

Hans cursed inwardly at what he knew Brandt was going to say next.

"If you kill me now, you have no right to take those trucks, so... enjoy your walk to Berlin," said Brandt triumphantly.

Hans glared at Brandt with pure hatred.

In anguish, he thought about the battalion and the rest of Anton Company. Of the beleaguered Berlin garrison desperately in need of relief. Of the dead old man.

Hans told himself that to leave behind the old man's trucks now would render his death in vain.

Finally, he lowered his gun and holstered it, his face burning.

"So glad you see things my way," said Brandt sarcastically. He brushed his hair and made to walk past Hans toward the men.

"Now, as the senior officer here, I will take charge...." Brandt started.

But Hans cut him off with an outstretched arm, blocking his way.

Without looking at him, Hans said through clenched teeth, "Let us be clear on one thing, Hauptmann. You may be greater in rank, but we are equal in appointment. In this company, *I'm* in charge."

Brandt looked like he was about to challenge that, then a sly look flickered across his face before it turned impassive.

"Of course," he shrugged nonchalantly, "Your company. I'll just tag along and help out where I may then."

Hans scowled at him suspiciously but could find no fault in what he said.

He raised his voice so the men could hear.

"Alright, bury this man, gather anything of use and load it up into the trucks. I want us to be on the road toward Berlin in an hour," he said.

The trucks were in better condition than they looked, and more importantly, they had full tanks of fuel and two jerry cans of extra petrol. Hans estimated they could make it all the way to Berlin with what they had with some to spare at the end.

Although how they came by the trucks left a sour taste in his mouth, he was quietly optimistic.

It wasn't just the speed they could now travel at. With the trucks able to carry equipment, supplies, and ammunition, his small band was becoming a respectable fighting force since they no longer had to abandon extra weapons and ammunition in favor of mobility.

The only snag they encountered was when one of the trucks had a flat tire, and they had no jack.

But when the men started talking about stopping for the night, it was Hauptmann Brandt, of all people, who chopped down a small tree and, cleverly levering the trunk against a rock, used it as an improvised jack to raise the truck enough so they could repair the tire.

They got on the move again, and by the end of the morning, they finally saw what seemed to be the first signs of functioning German forces.

A roadblock with three guards.

Chapter 29

The roadblock was more symbolic than anything else, considering the road it blocked ran through a completely flat and open field.

Even a civilian Volkswagen could readily drive around it without trouble.

The roadblock itself was a pathetic construction consisting of a long tree branch pivoting on a box with the other end resting on a rock.

Nonetheless, it represented structure in German units that had been disturbingly absent throughout their travel.

Upon sighting the trucks, one of the three guards ran toward a nearby hill where a tent was pitched—presumably to carry the report of their arrival to whoever was in charge.

The remaining two took on what they must have imagined to be threatening stances with rifles pointed forward and called out a half-hearted challenge to Hans and his company.

Hans ordered the trucks to stop and dismounted.

As he approached the roadblock and looked at the soldier who challenged them, Hans saw the two stripes and three diamonds on his shoulder epaulet and registered him as a Hauptmann.

But he seemed very young. Even younger than Hans.

"Excuse me?" Hans asked when the soldier mumbled something indistinct again.

"Password!" came the challenge again in a warbling baritone.

Hans was taken aback.

Password? In broad daylight with his company marching openly on the road? Forty of them against two? What sort of child's game was this? He had no password in any case.

And there was something very disconcerting about the officer in front of him.

"I am Oberleutnant Hans Wagner of 1st Battalion, 1034th Regiment, 59th Infantry Division," Hans began, saluting the Hauptmann, "With me are assorted troops from various units from the western front that got lost when all units were ordered to turn east. I am looking for...."

"Password!" the soldier interrupted, more insistently, raising his rifle to point at Hans.

Hans faltered as he stared down the barrel of the gun pointed at him. His mind reeled at the idea that, after surviving numerous battles with the Americans, his part in the war would end with a German bullet.

Then his brain slowly started catching up with what his eyes had been observing about the soldier before him. Besides looking very young, his uniform was not regular-issue for combat forces, yet it looked familiar.

So very familiar.

The thought struck Hans like a thunderbolt.

Hitler Youth!

This "Hauptmann" in front of him was a Hauptmann only in the youth organization for teenagers!

Hans rubbed his eyes wearily. Maybe he was more tired than he realized to have mixed the *Hitlerjugend* rank insignias with German Army ones.

Irrationally, the fact that Hans outranked the boy in front of him even as a Hitler Youth suddenly loomed large in his mind as he struggled to find the words to say.

"I am Hans Wagner, Unit Leader of the *Hitlerjugend.* I outrank you, so put down your weapon!" Hans began, then stopped at the sheer inanity of pulling rank on a pimpled teenager in the middle of a war.

He tried again to muster something coherent, "I am an officer of the real German Army and ..." and stopped again.

Finally, unable to contain his exasperation, he shouted, "WHERE ARE YOUR PARENTS?"

The Hitler Youth wilted under his glare and actually started crying. The other guard at the roadblock, now obviously Hitler Youth and even younger than the one who spoke, looked around uncertainly as his senior dissolved into tears and lowered his weapon.

Just then, Hans spotted two figures ambling down the hill.

One was a portly figure, clearly an adult male by his shape and manner, walking with a limp. He was led by the boy who had run off at the arrival of Hans and his company.

Impossible as it seemed, he looked even younger than the two he left to face Hans at the roadblock.

Hans peered anxiously at the approaching figures, hoping the older man was someone in authority and could take command. But as the man drew nearer, Hans's heart sank as he recognized the uniform he wore.

Polizei Berlin.

The unlikely pair reached the group at the roadblock, and without preamble, the older man asked Hans, "Who are you?"

Hans repeated his rank and details.

"I see," the older man said in acknowledgment.

"You are Berlin Police?" Hans asked.

"Retired," came the reply.

Hans closed his eyes and pressed his temples with his thumb and middle finger. There was no way he could leave his band with a retired policeman.

"What are you doing here, so far from the city?" asked Hans.

The retired police officer said, "When the Soviets started shelling Berlin, we evacuated most of the population out to the west. Then all able-bodied police were given rifles and absorbed into army units."

Hans's face fell at his answer. He knew Berlin was under attack by the Red Army, but for the population to be evacuated entirely meant things were worse than he thought. He gnashed his teeth in frustration at the thought of his beloved city coming under attack.

"Some of us retired ones reported to our stations to see if we could help, so they got us to take command of the boys here," continued the police officer.

The boys here, Hans thought grimly to himself. At least this man had no delusions they were anything remotely resembling a military force.

"What news of the forces passing by?" Hans asked, his voice a bit harsher than intended. "1st Battalion? 1034th Regiment?"

The police officer shook his head, "Don't know who went by. Some tanks and trucks, a couple of *Kübelwagens*, some troops on foot. They looked tired and footsore, but no wounded."

"How many?" Hans asked.

The police officer shrugged as if it were of no consequence, and Hans wanted to strangle him.

"Where did they go?" Hans demanded, struggling to keep his composure.

"That way," the older man said, pointing east toward Berlin. "I suppose to link up with the IXth Army in the city."

"The IXth Army? Do they hold the city still?" Hans asked anxiously.

The older man nodded his head, "They did when we left. We even heard of some SS Divisions pulling back to reinforce them, but the Red Army was also building up their forces by the day."

Then he added, "I don't think they can hold much longer if they haven't already fallen. We should leave. Head west."

Hans looked at the horizon toward the capital worriedly now. The thought of his beloved city under attack upset him greatly, but what should he do now? What *could* he do?

Just then, Hauptmann Brandt walked up. He had heard the last exchange and was furious.

"I would shoot you for treason, but we can't spare the bullets," hissed Brandt at the police officer.

Turning to Hans, he said, "What business do we have listening to cowardly old civilians? We are officers of the *Wehrmacht!*"

Pointing to the east, he said loudly, "There lies the IXth Army. The very core of our army. Reinforced by the SS bastards. Even *I* don't like them, but they are unmatched as a fighting force. More, our own 1st Battalion has probably joined them as well."

In a determined voice, Brandt said, "We should go. Rejoin our friends, reinforce them, inspire them, and face the Soviets. This is our duty as Germans and as officers."

Hans stared at Hauptmann Brandt, then to the east, a sense of anticipation dawning in his heart. Berlin was under attack. But all was not lost yet. How could he turn his back on his comrades and countrymen?

Hans made up his mind. The Americans would have to wait. Berlin must not fall.

"Orders," he said softly to the police officer without shifting his gaze. "You will gather what forces you have under your command. You will abandon this *lächerlich* roadblock, strip this position of anything that can be of use, and follow us."

Turning to face his company, he said with passion, "To the east lies the comrades we have been looking for. To the east lies the capital city of our homeland— threatened by foreign barbarians. To the east lies the

IXth Army—last of German strength holding out against impossible odds."

He paused to make sure he had everyone's attention.

Then he raised his voice and said fiercely, "There, we will meet with our friends! There, we will add our lives to those who defend our homes! There, we will take our final stand, and no one shall overcome us!"

"TO BERLIN!" he cried.

"TO BERLIN!" came the answering shout from his men.

Cheers and catcalls broke out as the men raised rifles and fists triumphantly in the air.

The police officer, tears shining in his eyes, drew himself straight and whipped off a parade-ground salute to Hans, then turned about smartly and marched off to gather his men.

Hans, too, turned about smartly and started marching toward the east, his face alight with a savage smile of joy as Hauptmann Brandt nodded approvingly.

Chapter 30

3rd May 1945—On the way to Berlin

By the end of the day, the new additions had found their places in the motley crew Hans was leading.

The retired police officers settled in with the soldiers, exchanging cigarettes and stories, while the three Hitler Youths followed Hans around like puppies with a new master and insisted on sitting in the front of the truck so they could talk to him in the passenger seat.

"I'm Wilhelm," said the eldest. "I'm one of the youngest ever to become Head Cadre Leader in the *Hitlerjugend*."

"I'm Josef," said the next boy. "And I..."

But the youngest boy cut him off excitedly, "I'm Tomas, and I can run fast! Even faster than Wilhelm and Josef! And they're older! That's why I was sent to fetch the Policeman... Not because I'm the youngest and I let them order me around, but because I'm the fastest. Yesterday, I saw a chicken and tried to catch it...."

"No, you didn't; it was trying to catch you!" exclaimed Josef.

"Only because I was trying to lure it to a better spot so I could catch it," said Tomas defensively.

"You were screaming as you ran...."

"To make sure I got its attention!"

Hans smiled at the prattle of the boys. Usually, it would have annoyed him no end, but with all the pain and chaos of the last few days, he found the sounds of something as ordinary as children squabbling among themselves soothing.

As the sun set, they pulled off the main road to settle for the night. The Hitler Youths, excited at the prospect of making camp with real soldiers, gallantly offered to stand guard at night so the men could rest.

Hans gratefully accepted and soon fell into a numbed sleep.

It seemed only an instant later that Tomas shook him awake and, with frightened eyes, reported that he heard men marching west along the road. But by the time Hans went with him to have a look, there was nobody there.

Annoyed as he was at having his sleep interrupted, Hans reminded himself that Tomas was just a boy. And even in the darkness, Hans could sense how crestfallen he was to have disturbed his great leader.

With a sigh, Hans ruffled his hair and reassured him he was doing an excellent job as a soldier. Tomas brightened up at the praise and returned to his sentry position with renewed determination and purpose.

There were no more interruptions that night, and the men woke up somewhat refreshed. After a quick breakfast, they loaded up and drove east until they came to a low ridgeline.

Hans deemed it prudent to check out the ground ahead on foot, so he ordered a stop. Quietly, the men dismounted, spread out, and started walking up the slope.

As the company approached the high ground, they heard a sound like distant thunder, except it was too regular, too measured. The men exchanged glances with one another.

Every soldier knew what it was.

Artillery.

And every soldier knew what it meant.

Fighting.

Specifically, fighting between cohesive and significant forces.

Nobody liked the sound of artillery nor what it usually meant.

But in the last two days, they had traveled along empty roads, devoid of all human life and, worryingly, devoid of any sign of organized German forces.

That artillery was being fired at all, even if *on* their own forces, meant at the very least, substantial operational German units still fought on in some measure.

All was not lost yet.

Carefully, Hans led his men up the ridgeline until they reached the top.

As he crested the peak and could finally see what lay beyond, Hans's heart soared as he looked across the valley to the next ridgeline beyond.

On it was the welcome sight of tents, equipment, and men moving about like ants.

Thankfully, that crowded position was not the target of the artillery attack they were hearing. Instead, the sounds of bombardment came from beyond. Hans's best guess was that Berlin itself was being shelled.

Just a few meters in front of him was a German machine gun trench with three soldiers huddled inside.

They were startled by the sound of Hans's approach from behind and turned to stare in amazement at him. Then they saw the rest of his company arrive, and their eyes widened even more.

A brief flicker of hope crossed their faces until they registered that, welcome as any number of friendly soldiers might be, they were not fresh reinforcements unexpectedly arriving in the nick of time.

They settled back into their trench and ignored the newcomers.

Annoyed, Hans walked up to the trench and tapped the nearest soldier on his helmet. The soldier turned in irritation to face him. Seeing it was an officer accosting him, he sullenly swung about to give him his attention.

"What unit are you? What's going on?" Hans asked.

"Clausewitz Panzer Division. 20th Corps. Wenck's XIIth Army. We were attacking Berlin."

Panzers! Germany's most potent divisions! There was a chance after all...

"Where are your tanks?" Hans asked excitedly.

"Down there," nodded the soldier to the valley below.

Dotted across the landscape were dozens of tanks.

Every single one was burnt out, ripped open, or broken into pieces. The sight of their shattered hulks caused Hans to shudder in horror.

Then, something even worse hit him as what the soldier said slowly filtered through to his exhausted mind.

With a growing sense of dread, Hans asked, "Wait, why were you attacking Berlin?"

The soldier looked at him, first in annoyance, then in sympathy, as he seemed to realize Hans and his men must have been out of touch for a long time.

"To break through to the IXth Army holed up there," he said softly.

"Break through?" Hans cried in astonishment, "You mean the Red Army...."

"...has surrounded Berlin," the soldier finished for him.

Hans was dismayed.

Surrounded!

Their last hope of salvation, trapped in their own city!

If the encirclement was complete, no supplies could get into the forces defending the city. Once they had consumed what they already had, they would be unable to fight regardless of morale or strength of will.

It would only be a matter of time. Weeks, maybe even days.

The situation was more urgent than Hans had feared.

"Then why are we waiting?" Hans railed at the soldier.

He pointed at the forces on the ridge, "We need to go in with all we have now! Smash through Soviet lines and link up with the IXth Army! Once combined, we can break the siege, or at the very worst, get them out of the city and regroup at the river Elbe…"

"Oberleutnant," the soldier interrupted him gently, "we no longer have the forces to do that."

Hans glared at him and pointed triumphantly at the men on the ridge.

The soldier looked away sadly and settled back into his spot in the trench as though the conversation was over.

Hans, his finger still pointed at the forces on the ridge, realized the soldier was no longer even looking at him. The triumphant look on his face took on a fixed quality, and his smile grew strained.

Slowly, he turned his gaze to follow where his finger pointed and looked again.

A cold, gnawing pit began to form in his stomach.

His finger started shaking.

It began with a slight tremor that built up to such a spasmodic shuddering that he could no longer point it straight.

His throat seemed to close upon itself, and suddenly his shirt collar seemed far too tight.

His heart slowed down into heavy, thudding beats, as though hoping to escape the horror of the world by becoming still, even if it meant stopping entirely.

Finally, his mind began to comprehend the horror of what his eyes saw.

The awful reality of what he was looking at.

The forces on the ridge were Soviet.

Chapter 31

3rd May 1945—West of Berlin

Hans dropped to his knees.

The shock of finding out the entire ridge was lined by Soviet forces instead of German caused him to sink into deep despair.

For the longest time, he stared at the ridgeline and said nothing, felt nothing, thought nothing. What could he do against such overwhelming odds?

Every time he attempted to plan something, the idea was defeated before it saw the light of day. Every time he tried to construct a coherent sentence, his mind shut it down before it finished.

Their only hope had been to reach the IXth Army in Berlin. The only plan that made sense was to concentrate all remaining German might to fight instead of letting their enemies take them piecemeal.

And now, their route to Berlin was cut off. The core of remaining German strength—trapped. And the last external force that could lift the siege—broken in the valley below.

Finally, it was only when a vaguely familiar face appeared in front of him, blocking his view of the ridgeline, that he came to his senses.

It was a boy, about fifteen-years old. And he was upset. Dimly, Hans heard sounds he did not understand, but after he paid closer attention, they eventually coalesced into words.

After a long time, he realized the boy was talking to him. Earnestly, pleadingly.

In a while, he managed to string a few words together to glean some significance from it, and they summed up to mean, in effect, "Please, Oberleutnant, what should we do?"

Looking at his tear-stained face, Hans felt a little sorry for him and decided to rouse himself. In another moment, he recognized the boy to be the Hitler Youth who was manning the roadblock earlier.

Prisoner of War

What was his name, Wilhelm or something like that?

Absently, he patted the boy on his shoulder and then slowly stood up. Then, shaking himself vigorously, like a dog coming out of water, he took a deep breath and looked around.

His company had settled down on the hill to watch the forces on the ridgeline. Some of his men were sharing cigarettes with the three soldiers in the trench. He noticed there were more regular troops too—probably in the same unit as the men in the trench—who had come to meet the newcomers.

Halfway down the slope, Hauptmann Brandt was in deep discussion with a sergeant as he looked critically at the defensive positions. Noting Hans had finally stirred from his stupor, Brandt gave him a wave and dispatched the sergeant to him.

The sergeant was a short, wiry man with a strange white streak of hair that ran from his forehead to the back of his head. It contrasted against his otherwise surprisingly dark, jet-black hair, giving him the appearance of a badger.

"I'm Sergeant Herbert Koch, 2nd Battalion of 106th Regiment. We were with the Clausewitz Division," he said by introduction, throwing a sloppy salute. "The Hauptmann down there says you're in charge and to talk to you."

"Yes," said Hans, nodding in satisfaction that Brandt didn't try to undermine him while he was in shock.

"Update, Sergeant," Hans ordered, finding some comfort in the familiarity of military form.

"The IXth Army is holding in Berlin," Sergeant Koch began, then qualified his statement. "More like trapped in the city, if you ask me."

He continued, "Soviet forces have all but surrounded the city. Some units have even linked up with the Western Allies. The IXth has been pounded by artillery for seven days straight and can't hold out much longer. Even aside from the artillery, they are running out of supplies and will soon have to surrender."

Hans nodded somberly.

Sergeant Koch said, "Before he died, Hitler ordered us—the XIIth Army—to break through Soviet lines from the south-west to link up with the Berlin garrison inside. Either to reinforce and resupply them or to pull them out. I don't know."

Looking at the tank hulks that littered the valley before them, the sergeant continued bitterly, "Not that it mattered. As you can see, we didn't break through."

His eyes went distant, and he said, "We did well at first. Our Panzers rolled away any opposition quickly. We took twenty-four kilometers in short order. We had momentum, and for a while, we thought we could really do it."

"It was only when we got here that we realized it had been so easy because *this* section of the Soviet forces was facing the city to prevent a breakout. Once they understood we were serious opposition, they turned around fully and faced us."

"It wasn't a fair fight," he concluded bleakly.

"Who's left then?" Hans asked.

The sergeant answered, "Of the XIIth? I guess General Wenke and the forces that weren't directly involved in this attack. There was supposed to be another attack further north—from the west of Berlin while the IXth would try to break out west to meet them, but I don't know if that succeeded."

Without pausing for breath, he carried on. "...maybe there might be some forces further north? The XXIst was holding there when I last heard, but I think they're too far to make a difference to us. If they're even alive. I mean, the British were up there too, coming from the other side...."

Hans cursed the loquacious sergeant and interrupted rudely, "I meant, who's left *here*?"

Sergeant Koch looked around and shrugged, "Remnants of the Clausewitz Division, some stragglers from other units. CO is dead. The command tent got spotted and shelled before the attack even began. All tanks were destroyed. We've salvaged some machine guns and *Panzerfäuste*, then we dug in up and down along this hill ...."

He said with a wry smile, "To be honest, if you and your men decided to attack our positions as you are now, you'd probably win by sheer weight of numbers."

Hans grunted in annoyance at the sergeant's attempt at humor.

"Who's in charge here then?" he demanded.

The Sergeant made a show of shielding his eyes and looking around in a full circle. Then he looked back at Hans and grinned irritatingly.

"Well, I suppose you are, Oberleutnant," he said.

Hans buried his face in his hands and swore.

It took him a few moments to compose himself before he could act.

Then, his training and natural leadership instincts took over.

For the time being, the Soviet units in front of them might as well be the entire Red Army compared to the meager forces at his disposal.

And, Hans thought gloomily as he looked north in vain for news of other elements of the XIIth Army, *we might well be the entire German Army now.*

Most importantly, the enemy on the ridge was clearly facing away from them, toward Berlin. They would not attack just yet, not until the IXth Army was defeated and Berlin fell.

So, technically that meant he was in a position to attack the enemy in the rear—an opportunity no commander of any level would pass up on—except for the mute testimony of a division's worth of smashed Panzers, some no more than 200 meters from where he stood.

He suppressed a shiver.

If this was the result of an entire German Panzer Division attacking the enemy from behind, what chance did he and his men have?

Then he spotted something below, and his heart sank even lower.

Amidst the twisted hulks of burnt-out German tanks and armored fighting vehicles lay the carcasses of soft vehicles. Transport half-tracks, trucks, vans, and even motorbikes, lay scattered about the battlefield like discarded toys.

On a mound of earth, Hans saw the remains of a lone *Kübelwagen*. As the sun began to set, it illuminated the black markings against the grayish-green of the broken door—R01.

Major Schmidt's vehicle.

There was no way anyone inside could have survived. Tears sprang to his eyes as he imaged the scene. How desperate it must have been that even the non-combat vehicles had charged the Soviet lines.

And how typical it would have been of Major Schmidt to have joined in at the last.

Hans heaved a deep, shuddering sigh and fought to keep grief from overwhelming him.

Fraught as their last encounter had been, Hans had always looked up to and admired the man. He now understood his anger at him was not the righteous anger of a junior officer disdaining the cowardice of a senior one—It was the anger of when his faith was challenged by someone he knew and trusted with his life. And perhaps, that person was right after all.

Hans choked back a sob and disguised it as a fit of coughing before the men could see.

But he needn't have bothered because at that moment, something changed.

It was subtle.

Like a change in atmospheric pressure or a drop in temperature.

He couldn't pinpoint it at first, but it left him uneasy.

Looking around, he noticed the men felt it too. Most were sitting up and seemed to be searching for the source of their disquiet.

Finally, in a piping voice behind him, Tomas commented, "It's so quiet now."

A dagger of ice struck in his heart.

Silence.

Ever since they arrived here and met up with the remnants of the Clausewitz Division, there was the steady whup whup whup and shaking in the ground that marked the explosion of artillery shells landing in the city.

It was so constant that after a while, they all simply got used to it as background noise.

Now for the first time, the guns fell silent.

The IXth Army was defeated.

Berlin had fallen.

And they were next...

Chapter 32

It was Hauptmann Brandt who spoke first.

He declared, "We should dig in, strengthen the existing positions, and set up new ones for those of us who just arrived. Withstand for a few days and see if we can get past them."

Hans looked around dubiously.

"This hill is not defensible. And now that they're done over there, they will come for us next."

"Am I not the master of defense?" said Brandt haughtily. "I see only infantry on the ridgeline. No tanks. We can hold."

"But if we can see them, they can certainly see us," chimed in Sergeant Koch, and Brandt shot him a black look.

Hans nodded worriedly.

Remembering Major Schmidt's tactics, he said, "And if they can see us, they can shell us at leisure, tanks or no tanks."

"We should at least reinforce for tonight, in case they attack..." began Brandt, but Hans shook his head.

"I'd like to get us as far away as possible, as soon as possible," said Hans.

He thought through the plan in his head, then announced, "Orders."

Sergeant Koch and some of the other men gathered.

Hans said, "We need to pull back. Well out of sight of the Red Army there and beyond the immediate range of their artillery. Pack up everything. We head west until the next defensible ground near the river and dig in there."

"That takes us very close to the Americans," someone said.

"The Americans will not attack. Too much of a risk of friendly fire. They don't want to make enemies of the Soviets and start another war before this one is done, eh?" Sergeant Koch quipped.

Hans's jaw tightened a little at the infuriating sergeant, but he had to admit he was probably right.

Another voice called out, "Maybe we should surrender to the Americans."

"No!" cried Hans and Hauptmann Brandt in unison, then they looked at each other in surprise.

"No," said Hans in a softer tone, but it was no less determined.

"The Americans are the enemy. Even if we do not have the strength to fight them now, we will never surrender to them. And I'll have the head of anyone who mentions the idea again," said Hans heatedly.

With that, they loaded up what they could into the trucks and started moving west. It was night by the time they reached the ridgeline where Hans and 1st Battalion deployed barely a few days ago.

Beyond it lay the river Elbe.

On the western bank, American forces were already fortified. But still, it seemed they were content to hold position and not cross the river.

To the east, a thin string of moving lights along the distant road told him the Soviets were on the move toward them.

Convinced the Americans weren't about to attack, Hans focused on organizing his defenses facing east.

Thankful for the clear sky and bright moonlight to work with, Hans started walking the ground to deploy his men.

It was here that Hauptmann Brandt's experience came to the fore.

While Hans only had experience conducting a defense at platoon level, Hauptmann Brandt was widely regarded as the Battalion's resident defense expert.

So, when Hans placed his primary machine gun position on top of a rocky outcropping where the gunners could see the furthest, Brandt intervened and advised repositioning them *behind* the high ground.

"But they can't see anything there," protested Hans.

Brandt shook his head and explained, "On top of this mound, they will be an obvious target and the first thing to be destroyed. But, behind it, they are hidden and protected, yet in a position to deliver enfilade fire when the Soviets try to rush the front trenches."

When Hans still looked dubious, Hauptmann Brandt said with conviction, "I, myself, will stay and command this position."

Hans grudgingly agreed and left him to it.

If Brandt were going to occupy the position himself, he would certainly be careful about where to place it.

And so Hans, with Hauptmann Brandt advising him, went about placing the men in fighting positions. As best he could, they were lined up to support each other if any one position came under attack.

Arcs of fire were determined and established, ammunition counted and redistributed. Crude traps and obstacles were laid.

More out of sympathy than any real tactical purpose, he positioned the three Hitler Youths in a trench behind him. Ostensibly to "cover for attacks from the rear" and to "dominate the high ground."

Even the boys didn't seem to believe that. But they were content to be near him and made no complaint.

Then it was time for digging. Nobody slept that night. The silence of the artillery on Berlin was all the warning they needed for the impending red wave of men and steel they knew would surely come the next day.

Every man dug desperately with whatever tools they had to hand. Every inch deeper was an inch more protection against the onslaught that would surely follow in the morning.

Somehow, Sergeant Koch had contrived to be within earshot of Hans's position. As they dug, he kept a running commentary about the forces facing them and what to expect while Hans grated his teeth at the continuous prattle.

Primarily Russian units, he told Hans. All pissed off, all hungry for revenge for what Nazi forces had done to them in the early stages of the war. For many, their actual homes and villages had been razed when the Germans went through. And many saw friends and family executed after a battle.

"Especially when the SS bastards went in, eh?" said Koch, conversationally, "Even *we* are scared of them. Can you imagine what they did to the Soviets then? No wonder they want to kill us so badly."

The sergeant stopped, and Hans fervently hoped he had a heart attack.

But Koch continued, his voice dropping in tone, taking on a reflective quality that held none of the banter and cheerful irreverence it usually had.

"When we went up against them, we thought we had a chance at first. We were fresh and on home ground. They'd been fighting for days, tired, and they had their backs to us."

"I was in the lead tank platoon. We moved in fast. Panzers first, as usual, rolling over anything that looked dangerous, then the infantry would follow on and mop up the remaining enemy."

"At least that was the plan," he sighed.

Then he continued, his voice cracking, "We first noticed something was wrong when our infantry didn't catch up after mopping up. It was only when their commander managed to radio us that we realized what was happening. They were getting bogged down by a counter-attack from the rear elements we had just overrun."

Sergeant Koch looked at Hans with horror in his eyes.

"Herr Oberleutnant, their cooks, storemen, and clerks, were attacking our infantry and *winning*!"

He fell silent again for a long time.

When he spoke again, Hans saw at last, beneath Sergeant Koch's irritating, voluble manner, was a broken man, trying to keep himself together with endless chatter.

"Then their real troops started attacking us. They didn't wait for us to smash ourselves against their defenses. They left the safety of their trenches to come at us! Soldiers charging tanks!"

"I have never seen such ferocity and hatred. It's in their eyes, Oberleutnant. I think these are the ones who have already lost everything, so they have nothing left to lose. They live only to inflict pain and death on those who caused them pain and death."

"Us," he finished in a whisper.

Hans was so spellbound by the sergeant's account that he did not notice the night ending until the sky grew lighter with the pre-dawn glow.

In another moment, a thin beam of light heralded the coming of the dawn.

In another moment, the sun cautiously peeked over the horizon as though dreading to start the day that promised such death and destruction.

In another moment, the sky was light, and the morning had arrived.

Chapter 33

4th May 1945—Eastern bank of the Elbe

They heard rather than saw the Soviet forces first. The rumble of tanks and heavy vehicles, the loud shouts and cries of men preparing for battle.

Louder and louder until, at last, the soldiers appeared on the opposite ridgeline, their bodies silhouetted against the dawn's light. Then the tanks emerged, guns pointing toward them. Infantry lined up as far as the eye could see, guns at the ready, bayonets attached. They were so thickly massed they blocked out the rising sun and formed a new horizon for it to break.

All forces deployed openly as they covered the entire ridge, not fearing attack from non-existent German artillery or the decimated Luftwaffe. They weren't even pretending to take cover nor bothering to get into any tactical formation for the attack.

Hans stared across the battlefield in despair.

How, he thought bitterly, *did it come to this?*

The call to attack sounded.

A single note on a whistle.

The Soviets cheered in response and then started trotting down the ridgeline. They moved in a jagged line, jostling with each other initially until they spaced out enough to move without tripping each other up.

Hans heard catcalls and banter and light-hearted shouting. There were no stern officers giving orders, no grizzled sergeants shouting to enforce discipline. Instead, the men streaming down the valley had the air of a carnival mob rather than a military attack.

Hans looked around desperately.

There was no help coming from the north. His men were terrified and stayed in place only by the thinnest thread of courage that remained.

He estimated the numbers approaching.... more than a hundred at least, bearing down on his sector alone.

Hans's mind went into overdrive as he calculated furiously.

He had three magazines on him, including the one already loaded in his rifle. Each of the three Hitler Youths just behind him had one. Each magazine had twenty rounds.

Even if every single one of their bullets found its mark in an enemy, there would be hundreds more for them to fight off with... what? His bayonet? His Hitler Youth knife? His bare hands?

The enemy line reached the halfway mark to his first trench.

A series of clanking sounds indicated the tanks had fired up and were charging down to meet up with the slower foot soldiers. They were timed to reach Han's positions just as their infantry got in range to start shooting.

Hans watched the tanks rumbling down the slope and then correct themselves as they hit level ground. Their turrets pointed toward German lines, and he knew his company was now within range of tank shells.

Mesmerized, like a bird transfixed by a snake just before it struck, precious seconds went by as he stared and stared at the approaching tanks.

Then his front-most trench opened fire, and battle was joined...

... except this wasn't like any battle Hans had experienced before.

Usually, there would be a sudden explosion of sound as, once two opposing forces came within range, both sides opened up with everything they had.

The shock of the initial barrage was crucial in blunting an enemy charge. If powerful enough, it could be sufficient in itself to stop the attack on its tracks entirely.

Likewise, overwhelming heavy fire from the assaulting force was needed to keep the defenders cowering and unable to aim effectively at the more exposed attackers.

However, the above scenario assumed that both forces were a respectable match for each other.

That was not the case today.

As the first trench started shooting, some of the nearest Soviet troops dropped to the ground and took cover, while the ones on either side laughed.

Laughed!

Machine-gun fire from the nearest tank suppressed that German trench. Two grenades flew in and detonated, and that was that.

The soldiers in the next trench didn't even get to start firing before a tank shell streaked into them and blew up.

Prisoner of War

A bang and a puff of smoke from another position revealed a *Panzerfaust* attack on that tank. The rocket hit the tank's tough front armor at an angle and glanced off, spiraling uselessly into the air.

Three tanks fired on that position and destroyed it before the deflected projectile landed back on the ground.

There was frantic movement in the next few trenches as their occupants decided they had had enough. Multiple grenades were hastily thrown at the approaching forces to distract them as the pairs that occupied the trenches climbed out and started running.

The tanks ignored them, leaving them for the infantry.

Another two men jumped out of their trench, hands raised high and shouting in crude Russian to surrender. They were cut down before they finished.

In the distant flank, Hauptmann Brandt's heavy machine gun opened up on the advancing Soviet line, providing defensive fire. But, as Hans watched in horror, a grenade flew in from behind the trench and exploded. The two-man crew slumped forward, and the gun fell silent. Brandt was nowhere to be seen.

Hans felt a dull thudding begin in his head.

Dimly, he was aware it was his own heart beating so hard that the pressure pounded up his brain. Somewhere further back in the recesses of his mind, he heard shouting.

Distant, forlorn, but getting closer and closer. With a start, he recognized the voice as his own.

His mind rebelled against conscious thought, trying to save him.

Calling out to him to see reality.

In front, a Soviet tank came to a stop lazily and traversed its turret until it pointed directly at the trench just in front of Hans.

A sudden burst of clarity hit Hans.

This was not a fight.

It wasn't even mopping up.

This was just a fox hunt, and the Soviets were attacking them for sport!

A split-second of sanity finally pierced through the fog of lunacy that engulfed his consciousness since the night he found out Hitler died. His body had gone on, but his mind had refused to accept the facts.

Now it all came crashing down on him in one single blow.

Turning to the terrified boys behind him, he drew a deep breath and screamed at the top of his lungs,

"RUUUUUNNNNNN!!"

The tank fired at the same time.

The T34 Soviet tank bearing down on them was mounted with the newer F-34 tank gun. The muzzle velocity of an armor-piercing shell from that gun was 680 meters per second.

In this case, though, the tank commander knew there were no tanks to engage. So he had ordered a high explosive tank shell to be loaded first. That only had a muzzle velocity of 325 meters per second. Less than half the speed of the armor-piercing shells.

However, for the hapless men in the trench at such close range, it might as well have been instantaneous.

In a split second, the shell slammed into the trench and exploded, destroying the position, its occupants, and everything in it, leaving an empty smoking hole as though nothing had ever existed there before.

The blast caught Hans just as he cleared his trench and started his run. The shock wave knocked him up and forward. He flew through the air like a human cannonball, arms flailing and legs pumping, and landed heavily on the ground.

Getting to his knees, he shook his head to clear it and risked a glance behind. The tank that fired seemed satisfied the target was destroyed and was slowly traversing its turret away, looking for more victims.

Looking forward, he saw three small figures racing ahead toward the river. Their progress was slowed by the treacherous footing of the rocky terrain, but at least all the boys seemed to have survived the initial tank shell blast and were able to run.

Hans had only one thought in his mind: To flee the tide of men and steel which he now knew he had no hope of defeating.

Chapter 34

Hans ran for his life.

Ahead, the three boys were making good progress despite the rugged rocky terrain.

Silently, he urged them on. Once they made their way through the treacherous stretch and reached the grassy river banks, they could run at full speed.

Hans risked another look behind. The Soviets were following but seemed in no particular hurry. The ground troops were content to stroll across the ground, shooting randomly, while the tanks took potshots at the retreating force.

When he looked forward again, he saw the boys had almost made it to the river bank. In another minute, they would clear the rocky ground and jump down over the ledge where they would be out of sight and safe.

Then to his horror, a tank shell exploded mere meters from them. All three flew in the air like rag dolls and disappeared from view into a gully in the ground.

"No!" Hans screamed and raced forward.

Wilhelm got up first and started running again on wobbly legs.

Clearly disorientated, he staggered off erratically at a tangent from his original path and drifted further and further to the left, like a drunk man trying to walk on a straight road and failing miserably.

By the time Hans reached the gully, Wilhelm was too far away, so he concentrated on the other two boys. Josef was sitting up, staring straight ahead, completely stunned. Tomas lay on the floor, not moving.

"Josef, Tomas, are you hurt? Can you get up?" Hans called to them urgently.

Josef stared at him blankly, then slowly nodded and started to get up.

Tomas's eyes opened as he stirred feebly. Then, his eyes rolled, and he slipped into unconsciousness.

Cursing, Hans slung his rifle, scooped the boy up in his arms, and started scrambling up the opposite side of the gully, making sure Josef followed him.

Hans staggered across the last fifty meters to the relative safety of the riverbank, praying no one would shoot him in the back.

It seemed like an eternity, but at last, he stood at the ledge.

Before him was a steep drop, and after that, the ground sloped gently down another four hundred meters until it reached the eastern edge of the Elbe and... American soldiers!

Sometime in the night, they must have crossed the river in force—and of course, Hans could not spare the time nor men to notice it.

Not that he could have done anything about it.

So, now American tanks and soldiers lined the water's edge—partially dug in and all at the ready.

The old fierce anger kindled within Hans again at the sight of the American Army displayed before him in full glory. Shifting Tomas's weight to his left arm, he struggled to unsling his rifle with his right while making his way down the steep slope.

He stumbled and lost his balance.

As he fell, he twisted awkwardly to make sure Tomas was cushioned from the fall with his own body but was startled when the boy's eyes flew open, and he screamed in pain.

Frowning in puzzlement, Hans gently lifted Tomas off himself and laid him on the ground. His eyes widened in horror as he saw an ugly piece of shrapnel protruding from the boy's chest.

How did he miss it earlier?

Reflexively he reached to pull it out, but Tomas screamed again when he touched it. The dark stain surrounding the shrapnel started widening ominously, and the boy's pale face became even paler.

Hans sank to his knees in despair.

He had seen enough wounds to know the boy was dying, and he could do nothing about it. The shrapnel must have lodged in his body when the tank shell exploded.

Then the fall probably drove it deeper until it cut a major blood vessel.

A fall because Hans tried to get ready to fight the Americans while climbing down... *NO!* Hans cut himself off.

It was the Soviets that did this!
It was the Soviets who must...

"Oberleutnant?" came a weak voice from in front of him.

"Yes, Tomas," said Hans gently, trying to keep the tears from his eyes.

"Am I dying?" asked Tomas in a frightened voice.

"No, of course not," lied Hans. "You've just got a concussion from the blast and a bad cut."

Tomas was silent for a while as blood oozed from his mouth. He tasted it and then said firmly, "I think I'm dying, Oberleutnant."

Hans didn't know what to say. He just nodded dumbly.

Tomas's face took on a waxy appearance, and a sheen of sweat appeared on his forehead.

He looked away as though embarrassed, then said, "I want to thank you for leading us, Oberleutnant."

Tears sprang to Hans's eyes as the boy continued, "But I'm done for. You can't help me."

"No!" cried Hans. "I'll get you out. I'll get help. You need to stay awake for a bit more."

Tomas smiled at his words, then coughed weakly, and more blood oozed from his mouth. Distant shouts in Russian came closer and closer.

"They're coming. Go, save yourself," he said in a fading voice.

"I'm not leaving you," said Hans furiously.

Suddenly a Soviet soldier appeared and jumped down the ledge. He seemed as surprised to see them as they were to see him. Hans reflexively fumbled to bring his rifle to bear on the man but knew he would be too slow.

The Soviet soldier raised his rifle.

A shot rang out, and Hans jumped, then closed his eyes, waiting for the pain to filter through to his brain to tell him where he had been shot.

When nothing happened, he opened his eyes and looked up.

His eyes met with the Soviet soldier's, who looked more surprised than anything else. Then a trickle of blood flowed from his lips, his eyes rolled, and he slumped to the ground, dead.

Behind him, Josef stood with his rifle pointed at the man, a thin trail of smoke coming from the muzzle. His face was white as a sheet. He looked at the dead man, then at his weapon. He threw his rifle down as though it were a live snake and his hands started shaking.

He pressed his hands together to stop them from quivering and whispered, "I've never killed anyone before."

"Pull yourself together, Josef," Hans snapped. "This is war. We do what we must. Now help me here with...."

He stopped short when he looked down at Tomas.

The boy's eyes were wide open, staring sightlessly at the sky.

An image of another broken body lying in a church surged to Hans's mind and became indistinguishable from Tomas's still form.

With the same brown eyes open and unseeing. With the same last words, urging Hans to save himself. And Hans, with the same last words, promising to stay by their side.

Only to be absent at the moment they died.

Hans took a deep, shuddering breath, gently placed his hands over Tomas's face, and closed his eyes.

His heart started pounding.

So loud it drowned out all else.

Vaguely in the background, he heard Josef saying, "They're getting closer."

He ignored the boy as a wave of white-hot anger washed over him, and he embraced it gladly.

He picked up his rifle and absently checked the weapon was loaded, and cocked it. Then, almost lovingly, he cradled it, so it slipped into his usual firing position, loosely held but ready.

A Soviet soldier appeared over the ledge, and Hans casually shot him in the face.

Another appeared, and Hans shot him too.

Then two slid down the sandy slope on the other side. He spun and fired two shots, taking each one in the head.

More cautious than his compatriots, the next soldier edged forward slowly, rifle first. Hans seized the barrel with his left hand and pulled hard. The owner of the weapon, too slow to release it, flew forward with his gun and died as Hans shot him in mid-air.

The soldier's body slumped in front of Josef.

"Oberleutnant," he squeaked. "Maybe we should go?"

"I'm not leaving," said Hans calmly as he switched magazines for his weapon, picked a bayonet from a dead Soviet soldier, and attached it to his own rifle.

"There are more of them coming," pleaded the boy.

Hans shook his head and looked at the body of Tomas. Then, he said, "I told him I wouldn't leave him. I won't break that promise."

Again.

Josef just looked at him in disbelief.

Two enemies jumped down behind him, and Hans fired into them, killing both. Then another appeared directly above him. Hans stabbed him with the bayonet and then fired into his body.

The man gurgled and died as Hans pulled out his weapon from his body.

The last man of the attacking squad peeped over the ledge, and Hans fired at him. He twisted to avoid the shot and slid down awkwardly, feet kicking to try and halt his descent.

His boot caught Tomas's face, and the dead boy's head slumped toward Hans, eyes half open again.

Hans, incensed at the desecration, screamed in outrage and savagely ran the man through with his bayonet and fired, again and again, emptying his magazine into the soldier long after he was dead.

Then he seized the light machine gun of one of the fallen soldiers, stood up to full height, and braced it over the ledge. He cocked the weapon just as the second squad started approaching.

Screaming obscenities, he fired into the men with deadly effect. Half the squad fell in seconds, dead or wounded, while the rest went to the ground and stayed low.

Hans fired until the weapon clicked empty. Then, as he looked around for more ammunition, the remnants of the Soviet squad got up, uncertain whether to flee or attack. Their hesitation was fatal as Hans reloaded and cut them down where they stood.

When he ran out again, Hans reloaded once more and fired again and again, screaming like at enraged animal, shooting in the direction of the Soviet Army even though no one was in sight.

Only when he felt a tentative touch on his shoulder did Hans jump and stop.

It was Josef.

The boy, seeing Hans covered in the blood of his enemies, appeared to be more afraid of Hans than the enemy.

"Please," he begged softly, tears in his eyes, "We should leave."

"I'm not leaving," Hans said harshly. "You go if you want."

Josef looked longingly at the river, then at his friend's body, then back at Han. He shook his head.

"Go now," snarled Hans.

Josef shook his head and said, "If you're not leaving, I'm not leaving."

Hans cursed and urged him to leave, smacking him on the head and shoving him roughly away, but Josef kept shaking his head.

Finally, with trembling hands, he picked up his rifle, looked at Hans, and said determinedly, "I'm not leaving you."

Hans swore and cursed again.

Then, looking over the ledge, he saw more soldiers forming up for an attack.

He looked at Josef, who was sticking his lower jaw out and trying not to cry.

Then lastly, he looked at Tomas, his body twisted on the ground after being kicked.

Swearing in anger, he gathered four grenades from the Soviet bodies around him and unlocked them one by one. Then he flipped their switches, arming them. Finally, with two grenades in each hand, Hans flung them toward the Soviets with all his might.

Then he turned to Josef and shouted, "Run!"

The boy took off at full speed.

As the grenades exploded into the Soviet ranks, Hans said bitterly, "And I will run with you."

Chapter 35

Hans raced after Josef, urging him on.

To his left, he saw Sergeant Koch sprinting at full speed toward the river, not bothering to duck or weave. To his right, he sensed rather than saw the rest of his company abandoning their positions to run away. Behind, he heard sounds of small arms fire punctuated with the occasional crack of the tank shell being fired in the utterly one-sided battle.

Ahead lay the river Elbe and the Americans.

When they saw Hans and his thin line of fleeing men, a shout went up from the Americans. Bayonets were fixed, rifles raised as the tank engines gunned loudly. A long note on a bugle sounded, and the American tanks and soldiers charged forward toward them.

Hans's heart sank.

He saw the Americans advance in dismay. If they had no chance in battle against the Soviets, they had even less against the experienced but fresh, rested, and well-supplied Americans.

Hans slowed down and, with a start, realized he still held his rifle in his hands.

A familiar, fierce anger surged in his heart as he gripped it tighter and thought about how best to fight the Americans, hopeless as it was. But the whiz of a stray bullet past his ear put paid to those ideas, and he started running again.

However much he hated them, at least the Americans weren't shooting at him right now.

Keeping low as he ran forward, he held his rifle in front of him. Careful to make sure it wasn't pointing at the US infantry now racing toward him, he was still reluctant to let it go, even though deep down, he knew the unthinkable was soon approaching.

Either he would surrender to his hated foes or die trying to fight them.

The latter, always an option in the earlier days of the war, was suddenly a lot less appealing and heroic than how he had previously envisaged it. It also made a lot less sense considering the last few days' events.

Sudden shouting ahead of him drew him out of his melancholy reverie even as his body ran forward without conscious thought.

Looking ahead, he noticed the American infantrymen were running forward in pairs instead of sections or platoons. The first German soldier to reach them was Sergeant Koch, waving his hands in the air, so his intentions were not mistaken while trying to run as fast as possible.

He tripped and fell on his face just before the approaching Americans got to him.

There was a hasty conversation, a few barked words in crude German by the soldiers, and a quick body search. To Hans's indignation, one American slapped Koch hard on his helmet, then they escorted him toward the bridge.

Things happened quickly after that.

As each fleeing German met with an American pair, one of them would point his gun at the German, covering the still-enemy soldier. The second would hastily check he had no weapons, confirm he was surrendering—often no more than a badly pronounced query of "*aufgeben*?", followed by a grateful *"Ja! Ja!"*—then slap a blue flag on his helmet, declaring him to be a prisoner of war.

The first soldier would immediately swing his weapon from the German toward the approaching Soviet forces, indicating he was now under American protection.

Hans now understood that Sergeant Koch wasn't being abused when he surrendered.

He was being marked for protection.

More and more German soldiers made it to American lines.

Or, in the case of those who were wounded and limping, American lines made it to *them*.

Before Hans's amazed eyes, the same dance was performed over and over.

As soon as a German soldier surrendered, an American pair would slap a blue sticker on their helmet and orientate their weapons toward the east where the Soviets advanced.

A few took an exceptionally long time divesting themselves of all their weapons—having stockpiled a formidable personal armory which Hans had no inkling about—to the consternation of the Americans accepting their surrender.

Prisoner of War

Stressed American GIs keeping a constant watch for the approaching Soviet forces would shout at them to hurry up before they arrived.

Others were too injured or exhausted to surrender properly.

In those cases, there was outrageous cheating where the Americans told them to lie still and pretend to be unconscious, then strip them of their weapons and "take" them prisoner.

One German corporal was hurling abuse at the Americans as he threw his rifle down in disgust and flung his magazines at them. Then, in the finale of his tantrum, he drew his bayonet out, slammed it into the ground to its hilt, and spat in the direction of his would-be captors.

It didn't seem to matter. The American pair capturing him, one looking annoyed and the other looking amused, nonetheless slapped the blue sticker on his helmet and then took him away. The first soldier led him to the bridge, and the other walked behind them, weapon trained toward the east.

Hans had slowed his run down to a walk now, partly out of a sense of responsibility to make sure his men were safe but more out of a reluctance to face his unavoidable encounter.

To his right, another German soldier had met his designated pair.

Fluent in English, he was chatting away amiably to the Americans and had seemingly announced his intention to surrender. But though he had shed his ammunition and bayonet, his rifle was still idly slung on his shoulders in plain sight. Either he had forgotten, or perhaps subconsciously, like Hans, he was still hoping against hope for the chance to somehow retain his freedom and fight on.

A shot rang out, and his head exploded in a spray of blood. He slumped to the floor dead as a Soviet sniper found his mark with ease. As the German still had not given up his arms, the Americans could not legally accept his surrender, so he was still fair game for Soviet bullets. The American pair cried out in anguish and frustration but could do nothing.

When the others saw this, panic rippled through the German and American lines.

American tanks, which had been holding defensive positions, roared to life as they moved forward to provide cover.

Prisoner of War

German soldiers who had been slow to strip themselves of their weapons suddenly couldn't get rid of them quickly enough.

The Americans, for their part, initially bending over backward to seem non-threatening, started shouting urgently to their would-be captives to surrender quickly.

Only once the blue stickers were on would they be declared prisoners under US protection and safe from Soviet bullets.

Hans started running forward again in a zig-zag until he crossed paths with two American soldiers.

One of them pointed to him with a shout, and rifles at the ready, the duo started running toward him.

Chapter 36

A more unlikely pair he had never seen.

One was small and wiry—of the same build and type as Sergeant Koch, and when he started speaking, Hans surmised, of similar personality too. He had bulging eyes set too closely together and buck teeth that gave him a comic appearance.

The other was fat. Far fatter than any active soldier in any army had the right to be. And he had a baby face to boot. He looked completely out of place on the battlefield.

Actually, Hans amended mentally, he looked completely out of place *anywhere*.

But here he was, dutifully pointing his rifle at Hans while the other skinny one attempted to process his surrender.

Hans's jaw tightened at the thought of what was going to happen now. A brief idea to negotiate instead of surrender crossed his mind, but the zip-zip of stray bullets snuffed that thought out before he had a chance to ponder more about it.

Bristling with animosity at the two Americans, he started to unload whatever he had on him. First, he ejected the magazine from his rifle, cleared it, and threw both down noisily. Then, taking out his pistol, he did the same.

Just then, the fat soldier's eyes widened in fear, and his gaze focused sharply behind Hans.

Hans instinctively turned and was sickened to see Soviet troops pouring over the horizon. The few of his fellow soldiers who were slow to run were brutally gunned down in short order. The most advanced elements of the attacking Soviets were actually closer to American lines than some of the fleeing Germans.

It was one of these that caused the fat soldier to gasp in alarm.

A Soviet soldier had appeared less than a hundred meters away and was walking briskly toward them with his rifle aimed squarely at Hans.

Gripping his weapon tightly, the fat soldier gingerly moved so that Hans was between him and the approaching Soviet.

At first, Hans was outraged at what he interpreted as pure cowardice—that the American was using him as a human shield. Then in a flash, he understood what was really happening.

Until he surrendered, Hans was technically still the enemy, and the American was obliged to keep his weapon trained on him. If the fat soldier were to point his gun at the approaching Soviet, he'd be threatening someone who was officially an ally.

To circumvent the predicament, the fat soldier drew nearer to Hans such that his rifle was practically over his shoulder, pointing at the Soviet behind. From a distance, he could plausibly claim to be pointing his gun at Hans—just very badly—when in fact, he was aiming at the advancing Soviet soldier.

The other soldier, in the meantime, did something even braver.

Walking around Hans as though inspecting him, he nonchalantly positioned himself between Hans and the

Soviet soldier and fearlessly showed his back to the approaching Soviet, denying him a clear shot at Hans.

The Soviet soldier shouted in displeasure as he was forced to divert his trajectory to one side to get a clean shot.

The thin American glanced back constantly and adjusted his position to block the Soviet soldier, all the while talking quickly to Hans, urging him to ditch everything he had quickly. Already, the thin American had a blue sticker in his hand, ready to slap it on Hans's helmet.

Hans hurriedly dropped his pistol without clearing it properly, took out a smaller one from his ankle, and just threw it.

The Soviet soldier came in fast, zig-zagging with his rifle braced on his shoulder, ready to fire the instant he had a clear shot.

He was eighty meters away and closing.

The thin American had dropped all pretense of casual interference and was playing a deadly game of cat and mouse, shamelessly blocking a possible shot with his own body while yelling urgently to Hans.

Hans ripped out his bayonet and flung it behind him. Done, he raised both hands and gave a half-smile to the fat soldier, expecting the slap on his helmet indicating the blue sticker was on, and that he was safe.

Instead, he heard the thin soldier behind him shouting, "Bayonet! Bayonet!"

In confusion, Hans patted himself down—he only had one bayonet—the one he had just thrown. How could he have another one?

The fat soldier was sweating profusely now and looking intently behind Hans.

Seventy meters.

Hans's hands patted the bulge in his front pocket where the thin soldier was frantically pointing, and his fingers grasped the handle of his Hitler Youth knife. He took it out, drew it from its sheath, and stared at it.

The broken blade. Damaged when his broken friend tried to free himself as he died.

The inscribed words. "*Blut und Ehre.*" So much Blood. For the *Führer's* Honor.

How could he give this up?

He looked pleadingly at the two American soldiers trying to take him in. Could he explain this to them? Could he persuade them to let him keep this one little thing?

But neither were even looking at him anymore.

Sixty meters.

The Soviet soldier had given up trying to shoot on the move and had decided to just run in and get close. The thin soldier, dancing around now frantically as he tried to block the Soviet soldier's line of fire, was screaming at Hans, "Drop the knife! Drop IIIITTTT!"

Fifty.

Hans willed his fingers to let go. But, still, they clung on to the handle.

Forty.

His other hand came over his first to release it but instead it simply gripped the knife even tighter.

Thirty.

Suddenly, the fat soldier's face turned pale. His face twisted in horror as he unmistakably mouthed the words, "Oh, shit!" and swung his rifle to his left, flipping the safety off as he did so.

Hans turned his gaze to follow where the fat soldier's rifle now pointed, and his hair stood on end.

Less than fifteen meters to his left, *another* Soviet soldier rose from the ground like a phantom, rifle at the shoulder and aiming straight at him. Hans spun around to face the new threat but knew immediately it was already too late.

His consciousness expanded exponentially. As if in its last instant of existence, his mind sought to savor as much sensation and experience it could possibly squeeze into this final moment.

The sun was blazing in the sky now. The cold dawn of the morning had given way to as fine a day as Hans had ever seen. The sky was blue, so very blue, broken only by the white ribbons of cloud that teased the very edges of the atmosphere.

Across the barren wasteland of the battlefield, there were still patches of greenery in evidence. Defying bombs, artillery shells, and merciless boots from all sides, they clung on tenaciously to life, some even daring to put forth small white flowers.

A shadow fell just next to the flowers, and his eyes followed it to the rising Soviet soldier that cast it. Russian probably, by the looks of him. His uniform was standard issue, though a patch on the right elbow was mismatched to the rest of his top.

Hans couldn't see his rank but sensed he had the bearing of command. Or at least confidence. He must be a corporal at least, if not a sergeant. But not an officer. Soviet officers didn't venture this far ahead of the regular troops.

Yes, a sergeant, Hans decided. If he had the wits and skill to make it this far without detection, he must be a sergeant. A good one.

He admired how calmly and delicately the Russian began to squeeze the trigger. Like he was playing an instrument of music instead of death.

At this range, Hans knew he would not miss.

A rumbling began from the back of Hans's head. Like the sound of a rushing waterfall getting closer, it surged to a deafening roar in his ears as his heart pounded blood to his brain at maximum capacity.

The Russian pulled the trigger.

Pain exploded in Hans's chest and shoulder, and everything went dark.

Chapter 37

Hans opened his eyes after... how long? He had no idea. All was still black. He blinked a few times but still could see nothing.

His mind reached around blindly, trying to make sense of his existence. He remembered seeing the Russian soldier pull the trigger. There was a loud noise and pain. Pain like he had never felt before exploding in his chest.

Am I dead? he thought. *Is this what the afterlife looks like?*

Perhaps not, he mused.

As though the memory of it made it come to life, he now felt that pain again. More to his left, toward his shoulder.

I shouldn't feel pain if I am dead, yes? Hans carried on reasoning. He winced as a sensation like lightning lanced through his shoulder when he tried to move.

Yes, certainly not this much pain, he surmised, quietly pleased with his brilliant deduction.

Then his eyes focused, and he realized it wasn't black, just dark.

He started making out a shape in front of him.

Enormous, menacing, looming.

And sound.

Sound was slowly filtering into his brain.

A sound that seemed tantalizingly familiar, as though in another moment, he would remember it with a satisfying, "Aha! Yes, *that's* what it is."

In an abrupt flash of consciousness, he suddenly became aware of two things: The looming shape in front of him was a tank. And the sound he heard was the chatter of machine-gun fire.

Scheiße! They were still shooting at him!

He twisted and flailed around madly, trying to cover his body and fend off bullets with his bare hands at the same time. He cried out as his frantic movements caused fresh agony to erupt in his shoulder.

Then he saw a face looming near his.

It was grinning and talking at the same time. In a moment, he recognized it to be that of the thin American serviceman. Then, in another moment of clarity, he inferred from his manner and apparent physical integrity that the thin soldier was not under fire, nor was he the one instigating it.

Hans sluggishly concluded that, therefore, he himself was safe for the moment. Patting himself guardedly, he was pleased to find no apparent wounds or holes in his body. Not even the supposed first shot that knocked him down. Did he even get hit?

As though reading his mind, the American interrupted his own monologue to answer Hans, "Oh, you were hit, alright. That Russkie fella had you in his sights real good. I couldn't get to 'im at all cos the first one was linin' up for the shot too, y'know? I thought you were a real goner then...."

Hans looked at him dazedly, struggling to understand his accent and piece together a coherent picture of the last few minutes.

The American drawled on, "Then the General 'ere himself comes chargin' over in his M4, knocks you over without killin' ya, and blocks the Russkie's shot! You shoulda seen the guy's face! So angry one minute for the block, then scared as hell the next when he realized he just shot at an American tank! Woohoo!"

The thin soldier was hooting with laughter now as his fat friend ambled by to stand next to him, smiling.

Thin Soldier (as Hans had come to think of him) continued, "Lucky it wasn't the General's favorite tank. Otherwise, there'd be hell to pay! He was just using one of the regular Sherman's today."

Fat Man (as Hans now named him) raised one eyebrow questioningly, and Thin Soldier, seemingly intuitively linked to his rotund compatriot, continued in response to his unasked query, "His usual tank ain't got the 37mm cannons on top. Just wooden dummies. I think he learned that modification from another general friend, so he's got more space to sit in.

"But today, he wanted to do some shootin' himself. I guess being a general and all, you don't get to shoot much yourself, so once in a while... hey, everybody's got to have fun sometime!"

As if to emphasize his point, the heavy cannons on the tank in front opened up at that very moment. Hans never imagined how a machine gun could sound half-hearted, but this one did.

Pointed into a small empty ditch directly in front of it, it stuttered and stopped erratically. Hans couldn't see the tank commander clearly, for he was silhouetted against the morning sun, but he could hear him clearly in between bursts of fire.

"Die German scum, die," he said calmly. The cannon fired out a few obligatory rounds, then swung to another hole in the ground.

"Got you now, you bastards," the commander intoned in a flat voice. The cannon fired again, almost apologetically.

The tank commander in the next tank, a huge black man, sat up straight in his position on top of the turret. Hans could only see his back but somehow got the distinct impression he wasn't happy.

"Oops, missed a few further up there. Quick. Let's get them before they attack our dear Soviet friends," called the first commander in a bored monotone.

His gun aimed further down the field and fired at one of the rearmost trenches of the original German positions.

This time the fire had more menace behind it.

The Soviet troops that hadn't quite reached that trench yet dropped to take cover.

The second tank commander sighed deeply while the first commander repeated the performance from left to right, effectively pinning down the entire Soviet line in that sector.

In the lull, the few remaining German soldiers were quickly "attacked" and overcome. They duly surrendered, had blue stickers stuck on their helmets, and were ushered to safety.

Thin Soldier looked at Hans and said, "Well?"

"Well, what?" Hans asked back in confusion.

"Bayonet?" Thin Soldier said, looking meaningfully at Hans's hand.

Hans looked down and saw that he still held the Hitler Youth knife in his hand. When he opened his palm, he could see see the pattern of the handle imprinted on his hand—so tightly had he held it.

A wave of emotions and memories threatened to flood him again, but this time he merely recalled the image of the Russian soldier literally triggering what should have been his death and how completely irrelevant the knife had been.

Worse than useless, it actually prevented the surrender that would have saved him. Only the timely and painful intervention of the General's tank stopped that bullet from reaching his heart.

He looked at his knife again and—in probably the biggest anti-climax in his life—simply handed it to Thin Soldier without any further ado.

Thin Soldier grinned, slapped the blue sticker on his helmet with a *thunk*, and hollered, "That's the last one of 'em! We're done here!"

Fat Man smiled happily and silently raised his fist in the air.

Chapter 38

The walk back to the camp was surreal.

Ten minutes ago, Hans stared down the barrel of a Soviet gun, poised to end his life. Then he surrendered to his most hated enemy, and suddenly it seemed he was immune to the might of the entire Red Army.

And now he was marching ... no, *strolling* across the bridge that spanned the Elbe, unarmed, in broad daylight, chatting to his captors.

Actually, only Thin Soldier was chatting. Fat Man was content to walk along beside him in silence, taking in the view of the Elbe like a tourist. And Hans walked in stony silence.

The Americans walked casually in pairs with their respective captives.

None of the prisoners were tied, cuffed, or otherwise restrained. Some who were injured were even helped onto a Military Police Jeep and driven back to camp.

The only moment of tension came when two tanks drove past them on the bridge to get back to base. There was confusion as men attempted to get out of the way and salute simultaneously while ensuring the shell-shocked prisoners didn't get run over.

This was made worse by the fact that the two tanks were driving across *abreast*, for no other reason, it seemed, than to facilitate conversation between the two tank commanders.

The first was leaning this way and that, constantly scanning the entire breadth of the bridge and muttering to the second commander, who did not seem to be listening. Hans recognized the silent commander to be the black man in the second tank earlier, and noted his rank as a Sergeant Major.

Sitting stiffly in a tank hatch far too small for him, the Sergeant Major, a behemoth of a man even taller than Hans, looked no happier than before as he pointedly ignored the first commander and seemed—there was no better description for it—to be sulking.

Hans, recognizing the voice of the muttering first commander, marked him as the one who knocked him over and shielded him from the Russian soldier.

Clearly an older man, his skin was sunburned, and deep lines creased his face. His eyes were hidden behind sunglasses, and he took off his helmet halfway to reveal a completely bald egghead. A glint from the helmet caught Hans's attention, and his eyes widened when he saw three five-pointed stars on its front.

They let a three-star general go into the front lines of a battle? What sort of foolery was this?

The General's tank slowed down as his driver threaded past a crowded knot of soldiers and prisoners who had not been able to step aside in time. Meanwhile, he was still looking around and talking to himself in an odd rhythm. Hans flushed with shame as he finally realized that the General was counting the prisoners.

Anger arose within Hans in an instant. Was he counting so he could gloat? So he could boast about how many enemies he captured? From the non-battle he had fought? He glared with hatred at the retreating back of the General.

Once the tanks drove past them, Thin Soldier beckoned for Hans to start walking again and said, "I'm Private Sam Lauren, and my friend here is Private Jerome Harding."

Looking at Fat Man knowingly, he said, "Together, we are Lauren and Harding." He gave a theatrical bow, then burst out laughing. Fat man—Jerome—simply smiled contentedly while Hans looked at them blankly, completely missing the reference to the famous American comedic duo.

When they were nearly across the bridge, everyone had to huddle to one side again when another tank roared by, heading in the opposite direction. Hans at once noted this was somewhat different from the other battle tanks he'd seen before.

For one, its 37mm cannons were just clever wooden replicas of the ones that were used to intimidate the Soviet forces minutes ago. And, more obviously, two flags were flying proudly on the front. One had three stars against a plain background, and the other had the XVI Corps emblem stitched on it.

Sam, noting his interest, said, "That's the General's tank alright, the one he usually rides in."

"I understand that, herr Lauren," Hans said aloud, "but the General just went back to base, so why is his tank going *there*?"

He pointed to the bridge's eastern end, where the tank had reached, and slowed down to perform some mysterious maneuver.

"Oh," said Sam as he understood.

Off-handedly, he replied, "Parking," as though that explained everything.

Hans waited for Sam to continue, but for once, he seemed to have nothing else to say on the matter and looked like he was going to move on to the next topic of interest that caught his attention.

Losing patience, Hans said sharply, "Parking? What do you mean? Explain yourself."

Sam stopped walking and motioned for Hans to do the same. They both turned to look at the tank. It slowed down as it reached the end of the bridge, then edged ahead until the tracks left the bridge and touched the banks of the river.

Someone, presumably the commander, climbed out of his hatch and stood on top of the turret, looking at the floor. He started shouting directions to the driver, making vigorous signals with his hands even though no one inside could possibly see them.

After some confused shouting and movements, eventually, they got the job done.

The tank was parked perpendicular to the bridge, sprawled across the ramp leading to it. Somehow, they had placed it so that it caused maximum obstruction to anyone seeking to cross. A single file of soldiers could walk past, of course, but vehicles and certainly other tanks could not pass.

More significantly, the tank was only just, but definitely so, on the banks of the river and not just the bridge itself.

The tank commander climbed down the tank. The driver climbed out. And they both started complaining loudly about each other's respective skills as they trudged back across the bridge.

"They're just going to leave it there?" Hans asked incredulously.

"Not quite," came the cheerful reply from Sam. Jerome chortled softly beside him as though in the know about some funny joke.

A Military Police jeep drove past them onto the bridge and sped across directly to the parked tank.

Two MPs jumped and walked around it, complaining loudly. One banged his fist loudly on the side of the turret, shouting for a response from the non-existent crew. The other climbed on the tank, opened the hatch on top, made a show of looking in, then shook his head at the other.

Then, to Hans's bewilderment, they both went to the front of the vehicle, placed their hands on the lower front plate, and tried to push the tank.

They heaved and strained for a few seconds before giving up in apparent exhaustion. Conferring vigorously between themselves, it looked like they were having a heated argument.

One officer checked his watch and gestured at it. The other seemed to give up arguing and threw his hands in the air, walking back to the jeep.

The first officer took out a writing pad and furiously scribbled on it. Then tore off the sheet he was writing on and stuck it on the driver's hatch in the front. He strolled back to the jeep and got in. His companion had already started the engine and drove off in a huff before the door was even closed.

They were grinning ear to ear as they sped back to base.

"*Now* they're just going to leave it there," concluded Sam, chuckling along with Jerome.

Chapter 39

Completely baffled now, and feeling annoyed that everybody seemed to be in on the joke except himself, Hans asked sulkily, "I suppose you cannot tell me what all that was about? I am just a prisoner now...."

"Oh no, no, nothing like that at all," said Sam soothingly. "But we thought it'd be obvious to you what was going on."

Hans frowned and shook his head.

"Well," began Sam, warming up to his favorite pastime—telling people what was happening, "It goes somethin' like this: The Soviets and us have an agreement, see? They get Berlin and everything up to the east of the river, and we get everything to the west of the river. I'm not sure who owns the river itself, mind you...."

Hans turned pale and staggered- *Mein Gott! They had already divided our land among themselves before they'd even finished us off!*

Oblivious to his distress, Sam continued merrily, "...not that it matters, I mean who really cares? But, in any case, we got orders from on high—from Ike himself—to stop here at the Elbe, not cross it, and definitely *not* push on to Berlin."

Hans nodded, recognizing the nickname for General Dwight Eisenhower, Supreme Commander of the Allied Expeditionary Force in Europe.

"When TB... I mean, the General, heard it, he was furious," Sam said in a low voice, "the men say he was shouting about it with the Sergeant Major and some of the Division Commanders. Somethin' about we can't let them Russkies get Berlin—we can get there before they do, 'specially since the Germans are fallin' over themselves to surrender to us!"

Sam said, "Well, you were, weren't you?"

Hans nodded slowly, remembering that stormy night in the Battalion Command Tent when he received orders to turn and fight the Soviets so that more could surrender to the Americans.

Sam continued, "Someone said TB was yelling at Ike on the phone, 'Hell, the Berlin Garrison would open the door and welcome us with both arms open, except they need one hand to keep shooting at the Russians!'

"I dunno, that day, it looked like he was gonna throw the 9th Army across the river and go take Berlin by himself."

Sam slowed down for a rare moment, and his eyes turned reflective, "You know what? I think he could have done it."

Looking squarely at Hans, he said, "*We* could have done it."

There was an awkward silence as Sam realized what he was saying and to whom. Finally, he coughed and looked away in embarrassment.

Then he slowly resumed walking toward the base and was clearly relieved when Hans followed him.

"Anyway, we're not supposed to cross the river to attack Berlin, but when you guys showed up, the General says, 'Ooo, the Germans are massing to attack. Well, we're not gonna wait for that. We're gonna take the fight to them.' That way, we ain't crossing the river to take Berlin. It's all just in self-defense, see?" explained Sam.

Warming back up to his story, Sam continued, "So now that we've crossed the river—purely in self-defense, of course—and captured all you Germans who might have attacked us, the threat is gone. We're all supposed to go back across the river to our side, good and proper cos there's no more enemy on the other side, right? There's only Red Army there now."

Hans nodded, still not sure where all this was going.

Sam kept talking, "So the General orders his own tank to go across and take one last look, just to make sure everything is OK, and everyone has left. Him being a good leader and all, first in, last out, that sort of thing."

Hans nodded again, more impatiently this time.

"Then he forgets he left his tank there," said Sam with a straight face.

"Forgets?" Hans asked in confusion.

"Yes. And unfortunately, it's blocking the entire bridge so no one can cross over," said Sam, still with a straight face. "And it's also on Soviet-controlled territory now, not just on the bridge, and that's a no-no."

"Aren't you afraid they'd shoot it?" Hans questioned.

Sam shot Hans a withering look that said better than words: *They wouldn't dare!*

"No, no," he explained. "If they shoot an American tank, it's an act of war. Allies or not, we start fighting here and now.

"We've got the 2nd Armored Division—'Hell on wheels,' I tell ya, just next door and ready to roll across and run over whatever they've got over there. Then the rest of the 9th Army's gonna swarm across, take Berlin, then send the Reds back to Mother Russia herself."

Hans shrugged and tried to look unconvinced. But having been on the receiving end of what the 2nd Armored could do more times than he cared to remember, he grudgingly admitted only a fool would start shooting at the Americans now.

Especially *these* Americans.

"They could just move it?" he suggested.

Sam dismissed the idea, "Nah. Any other American tank, maybe. But this 'ere is ol' TB's tank itself. Marked with flags and all. Everybody knows whose it is, so they can't move it. Some courtesy thing between generals and all."

"But it's still an American tank in Soviet territory now," protested Hans.

"That's right, that's right," said Sam, clearly relishing the build-up to his punch-line, "blocking the bridge, on their soil… that's no way to behave. But they can't do nothin' about it. They can't move it. They can't blow it up. It's just sitting there like two fingers in their faces."

"In fact…" Sam paused, shielding his eyes to look at the tank, "Yes, I think the turret is pointing one way and the machine gun another to form a 'V' shape …."

Hans exclaimed, "But surely, they would report this to their High Command, to Moscow itself, and they will call your President, and the General will be punished for invading Soviet territory?"

"Oh yes, yes," agreed Sam vigorously, "Let it never be said the US Army doesn't take discipline seriously. Even at the highest levels."

Using a mock scolding voice, Sam piped like a schoolteacher, "There will be an official investigation into this serious matter, and if found guilty, the General will be punished according to the fullest extent of United States Military Law. And we will make sure it's all done open an' proper so everyone can see justice is served."

He broke into a grin and reverted to his normal voice.

"Of course, since we're allies and all with them Soviets, this is technically not an invasion, or wossit, a breach of sov'renty at all," said Sam, struggling to contain his laughter now, "it's just a civil offense."

"More like breaking traffic rules with bad driving, or stopping a vehicle in an inconsiderate manner which blocks the road and so...ha...ha," Sam snorted as he tried to stifle his giggle. He gave up trying to finish the joke, and circled his right hand at Hans for him to take over.

"...and so, the parking ticket," finished Hans dryly.

Sam doubled over and howled with laughter, tears running down his cheeks. Even Jerome chuckled softly beside him.

Hans, wondering how such inane people managed to push back the entire German army, waited until Sam stopped laughing but still could think of no suitable reply to the absurdity.

Sam, gasping as he caught his breath, started talking again.

"Y'know, the thing is, I think TB ain't too fond of the Soviets either. I know they're on our side and all, cos we're all fighting the Naz...., I mean the Krau...," he floundered, "...uh... fighting you Germans, so that means they're our allies. But from how he talks of them... I dunno... sometimes it sounds like he thinks *they're* the real enemy, and you guys just got in the way."

Hans said nothing as a memory stirred from long ago.
Of talk between drunken celebrating officers.
One lone, dissenting voice.
And the click-clack of the boots of the SS Officers.

Chapter 40

They reached the outskirts of the camp on the western banks of the Elbe without exchanging another word.

As they approached the camp itself, Hans viewed the defenses with a professional eye.

They were formidable.

Triple layers of barbed wire lined the entire camp, making it impossible for infantry to storm without first cutting or blowing up the barricade. Palisade walls, interspersed with concrete strong points, formed the inner perimeter. Sturdy wooden watchtowers framed the main entrance and marked the four corners of the camp.

The camp would be costly to take, even without accounting for the inevitable counterattack from armored units as soon as the alarm was raised. Forcing a way in was not a viable option.

Finding a way out, however, might be a different prospect altogether.

Security to stop prisoners from escaping seemed non-existent.

For one, no one was bound or restrained. There seemed to be no restrictions on prisoners talking to one another. There did not even seem to be dedicated guards once they crossed the bridge.

If things were as lax inside, escape was a very real possibility.

To that end, Hans shook off his numb exhaustion and tried to take in every detail he could.

In the meantime, the prisoners reached the camp perimeter. There, they formed a line and gave their names, ranks, and unit number to a young American officer with a clipboard.

When the last prisoner was registered, the officer gathered everyone together, stood on a box, and began briefing them in passable German.

"Welcome to the US 9th Army Headquarters. This is also your POW Camp for now."

Hans looked down in shame at his bare hands, empty of any weapons to fight with.

The officer continued, "As prisoners of war of the US Army, you are entitled to food, water, shelter, and medical care. You are also under our protection against those who seek to harm you, such as the Soviets we just rescued you from.

"In camp, you will be organized according to platoons and companies with your own officers in charge. Your countrymen who are already here will split you accordingly and manage your schedules. Wash and wear back your own uniforms—we have some plain fatigues you may use until your clothes dry."

Then the officer said, "You are free to leave at any time...."

What? thought Hans incredulously.

"...but no weapons, of course. You'd have to remove your blue sticker, indicating you are no longer our prisoner of war but are instead an operational German soldier."

Excited murmuring broke out amongst the men but was cut short with the next sentence.

"Since we would then be technically at war against you again, we cannot release an enemy within our lines.

Therefore, we can only release you to cross the bridge to the other side. After which, you are beyond our jurisdiction and free to do what you want."

Hans thought excitedly, *Free to go! Just like that!*

But only across the river where the Soviets waited. Anyone crossing would be captured or killed by the Soviets in short order.

The officer gave his last instructions with a slight smile, "Otherwise if you're staying, head down that entrance to the main camp to wash up and get some hot food."

A weak cheer sounded from the men, and they drifted toward where the officer indicated. Grins broke out amongst the men at the prospect of their first hot meal in days, and happy chatter sounded at the chance to wash at last.

But Hans didn't move.

Something was wrong. So very wrong.

He looked at the smiling face of the clipboard officer and the other guards as they ushered the prisoners toward the entrance, and his mind screamed in warning at him.

Prisoner of War

He looked at the smiling faces of his countrymen, eager for a shower and food, and alarm bells sounded in his head.

A revolting memory of stories that shook him to the core crept into his mind.

Of sick prisoners in the Ohrdruf Concentration Camp. Led to a courtyard with the promise of food, so it was easier to shoot them. Of women and children in Auschwitz, taken to rooms with the promise of a wash, only to be gassed to death.

A sudden chill seized his heart as another realization hit him—The Americans must have passed through Ohrdruf!

With sudden certainty, Hans was convinced of one thing. The Americans were going to kill them all.

In a panic, he suddenly knew he had only one chance of survival, and that was to make himself useful.

Spotting an opportunity to the left of the entrance, he abruptly changed direction and headed toward the sandy patch of ground. Ignoring the young officer's indignant "Hey!" he walked on briskly and half-closed his eyes, anticipating a bullet in the back for his disobedience.

None came.

He sensed rather than heard surprise from some guards behind him, but no alarm.

Unchallenged, he made it to the sandy patch of ground.

There, he spotted the object of his salvation, seized it with both hands, hefted it over his shoulder, and slammed it into the ground.

Then he hefted it over his shoulder and slammed it into the ground again. And again. And again.

Having ushered the rest of the prisoners on their way, the clipboard officer tucked his pencil behind his ear, folded his clipboard under his arm, and marched toward his one and only errant charge, muttering to himself as he approached.

Hans had been digging furiously for five minutes now with the grub hoe he found and actually had made a respectable hole in that time. As he worked feverishly, his mind played through a fantastic narrative that no longer had any context or relevance to his actual situation. His emotions were a roller-coaster totally disconnected from reality.

He had started with panic.

Then, when he was not immediately shot for disobeying his captors, this went to elation that his ploy had worked and he was still alive.

Then, this went to uncertainty at how he was to phrase his answers when he was inevitably challenged.

Then, he was filled with the fear that he was not working hard enough to justify his survival and would still be shot later anyway. This sparked a furious effort to dig deeper and faster than he ever did until he was utterly exhausted.

By the time the young officer with the clipboard reached him, Hans had just transitioned from tearful self-pity to bitter resentment.

"Hey, you," came the irritated call of the American officer, "Get inside, shower down, and get something to eat."

Hans ignored him.

"Hey, HEY!" the American officer called out, annoyed now, "Take a shower and get some chow. Those are your orders!"

Hans stopped digging, then glared back at the officer.

"Don't pretend to care for us, *Ami*," he growled in English. "I know what prisoners are meant to do. We dig trenches. We work until we die."

God knows that's what we did to ours, thought Hans.

He dug out a few more handfuls of soil, turned back to the American, and shouted, "Well, what are you still doing here? I have surrendered. I am your prisoner. I am doing what you want!"

The American looked helplessly at him in frustration, then shrugged and walked off into the main camp.

Chapter 41

Another hour went by before Hans paused for breath.

But still, he would not stop.

He cursed the Americans as he wearily resumed digging.

Of all the scenarios he had expected—being beaten up, dragged away kicking and screaming, or threatened with a bullet to the head on the spot—this was the only one he had not predicted: He was left entirely alone.

And now, utterly spent with his efforts, he desperately wanted to stop but was too proud to do so.

"Still doing things the hard way, I see," came a calm voice in perfect German from behind him.

Hans jumped and turned around.

Against the glare of the midday sun stood Major Wolfgang Schmidt, in full military uniform complete with overcoat and officers visor cap, looking down at him in disapproval.

Hans was so shocked at seeing his commander standing in the flesh that he dropped the hoe on his foot. With a yelp of pain, he clutched at his foot and hopped around in the mud, relinquishing whatever dignity remained.

Dignity he had hoped to preserve against the Americans and, as he recalled the harsh words of their last parting, against Major Schmidt too.

Shock turned to genuine relief at seeing him alive, but pride quickly turned relief to bitterness. Hans burned with curiosity at how Major Schmidt came to be here, but he forced it down to make way for the resentment he had been building up.

"Do you have a better idea?" snapped Hans back.

"Yes," came the crisp reply. "Follow orders, take a shower, get some food."

"No," Hans said stubbornly.

An American soldier appeared at the entrance to the camp and, noticing the two men talking, stopped and watched them uneasily.

For his benefit, Hans switched to English and raised his voice, "I will stay here and dig this stinking trench until I die! That is what prisoners do."

The American soldier looked alarmed and started to get agitated.

"This stinking trench is a latrine that they are finished with and have covered up," Major Schmidt said evenly.

Hans blinked and looked around carefully. No wonder the smell had been so bad.

"You are literally digging up *Kácke* someone had just covered," said the Major. "Now, get out of that trench, shower, and get some food."

Hans sighed, then threw his hoe down and sulkily followed Major Schmidt, who had already turned and was walking to the entrance of the main camp.

"All yours," he said kindly to the American at the open tent flap. The soldier smiled his thanks and hurried out past the two Germans, unbuckling his trousers as he went.

The two of them made their way inside in stony silence. Following where Major Schmidt pointed, Hans soon found himself in the showers.

Not just a designated washing-up area, but a set-up with real showers.

With an unlimited supply of water just next to them, it seemed the Americans were quick to capitalize on this luxury and had set up a system of pipes with crude, improvised showerheads to spread the water out a little so one could wash more thoroughly.

Each shower had a small tank set above it on a rack and a simple lever to start and stop the water flow. The area was exposed to the open sky and loosely walled off with stakes over which old sandbags were stretched and tied.

Clearly, these were more for the appearance of privacy than for meaningful security. There were huge gaps on either side of the sandbag wall where one could just walk through and leave.

"Each man gets one jerry can of water for showering, no refills," came a bored voice from behind him.

Turning, Hans saw a portly lance-corporal heft the twenty-liter container toward him and leave it by his feet.

"You pour in there," he said, pointing to the water tank. "You wash," he said, miming someone scrubbing themselves. "Then you wear these," he continued, handing Hans a small towel and his prisoner fatigues. "Then you wash your clothes in the river," he finished, pressing a small lump of soap into Hans's hands.

He ambled off without waiting to see if Hans understood.

Hans understood well enough. He was filthy beyond belief.

Quickly filling the tank, he stripped off and pulled the lever. It released a steady stream of water that was just enough to wash with without draining the tank too quickly. The water was cold, of course, and slightly brown, being straight from the river. But Hans didn't care.

It was the most heavenly sensation he had felt in weeks. He stood there for a while, reveling in the joy of dirt, mud, and stale sweat starting to loosen as cool water poured onto his head and trickled down his body. Then he scrubbed himself down and got reasonably clean before the water ran out.

He dried himself down using the small towel and put on the prisoner fatigues. They were well worn and faded but clean. Most importantly, they fit his large frame.

Washed and dressed, Hans couldn't recall the last time he felt so refreshed. Picking up his uniform, he looked around to see where to go next. There was no one in sight to ask. Did the Americans not even bother to guard them?

Cheerful shouts drew his attention. He walked past the gap on the left side, looked down toward the river, and his jaw dropped.

At the water's edge were no less than ten men dressed like him, washing assorted uniforms in the river. Hans looked for the American guards and saw there were only two.

One was shouting at the men in the water like a vexed mother, while the other was more alert, weapon held loosely but ready. However, it wasn't the playing men he was watching but the other bank of the river, eyes alert for movement and any signs of danger.

Uncertainly, Hans approached the party with his dirty uniform in hand until he heard a cheery "Guten Tag, Oberleutnant!"

Sergeant Koch!

Was there no getting rid of the man?

"What's all this then?" asked Hans and instantly regretted it as the garrulous Sergent opened his mouth to explain.

"So glad you survived, Oberleutnant. Where have you been? After we came in, we were organized according to a simplified version of a typical infantry unit. Ten men to a squad, three squads made a platoon, three platoons made a company, and three companies made a battalion."

"We are Caesar Company," Sergeant Koch grinned. "Pretty much made up of those of us who came in this morning. It's a credit to you, Oberleutnant, that enough of us made it here to form a brand-new company all by ourselves!"

Hans thought moodily, all he did was tell them to run. Hardly the pinnacle of tactical genius.

"Berta Company consists of my friends from the Clausewitz Division, the ones who survived that ill-fated assault on the Soviets a few days ago. Anton Company is pretty much everyone else who was here before the rest showed up.

"In fact, I don't think they were Anton Company at all, to begin with. Only when the remnants of the Clausewitz Division came were there enough numbers to make the Americans rethink how to deal with us.

"Then, their General came up with this idea of making us look after ourselves. Plus, there was a senior enough officer to make it work."

Koch spread his arms to indicate the rest of the men here, "So here we are, Squad One of Platoon Two, Caesar Company, on laundry duty. Squad Two is clearing up where we will sleep, and Squad Three has gone off to draw supplies for all of us."

"So where do I go then?" asked Hans.

"Probably with him," said Koch, looking past Hans toward the camp.

Hans turned to look, and he saw the Clipboard Officer trudging toward the river, making straight for Hans.

As he reached the group, he asked, "You are one of the officers?"

Hans nodded.

"Come with me, please. The General wants to see you."

"Leave this with us," said Koch kindly, taking Hans's dirty uniform and passing it to one of the men. "We're on laundry duty anyway."

As Hans followed the Clipboard Officer back to the camp, he glanced back to where Sergent Koch and Squad One were washing clothes, enjoying the fresh air and cool water, under the watchful eye of their two guards.

He got the distinct impression that the guards were not watching them but watching *over* them.

Chapter 42

Clipboard Officer led Hans through the camp until they reached a large tent.

As they entered, Hans was surprised to see the General himself sitting behind a large desk and even more surprised to see Major Schmidt next to him, deep in conversation.

Hans saluted stiffly and went to stand at the side of the room to the General's right. Major Schmidt hastily concluded his conversation with the General and went to join Hans, his expression grave.

The General nodded, and the two burly MPs in the room moved quickly. One placed a chair two meters in front of the desk while the other ducked out and returned shortly with another German prisoner in tow.

Hans raised an eyebrow as Hauptmann Brandt entered the room, still in uniform, his face set in its usual sneer.

The General spoke to him, "Please sit. I've invited all your fellow officers to be present at this interview so there can be no confusion or misunderstandings later on. You two are content to stand, yes?"

He directed the last sentence to Major Schmidt and Hans. Schmidt nodded in assent. Hans nodded automatically, too, but was baffled. Why did he and the Major have to be present?

Hauptmann Brandt inclined his head in understanding and sat down but said nothing. His eyes were watching and waiting.

Opening the folder in front of him, the General picked up a pen and followed the words on the papers as he read out, "Hauptmann Adolf Brandt. Berta Company Commander, First Battalion, 1034th Regiment, 59th Infantry Division."

No reaction from Brandt.

The General continued, "Born in 1913 just before the Great War broke out. Your father was Otto Brandt, an officer in the Imperial German Army. He later distinguished himself in the Great War and survived it. Your mother was Anna von Graf, daughter of a minor Prussian noble, whom he married in 1913."

Brandt still said nothing, but his jaw tightened.

Hans started to pay attention. While this was all new to him, why would the General bother with such details when processing prisoners?

"Otto and Anna were tragically killed in a mysterious accident when their boat sank. After that, you were raised by the housemaid, Natalia Belyaeva. Natalia had been with your family for years, even before you were born," said the General.

Hans felt a pang of pity for Brandt but was puzzled why he was becoming more agitated. There was nothing to be ashamed of. Being orphaned at a young age was worthy of sympathy, not judgment. Why did he look like a caged animal?

Looking down at the folder again, the General said, almost gently, "You look like your mother."

Now Hans was perplexed. From his vantage point, he could see a copy of two photographs in the folder. One of a handsome young man in Prussian Army uniform and another of a plain-looking but well-dressed woman with a stiff smile.

Both had dark hair and eyes.

At last, Hauptmann Brandt spoke. Haughtily, he said in perfect English, "You insult me, Herr General. I look nothing like my mother. While it is uncommon for Aryans to come from dark-haired couples, I...."

"I meant your real mother," interrupted the General, raising another photograph.

Hans gasped in surprise as Brandt turned pale.

The black and white photo was faded, but in it was an attractive woman in a plain uniform, with fair hair and pale eyes. It was such a spitting image of Brandt that it could only be his mother.

Neatly printed under the photograph were two words: Natalia Belyaeva.

With the suddenness of a cat pouncing, Brandt's lunged forward toward the General, hands extended like claws, his face twisted in a mask of rage.

Immediately, the General's arm shot forward, pen firmly held in hand, pointing directly at Brandt's face.

The angry German, suddenly aware he was going to impale his eye on the General's pen, ducked in mid-leap and crashed on the table. He bounced off straight into the arms of the two MPs, who quickly wrestled him to the floor.

The General calmly put the pen down and carried on reading the folder as though nothing had happened.

Then he said, "Your father was engaged to be married to Anna von Graf but was in a relationship with a pretty but lowly Russian serving girl. He got her pregnant, but she refused to abort the baby. So, to cover the scandal, he quickly married his official betrothed so that when you were born, it would seem to be within the marriage.

"Anna and her family, equally keen to hide the disgrace, went along with it. Natalia stayed on as the family maid, allowing her to see you grow up, even if she was never acknowledged as your real mother."

The General continued sadly, "When Otto and Anna died, she was the only one left to raise you. Otto had no other family. And the von Grafs were only too glad to be rid of their illegitimate descendant."

"In effect, she got what she wanted in the end. To raise you as her own, as a good Russian boy," finished the General.

Hauptmann Brandt, struggling futilely against the two MPs sitting on him, sagged and started sobbing.

Bitterly, he said, "You Americans, so proud, so full of yourselves. You join a war that had nothing to do with you. A war we should have won with ease! Then when the victors bled us dry with their demands for war reparations, you had the audacity to come in to lend us the money to pay for them!"

The General answered quietly, "We were trying to help."

"You were facilitating our national humiliation," Brandt shot back angrily.

Then he twisted and tried to look at the General from under MPs, "Then, suddenly the money dries up, and you demand payment back from us when the entire world is reeling from a financial crash of *your* making because of *your* greed!"

"Just when we are least able to weather the storm, you betray us to save your own skin. All well and good when you come in to save the day. All well and good to lend to us when there is money to be made. But when your avarice comes back to bite you, you recall your loans to us and collapse our economy," snarled the angry German.

At this, the General looked genuinely regretful.

He said sadly, "I'm just a soldier. I do not pretend to understand the complexities of the financial world. But yes, my countrymen did get greedy. We made mistakes...."

"We had to beg for food because of your mistakes!" yelled Hauptmann Brandt.

"When all the German Reichsmarks my parents saved became worthless, my mother took on two jobs, cleaning for Jews, so that she could feed us. If it weren't for the Russians in Berlin who took pity on us, we would have starved," he continued angrily.

"In the end, using my father's legacy as a war hero, I joined the German Army and prospered there. There was no other work to be had," he said.

The General said quietly, "For what you and your mother went through, I am truly sorry. However, it is one thing to hate us and fight us. It is another entirely to betray your own people."

Hans gasped in surprise at the accusation.

Brandt growled, "I betrayed no one. On the contrary, I faithfully served my father's country until it became apparent, once you *Ami* decided to join the war and swing the tide again, that it was doomed. But my heart was always with the country of my mother. It was Russian hands that fed us in our hour of need."

Staring with open hatred at the General, he said, "And it is Russian hands that will destroy you in *your* hour of need."

"Which is why you tried to join them yesterday, isn't it?" asked the General. "What happened?"

Hans's eyes glazed over as things started falling into place.

Brandt's unflagging drive to get to Berlin. Not to help the German garrison but to join the Red Army.

Casting a baleful look at Hans, Brandt said bitterly, "I didn't get a chance to cross over at night because *somebody* decided to retreat to the river, fearing a Soviet attack."

Brandt's strange eagerness to dig in so close to the Soviets in the first position.

"At the river, when it was clear they were following and going to attack, I prepared to surrender to them, counting on my fluent Russian to see me safely received by them. That, and the fact that I made sure our position was easy for them to overrun, as a gesture of good faith when I surrendered to them," Brandt said.

The General said thoughtfully, "My scouts did report your unusual defensive positions. Almost as though you were inviting them in."

Brandt's odd positioning of the men in his sector.

Brandt continued, "But the attacking Soviets were in no mood to listen. They simply shot at anything that moved. They weren't taking any prisoners. Even when I threw a grenade at our machine gun nest and destroyed it to prove I was on their side."

Hans was stunned when he heard that.

In German, he whispered in shock, "You killed them. You killed our men just to save your own skin."

Brandt smiled at him and replied nastily, "And pity it wasn't you in that trench or those stupid boys who follow you around like puppies."

"You two-faced, traitorous, Soviet *spy*," cried Hans as he suddenly surged at Hauptmann Brandt in rage.

But the General was even faster.

His arm shot out again, fully extended, pen firmly in hand, pointed at Hans's face. Hans just managed to halt his movement in time to avoid impaling his eye on the pen, inches away from his face.

The General calmly waited until two more MPs moved behind Hans and held him securely before lowering his arm and writing a few notes on the folder with his pen.

"Soviet sympathizer. Not spy," corrected the General absently, picking up enough of Hans's exclamation to understand. "He wasn't actually sent by the Soviets. It's just that's where his true loyalties lie."

"He is a German traitor, a murderer of my soldiers," fumed Hans in English to the General. "And a murderer of yours too. Prisoners of war we captured."

"Is that so?" said the General, his eyes narrowing.

An awkward silence filled the room while the General leaned back in his chair and pondered what to do.

Looking at Hans and Major Schmidt, he said, "Thank you for your presence here. You may return to your men."

Hans looked at Brandt and said harshly, "What about him?"

"As a self-confessed Soviet sympathizer, murderer of his own men, and possibly mine, he is a suspected war criminal and will be held separately in a cell to face charges for war crimes," said the General.

"Release him to be with the rest of us," said Hans suddenly.

The General frowned in surprise, "Why?"

"To face me," said Hans as his eyes burned.

"Not a chance," said the General, shaking his head. "I have enough plans for you to keep you busy without starting a riot within my camp. He stays in a separate cell from now on."

Hauptmann Brandt smirked at Hans.

"Unless we hand him over to the Soviets," said the General.

Brandt's smile froze.

The General said benignly, "Since they are our allies, we tell them we think he is one of their spies and thank them for the information he has passed on to us. At best, they don't believe that, in which case he can join the other German POWs in a Gulag. Or they believe us and think he's a *failed* spy who has told us everything, in which case things will be a lot worse than the Gulag."

Brandt's face fell in horror as the General nodded and the MPs took him away.

Chapter 43

After the General dismissed them, Major Schmidt led Hans unerringly to the mess hall where the last of the lunch crowd was getting their food. Silently, they joined a queue comprising both soldiers and prisoners, and in short order, they got their food.

Hans was famished and wolfed down his hot stew almost before the Major started on his. He looked regretfully at his empty plate, then longingly at the serving station.

The Major noted his consternation and nodded toward the cook, "If there's extra, they don't mind giving seconds. Less for them to wash up."

Hans needed no further encouragement. In a flash, he took his tray, got it refilled with another heap of steaming food, then returned to his seat and started eating. Major Schmidt picked at his lunch half-heartedly to keep him company.

Between mouthfuls, Hans asked, "Did you know about Hauptmann Brandt?"

Major Schmidt shook his head ruefully, "I'm afraid not. I never liked him, and he was a nasty piece of work, but as long as he did his job and looked after his men, I left him in command. I didn't expect him to be a traitor."

Hans said, "I hated him. After he killed those prisoners, then abandoned my men, I wished him dead. Then he killed a civilian when we met again, and I hated him more. But he was so helpful as we tried to catch up with you...."

"Well, now we know it was for his own purposes, not yours," concluded the Major dryly.

Hans ate slowly while Major Schmidt rose and walked to the serving station. He got two mugs of coffee from the cook, placed them on the table, and sat down again.

"How did you come here?" Hans asked as he took a sip. "How did you survive? I saw your *Kübelwagen* destroyed...."

The Major scratched his chin and looked away, "You know what Hans? I really don't know either. But, by rights, I should be dead."

He leaned back in his chair and sighed, "After you left, we packed up and moved east, met up with some local militia—police and Hitler Youth…."

Hans smiled at the reference to that motley crew and their ridiculous roadblock.

"… spoke with them a while, helped them set up a roadblock…."

Hans's smile froze, then he burst out, "*You* got them to set up that *beschissen* roadblock?"

"It gave them something to do," said Major Schmidt defensively, "Otherwise, they would have come with us."

He continued somberly, "It's one thing for us to go on and fight to the end. But those Hitler Youth…. they're just boys. There was no way I was going to lead them to their deaths. So, I had them cut a tree down, told them to build a roadblock, and man it. Then I told the retired policemen that the boys needed someone to look after them—that way, a few more of them stayed back and were spared. I hope."

Hans nodded silently.

The Major said, "Eventually, we joined up with real army units. Clausewitz Division. Good unit. Their infantry was made up of veterans who were injured early in the war and recovered. The tankers were former instructors, so they knew their stuff. They were short of equipment and ammunition as everyone was, but they were fresh and ready to fight.

"There, we found out Berlin was virtually surrounded, and it wasn't so much a question of 'could we reinforce the garrison there' as 'could we get them out?'. We reached those units the night before they were going to attack toward Berlin and try to break the IXth Army out of there.

"Since they were short of men, we just joined them and filled whatever gaps they had. The Division Commander let me keep my *Kübelwagen*, but the rest of the battalion was dispersed from there on."

Major Schmidt looked thoughtful, then sighed, "At first, it went well, mainly because the enemy was facing Berlin, anticipating a breakout attempt from the inside. But when they realized we were an operational Panzer division in their rear, they turned to face us squarely. Nevertheless, the Clausewitz Division still attacked them head-on, hoping the other divisions could go past them and push on to Berlin."

The Major's voice had dropped to a monotone now, and Hans could sense this was his way of dealing with the horror of what followed.

In hushed tones, he said, "The Soviets deployed on the ridgeline. Infantry. Dug in. But we saw no tanks. So we placed our heavy machine guns on our ridgeline since they were useless in a charge, while our tanks and armored fighting vehicles simply lined up and moved into the valley to attack.

"Only when our tanks were midway across did the Soviet tanks appear. They had been hiding just below their ridgeline. At that point, we were committed. There was no turning back. Either we broke through Soviet lines now or died trying.

"I ordered my driver to drive our *Kübelwagen* in to join the attack. Many of the soft vehicles joined in too—either following me or commands from above—I do not know. I stood up in my *Kübelwagen* with my rifle, trying to look threatening. No way I was going to hit anything with the vehicle lurching all over the place, but any shot directed at us would be a shot away from our tanks. Our Panzers were our only hope. If they died, the attack died."

Hans cringed at what he knew would be his commander's next words.

"They died," he said flatly.

There was a long silence as Major Schmidt picked up his mug of coffee and drained it.

Then he said, "The Soviets weren't stupid. They knew the tanks were our main threat. Our *only* threat against them. So, their tanks systematically targeted ours and ignored the rest of us who were driving around like mad, trying to distract them. Once our tanks were gone, their infantry could advance and mop up."

He shuddered as he said, "Their infantry didn't wait for their tanks to finish ours. They were so hungry for blood they left their positions to attack the tanks themselves. Soldiers against tanks. Men in hand-to-hand combat against machines. I've never seen anything like it.

"At that time, I knew the battle was lost, and it was time to run. I ordered my driver to take us back. He turned too fast, hit a pothole, and I flew out. Amazingly I landed on my feet in a soft patch of ground. As I rolled with the fall, a shell hit my *Kübelwagen* and destroyed it. My driver died instantly. I ran for my life."

He said the last sentence in a matter-of-fact tone.

Continuing, the Major said, "A few of us regrouped back on our ridgeline where we left the machine gun crews. The Soviets didn't bother to follow. The division was finished. All the tanks and AFVs—gone. All senior officers—gone. Of the last viable fighting force of any significant size, less than a hundred men remained, and the three machine gun crews that covered the retreat.

"I was the most senior officer remaining. We had no communication with anyone above us. We weren't even sure if there *was* anyone above us anymore. So I decided to march us west and surrender to the Americans."

Major Schmidt stopped here a little defiantly as though expecting a retort from Hans.

When none came, he carried on, "We gathered whatever supplies we could find and moved out. The main fear now was the Soviets would take the trouble to give chase. Plus, we had wounded who were too hurt to move.

"One of the tanker sergeants—I don't know how he survived the first charge—volunteered to stay back and command the machine guns and look after the wounded until the Americans came east, or they died. His job was to hold off the Soviets and delay them as best he could and, if possible, get word to us of pursuit. Short man. Funny white streak of hair. Talked a lot."

Koch, Hans thought to himself.

Major Schmidt said, "He made it back with your group. Still talks too much, but a good man for what he was willing to do. He's already been making himself useful since he came in this morning."

Hans burned in shame. How badly he had misjudged the little sergeant.

"Anyway, after that, it was fairly straightforward. The rest of us marched west, crossed the river, and surrendered ourselves to the first American unit we came across."

"And this?" Hans asked, tugging at his prisoner fatigues and looking at the Major's uniform.

"Oh this," Major Schmidt said dismissively, "There are so many prisoners now they don't have enough fatigues to go round. So, you wash what you came in with, and once it's dry, you put it back on and save these for the next lot. It helps with the organization of the prisoners. Then people can recognize who's who."

Hans raised a questioning eyebrow.

The Major explained, "There's too many of us to guard in the usual ways. They'd need an army four times this size to hold all of us if they followed their own protocols. So, the General got it into his head to let us organize ourselves according to rank and file within the camp. That way, we maintain our own discipline, manage our schedules, food, exercise... everything.

"We are happier in a structure we are familiar and comfortable with. The Americans are happier because they don't have to babysit us as much, and...."

The Major looked thoughtful here as he mused, "I suspect he might even have something in mind for when the war is over. When we rebuild, we will need men and order more than anything else. No point destroying, then remaking, something that can be readily preserved here."

Hans was jarred by how casually the Major had said, "when the war is over."

But his irritation vanished when a thought struck him, "If all prisoners here are functioning as a unit, but without arms, as senior officer here, that would make you...."

"...Commanding Officer of the US 9th Army Prison Battalion," Major Schmidt finished for him with a wry smile. But his face turned serious as he made the following comment.

"That would also make you the next senior officer in the camp."

Hans looked startled.

Major Schmidt said, "You shouldn't be surprised. When the General interviewed Brandt, it was in the presence of all German Officers in this camp. That's just the two of us."

Looking at Hans, he said, "I need a second-in-command. And soon. We increase in numbers by the day. So, as the CO of the prisoners, I hereby offer you the job. Just like old times, eh Hans?"

The familiarity touched Hans, and the promise of order and structure after days of deprivation and chaos was enticing.

But what got him more excited was the idea of something else.

Looking around carefully, he returned to face his commander and said in sotto tones, "Then we escape."

"Yes... No! What??" the Major cried out, flabbergasted.

Leaning forward, Hans pressed on in low tones, "With the two of us in charge, and the Americans so lax in control, we can escape easily. Maybe even gather the best of the men and bring them with us...."

Major Schmidt stared at him, appalled.

Regaining his composure, he said, "Finish your food, get some rest. We will talk again when you come to your senses."

With that, he got up abruptly, took his tray, and left. It was clear he did not want Hans to follow him.

Chapter 44

Hans did not see Major Schmidt again that day. After he finished his lunch and returned his tray, someone directed him back to where the other prisoners were camped. It was a large area under a series of tents, with a pile of blankets and groundsheets in the corner.

Sergeant Koch seemed to have been appointed platoon commander and was clearly in charge as he directed the men to stake out the groundsheets in neat rows and place two blankets on each. In minutes, the job was done, and most of the men, exhausted from the trials of the last twenty-four hours, curled up and slept.

Finding the nearest empty groundsheet, Hans rolled one blanket up as a pillow, lay down, and tried to spread the other one over himself. He was asleep before he finished.

When the sun rose the following day, Koch got everyone awake and lined up as the Clipboard Officer arrived and counted heads. He marked the numbers down on his notepad and walked off.

That was it. No shouting, no threats, no warnings. He just left them alone.

Hans began to ponder again about the complete lack of supervision the Americans gave the prisoners. How could Major Schmidt not see? Escape was not only possible; it was a very real prospect. And did not the Clipboard Officer say they were free to walk out? Had no one thought to test that offer?

Meanwhile, Koch began to rattle off the day's activities to the platoon.

"Breakfast is at 8 am," he began. "After the American soldiers have had theirs—because they have real work to do. But before the senior officers come in—because it wouldn't do for an American General to be surrounded by a hundred Germans and taken out in his own camp."

Amused chortles broke out at this.

"After that, there will be area cleaning to do, washing of clothes and fatigues, and for a few lucky ones, some latrine digging duties."

He said the last with a straight face, and Hans suspected it wasn't actually a joke. Used to the hustle and bustle of an active unit in the middle of a war, he wasn't sure he even knew how to literally sit and do nothing.

Even though the old military adage remained true: Soldiers either rush to wait or wait to rush, Hans found that in the lulls, there was always a sense of purpose and expectation. Even if nothing could be done now, there was always something to achieve later.

But, as a prisoner now, if they weren't going to be tortured or pressed into work as slave labor, what *was* there to do? So digging latrines might be a welcome diversion.

The hourly gong sounded then, and the men streamed toward the mess hall for breakfast, just as most of the American servicemen were leaving.

There were no apparent restrictions as to where one could sit except for one table in the corner, set slightly apart from the rest, which had a white tablecloth. This was obviously the Officers' Table, reserved for senior officers or dignitaries.

Hans was shocked to see Major Schmidt dining at that table in quiet conversation with the Clipboard Officer. And, as Hans registered a second later, the American officer was too junior to sit at that table. It seemed he was there at Major Schmidt's invitation.

As Hans came in, the Major's eyes flicked in his direction, but otherwise, he gave no indication he noticed Hans. Hans felt a little surly about that and, after getting his food, set his tray down and sat deliberately with his back to the Major.

Halfway through the meal, another platoon of prisoners arrived with Josef amongst them. Hans smiled genuinely for the first time since coming in at seeing the boy unharmed. He raised his hand to call out to him, but Josef looked at the Officer's Table instead.

His eyes widened when he recognized the man who got them to build the roadblock and trotted over eagerly. Sergeant Koch appeared out of nowhere and good-naturedly blocked his path with a gentle reminder about protocols when approaching senior officers, especially if they were talking to someone else.

But Major Schmidt spotted the boy and rose to meet him with one fluid movement. He called out to him, delight obvious on the older man's face, and Josef and Sergeant Koch went over. The three of them stood in the middle of the mess hall and exchanged warm words, an intensely private circle of communion despite the loud noises of many men about them eating their meal.

Hans watched with a surge of jealousy.

He knew the Josef too.

Did I not lead him to battle and glory... he stopped the thought there as the memory of Wilhelm running off in a daze came to his mind, followed by the image of Tomas's dead face.

Hans looked down in self-loathing and shame.

Josef was here *despite* Hans's actions, not because of them.

Trying to force down his feelings, Hans then looked at Sergeant Koch and thought defensively, *did I not take over command of the ridge from the grateful sergeant? Did I not command the defenses which...* he stopped there.

They all almost died.

Lost in thought and brooding about how to force the facts of the past few days to fit into his perceptions, he did not see the little group disperse, and the Major walk over to his table. Sitting down across Hans with a grunt,

Major Schmidt clasped his hands around his coffee mug and said, "Well?"

"Well, what?" was Hans's surly reply.

"Are we going to do this again?" snapped the Major.

"Do what again?" Hans said coolly.

The Major looked to be biting back a retort.

Softening his tone, Major Schmidt said, "We lost. We just have to accept that. Lost to the Red Army, lost to the western allies. For us, the war is over. There is no need to fight anymore."

Drawing a slow breath, he said, "Not with them, not with each other."

Hans sat still, clearly listening but looking past the Major, glowering.

Major Schmidt said, "We are fortunate beyond belief that the Americans have taken us in."

Hans stiffened, and his face flushed.

The Major pushed on, "The Soviets are ready to murder us on sight. You heard the reports of what happened in Moscow, in Stalingrad, and the rest. They are not going to forgive us for that. The Americans were at least willing to accept our surrender and not execute us immediately. From a purely tactical point of view, you know it was the right choice. Would you lead your men to pointless death or lead them to safety?"

Hans bristled, "A good soldier is willing to die for...."

"... for what?" cut in the Major, "A dead leader? A lost country? A fallen city?"

Looking him squarely in the eye, Major Schmidt asked again, "Would you lead your men to a pointless death?"

Hans reluctantly shook his head.

"Then why are you looking to do that to yourself?" came the poignant question.

Squirming uncomfortably, Hans fell back on fundamental beliefs he knew to be true.

Defiantly, he said, "We should escape."

"To where?" the Major countered.

Where indeed, Hans's mind churned. To Berlin? Filled with dead German soldiers and live Soviet ones seeking to add numbers to the former? To the west? Where even more American forces awaited? To the non-existent *Wehrmacht*? There were no German forces left.

Slowly, stubbornly, Hans repeated, "We still should escape."

"For what?" the Major pressed.

For what indeed? To lead a resistance? Find weapons, hide and snipe from a distance, disrupt enemy activities? For what conceivable purpose? There was no victory to be had. No glory in such craven battle.

"To fight the Soviets," blurted Hans, seizing on a random thought. "How can we call ourselves soldiers when we hide here in safety while our countrymen are being slaughtered by the Soviets?"

Through clenched teeth, the Major said, "Can you not see that fighting is not the answer anymore? The best thing we can do for our countrymen is to let this damned war end!"

Floundering in confusion now, Hans's mind raced until he settled at last on something he was absolutely sure of. Something he could triumphantly present as justification.

Leaning forward closer to the Major, he snarled, "The Americans are the enemy. They've bombed our cities, destroyed our homes, pissed in our rivers, killed our soldiers, my soldiers...."

With a bitter grimace, he added, "...your soldiers."

"Yes, the Americans are the enemy," Hans finished with satisfaction at his own wisdom.

He sat back and folded his arms as if daring a reply to his assertions.

Major Schmidt was silent for a long time. He stared deep into his mug as though in despair.

Finally, he said in a broken voice, "I cannot reach you. For all the respect I once commanded from you, for all the trust built up throughout countless battles, for all the times we have saved each other's life, I cannot reach you."

Hans, sensing victory, said one more time with a cruel smile on his lips, "The Americans are our enemy, and we are theirs."

"*Wir haben es begonnen*," retorted Major Schmidt, and he stood up abruptly and left.

Hans was left sitting in his seat with his smile frozen on his face, the Major's last words haunting him.

Wir haben es begonnen.

We started it.

Chapter 45

Hans was aghast.

Could he have been so wrong all this time? All the fighting, all the deaths because of his obstinate hatred of the Americans?

But they deserved it! They killed his friend! Why should he let go of his hatred? It was the only thing that gave his life meaning now. The only thing that could replace the emptiness he felt whenever he thought about Erich. The only thing that gave his life purpose since his father died.

Then Josef appeared in the mess hall, looking around. He spotted Hans and walked over to him. Drawing near, he held out something in hand and offered it to Hans.

"Look, Oberleutnant, I found your knife and cleaned it up for you," he said shyly.

Hans stared in disbelief at the little item in the boy's hand.

In a trembling voice, he asked, "Where did you find it?"

"In the rubbish ditch," said Josef. "I was on duty to clear the rubbish when I spotted it there. Someone must have thrown it away."

Hans just kept staring at what used to be his most precious possession. The unmistakable scratched out star on the pommel, the familiar inscription, the broken blade. How much toil and suffering he went through to earn it. How much he held it for inspiration before battle. But he was forced to give it up by his own hand in the end.

"My leader always said we should keep our knives with us to help us remember who we are," said Josef proudly.

Now Hans stared at him in amazement.

Who we are? Who we are? *Good little Nazis from a city overrun with the enemy? Loyal Hitler Youths named after a man who was dead? Good Germans defending our land in a war we instigated?*

In growing horror, Hans read the face of the boy in front of him, seeing in him the same pride and growing confidence he once had in his *own* identity. The arrogant sureness of his own righteousness reflected back to him in the face of youth.

"Why?" Hans whispered hoarsely, and Josef frowned in confusion.

What was the point of holding on to the old ideas?

"Why?" he said louder, rising ominously from the bench, and Josef backed off uncertainly.

Old ideas which caused the deaths of so many he cared about and owed a debt to.

"WHY?" he roared and lunged at Josef, seizing him by the shoulders and shaking him until his teeth rattled. He looked like he was going to strike the boy.

The men around him, a mixture of American soldiers and German prisoners, quickly leaped on Hans and brought him crashing down as Josef pulled away, eyes wide in fear.

Hans shouted in fury as he thrashed and struggled against the bodies.

Bad enough, he believed in a lie. Bad enough, his misplaced faith brought all this pain and destruction to those around him. Yet, a part of him still wanted to hang on. He knew no other way to live. And maybe, it was fitting for him to follow it to the bitter end.

But to see it coalesce again in Josef was intolerable. For this to pass on to the next generation was something he simply could not bear.

Then he broke down and wept. The men holding him down slowly released him when they saw he no longer struggled. He gnashed his teeth and sobbed in anguish while the bewildered Josef looked on.

After a few minutes, Hans finally composed himself enough to pick himself off the floor. Then, pushing his way past the curious onlookers, he mumbled, "I need to think," and made his way out of the mess hall.

In a daze, he stumbled around the camp randomly, trying unsuccessfully to find a quiet space he could sit down and be alone. But it was in the late afternoon by now. Everybody, POWs and American soldiers, was up and about, busy with chores and routines.

So finally, he made his way to where a series of cells had been set up—the Real Prison—Sergeant Koch had called it.

Each was separated by thick wooden boards, with gaps large enough to see through but not enough to reach through. The doors were sturdy metal grills that allowed a full view of the cells within from the front.

One guard was sitting at the desk, peering at some papers, while another two were walking around the cells slowly, weapons held loosely but at the ready.

Stepping up to the guard at the desk, Hans pointed to an empty cell and asked, "Can I sit in there for a while?"

The guard stared at him in surprise and looked like he was about to refuse, but he must have caught something in the clenched hands and desperate eyes of the big German in front of him that made him change his mind. His expression softened, and he said, "Sure, go ahead. It's not locked."

Hans muttered his thanks, leaving the bemused guard wondering whether his actions would get him in trouble. Then he shrugged and dismissed his worry. So he was letting a prisoner go into a prison cell. How wrong could that be?

Hans entered the cell and sat down on the floor in relief. He was still within sight of the guard at the desk, but better one stranger than many. At least here, there was a slight modicum of privacy. Sighing deeply, he leaned back against the cell bars and unclenched his hands.

In the right one was his Hitler Youth knife.

Hans couldn't believe it. In all the confusion, he must have snatched it from Josef in a desperate bid to keep the boy away from the madness the knife represented. A madness that prevented his surrender from being accepted and nearly cost him his life.

Reflexively, he opened it and examined the broken blade.

"We can use that to escape," came a sudden whisper to his right in German.

Startled, Hans looked toward the voice and saw a familiar figure.

Hauptmann Brandt was in the next cell. He was unshaven and disheveled, but looked relatively clean and well-fed.

He crawled over to the wall separating them and put one eye against the gap, staring hopefully at the gleam of metal in Hans's hand.

"Use the knife to kill the guards, get the keys and get me out of here, then we can escape together," said Brandt eagerly.

Hans looked at him as though he was mad.

"There is no need to kill anybody. The Americans already said we are free to leave anytime," said Hans coldly.

"Not me, not me," whimpered Brandt.

"Look," he said with sudden eagerness, "Maybe there's no need to kill anybody, but you can steal the keys, release me, and help me escape. Then you can walk out and join me."

Hans was incredulous and said, "And why in the world should I do that?"

"So we can be free," came the reply.

"Free to do what?" asked Hans in exasperation.

"Free to fight on," said Brandt.

"Against whom?" asked Hans. "The Soviets? Did you not see their strength when we were running for our lives? We are powerless against them. The Americans? Are they not treating us better than we could care for ourselves?"

Brandt said haughtily, "It is our duty as loyal German soldiers and officers to escape and carry on when we can. It is what the *Führer* would expect of...."

"The *Führer* is dead," said Hans flatly, cutting him off.

Brandt pressed on, "We have a duty to defend the country...."

"Berlin is fallen," said Hans in a harsh voice.

Brandt tried again, "We owe it to our countrymen, our fellow Germans ...."

"You are not even German," said Hans hotly. "You are a Soviet sympathizer who has been rejected by your own side, yet you want to crawl to them again and try to join them."

Brandt looked away guiltily. But he quickly adjusted his expression and spoke smoothly, "Perhaps, but if you come with me, I can vouch for you. I can say you helped me escape and that you want to join them too."

Hans couldn't believe the gall of the man. Defeated. In prison. Powerless. Proven to be a liar and a traitor. But he still had the audacity to invoke duty to the very country he betrayed, to try and deceive Hans once more.

Hans shook his head in amazement. Shocked at the shameless lies of his former comrade. But even more, he was rattled as he recognized Brandt's words as his very own.

Was this how Major Schmidt felt when they spoke earlier?

Getting up slowly, Hans said to Brandt, "We're done here. I will listen no more to your lies."

Hauptmann Brandt grasped the bars that held him and rasped, "I will still be here. You can come back anytime you are ready, and we can do this."

But Hans just opened the door of his cell and walked out.

As he passed the guard at the desk, he placed the broken knife on the table and said, "One of the boys found this. I would appreciate it if you could dispose of it as you see fit."

Then he walked off.

Chapter 46

5th May 1945—American Camp

That night, Hans tossed and turned restlessly, unable to drift off to oblivion.

His mind writhed in agony, twisting one way then another, desperately trying to find an answer to the shambles of his life. Trying to make things fit into what he had always known.

Or thought he knew.

He considered the physical situation he and his countrymen were in.

Even though it was only his second night in camp as a prisoner, he grudgingly had to concede they were treated very well. In fact, they were arguably better off than when they were in the field as combatants even in the early days of the war, let alone during the chaos of the later ones.

Then a pang of guilt seized him.

Better off than any German soldiers left out there.

He thought about the shame of surrendering.

But even that had been assuaged somewhat by the fact that not once had he been taunted or jeered at by the Americans. They mostly ignored the prisoners, or if there were any interactions, it was like that of a harried schoolteacher with unruly children rather than triumphant victor to humiliated foe.

Why weren't the Americans the demons he had been raised to believe they were? Why weren't they mistreating them as he'd expected, the better to confirm his accusations against them? The better to justify the satisfaction he felt when he fought them?

But if he couldn't fault their treatment here, at least he could fall back on the outrage he felt at the deaths they had inflicted on his countrymen and the soldiers in his command.

Yes, in this war, they had indeed killed so many... then Major Schmidt's words came back to haunt him.

We started it.

But *before* this war then, with all the suffering his country went through, surely the blame fell on them?

Hauptmann Brandt, for all his duplicity, had a valid point of grievance.

Germany was already on its knees after the devastation of the Great War. Then it was forced to make crippling reparations even as the citizens tried to rebuild. The Americans caused the Great Depression with their greed, and everyone suffered.

Did they get punished? No, they simply called in their loans. So when his country could least afford it, it was made to pay. For American avarice. For a war that it had lost. For a war that…. Major Schmidt's voice cut in again in his mind.

We started it.

Hans groaned in despair. A depressingly recurrent theme was emerging from his ruminations.

Again and again, it came up. Endlessly pounding at whatever arguments he sought to raise against reality.

Mentally stumbling blindly now, he moved on to the Soviets.

Were they not friends? Had they not invaded Poland together and carved up the country between them?

Were they not allies? But that too fell apart when Nazi forces invaded the Soviet Union, so...

We started it.

But not me, pleaded Hans. It was High Command! It was the *Führer*! I had nothing to do with it! I never wanted to fight the Soviets!

But once again, Major Schmidt's voice cut in. *If we want to share in his victories, we must share in his mistakes. If we want to share the spoils, then we must share in the loss. If we unite ourselves with him to rise to glory, we must be prepared to go down with him in defeat.*

Hans was screaming in his head now. *I am a good soldier! An honorable officer! I cared for those under my command! I fought with integrity and distinction!*

Then he thought of the men he led in the final battle.

More like led *to* the final battle.

His thoughts turned bleak as his own mind started accusing him.

We could have surrendered earlier to the Americans. How many men died in that pointless battle against the Soviet forces? How many boys? Tomas was dead. Wilhelm was gone. Josef, and the ones that survived—only by the mercy and courage of the Americans.

And even so... the picture of Josef proudly showing him his Hitler Youth knife came to his mind, and Hans wanted to vomit.

Not him. Not the boys. Never mind if I die now for my sins. Don't let it pass on to the next generation.

Hans shut his eyes tight and covered his ears as though to shut out the voice in his head. Curling up in a fetal position, he suddenly felt he couldn't breathe.

Faced with the prospect that his entire life had been a lie, his consciousness simply rebelled and attempted to shout down the truth by shutting down his body.

His heart slowed, and his hands went numb. Like a deer caught in brambles eventually stops struggling and accepts the end of its existence, Hans's breathing slowed down and almost stopped entirely as he literally tried to die.

But death would not take him.

Finally, his eyes stared sightlessly into the near pitch-darkness of the platoon tent in utter despair and utter defeat.

There was nothing left to fight for.

Hitler was dead.

Berlin had fallen.

There was nowhere else to go.

Then he cried.

At first, the tears did not flow. It was just a spasming of his chest and stomach that cramped him over and made him curl up even more tightly than before.

Then his hands started shaking, and he drew in a deep, shuddering breath. The filling of air in his lungs brought life and pain back to his body, and he gasped, then shook again.

He uttered a hoarse curse, gulped as his dry throat rasped against the words, then retched. Nothing came out, but his empty stomach still heaved wretchedly. Then, at last, with one pathetic wail, the tears started flowing, and he could cry.

Like a dam that had burst, the tears flowed freely down his face and formed a puddle on his groundsheet. He sobbed in spurts and fits, mourning for all the waste.

Waste of German lives that had been brutally lost in this war.

Waste of so much of *his* life spent in so much hatred.

Waste of following a madman to the depths of insanity and jeering at others who didn't.

Worst of all, the waste of fighting against those who would be kind to him if only he hadn't been so busy trying to kill them.

He wept bitterly for a long time, working out the demons that had haunted him since his youth.

Then, like a frightened child finally accepting he was truly all alone, Hans let the darkness take him, and he rocked himself to sleep.

Chapter 47

6th May 1945—American Camp

Hans woke up abruptly.

And regretted it.

He felt like he had the worst hangover in his life.

His eyes were swollen and puffy to the point where he had to squint to see where he was going. His face was drawn and pale. His mouth was so dry he could barely draw a breath.

Like a ghoul, he followed his platoon into the mess hall and sat down morosely facing the tent wall. While the others got their food and ate, Hans didn't move.

At the Officers' Table, Major Schmidt spotted him, sighed, and cleared his tray. Then he refilled his mug of coffee and went over to Hans, and sat next to him.

Together, they stared at the camouflage green of the tent in heavy silence.

His platoon finished breakfast and left. The next platoon came, had breakfast, and left. A few senior officers strolled in and got their food, and ate.

Finally, after even the senior officers had left, Hans spoke his first words that day.

"Why didn't you tell me?" he asked in a hoarse whisper. He did not take his eyes off the tent wall.

Major Schmidt paused then said, "I think I tried to."

"Why didn't I listen?" he asked in a haunted voice.

The Major kept silent.

"I don't know what to do," Hans said softly.

Still, the Major kept silent.

"I... I can't see past the darkness," Hans whispered, choking back a sob.

The Major spoke at last, "You are not alone."

The two men sat in silent solidarity for a long time.

Lost in their thoughts but, at the same time, in a strange, comfortable silence that was almost intimate.

"We have to help them," said Hans, sitting up straight slowly.

"Who?" asked Major Schmidt.

"Our soldiers. Our fellow countrymen. The ones still out there across the river," said Hans, with building passion. "I cannot sit here and abide in the comfort and safety of the Americans while they remain at the mercy of the Soviets."

Major Schmidt nodded speculatively.

Hans continued, "They said we could walk out of here. Well, let's walk out of here. We tear off our stickers. We cross the river. We find those we can. We bring them back here to safety. Then we go out again and find more. We go until there are no more left to save."

"If we encounter any Soviet forces without our stickers, they can, and will, kill us on sight," warned Major Schmidt.

"We'd be no worse off than we would have been without the Americans," Hans argued. "But this way, at least *some* of our comrades have a chance."

Major Schmidt shook his head and asked, "Still doing things the hard way, Hans?" But there was kindness in his voice.

Hans frowned at him.

"How much good do you think we can do on our own, going in blind, unarmed, unsupported? How many can we save if we can't even save ourselves at first contact with the enemy?" asked Major Schmidt.

He continued, "I admire your intent, and I agree with it. I admire your courage, and I applaud it. But if we just go like this, we would simply be killed. How much good would that do for our compatriots then?"

Hans said in frustration, "So, you are saying it cannot be done. The enemy is too strong. Too prevalent. We cannot hope to cross the river and expect to save even one soldier. Those that remain are trapped there and doomed."

"We can't do anything about it..." said Major Schmidt, nodding in agreement.

Then he looked to the door just as the General and the Sergeant Major walked in.

"...but maybe *they* can."

The entire mess hall fell silent as everyone rose to salute the General. He quickly returned the salutes and waved everyone to be at ease.

To Hans's surprise, Major Schmidt signaled to them, and both men came over immediately. The Sergeant

Prisoner of War

Major stood to one side while the General noisily dragged out a chair, reversed it, and unceremoniously sat down on it back to front, facing the two Germans.

"Yes?" he asked mildly.

"Hans here has something to say to you," said the Major casually.

"*What?*" blurted Hans, completely taken off guard.

But it was too late. The General was already looking in expectation, and the massive Sergeant Major's eyes were boring into him.

Resisting the urge to kick Major Schmidt under the table, Hans drew a deep breath and said, "First, I'd like to say, for saving my men and me and treating us with kindness, I thank you. We owe you our lives."

"But glad as I am to be safe here, there are more of my countrymen across the river who stand to be butchered by the Soviet forces there. I have to try to help them. It is a debt of honor I must repay or die trying," said Hans earnestly.

Trying to keep his voice from shaking, Hans said, "To that end, it is my intention to remove my blue sticker, leave the camp, and head across the bridge to aid those I can find."

"You'll be dead before the sun sets," growled the Sergeant Major softly. But there was no malice in his voice.

Hans nodded in acknowledgment and said, "Nonetheless, I must try. You saved me. I cannot repay that. But I can save others."

The General looked thoughtful for a while, then he said, "You say we saved you, and we did. You say you owe us your life, and you do. *I* say you honor us better if you do not throw it away needlessly."

Rising from the chair, the General said, "Come with me."

Completely confused now, Hans got up and followed the lanky General, with Major Schmidt and the Sergeant Major just a step behind. They reached the Command Tent and entered it.

Inside, Clipboard Officer was making some markings on a large map on the wall. He saluted instantly when the General walked in, but his eyes widened when he saw Hans.

Frantically, he tried to cover the map on the wall while still holding the salute. Soon, he gave up and, with a guilty expression, allowed the map to be seen by Hans.

It showed the American area of operations. At the center was the bridge that spanned the river Elbe. On the left were numerous markings in blue that covered that entire side of the map. On the right, across the river, were multiple markings in red. Between the sea of blue symbols and red ones was a handful of small, yellow ones that lined the river's eastern bank.

The General walked to the map and pointed as he spoke.

"The blue markings are our forces. We've been here for weeks now but have not been allowed to cross the Elbe in force, so we're quite heavily built up on the western bank now," he said, his voice betraying frustration.

"The red markings are Soviet forces...."

Hans was startled by that revelation.

Red markings always indicated enemy forces. At first glance, he should have known the red symbols were far too great in number and strength to represent German units. But weren't the Soviets and Americans allies?

"...while the yellow markings indicate where our reconnaissance have spotted German units," finished the General.

Yellow, thought Hans, *for unknown or pending forces, instead of red*.

Major Schmidt looked at the map speculatively, "Too few and too scattered to justify crossing the river in force as you did for Hans's company. If you did, the Soviets would have no choice but to respond by sending more forces into the area....."

".... which, aside from the trouble the General will get into with his superiors, will also spell the end of any hope the Germans there have of evading the Red Army when they come in force," concluded the Sergeant Major.

Hans was crestfallen at how the conversation was going.

Then the General said speculatively, "However, a smaller group *could* go across the river for a variety of perfectly legitimate, non-military reasons which the Soviets should not object to too strenuously."

"And if such a group *happened* to encounter any German soldiers, who *happened* to surrender....why, we'd have no choice but to take them in, won't we?" said the General innocently.

"So, will you come out with us to help rescue the German soldiers that remain out there?" asked Hans anxiously.

The General grinned back at him and said, "I was just going to ask you the very same thing."

Chapter 48

"You planned this all along?" Hans asked in exasperation as he and the Major left the Command Tent.

Major Schmidt replied sheepishly, "Well, yes. Not just me, of course, but the General and some of his staff. They did the big operation that saved you and your band all by themselves.

"But the next day, we spoke seriously about smaller missions to cross the river to do the same. But we weren't sure if we could actually go ahead with it unless you were on board."

"Why me?" asked Hans suspiciously.

Major Schmidt replied, "Because the General won't risk me going out since I'm supposedly commanding the prisoners here. Of everyone left, only you speak English well enough to translate efficiently under pressure. Plus, as an officer, you will be a more convincing advocate than the others."

"I feel used," Hans complained.

"You *are* being used, but if it's for a good cause, what's wrong with that?" asked Major Schmidt brightly.

In less than an hour, Hans found himself standing in front of an open-top American M3 half-track Armored Personnel Carrier, waiting to board.

He was back in his German Army Uniform, complete with Oberleutnant rank insignia. He was unarmed, of course, with no battle webbing and gear, but he had his helmet on.

It still had the original blue sticker of surrender on it.

Sam tapped him on the shoulder, then climbed into the APC. When Hans followed him in, he was not at all surprised to find Sam's chubby friend already inside, waiting for them. Sam and Jerome were inseparable and somehow always contrived to be deployed together.

Prisoner of War

The rest of the cabin was empty. They could easily accommodate another eight passengers seated with room to spare for many more sitting on the floor.

The rest of the convoy consisted only of two M4 Shermans. The one directly in front of them was commanded by the Sergeant Major. The other tank leading the column was one familiar to Hans from his previous brush with it the day he surrendered.

Brush it was for the tank. For Hans, it was more like being hit by a car.

He rubbed his shoulder absently where it still ached a little from that encounter. The General himself, of course, commanded that tank, complete with one flag with three stars on one side and the XVI Corps Emblem fluttering proudly on the other.

With a quick glance to check all behind him were ready, the General called to his driver, and his tank moved off. The other Sherman followed, and Hans's APC lurched after it.

Behind them were two military jeeps. One with one driver and the Clipboard Officer—whom Hans now knew to be a Lieutenant Harris—in the passenger seat. He was operating its large radio and assorted communication equipment.

The other jeep had one driver and three soldiers—presumably as scouts or messengers.

A half-ton field ambulance followed the jeeps with the Red Cross emblem clearly displayed on both sides and the roof. Taking up the rear was another APC identical to the one Hans was riding in.

The General headed across the bridge and turned left, leading the convoy north along the eastern bank of the Elbe.

To Hans's relief, the first few encounters were almost routine.

Upon seeing a German officer in full uniform urging them to lay down their arms, the German soldiers they encountered would usually surrender immediately. Then, the Americans would slap blue stickers on their helmets and take them into the APCs.

It was noon when things got decidedly tense.

A machine gun nest with four men—the largest group so far—proved more tricky.

The Americans had approached cautiously, turrets deliberately pointing east instead of toward the trench. With lots of waving and friendly calls, they got close enough to communicate without incident.

Hans's APC moved closest to them so he could lean over the vehicle wall and talk to the men. The rest of the convoy stayed behind respectfully while the three men in the second jeep dismounted and went off to scout the woods.

The initial exchange was brief and concise.

The four soldiers in the trench readily accepted the Americans weren't interested in attacking them. They believed the offer to receive their surrender was in good faith and that they would be well treated. They appreciated the kindness the Americans were trying to show, but they had to politely refuse.

Against all reason, they felt it was their duty to hold their position to the last man against the Soviets. With a stubbornness that Hans found vaguely familiar, they turned their backs on the Americans and settled in to wait for Soviet forces.

One of the American soldiers came running back at full pelt.

"Soviets! Three hundred meters and closing fast!" he called out breathlessly to the entire group. Then, without breaking stride, he angled to the General's tank to give further details.

The General questioned him quickly, then signaled to the Sergeant Major.

He raised his three middle fingers, patted them against his left upper arm, then barked, "Tank platoon. Non-Comm Commander. George, you're up!"

The Sergeant Major nodded and dropped down into his tank to give orders to his crew.

Hans quailed at the thought of facing the Red Army again.

He knew they were supposedly allies of the Americans. Therefore, German prisoners such as himself were theoretically not at risk.

But the stubborn, *uncaptured* ones in the trench, still resolutely holding out against the Red Army, could be a convenient excuse for the Soviets to start shooting.

Hurriedly, he told the four soldiers that Soviet tanks were approaching and urged them to give up quickly.

Prisoner of War

But instead of surrendering, they got very excited. Hans clenched his fists in frustration when he realized all he had done was make them more determined to fight.

Two soldiers lined up with rifles at the ready while the other pair struggled to get their machine gun in place.

There was no time to convince the four in the trench to surrender now. They would probably start shooting as soon as the Soviets appeared, who, in turn, would be obliged to shoot back—with the Americans in line of fire.

Hans sank down in the APC grimly. The situation was deteriorating very quickly. Briefly, he considered leaving the vehicle and jumping into the trench to knock some sense into his countrymen, but he remembered his standing orders to stay out of sight if they encountered any Soviets.

"If you wouldn't do it for your own safety, at least do it for ours," the General had sternly warned.

At a curt signal from the General, the convoy took up defensive positions alongside the German trench. The Sergeant Major's tank turned and rumbled toward the tree line to meet the incoming Soviet forces.

This won't work at all, thought Hans in sudden panic. *As soon as the Soviets spot the German trench and the*

Americans not *attacking it, their cover story of "overrunning enemy positions" would be completely implausible.*

A bright flash of inspiration hit him suddenly, and he called out to the General urgently to outline his plan.

The General listened carefully, then raised an eyebrow and said, "Are you sure?"

With some pride, Hans replied, "General, this is a *German* infantry trench. We construct them for precisely this situation."

Still looking dubious, the General called out orders while Hans's APC took up station north of the German trench.

The Sergeant Major drove his tank and took up a position east of the trench, drawing curses from the four soldiers as he now blocked their line of sight to the approaching Soviets.

Their curses soon turned to screams as the General's tank rolled forward and, without pause, calmly ran over their trench, machine gun and all, and stopped there.

The tank driver popped up to check his position with no more concern than he might have while parking a car, then dropped back down and turned his engine off.

In the meantime, the Radio jeep pulled just ahead and to the left of the General's tank. The driver killed the engine and leaped out with a toolkit, scattered tools over the body of the General's tank, and started banging noisily underneath it.

The General, for his part, stood high in the commander's hatch and scowled impatiently.

Hans settled down and prayed the General understood his suggestions and didn't improvise too much.

The ground shook. A deep, rumbling noise that announced the arrival of the Soviet platoon of five tanks.

The lead tank commander was a thin, sour-looking First Sergeant. He pulled right in front of the Sergeant Major's tank and called out harshly in heavily accented English, "What are you doing here?"

"Broken down," replied the Sergeant Major ruefully.

"I can see that," said the First Sergeant, "I meant, what are you all doing *here*? On this side of the river?"

The Sergeant Major said, "Visiting your division commander. Do you happen to know where he is?"

The Soviet commander was taken aback, "Visiting? No, I know nothing of that. The Division Commander does not answer to me."

The Sergeant Major heaved a long-suffering sigh and said, in a lower tone, "*We* know nothing of it either. General makes one call, brings everyone along as escort, and doesn't bother to tell us where to go, who to contact, when to meet... and then gets angry when he has to wait. You know how officers are, eh?"

The Soviet commander grunted in agreement.

Hans jumped as the General, apparently in a fit of pique, suddenly shouted at the driver repairing his tank and threw his helmet at him in disgust. Then he spun around and spotted the Soviet tanks.

The Russian commander blanched as he suddenly became the focus of attention of the angry General.

The General's eyes widened in outrage. Pointing to the Soviet First Sergeant, the General called out to his Sergeant Major in a haughty tone, "What does *he* want?"

"Nothing, nothing, Sir, they're just on patrol," said the Sergeant Major hastily, with an apologetic glance to his counterpart.

The General barked at the Sergeant Major, "Does he know anything about my meeting? Get him over here!"

"No, no," called the Sergeant Major back in a harassed voice. "He's just a non-comm like me, Sir. He knows nothing either."

In a low tone, he addressed the Soviet commander, "You'd better go. He's difficult when he's in such a mood."

The Soviet First Sergeant nodded in sympathy.

"*Da, da*, I can see that," he said and quickly got his platoon moving before he got more involved with a spoilt American general.

Five minutes later, the Soviet tanks withdrew.

The Sergeant Major deemed it safe and gave the signal. The General's tank made a miraculous recovery and rolled off the trench. The four Germans underneath clambered out shakily and begged to surrender. Their helmets were stickered, they were loaded up, and the whole convoy wheeled around and drove off as fast as they could.

Chapter 49

It was late afternoon when an almost identical scenario unfolded.

This time, it was just two German soldiers in a shallow ditch.

Unlike the earlier quartet, they were not deeply dug-in in a structured trench, so there was no option to just roll over them as they did with the previous group.

But they were well-armed and scared, and the General ordered Hans to talk to them from the APC rather than get off and expose himself to fire. Hans cursed the stubbornness of his countrymen as they steadfastly refused to surrender.

The rest of the convoy casually deployed around the German pair while the three scouts started their sweep of the surrounding area. They returned hurriedly with stern expressions.

The lead scout used his hands to signal *tanks*. Then made three stripes with his fingers and placed them on his shoulder. *Led by a captain*.

The General nodded in acknowledgment and raised his hand.

"Parade formation," he called tersely.

His tank crew immediately raised a large American flag and attached it to their machine gun. The Sergeant Major's crew did the same. At the same time, all the other vehicles moved to line up neatly in front of the Sergeant Major's tank, blocking the two Germans from view.

Just then, the first Soviet vehicle peeked out from the tree line. The General said, "Go." And his tank lurched forward and charged toward the Soviet tank at full speed.

Without thinking, Hans suddenly leaped over the APC wall and dived into the ditch. Slapping the two soldiers on their helmets, he berated them furiously for their intransigence, then threatened and cursed them until they gave in.

Looking up at Sam, who was looking over the wall of the APC anxiously, Hans called softly, "They surrender. You can take them now."

"Stay there," Sam said, glancing nervously behind, "We're already in sight of their tanks. If they see us loading up prisoners, they'll know what we're up to, and there'll be trouble, I tell ya."

Motioning for the two soldiers to stay low, Hans crawled toward the APC and peered through the tracks just as the General reached the first Soviet tank.

Even from the distance, Hans could hear the General shouting words like "no show," "insult," and "outrage" to the lead tank commander, who was looking confused and apologetic.

Hans sighed in relief. The more this encounter was about courtesy and etiquette, the less likely it was to become a shooting matter.

In moments, the General haughtily turned his tank away from the hapless Soviet Captain and started driving back to the convoy. Hans could have cheered as he saw the Soviet tanks forming up to leave.

He was just about to tell the two Germans soldiers to prepare to load up when a movement caught his eye.

Prisoner of War

A Soviet GAZ-67 four-wheel-drive vehicle sped in and pulled up at the left of the General's tank just before it reached the convoy. The General stopped his tank as a hawk-faced Soviet Colonel stepped out of his vehicle.

"Comrade General, a moment of your time, please," came a sharp and commanding voice. "I am Colonel Dorokhov, 3rd Regiment, 395th Rifle Division. This is my sector of responsibility."

"Ah, Colonel," began the General, "So glad you are here. We came to meet your Division Commander for lunch to cement the friendship and alliance between our two nations. But when we got to the rendezvous point, there was no one there to meet us!

"Since then, we have been driving around looking for any Soviet units to establish communications and get an explanation for this outrage! Your tank Captain there says he has no idea of this *most* important meeting."

"I know of no such meeting, Comrade General, and am mortified at this breach of protocol. Rest assured, I will forward this message to my superiors as soon as possible, vigorously pursue the matter and see to it the appropriate persons are punished." replied the Colonel quickly.

Hans started to worry.

The General had evidently bullied the tank captain with little difficulty, but this Colonel would not be so easily intimidated. In a single stroke, he had deflected and nullified the main thrust of the General's ploy to distract the Soviets.

Smoothly, the Colonel carried on, "However, of greater concern now is your personal safety, Comrade General. We have reports that there are German forces about. Have you, by any chance, encountered them?"

"A few stragglers here and there," replied the General airily, "We dealt with them. No trouble at all."

"I commend you on your efficiency and rejoice at your safety, General," said Dorokhov in a tone that meant anything but that.

With the suddenness of a viper striking, he abruptly changed tack and asked, "So did you kill them?"

Hans flinched at the venom in Dorokhov's voice, and he started to shiver. He had seen eyes like his before. Like those of Hauptmann Brandt. Cold, merciless, bent on killing their victims.

And utterly relentless.

Meanwhile, the General maintained his pose and replied loftily, "Probably. I don't take Sit-Reps from privates and corporals. What do you think my junior officers are paid for?

The Colonel started to stroll casually toward the convoy.

Hans was seized by fear as he realized the Colonel intended to check them out thoroughly and would not let them go until he finished! In another minute, he would walk around the APC and spot Hans and the two men in the ditch. There was no way to load and hide them in the APC unless...

Urgently, Hans called to Sam in a hushed voice and said, "Shoot us!"

"What?" came the startled reply.

"Shoot us! The only good Germans here are dead ones," he hissed and jumped back into the ditch, joining the two men.

Dorokhov drew closer to their APC.

In a conversational tone, he asked the General, "Are you sure there are no more Germans here?"

"No more Germans," replied the General.

Suddenly, Sam burst out of the APC, jumped into the ditch, and fired three times at the Germans' heads before they could scream.

"No more *live* Germans," amended the General blandly, without skipping a beat.

Hans hissed to the two men, *"Stell dich tot!"*

Play dead.

Hans slumped to the ground heavily, his helmet rolling off his head, and the other two men followed suit without hesitation. Sam motioned for Jerome and the three scouts to help him, and they hurriedly started to load the bodies onto the APC.

Dorokhov, surprised at the unexpected action, recovered and started walking closer again, but the Sergeant Major was there.

He had started moving as soon as Sam fired and cut directly in front of the Soviet Colonel, blocking the Soviet officer's path to the APC with his tank.

"Get that soldier here in front of me, NOW!" thundered the Sergeant Major. Sam passed the body he was carrying to Jerome and ran over to the Sergeant Major's tank, nearly tripping in his haste.

"Of all the blind, incompetent, useless soldiers in the great American Army, how did you come to be in my detail?" roared the Sergeant Major at Sam.

Getting red in the face, he continued shouting, "How could you miss three Germans sitting in a ditch behind your back? The General could've been killed! *I* could've been killed! You don't call clear until you've bloody cleared the area!"

"Sir, yes, sir!" Sam cried out desperately.

The Sergeant Major's voice dropped to a low menacing snarl, "God help me, but if I could demote you, I would."

Then he raised his voice to a shout, "But you're already as low as it gets in this army, so I'm just going to have to punish you the old-fashioned way when we get back!"

Sam went pale, and he shook so hard that his teeth chattered. "Sir, yes, sir!" he shouted.

"Now, get out of my sight before I shoot you myself!" yelled the Sergeant Major, fumbling at his sidearm.

Sam fled into the APC with the dead Germans and slammed the door shut.

The General turned back to face the Colonel and said grumpily, "Forgive the scene, but my Sergeant Major gets twitchy when my men can't see to the safety of their own general."

Shaking his head in resignation, he looked around and said, "I can see there is nothing left for me to do here. Please convey my regards to your superiors, but I have lost my appetite for lunch. Tell them we will have to meet another time."

With that, he wheeled the tank around and drove off without waiting for a reply.

In the APC, Hans held his breath until the convoy started moving.

Then, sitting up, he glared at the two new prisoners in his vehicle, whacked the nearer one on his helmet, and began scolding them for their stubbornness that could have gotten all of them killed. The two soldiers sheepishly nodded their thanks to him and the Americans.

The APC picked up speed, and Hans relaxed a little, enjoying the coolness of the wind blowing through his hair.

Wait. Wind? In his hair?

With a start, he suddenly realized his helmet was missing.

He must have dropped it when Sam fired at him in the ditch.

Reflexively Hans popped his head up to look back and gasped. The hawk-faced Soviet Colonel had picked up his helmet and was curiously examining the blue sticker on it.

Then he abruptly looked up toward the retreating APC before Hans could duck, and their eyes met for an instant.

Hans's heart sank when he saw a slow, cruel smile cross Dorokhov's face just as the APC accelerated and took him out of sight.

Chapter 50

"He knows," said Hans quietly to the group as they gathered in the General's tent for a debrief.

"Are you sure?" asked Major Schmidt, who had been waiting for them when they returned and joined them.

Hans nodded miserably, "The Soviet Colonel saw me."

"But if he didn't see the rest of your uniform, he wouldn't know you were German," said Sam hopefully. "Especially since you didn't have your helmet on."

"That's because *he* had my helmet, sticker and all," said Hans gloomily.

The room fell silent as everyone digested the information.

Lieutenant Harris began, "So he knows one of the "executed" soldiers was already a prisoner. It wouldn't make sense for us to shoot him after we stickered him. And if he saw him alive in the APC, then ...."

"He knows," finished the General firmly, echoing Hans. "I saw his eyes. We weren't fooling him, even without the antics of those two in the trench. He just didn't have an excuse to challenge us openly."

"I'm sorry, everyone," said Hans regretfully. "I've compromised everything."

The General said, "But nevertheless, you helped with everyone we saved today, and we all got back safely."

Hans nodded, then said worriedly, "But there are still more Germans to the south. So we need to go again. Tomorrow's mission...."

"Is tomorrow's problem," said the General. "We'll deal with it once we get more information."

With that, the General dismissed the group to rest.

Later in the evening, when the intelligence report was collated and ready, the General gathered the officers together first to review what information they had for the next day's missions before the rest of the men arrived.

"Any idea which unit they are?" asked Major Schmidt.

The General showed him the intelligence report.

The Major pursed his lips as he read it.

"I know those markings. 2nd Battalion from our sister Regiment. Tough unit, which explains why they're still around. But probably reduced to company size now," he said, still scanning the report.

"How likely are they to surrender?" asked the General.

"They're not," said Major Schmidt flatly. "The CO would be better suited in an SS Division, and his company commanders are all the same. Tough, die-hard bastards. They're just as likely to shoot at you as the Soviets."

"Then we'd better go in first and talk to them, right?" asked Hans.

"They're just as likely to shoot at us, too, if they see us in German uniforms, unarmed, with a blue sticker. They don't take kindly to desertion or surrender," said Major Schmidt moodily.

Lieutenant Harris asked, "What if *we* surrendered to *them* so we could get close enough to talk?"

Major Schmidt shook his head, "They weren't taking prisoners the last time I checked. And that's when things were going well for us. I won't let you risk yourselves for my countrymen in that way."

He paused and said thoughtfully, "I'd better come along for this one."

The General protested immediately.

"No can do, Wolfgang, it's too dangerous. You're in charge of the prisoners here. We'd be idiots to risk our highest-ranking officer out in the field like... uh..." and faltered as Major Schmidt gave him a withering look.

"...like you Americans do?" asked Major Schmidt, coolly.

Hans hid a smile as the General squirmed.

"Oh, alright," said the General irritably. "You can come along, but no heroics, understood? I already have my hands full with this one here jumping into trenches against orders."

He said the last comment nodding to Hans, who grinned ruefully as the rest of the rescue team filed in for the briefing.

"Alright, if everyone's here, let's begin," said the General.

To Hans's surprise, it was Major Schmidt who took the floor.

Moving to stand by the map on the wall, he picked up the pointer and began speaking in crisp, near-perfect English.

"Gentlemen, tomorrow we intend to head out again across the Elbe to see if we can find more of my errant countrymen. This time, we turn right and head south where there are reports of significant German units holed up here," he slapped the map with his pointer, "and possibly here," indicating a section further east.

"Our aim is to engage German forces in the first location, where the terrain is suited for defense," he said.

"Those in the second area, if they have not yet retreated back to the first position, are already dead men," he said bleakly, "We can do no more good there."

He pointed at the first position again, "There might be up to a reinforced company left still fighting. Not a threat to the Soviet forces lined up to their east, but certainly more than enough to destroy our little band should they choose to engage."

Major Schmidt carried on, "If we know they are there, the Red Army certainly knows they are there too. Up till now, they hadn't moved to destroy them. Perhaps they don't want to waste more men and are just waiting for the war to be over? Or perhaps they are saving this last morsel for dessert."

There was no humor at all in his last comment.

"However, if the Soviets are aware of what we have been doing and what we intend to do tomorrow, that may change," said Major Schmidt. "They may decide to wipe out this last pocket out of spite rather than let them fall into our hands."

Drawing vertical lines with his pointer, the Major indicated, "German defenses, such as there might be, will be deployed along the north-south line facing east. The terrain dictates it. Think of a series of large solid waves, and you'd have an idea of what it really looks like. A frontal attack against such a line of defenses would be a bastard to conduct. But with a full division, the Soviets could do it easily."

The General stood, and Major Schmidt nodded, giving him the floor.

"Here's how things stand then, gentlemen," said the General. "First and foremost, great job today. Nobody got hurt. We saved quite a few. And most importantly, while we're quite certain they know what we are doing, the Soviets don't *quite* have enough reason to accuse us openly. So for now, we're still allies, and we'll play that card as hard as we can until we can't play it no more."

His voice became serious as he said, "But tomorrow will be a different situation. Aside from the Soviets, we are coming against a German force large enough to obliterate us instead of the small pockets of soldiers we met today."

One of the men raised a hand, and the General nodded for him to speak, "Sir, what about going in with a larger force. A full tank battalion? No way they're are gonna fight that. At least we take the possibility of the Germans blowing us up out of the equation?"

The General was already shaking his head before he'd even finished.

"We can't do that," he said. "If we bring in any force large enough to make a difference in a fight against the German company, we become a real threat to the Soviets, and they'd have to respond. We don't want to fight the Soviets. Yet."

Drawing a breath and puffing his cheeks as he exhaled, the General continued, "No, if we do this, we have to do it the same way. Same force, same drill, hope the Soviets don't ask too many questions before we get the Germans, hope the Germans don't start shooting before we can talk to them. We'll see what we can do."

Looking around the room so he made eye contact with every man, the General said earnestly, "Like today's operation, tomorrow's mission is strictly volunteers-only.

We have no official backing from our government or anyone above me. If it goes wrong and anything happens to us, we're on our own. You have all given of yourselves admirably today, and I can ask no more of you. If anyone wants to sit this one out, you can just say so with your head held high."

The Sergeant Major, who until now had been completely silent as he loomed in the back of the tent, rumbled, "Of all the cockamamie schemes you've ever come up with, Sir, this one takes the cake. You want us to go out tomorrow, rescue a German company that might not want to be rescued, are strong enough to wipe us out, might just try and do that, while facing off an entire Soviet division, who, once they find out what we're up to, will probably want to wipe us out too."

The General grinned wolfishly, "That's exactly what I'm saying, Sergeant Major. Well, are you in?"

The Sergeant Major grumbled irritably, "Well, somebody's gotta watch your ass, Sir."

The men chuckled and nodded as murmurs of assent rippled around the room.

"That's it then. We leave at dawn," said the General.

"Attention," called the Sergeant Major, and everyone scrambled to their feet as the General waved "at ease" as he left.

In a few moments, the room was empty except for Hans and Major Schmidt.

"I sure hope we don't accidentally kick off another war before this one's even ended," said Major Schmidt gloomily.

"Would that actually happen?" asked Hans skeptically.

Major Schmidt sighed, "The Americans and Soviets hate each other with a passion that is almost holy. They were already squaring up to fight each other until we got in the way....

"We just *had* to attack them *both* first, and look what happened. Now that they're done with us, I think they're going to fight each other."

But Hans wasn't listening anymore.

Instead, he stared at Major Schmidt as though seeing him for the first time.

He had stopped short when he found the Major's first remarks startlingly familiar. The wheels of his mind turned, and memories clicked into place like the final pieces of a jigsaw puzzle.

Of his commander's seemingly encyclopedic knowledge of matters far above his station. Of how the officers senior to him, even the American General himself, often deferred to his opinion.

His memories flashed to his graduation day. A heated conversation overheard. The click-clack of Gestapo boots. A one-star general arrested....

Suddenly, Hans *knew.*

"If you say so... *Generalleutnant*," replied Hans softly.

Major Schmidt stiffened, then looked at Hans and nodded his head slowly.

"So now you know who I really am," he said heavily.

Hans said, "I was there by the door that day."

The Major sighed and nodded soberly.

They walked in silence for a while, passing Sam and Jerome as they prepared their APC for the next day's mission.

"Why are they doing this?" Hans mused to the Major.

"I don't know," said the Major, shaking his head.

There was an awkward silence.

"Why are *you* doing this?" Hans then asked.

The Major looked reflective for a while, then replied, "The same reason you are."

Hans nodded. There was no need to explain. It was clear enough to both of them.

Saved from extinction by the very ones they fought and tried to kill, shown mercy beyond anything they had a right to expect…. They both knew such grace could never be repaid.

But it could be passed on.

So the least they could do now was to help save as many of their countrymen as possible. If they died in the attempt, well… that was what should have happened to them anyway. They would not lose anything they could rightfully keep.

"That was a good briefing just now, Generalleutnant," Hans said cheekily.

"Of course," said Major Schmidt modestly, "he was one of my best students after all." And he strode off, leaving the flabbergasted Oberleutnant behind, jaw hanging open.

Chapter 51

7th May 1945—East of Elbe

The next day, Hans found himself in the APC again with Sam and Jerome for company. Major Schmidt had found another helmet and given it to him before getting into the other APC, and Sam dutifully slapped on a blue sticker when Hans boarded. Then the rescue convoy drove across the bridge, turned right, and headed south.

Soon, singly or in pairs, tired and frightened German soldiers emerged from hiding holding white flags. They were quickly stickered and loaded up in the vehicles.

It was late morning when they encountered more serious trouble.

The convoy rumbled to a stop, and word filtered back to Hans's APC that a lone German soldier was ahead. He was deeply entrenched, armed to the teeth, including a mounted machine gun, and had already fired his rifle at the General's tank.

As a purely physical threat, he wasn't much of one against a tank.

Especially since his first shot had missed.

However, as he had shown a willingness to shoot first and talk later, the General refused to let Hans or Major Schmidt expose themselves to speak with him.

Instead, he moved his own tank closer so he could talk to the lone soldier.

As he did, Hans overheard the driver yelling to Sam that Soviet forces were spotted less than one kilometer away and headed toward them.

Hans tuned in anxiously to the encounter at the trench. As things were going, while the General could speak some German, it wasn't anywhere fluent enough to convince the increasingly agitated soldier they were trying to help him.

And, from the halting English coming from the soldier, it was clear he spoke even less English than the General did German.

It was also clear that as his voice rose higher and higher, he was getting more upset. It sounded like he was going to cry.

Hans looked on worriedly as Jerome reluctantly cocked the vehicle-mounted M2 machine gun and took aim. The German soldier was close to panic and could start shooting soon. And with the Soviet forces approaching, there was no time to talk him down.

Hans gnashed his teeth in frustration as it looked like, for the first time, the rescue convoy would have to shoot a German soldier they were trying to rescue.

Then, the soldier's voice broke as he started sobbing in a warbling baritone.

Hans had a strange sense of having experienced this before.

So he took a risk and peeked over the armored wall of his vehicle to get a look. His eyes widened when his eyes fell on two stripes and three diamonds on the soldier's epaulet, then onto a familiar face, in a very familiar expression.

He stood up in his vehicle and bellowed, "YOU!"

With a speed that belied his size, Hans vaulted over the vehicle's side and landed on his feet. He rose to full height, face red and eyes ablaze, and he began to stride toward the trench like a god of war.

"Idiot! Imbecile!" Hans screamed in German. "You cry like a baby when threatened with death, but now when someone is trying to save you, you decide to show backbone?"

Then he unleashed a string of curses that had the German prisoners who heard them wincing uncomfortably.

In the trench, Wilhelm Hahn, youngest-ever Head Cadre Leader in the *Hitlerjugend,* blanched and tried to scramble up the other side to flee the coming wrath. But he missed a step, slipped, and slid back down miserably into the trench.

Wilhelm desperately tried to crawl away, but Hans jumped into the trench and actually stepped on the boy's feet, pinning him down with his size 14 boots.

Then, grabbing him by the collar, Hans pulled him close and snarled at his face, threatening the boy with oblivion by his own hand if he did not have the sense to surrender to save his own life.

Releasing Wilhelm's feet and climbing out, Hans imperiously pointed at all the equipment and weapons in the trench, demanding *immediate* action from the boy, making clear that the threat of annihilation had not been abated, merely forestalled.

As they deployed in a defensive formation, the Americans couldn't help grinning as the boy scrabbled about in panic, trying to unload his rifle, dismantle the machine gun tripod, and surrender his spare magazines all at the same time.

Needless to say, he failed in all three. Then, to the amusement of the impromptu audience, Hans roared in impatience and leaped into the trench with another long, single-breathed ripple of oaths.

He snatched whatever Wilhelm was holding in his hands and threw them out of the trench. Then, swearing furiously, he rummaged around some more, tossing out yet more offending items.

Out flew two magazines and the tripod. Then a pistol, a grenade...

GRENADE!

As one, the Americans dived down hard for cover. Even the General and Sergeant Major ducked down into their commander's hatch.

When nothing happened after a few seconds, the men slowly and shakily rose to their feet. Hans, still bent over, was muttering and throwing more items out. Rifle, machine gun, more magazines...

The Hitler Youth knife sailed a particularly long distance through the air before clattering off a rock.

Lastly, out flew the Hitler Youth Captain himself as Hans flung him out of the trench. The men watched in amazement as the boy careened through the air, legs swinging wildly.

He landed on his feet in a run, dashed to the nearest American soldier, and hugged him tightly, almost knocking him over as he tried to put the American between Hans and himself.

The amused soldier stickered the boy as the Sergeant Major barked at them to get moving.

Hans, utterly spent now, climbed out of the trench and grumpily mounted his vehicle.

He was not at all surprised when Wilhelm chose to sit in the other one.

They drove off just as the first Soviet soldier appeared at the tree line, too far away to interfere with the small convoy of American vehicles tearing off south at full speed.

In his vehicle, Hans allowed himself a few tears.

Of relief at finding Wilhelm unharmed after presuming he was dead.

But of regret too.

For all his bravado and heroics, his example to the boys had been a sham. Pure, deluded hubris. And worse than a pointless lie was one that destroyed the liar and all those around him.

In a flash, he saw Tomas lying dead on the ground, a consequence of Hans's foolish pride and hatred. Then, in Josef's eyes, he saw his own mindless faith in a madman when the boy returned him his Hitler Youth knife. In Wilhelm, he saw the same stubborn defiance and enmity against those who would save him.

Shaking his head to himself, Hans decided from now on, if he was ever going to fight, it was only be to rescue others. And he prayed that would be enough.

Chapter 52

Less than an hour later, they heard the unmistakable chatter of machine-gun fire coming from the southeast. As the convoy was due north of the German company, the sound of fighting in that direction meant the second, more eastern German position was being attacked.

Without speaking to each other, the General and Sergeant Major gave quick commands to their drivers, and both tanks roared off at full speed. The remaining vehicles gunned their engines to keep up. In minutes they came up within sight of the entrenched German company.

They all paused to take in the sights and sounds before them.

To the south, directly in front of them, was the last operational German company. As Major Schmidt had predicted, the land around that area rose and fell in shallow humps like waves approaching the river. The soldiers were deployed in four lines parallel to the river and nearly in line with the American convoy.

To their left, the sounds of fighting drew closer and closer. Obviously, the eastern position had been overrun, and any survivors were fleeing for their lives. Shouting came from the main German position, and there was a series of click-clacks as every soldier cocked his weapon and settled down into firing positions.

It was clear they were only waiting for their fleeing comrades to reach them before they started shooting freely at their pursuers.

We're too late, thought Hans in dismay.

The General and the Sergeant Major exchanged a single glance.

Without words, they communicated and decided what to do. The General nodded once at Lieutenant Harris, who gulped and frantically began to work his radio. Then he turned around and looked every man in the eye.

"I'm going in," the General said simply. "Are you with me?"

Shouts of "Yes, Sir!" and "Aye, aye!" resounded from the little group. His gaze rested on Hans and Major Schmidt, and they both nodded solemnly.

Addressing Major Schmidt, he asked, "Still think your countrymen would shoot you as you are?"

"Yes," replied the Major tersely. "Nonetheless, we have to try. Drop us just out of range of their weapons. We'll run in from there."

The General shook his head and said, "Too dangerous. Tanks to hold off the Soviets and buy you some time. APCs to bring you right into their lines so you can talk to them up close within the vehicles."

"You will be fired upon, General," said Major Schmidt softly. "It is better that Hans and I just go openly."

Again, the General shook his head and said, "No can do. They'll just shoot you as you run in."

Major Schmidt looked like he was going to argue when Hans suddenly cried, "Wait!"

Everyone looked at him in expectation.

"I have an idea," he said.

Looking to Major Schmidt, he asked urgently, "Do you remember my raid on the Division HQ?"

Prisoner of War

Major Schmidt frowned in confusion, then realization dawned on him, and he grinned viciously and nodded.

Hans took off his helmet and started trying to peel the blue sticker off, but his large fingers couldn't find an edge. Absently, he tossed it to Sam and told him, "Get the sticker off, please." Major Schmidt passed his to Jerome with the same instructions.

Then they both took belts from the recently captured Germans and started putting them on.

Hans explained as he donned battle gear for the first time since he surrendered.

"That German company would view captured German soldiers as no better than deserters and shoot them on sight."

Then he said, slyly, "German *reinforcements*, however, are an entirely different matter."

"If they see us running in as active soldiers joining the fight, they'd welcome us with open arms. Then we can get close enough to talk to them," concluded Hans.

The General objected, "The Germans might not shoot at you, but the entire Soviet Division will. It's too dangerous. I forbid it."

"With respect, General, we weren't asking for your permission," said Hans calmly as he took back his helmet from Sam and strapped it on his head.

The General's eyes bulged in surprise.

"You *did* say all prisoners were free to leave at any time, but only to the east of the Elbe," said Major Schmidt with a grin as he strapped on his helmet. "We are east of the Elbe, and we are leaving now."

"I also said no weapons," grated the General, realizing what they were about to do.

"No weapons as we leave," said Hans reassuringly, showing his empty hands as he and Major Schmidt climbed down from their vehicle. "There, we've left."

Then he picked up a rifle and said, "Oops, where did this come from? I'll just hang it to it now. Nothing to do with you."

As he spoke, shouting erupted from the German lines as the last survivor of their front position made it back.

With no friendlies to watch for anymore, their longer-range weapons engaged the approaching Soviet forces without restraint. Heavy machine guns opened up as the first line of Soviet troops appeared over a ledge.

Two were hit. The rest dropped for cover and started firing back, and battle was joined.

Hans looked back at the General, his expression serious again. "We have to do this, General. Please don't stop us."

The General glared at Hans, then he said through gritted teeth, "Alright, you have three minutes. Then we're coming in whether you like it or not."

Hans nodded and saluted. Then, cocking his rifle, he turned to Major Schmidt and said, "Ready, Major?"

"Just like old times, Hans," laughed his commander.

And they both raced off toward the German company.

Hans had a strong sense of deja vu as he approached the German company's left flank.

Memories of his daring raids in American uniforms invaded his mind. The mouth-drying fear as he met with the victims he would outright defraud and trick. The heart-pounding tension when he played his hand and prayed he wasn't found out.

Why was it then, now that he was playing the part of himself, closing in on his own comrades, did he feel even more terror at being found out?

As the first German soldiers spotted them and yelled, Hans dutifully fired a few rounds in the general direction of the Soviets. Major Schmidt did the same. Then they both sprinted toward the beckoning soldier in the rear of the German formation.

Hans reached the man and breathlessly explained who he was and what he was doing. Pointing excitedly to the north, he urged those within earshot to head down to the river itself, where they could make their way to the American convoy out of sight of their attackers.

In the meantime, Major Schmidt, with typical confidence and efficiency, simply ordered the men he encountered to flee, and they did.

He probably outranks the commander here so he can get away with it, thought Hans enviously as he resumed persuading the first group of men.

The first two needed no further invitation and took off, abandoning their heavy machine gun position. The following two hesitated. One with a look of contempt for Hans, the other with a look of concern toward the front lines.

Now Hans faltered.

All along, the obstacles anticipated in this mission had been centered around getting him safely to German lines rather than what to do once he got in.

He never imagined that any German soldiers under fire would refuse a genuine offer of safety from imminent obliteration. The first soldier undoubtedly thought he was a coward—which Hans found particularly galling, while the second was obviously concerned for his fellows in the front. Despite his pleas, both refused to move off and surrender.

"Some of these idiots don't want to surrender!" he shouted to Major Schmidt as the Major dispatched yet another soldier.

"Remind you of someone?" came the curt reply.

Hans grimaced. He had walked right into that one.

Sighing to himself, he squared his shoulders and quickly thought of another plan.

"Americans to the left, fire!" Hans shouted suddenly and fired a few rounds toward the north, praying those in the convoy were keeping low. A few heads popped up, and, seeing a tall, blond Oberleutnant taking command, rallied to him.

"Left flank, by the river, follow me!" he yelled and rose from the ground. Five men followed him as he dashed toward the river and ran along the water's edge.

After a lung-bursting sprint, Hans deemed they were almost back at the convoy's position, so he cut right sharply and ran up the bank, straight into full view of the two tanks and APCs.

When the men following him caught up, they found themselves in front of and very exposed to a small but powerful American armored force. So when Hans threw his guns down and raised his hands, they quickly followed suit.

Quickly, Sam stickered them and sent them toward the ambulance where the rest of those who surrendered waited.

Hans huffed and puffed as he tried to catch his breath and prepare to run back when the General called to him.

"You're doing a great job, Hans, but we're out of time. Look," he said, pointing to the battle.

Hans's heart sank as he saw what the General was pointing at.

Prisoner of War

The Soviet forces had formed up and were attacking the German front lines head-on, and a furious firefight was unfolding. The Germans held against the first wave, but the left flank, bereft of their heavy machine gun, and the soldiers Hans had convinced to surrender, was under tremendous pressure.

Hans cursed. Could he do nothing right? All he had done was make things worse. The very success of his mission to save German lives made it easier for the Soviets to break through and butcher everyone else.

The General plainly came to the same conclusion.

Pointing to Hans, then to the APC, he said in a tone that brooked no argument, "Get in. Now."

Chapter 53

As he climbed into the APC, Sam and Jerome welcomed him warmly. Hans automatically checked his weapon. So far, he had fired it only for show. But, he prayed, when this day was over, he would not need to fire it in anger.

Peering over the vehicle wall, Hans saw the convoy was preparing to move, but, for some reason, all eyes were on the Comms Officer in his jeep. Suddenly Lieutenant Harris looked to the General and gave him a quick thumbs up.

The General squared his shoulders, took a deep breath, and muttered, "Let's go."

Engines roared to life as all vehicles throttled up and charged directly toward the German lines even as the Soviet forces regrouped and started working their way across the field, getting ever closer to the Germans.

Prisoner of War

They were no more than a hundred meters from the defenders now.

The two American tanks lined up and headed directly toward the center of the German formation between their second and third ranks, heedless of any small arms fire coming their way from the Germans.

The unarmored jeeps sped toward the last row and veered off at the last minute. The three scouts jumped off and started running in, staying low.

The slightly slower APCs angled toward the very front line instead.

As his M3 Halftrack raced across the field, Jerome loaded and cocked the vehicle weapon. Then, with an ear-splitting cry that rose above the sounds of battle, he let rip with his Browning 50-cal machine gun.

Hans stared in amazement at the portly soldier in front of him. Chubby Jerome. Baby-faced Jerome. Never-ever-heard-him-speak Jerome... was suddenly transformed into a fighting machine.

His eyes were alight with a fierce, vicious joy. His face was curled up in an intense scowl as he screamed, seemingly without the need to pause for breath. His battle cry was like an eagle's screech, piercing through the sounds of weapons firing and men shouting. Hans was overcome with awe at the sight of his friend in a battle frenzy.

But soon, he saw this was far more than just a soldier in a berserker rage.

With a precision that should not have been possible, Jerome delivered a steady line of fire inches in front of the German positions without actually hitting them. Occasionally, he would apparently lose control and let the line of bullets drift toward the advancing Soviets, who had no choice but to take cover.

He effectively kept the two sides separate with a steady stream of bullets up and down the line. They could still shoot at each other, of course, but the Soviets could not overrun the German lines.

Only now did Hans realize that in the entire Corps, there was no better man to have on the 50-cal cannon than the quiet and unassuming Jerome Harding.

Then Sam slapped him on the helmet and yelled, "Go, go, go!"

Hans noticed with a start that they had stopped just meters from the German positions.

He was on.

Prisoner of War

Jumping off the side of the APC while Sam scrambled out the back door, Hans landed on his feet and sprinted toward German lines once again, keeping low and shouting in German for his countrymen to surrender to the Americans.

By now, most needed no further encouragement. The few that hesitated only had to look to their front to see the seething mass of Soviet troops gathering before they capitulated and surrendered.

Sam quickly slapped on blue stickers and urged the prisoners to retreat to the rear positions.

As the fleeing soldiers crawled over the trenches behind, they spread the word of their rescue, and their comrades began to surrender too, dropping weapons and lowering their heads for the American soldiers to slap stickers on without even asking.

For now, it looked like the rescue was actually working.

Held off by fire from Jerome's 50-cal, the Soviets could not mount a direct charge on the Germans. And with the two American tanks apparently attacking well within the German position, they didn't dare fire freely for fear of hitting allied tanks, especially the one decorated with a three-starred flag.

Hans grinned as he watched the General and Sergeant Major dutifully attack each trench with machine-gun fire, but always *after* the occupants had fled.

Careful to stay hidden from Soviet sight, Hans moved deeper in, using the tanks to conceal himself. He called urgently to his confused countrymen and sent them back to safety.

In this fashion, with Hans keeping abreast of the tanks, they slowly but steadily made their way south, systematically clearing the German company.

At last, they edged up the incline until they reached the largest trench, situated on a slight rise, defended by a heavy machine gun. It was obviously the Company Commander's position.

Major Schmidt was already there and looked like he had just finished a furious argument with the company commander, a fierce-looking Hauptmann.

Reluctantly, the company commander shouted a few orders, which were quickly relayed to the remaining men around him. In response, the machine gun crew and the Company HQ abandoned their weapons and quickly made their way to the river.

Prisoner of War

Major Schmidt spotted Hans and gave a thumbs up. Hans grinned back in delight. They had done it!

But his smile froze on his face as, to his amazement, the German company commander climbed out of this trench and started running south, *away* from the Americans, shouting as he went.

Baffled, Hans ran up to the top of the high ground to see what was happening. He reached the heavy machine gun nest at the crest of the incline and finally had sight of what lay down the other side of the slope.

His cried out in despair.

Below were *more* German soldiers deployed in trenches. At least a platoon strength. Blocked from view by the high ground where the Company HQ had dug in, the Americans hadn't seen them at all.

To the left, out of reach of Jerome's cannon fire because of the high ground between them, the leading Soviet line was attacking the German platoon unhindered by American interference.

Scores of dead bodies littered the field in front of the German line, testimony to their tenacious defense, but more Soviets were forming up behind. It was only a matter of time before they broke through and killed everyone.

517

The General had obviously come to the same conclusion as his tank roared to life and surged forward, the Sergeant Major's just seconds behind him.

Together, they charged across the German front line, carefully firing their machine guns between the two battling forces as they went, frustrating the Soviet attack with their apparently inept maneuvering.

Then, from beyond the German platoon's position to the south, a Soviet flanking force appeared. And many of them held in their hands a bulbous shape that was all too familiar to Hans.

A German *Panzerfaust*.

How often had he delighted at the sight of the German single-shot anti-tank rocket fired against American Shermans with deadly effect?

Now, presumably captured by the Soviets, at least three were being clumsily prepared for use. And from how the Soviet squad looked and pointed, it was clear the lead tank was their target. The two American tanks, busy trying to keep the Soviet main attack back, seemed oblivious to the danger.

His heart in his mouth, Hans panicked. What could he do? The tanks were too far for him to alert in time. And even so, what could *they* do? Attack the Soviets openly? It would be a declaration of war.

Hans looked at the rifle in his hand. Up till now, it had been a prop for his charade as an active German soldier. He had studiously avoided any direct action against the Soviets, lest his status as a POW would be compromised, if not in their eyes, then at least his own.

To fire now would invite the wrath of the Soviets upon himself, and not even the Americans would be able to save him this time.

But to do nothing would be the end of the man who saved his life.

In the end, Hans realized there wasn't really any choice at all.

He threw down his rifle.

Chapter 54

Hans jumped into the machine-gun nest, swung the weapon to the right, cocked it, and fired.

A hail of bullets whizzed into the Soviet flanking force, and the men dropped their *Panzerfäuste* and dived to the ground. Hans kept a steady stream of fire, pinning them down.

The German squad at that edge, alerted to the threat on their right, charged the enemy. Hans stopped firing for fear of hitting them, then cried out in anguish as half of them died destroying the flanking force.

The two American tanks, having reached the edge of the German position, turned sharply right and circled back, rolling over the second and third line of trenches like sheepdogs herding sheep to safety.

Prisoner of War

At one position, one soldier was so engrossed in the battle that he did not see the Sergeant Major's tank looming from his right. The tank had to stop when he did not flee. Out popped the Sergeant Major like an angry bear and threw a magazine at the soldier.

It hit him squarely on the helmet. The soldier turned to see an American tank a few feet away and scrambled to the rear in panic.

The Sergeant Major sank back into his commander's hatch and perfunctorily fired into the empty trench as his tank slowly moved on.

The remaining German soldiers started to abandon their positions and crawled to the rear under cover of the tanks. But it was the wounded that were making painfully slow progress, if at all. A few were helped by their comrades, but some simply collapsed or gave up.

Hans got ready to run down and help them, but as the tanks turned, the Soviets renewed their attack.

Cursing, Hans jumped back behind the machine gun, swung it left, and fired, raking the ground just in front of the attacking Soviet line, halting one section of the charge.

But, as he was firing virtually head-on toward the Soviet line, he couldn't cover all the angles at the same time. Soon, two groups gathered to the left and right of Hans's arc of fire and prepared to run in. Hans's thoughts raced as he tried unsuccessfully to resolve the quandary: To pin one group down would allow the other through.

With rising panic, Hans realized that he would soon have to kill Soviets, or let them through to kill Germans. His face pale, Hans mechanically cleared the gun as it jammed, cocked it again, and took aim at the group on the right, its frontmost soldier in his sights—the first Soviet he would kill. He closed his eyes in anguish and prepared to pull the trigger.

Then Jerome was there.

As the main German position was cleared, his APC had moved up the slope to see where their tanks had gone. It crested the high ground just as the Soviet line was preparing to stream around Hans's arc of fire.

With another shrieking battle cry, Jerome fired his M2 machine gun furiously into the front trenches, creating a wall of bullets that prevented anyone from getting through, buying the retreating Germans precious seconds.

Prisoner of War

Hans seized the opportunity to race down to the wounded soldiers.

Then Jerome's weapon jammed, and the Soviets readied themselves again.

But the General swung into action. From his position between the second and third row of trenches, he swept an arc of heavy machine-gun fire across the entire stretch of the now-empty first row. The approaching Soviet infantry happened to be in the line of fire and had no choice but to dive for cover.

Before anyone could react, the General's tank lurched forward a few meters toward the Soviet line and swiveled its turret a hundred and eighty degrees to face the German trenches.

Then, the tank's heavy cannon opened up again, strafing the empty ground wildly.

Jerome cleared his weapon and started firing again, once more cutting off Soviet access to the German soldiers and American tanks.

Meanwhile, Hans reached the first wounded man, hoisted him on his back, and ran down to the river bank. He found Sam and the three scouts hurriedly putting stickers on the surrendering Germans.

"Many wounded," was all Hans had breath to say. Sam nodded and called to the scouts, and they all followed Hans back to the battlefield and fanned out, looking for the wounded.

Hans saw each scout quickly find an injured soldier, sticker him and help him back to safety.

Then he found the next wounded soldier a little further ahead. Sam dashed in, and Hans waited for him to put a sticker on, but instead, the thin soldier shook his head and said plaintively, "I'm out of stickers. We didn't think there'd be so many here."

Hans swore.

"We'll just have to carry them back and hope no one sees us then," he snarled.

Hurriedly, Hans and Sam hoisted the casualty to his feet and were prepared to carry him when the battle suddenly took on a strangely subdued turn that made them pause.

The General and Sergeant Major were still assiduously shooting into empty ground, while Jerome—his face fixed with an apologetic smile and studiously avoiding eye contact with anyone—staunchly maintained a steady stream of fire in front of a Soviet line that was now standing and jeering at him.

The scene now resembled an angry crowd at a concert baying for a sub-standard act to get off the stage and let someone else come on.

Then an odd movement caught Hans's eye, and he stared in surprise. And surprise quickly turned to fear as a single figure, coming from somewhere in the middle, started walking forward calmly toward the General's tank, seemingly unconcerned about everything around him.

Dressed in an immaculate heavy overcoat proudly displaying three crests on each shoulder, the Soviet Colonel wasn't even wearing a helmet.

Instead, he wore a formal dress hat with a visor and carried no rifle.

With a single cutting gesture of his left hand, all fire from the Soviet forces ceased. The only sound now was Jerome's 50-cal thudding away, still maintaining the line of fire. It sounded terribly lonely now as even the American tanks ceased fire.

The Soviet Colonel walked toward the General without speeding up or slowing down, seemingly paying no heed to the line of bullets whizzing in front of him.

Jerome shifted his fire to the right to give more space between his line of fire and the Colonel, but the officer simply walked on, as though daring the American gunner to shoot him in plain sight. Jerome shifted his line again to the right even more, then gave up and stopped.

The Colonel had called his bluff.

At five meters from the General's tank, he stopped and stood with legs shoulder-width apart and his hands clasped behind his back. "Comrade General," Colonel Dorokhov called in a falsely light-hearted tone.

The General himself didn't move, but he turned his turret one hundred and eighty degrees around until he faced the Colonel squarely, the tank's main barrel pointing directly at him.

"Yes?" he answered mildly.

If the Colonel was intimidated by the tank gun aimed at his chest, he did not show it.

"What, may I ask, are you doing here?" he asked with deceptive calm.

The General made a show of looking around and answered, "Joining your attack on this last German position."

"With two tanks and two APCs," said the Colonel sarcastically.

"Yes," said the General with a straight face.

"Such a small force to attack with," said the Colonel in a derisive tone.

"You needed more help then?" the General asked innocently.

The Colonel grimaced, and his face went red in embarrassment.

Impatient with the fencing with words, he switched to the direct approach.

"We could have overrun them ourselves in minutes if you didn't get in our way with your... timely arrival," the Colonel said.

"My apologies if we held you back. We found ourselves in a position to flank them, and as field commander of this force, I made the decision to exploit that," said the General calmly.

"Your tanks were spotted deep within enemy positions," noted the Colonel.

"Overrunning the enemy with a quick, powerful armored thrust," said the General, quoting military doctrine.

"Your other tank actually stopped," pressed the Soviet officer.

"Checking to make sure there were no live Germans in that area," countered the General.

"Your APC gunner was shooting across the front of my soldiers…" began the Colonel.

"…suppressing the German front line and preventing a German charge on your men," finished the General.

"He kept shooting after they all retreated," grated the Colonel.

"He's a little… you know…slow," floundered the General unexpectedly and tried to look embarrassed.

Jerome quickly let his jaw go slack and stared blankly at the floor.

Dorokhov glared at Jerome, then looked back to the General and said accusingly, "*Your* tank shot at my men!"

"Attacking the German lines in the rear," answered the General coolly.

"Then you charged at my soldiers!" shouted the Colonel.

"Merely getting in line so as to avoid misunderstandings," explained the General.

Switching to his most reasonable tone, the General said, "You said so yourself, Colonel, that we were getting in your way. I thought it best to stop doing so."

Hans held his breath as he waited for the Colonel to respond.

By addressing the Colonel by rank now, in the most farcical part of the conversation, the General created an opening for a face-saving exit for the Colonel.

Hans desperately prayed the Colonel would accept the offer and call it a draw. But he didn't seem to be thinking about it.

In fact, he wasn't even looking at the General anymore.

A strange expression had come over his face.

A fierce hunger of unimaginable malice.

With a sudden chill, Hans realized Colonel Dorokhov was looking straight at *him*.

Chapter 55

Time stood still.

It took Hans a few seconds to fully understand what was happening now.

Dread rose in his heart as awful comprehension surfaced in his mind.

Scheiße, Scheiße, SCHEIßE! Hans thought frantically.

All along in these missions, he had been set on his task of talking to fellow Germans to convince them to surrender. So he never noticed the care the Americans took to make sure he was never exposed. It wasn't just to protect him from attack by frightened Germans; it was also to avoid observation by Soviet forces.

As a prisoner of the Americans, he was under their protection. But if he were seen participating in operations, he would be regarded as active personnel.

Prisoner of War

Active German personnel.

And active German personnel were fair game for Soviet bullets.

And here he was, caught red-handed with Sam, helping a wounded German who didn't have a sticker on his helmet.

Then, he went sick in the stomach as another realization hit him: He didn't even have *his* sticker on anymore!

With a wicked smile, Colonel Dorokhov faced the General again and said, "There seems to be some collaboration between your soldiers and the Germans, Comrade General."

"Perhaps," grunted the General noncommittally.

"In which case, I might be entitled to attack not only those Germans but also your men," said the Colonel.

"The Germans are my prisoners. My men are merely guarding them," said the General sternly.

"But I do not see blue stickers on those two Germans," said Dorokhov nastily.

"Take off your helmet," hissed Sam to Hans suddenly.

"What?" asked Hans, confused.

"Take off your helmet," repeated Sam insistently.

Hans slowly took off his helmet and stared, dumbfounded, as he saw his blue sticker loosely stuck inside.

"Didn't know where to put it just now," shrugged Sam apologetically.

Hans turned his helmet toward the Soviet Colonel and showed him the sticker.

Dorokhov looked like he had been slapped.

His face flushed as he growled, "Very well, that one is yours, but the other is mine. Mine to keep if he surrenders. Mine to kill if he doesn't."

The wounded soldier gasped in dismay and sagged between Hans and Sam, weeping as he did so.

Dorokhov's lips curled into a malicious smile of triumph as the soldier started babbling and begging incoherently.

But Hans, face drawn and pale, reached inside his helmet to pull the sticker off.

Sam realized what he was about to do and whispered, "You don't have to do this."

Hans replied in a shaking voice, "I know."

"But I want to."

And he slapped his sticker on the wounded man's helmet.

Dorokhov stared at him in shock; then, a sly look crossed his face.

He addressed the General again, but his eyes never left Hans.

"It seems we have an awkward situation here now, General. One of your prisoners has chosen not only to be active in a battle situation, but he has also chosen to leave your care."

"Perhaps," repeated the General, undisturbed.

"You, therefore, no longer have jurisdiction over him. Under the rules of combat, he is to be treated as an active combatant, or he may surrender to me!" said the Colonel gleefully.

The General leveled at him a steady gaze.

"No."

"No?" said the Colonel, raising his eyebrow theatrically.

"NO?" he said again as his voice went up an octave.

Hans felt sick.

Not only was his life forfeit, but his very presence risked the men to whom he owed his life. With a sinking sensation, he knew there was only one thing he could do.

"Stop!" called out Hans suddenly.

Looking regretfully at the General, Hans nodded his thanks to him with tears in his eyes and hoped he understood. Then he faced the Soviet Colonel and raised his hands in surrender.

"There is no need to involve the Americans in this," said Hans to Dorokhov in a trembling voice. "I surrender to you."

"I appreciated the gesture, Hans," murmured the General, "but no can do this time. Stand down."

But Dorokhov cried with mock regret, "Comrade General, if you do not agree to this, you are complicit in this man's rebellion and a renegade to your own forces. As a loyal soldier of the USSR, which is in alliance with the USA, I have no choice but to engage in capturing or destroying these renegade forces of my beloved allies."

"Do you know what your beloved Allies think of that?" cut in the Sergeant Major, snarling. He had slowly driven his tank nearer until his tank gun and coaxial cannons were pointed directly at Colonel Dorokhov.

"Threats, Sergeant Major?" said the Colonel nonchalantly, "You should be helping me arrest your General. Or are you in this too?"

Neither American said anything.

The two American APCs slowly moved in, easing in line with the two tanks facing the Soviet forces. There was a loud click-clack as Jerome changed the worn-out barrel of his M2 machine gun, reloaded a new ammunition belt, and cocked the gun meaningfully. He leaned casually over the butt of the weapon, but the threat was clear.

There was nothing slow on his usually placid face.

With rising apprehension, Hans realized it wasn't just the General who was willing to stand up for him now, but all the Americans here.

Desperately, he looked around for any way out, but like a mouse trapped in the gaze of a snake, he was utterly powerless to make any difference now.

"Come now, General, your men wish to fight?" the Colonel laughed.

"So loyal, so predictable, so *American*," he sneered.

Dorokhov scoffed, "Your two tanks and APCs might pose a challenge for an infantry company, but I have my own regiment already here on the field. And behind me is my entire division! We could wipe out your tiny force without loss and claim it was just an unfortunate accident!"

"And I don't even have to do that myself!" he exulted.

The Colonel gave a signal and pointed dramatically behind him at a ridgeline.

"Behold, the mighty Soviet armored forces!" screamed Colonel Dorokhov, still pointing as a Soviet tank company rumbled into view and lined up.

As though on cue, the lead tank's commander hefted a heavy wooden pole and raised his regimental colors high.

Hans jumped as Jerome cracked off a single shot from his 50-cal and the flagpole shattered. The Soviet captain stared in astonishment at the stump of wood remaining in his hand as the regimental colors flew in the air and landed on the ground.

Dorokhov spun around to face the Americans and shrieked, "You dare? You DARE? YOU SHOT AT MY TANK!"

Regaining his composure, the Colonel issued quick orders in a harsh voice.

Then he faced the Americans again as the Soviet tank company formed ranks and advanced menacingly. In seconds, the Colonel stood triumphantly in front of a solid wall of thirteen tanks.

He took a step forward and said in an official tone, "General, as the ranking officer of all Soviet forces here, I declare that German officer to be an escaped prisoner and subject to the rules of open combat."

"I think not," replied the General softly.

The Colonel flushed and snarled, "General, since you stand in my way, as the ranking officer of all Soviet forces here, I declare you and your men to be renegade American troops and subject to the rules of open combat."

"I think not," replied the General firmly.

The Colonel turned bright red and shouted, "General, as the ranking officer of all Soviet forces here, I will shoot you where you stand and all your friends NOW!"

"I. Think. Not." said the General grimly, with death in his eyes.

Suddenly, two P51 Mustangs appeared across the river, flying fast and low. Hans ducked instinctively as the planes zoomed directly over their position before pulling up into a steep climb, wagging their wings in salute as they did so.

Dorokhov had also ducked as they passed over, but the General remained upright in his tank, eyes fixed on the Colonel.

Then the Soviet tank commander gave a strangled cry and called, "Colonel...?" It sounded like he was speaking through clenched teeth and trying not to move his lips. Dorokhov turned in irritation to face him, then looked to where the captain was nodding.

Hans followed his gaze and gasped in amazement.

In the north, a column of American tanks rumbled into view and lazily spread out in a line pointing toward the bunched-up Soviet tanks. Hans tried to count but stopped when he reached thirty. It was at least a complete tank battalion.

"What... how dare you invade...." spluttered the Soviet Colonel indignantly.

"Search and rescue party," said the General smoothly. "When I didn't return from my battle with the German company despite Soviet help, they came looking for me."

Then, the all-too-familiar whistle of artillery suddenly sounded, and everyone looked up nervously except the General. Small eruptions appeared high in the sky behind them, over where the rest of the Soviet division was deployed.

There was a collective sigh of relief when everyone saw they were only illumination shells.

But the message was clear.

They could just as easily have been 105mm Howitzer High-Explosive shells raining death on the Soviet 395th Division.

"What are...." began the Colonel again.

"Celebrations," said the General genially. "Haven't you heard? German High Command has surrendered."

"No," the Colonel gasped, and his face twisted in anger.

Pointing imperiously at the General's tank, he shouted at his tank commander, "Destroy the American tank!"

The Soviet tank commander's jaw dropped at the command.

Looking at his superior in disbelief, he jerked one thumb and nodded his head toward the thirty-plus Sherman tanks pointed at him. Then, shaking his head in disgust, he sat down grumpily and folded his arms, clearly intending to ignore the order.

In a rage, the Colonel fumbled to open his overcoat and reach for his pistol, but the General said, "If you attempt to shoot me yourself, you'll be dead before your sidearm leaves its holster."

"By your own men," he finished, looking meaningfully at the Soviet soldiers in the front line. The Colonel turned and saw hostile and angry faces staring back at him.

Not many of his soldiers understood English well enough to follow the conversation, but the Colonel's suicidal order to attack was given in Russian. Nobody seemed pleased at all.

The General spoke again, "If you choose to start a fight here, you might get a lucky shot, and I don't survive."

Leaning forward in his hatch, he asked, "The question is, will you?" glancing at the Shermans on his left.

"Will they?" he nodded toward the Soviet troops in front of him as the Mustangs flew by again.

"Will your division?" he asked as more illumination shells exploded harmlessly over the Soviet positions.

In almost a whisper, he said, "Will Moscow?"

High in the sky, almost too small to see, a squadron of B-17 Flying Fortresses droned toward the east, leaving small contrails in their wake.

The Colonel, raging like a trapped animal, looked like he was going to leap and attack the General with his bare hands.

But the General leaned back and said coolly, "In any case, when I said "I think not" earlier, I wasn't talking about all this."

The Colonel raised a questioning eyebrow.

The General smiled, "I was referring to your assertion of your position as ranking officer on the field."

Chapter 56

As Colonel Dorokhov spluttered in outrage, another Gaz-67 pull up, and a figure stepped out. There were gasps of alarm as the front ranks of Soviet soldiers saw him and hastily snapped to attention. A slim man in an immaculate Soviet Army overcoat and commander's hat strode toward the General and Colonel.

There was one star on each of his shoulder epaulets.

"What's this, Dorokhov? Trying to start a war in my absence when we've just finished a big one?" said the man.

"General Korusevich! I thought you... you were in Moscow!" the Colonel stammered.

Then, trying to salvage the situation, Dorokhov pointed accusingly to the top of the Sherman in front of him, "This American general here has..." but stopped when he saw no one there.

The General had already climbed down the tank and was walking toward them, eyes fixed on the new arrival. The Soviet general stiffened as the American approached. Then, he snapped to attention and threw a smart salute.

"General Simpson," he said in a cautious greeting.

The General stood to attention and returned an equally smart salute.

"General Korusevich," he replied courteously.

They stared at each other for a while, then, to the astonishment of everyone there, embraced each other warmly.

"Aleksei! So good to see you alive and well!" exclaimed the General, slapping him on the back.

"William! It's been too long, my friend, too long! You're completely bald!" said the Soviet general at the same time.

Then pushing the American back and holding him at arm's lengths by the shoulders, The Soviet general looked critically at his counterpart's shoulders.

"So, they made you a three-star general then, is that what the American Army has come to now?" he said, wrinkling his nose.

"Maybe, but that means I can still get you to polish my boots, you lowly brigadier general," shot back the General, making a face.

Pointing to the stars on his shoulders, the Soviet general said ruefully, "And I only got these last month too!" And both men chuckled.

The General winked at the completely bewildered Colonel. "Yesterday, when I said I was looking to have lunch with your Division Commander, I wasn't kidding."

"But I may have gotten the day wrong, though," he mused thoughtfully, then resumed bantering with the Soviet general.

Hans, forgotten by all for the moment, lowered his hands in confusion. Clearly, things had escalated far beyond even what Dorokhov had imagined.

Then, out of the corner of his eye, he saw Major Schmidt walking toward them with a determined expression on his face.

Frantically, Hans tried to wave him back without drawing attention, but it was too late.

Prisoner of War

Dorokhov saw the Major and gasped.

Hans groaned.

Surely, even a friendly Soviet general could not overlook American collaboration with a senior German officer.

But to his amazement, General Korusevich uttered a cry of recognition as he spotted Major Schmidt, "Wolfgang! I thought we blew your Kraut buttocks from here to kingdom come last year!"

"I can still kick your skinny backside anytime, Aleks," said Major Schmidt, grinning as he walked forward to embrace the Soviet general.

"Your boys very nearly did at Stalingrad," said General Korusevich, "If *you* were there, I think they could have done it."

His comment struck a chord in them all, for suddenly, the mood turned solemn as all three men stood in silence for a while, ignoring the armies waiting around them, each deep in thought.

Hans strained to hear but could not catch most of what was being said.

Evidently, they all knew each other, probably from a training stint together, unlikely as it seemed. And a firm friendship had been built that endured even the bloody war that just ended today.

Hans sighed to himself.

Maybe this was what being a soldier was truly about. The friendship and camaraderie of those who, by necessity, have to take lives and be prepared to give their own.

It was not defined by a blind hatred of complete strangers as the Soviet Colonel and he had done. But by simply striving to do the best they could, for their own men and, if at all possible, for the other side. How different would the last six years have been if these three had been in charge of their respective countries?

The senior officers talked for another five minutes, in which time the topic had clearly shifted from past reminiscences to the current situation.

Hans fidgeted self-consciously when at one point, they all turned to look at him. Dorokhov almost fainted when the General pointed at him, and the trio turned again to gaze appraisingly at him.

They shook hands warmly and embraced when they finished, promising to keep in touch, then each went their separate ways.

General Korusevich walked briskly back to his own vehicle, waving to his discredited subordinate. "Come, Dorokhov, there will be no more fighting today, my bloodthirsty Colonel," he said lightly.

Then in a cold voice, he added, "I think you dropped your flag."

The Colonel sagged in utter defeat as his commander drove off.

Major Schmidt went off to look for the German Company Commander to organize the new prisoners. The Sergeant Major had circled his hands in the air in the universally understood signal of "pack up, we're going home" and moved off.

This left Hans the only person within the vicinity of the General, who simply stood with his hands behind his back, watching his men ready themselves to depart.

Hans moved hesitantly beside the General and joined him in watching the men.

"You... knew Major Schmidt before. And the Soviet Division Commander," Hans said. It was not a question.

"Wolfie and Aleks?" the General said, snapping out of his reverie. "Yes, we met in an officer training exchange program when we were junior officers."

His eyes went distant again as a rush of memories engulfed him.

"Aleksei and I are actually a few years older than Wolfie, but I was slow, and Aleks was held back by Soviet bureaucracy and class discrimination, so when we arrived, we were lowly lieutenants.

"Whereas your Major over here was some up-and-coming rising star in your army and was already a captain. That, and also because your country was mobilizing for war, though we didn't know at that time," he said darkly.

Shaking himself, the General continued, "Anyway, because the training course was run by a very fussy officer, he only saw ranks and not age, so Wolfie was put in charge of us. He was even made an instructor for one of the modules we had to take."

Hans smiled in anticipation of what must surely have happened next.

"Aleks and I made his life hell for that," the General chuckled, then amended, "Or at least we tried to."

"We would heckle and hiss whenever he taught until two things happened. One, we soon figured out he actually knew what he was talking about, and it was worth us shutting up and learning...." said the General, holding up one finger.

Then, counting off a second finger, he continued, "Two, after one lecture where we, to be honest, *did* go too far, he took us out to the back and beat us up. Both of us. At the same time. We never disrupted his lessons after that."

Something had Hans puzzled. He asked, "When did all this happen, Sir?"

"Before the war," came the reply.

Hans frowned, "But Hitler would never have let his officers mix with foreign officers. He feared corruption or undue influence or...."

"Before the *first* war, young man," said the General, primly.

Oh, thought Hans. *Of course.*

The General continued, "We were all in the Great War, of course, but far too junior to know what was going on, and I don't think we made much of a difference then. Then we all rose in rank and started coming across each other again. If not face to face, then as subjects of intelligence briefings as potential adversaries.

"That was hard to take. I didn't want to have to fight my friends. Especially Wolfie. I *really* didn't want to have to fight him."

"You were afraid of him," Hans said, surprised he had the nerve to say it.

The General didn't take offense.

Instead, he nodded grimly, "Yes. Yes, I was."

"Don't get me wrong, Oberleutnant, I hold my head high as a tactical and strategic commander, and I would bet my command against any other. I didn't get three stars for being a wuss.

"But Wolfie is another matter entirely. He doesn't just have the technical knowledge. He has incredible battlefield awareness, and most of all, he has the love and respect of his men. That makes him a dangerous foe. The most complete opponent."

Hans nodded in appreciation. He, of all people, understood precisely what the General meant. He had modeled his own style of leadership after Major Schmidt's.

"I modeled myself after him," said the General, unwittingly echoing Hans's thoughts. "Because he was simply the best there was. If he were on our side, we would have reached Berlin months ago. If your High Command hadn't been so stupid as to demote him, we wouldn't have made it this far."

Making a face, the General said, "As it was, even as a lowly battalion commander, he made our lives miserable. We paid dearly for every yard we took from him. Otherwise, sometimes he'd tie up entire divisions for days in ridiculously defensive positions, then disappear without loss when we finally got round to digging him out."

Looking sideways at Hans, he said dryly, "And apparently, there are reports he had a young, blond, and very savage junior commander as his sidekick wreaking havoc in American ranks whenever he raided."

Hans had the grace to blush at that.

The General continued his recollections, "Aleksei rose in rank as well. He's as good as they get. Solid, dependable, not as dynamic as Wolfie, but perhaps more suited for the Red Army. His rise was stunted by his peasant family background and his devotion to the country rather than Stalin. I'm glad he survived Stalin's Great Purge in '37."

He said, "And once the shooting started, I don't think they bothered to check too deeply about his personal loyalties then, as long as he could command.

"Wolfie survived his own indiscretion, too, talking against going to war with us. I'm glad he survived, but I'm not all that sorry he got demoted. He would have been Corps Commander or higher by now, and I would not have liked to face him on that level. An unbeatable enemy battalion commander was hard enough for me to deal with, thank you very much."

The General fell silent again.

"Sir, why do the men call you TB?" blurted Hans out suddenly, then bit his tongue as he feared he had pressed too far.

But the General just grinned at him and drawled, "Well, in America, William is often shortened to Bill. And I'm from Texas, you know...."

Texas Bill? Hans shook his head. He would never understand these Americans.

Hans waited respectfully for a while, then clearing his throat, he said self-consciously, "Sir, I wanted to thank you for saving my life. Twice at least now. For saving all our lives. And sorry for the ...ah... trouble we caused. *I* caused."

Prisoner of War

The General was still for a moment, then answered quietly, "No need to thank me, soldier. That's what we're all fighting for here."

"Life itself?" asked Hans tentatively.

"Well, actually, I was going to say freedom," muttered the General, scratching his chin, "but you're right. If there ain't anyone alive to be free, there's no point there either, is there?"

Hans didn't know what to say.

The General spoke again, "If men like Hitler and Stalin want to rule, I've no gripe with that. It's when they want to oppress their own people that I start to take issue. And when they start wanting to oppress *other* people, then that's when I get ready to fight."

Hans held his breath, wondering where the American General was going with this, to mention Hitler and the Soviet leader in the same sentence, in the same way.

The General was speaking softly now, almost to himself, "There will be another war soon. I just don't see how it can be avoided."

Looking at Hans, he said seriously, "You know, I think it's already begun."

Epilogue

9th November 1989—Federal Republic of Germany

The report ended.

The old man turned down the radio, and quickly switched on his television in time to see the special news bulletin that confirmed what the excited radio presenter had announced.

Then he looked outside the window to check the weather. It was chilly, but thankfully not raining. With calm efficiency, he started getting dressed.

Four years shy of his seventieth birthday, he looked at least ten years older. Tireless work rebuilding his country took its toll on his body, but not his mind or spirit.

His thinning blond hair was cut short to military standard and highlighted piercing blue eyes that remained undimmed with age, even though the rest of his face bore the ravages of time.

A large man by any standard, his back was stooped, and he no longer towered over other people like he used to. An arthritic knee gave him trouble in damp weather, and he needed a walking stick to get around, even for short distances. A voice that once commanded warriors to battle was now feeble and frail.

But none of that mattered to him now as he put on his old trousers and shirt. He dusted off a worn, faded overcoat and shrugged it on, then finally reached for the last piece of his attire from the hat rack and stepped out the door.

The sun was bright. The air was cold and bitter, but there was a crispness and freshness to it. The old man walked as quickly as he could toward his objective. The street where he stayed was empty, but when he reached the main road, the crowds had already started to gather and were drifting in the same direction as him.

Many paused and stared at the apparition walking down the central boulevard of the town. An ancient and grizzled soldier in full battle gear making his way to the east. Always to the east. Like a ghost of a past age come to life, the only things that marred the image were the walking stick in his hand instead of a rifle and, most incongruously, a tattered blue sticker on his helmet that vaguely resembled an American flag.

No one called out to him.

No one dared to approach him.

Something in the set of his body spoke of an inescapable mission, and people automatically gave him space.

Soon, as if by some unspoken instinct, the crowd had settled into a rhythm and formed a circle around him like a guard of honor, escorting this strange old man to the destination they all knew he, and they, were heading to.

At last, in the distance, rose the barrier that stretched to the left and right as far as the eye could see. The old man's pace increased as he caught sight of the ugly structure. His breath came in short gasps as his lungs struggled to keep up with the exertion. His face was flushed, and he started perspiring, even in the freezing cold.

Twenty meters from the barrier stood the police cordon. A mixture of small portable fences linked with bright yellow police tape. A large throng, many meters deep, had already gathered in front of the police barricade.

As the old man approached the back of the crowd, he only had to slow his pace slightly as his impromptu escorts streamed ahead of him and gently cleared away other onlookers from his path.

At the police line, Probationary Constable Simmons—young, pink-faced, and only a month into the job—was alert to the approaching would-be intruder and moved to block his path.

But his sergeant, a much older man of great experience, had sensed the shift in the crowd's mood long before he saw anything in the front. With a barely perceptible shake of his head, the senior policeman instructed his junior to let the old man pass.

Probationary Constable Simmons stood aside reluctantly as the crowd opened up like a curtain. The old man reached the police line and marched through like it wasn't there. Yellow tape stretched and snapped and fell to the ground, trampled under size 14 combat boots that better belonged in a museum.

A hush fell over the mob as he walked the last twenty meters to the barrier itself. In the silence that ensued, disorganized singing and cheering could be heard coming from the other side, but all eyes were on the old man as he put one gnarled hand on the wall, feeling its smooth surface.

So cold. So immovable. So uncaring.

He looked at the crowd behind him and drank in the sight of their faces. Young and old, men and women, children scattered here and there. Mixed expressions on their faces.

Curiosity, contempt, pity, compassion... no one single emotion dominated.

But what stood out was that no one was afraid to show what they felt.

Unlike their brethren on the other side.

The old man made up his mind.

He spied a sledgehammer on the floor. Abandoned by some youngsters who tried to use it earlier, but were chased away by the police, it was plain and worn but serviceable. Bony fingers grasped the handle, and the old man hefted the heavy tool over his shoulder with a grunt.

He swung the sledgehammer hard, and it bounced off the wall, leaving only the faintest of marks where it hit.

He swung it again, harder this time, with no perceptible effect.

With a shout of frustration, he lifted the hammer and struck again and again. Within a few blows, he felt tired and spent, but he refused to stop. Like a warrior caught up in battle, he went on, ignoring the warning signs his body was giving him.

A strange calm settled over him as his focus zoomed in on the mark on the wall like a sniper taking aim. His arthritic movements smoothed out, his joints ceased hurting, and his muscles swelled as he swung the hammer repeatedly.

Sweat poured down his face as he found his rhythm. *Clack*, *clack*, *clack*, went the sledgehammer. The steady, relentless pounding pitted the wall's defiance against an old man's stubborn refusal to give up. The years fell away as his worn body found a new life and cadence, striking again and again at the wall.

The initial ferocity of his assault settled into a calculated, ruthless attack to cause maximum damage in the shortest time possible. Decades of pent-up frustration found expression in the cold, controlled fury that now galvanized the old man.

On and on he went, hammering at the unyielding barrier before him with force men half his age would have struggled to muster, let alone sustain for so long. Like a marathon runner getting his second wind, his body found the perfect rhythm, and settled into it.

Every unnecessary movement was forsaken. Every breath was timed to maximize efficiency. Every action was designed to augment the efficacy of each strike.

Unconsciously drawing on old skills honed in battle, the old man made war upon the immovable barrier with a grim determination that knew no surrender.

The crowd was completely silent now, mesmerized and awed.

It seemed like a titan of ancient times walked among them again as the old man stood tall and swung the hammer again and again at the wall. For a while, it seemed he would go on until the wall was rubble at his feet.

Yet, there were physical limits after all.

After three full minutes of relentless pounding, his chest began to hurt. His breath came in short, sharp gasps, and his arms started to cramp.

Nein, nein, nein, NEIN! he thought as his body started to protest against the abuse he was inflicting on it. In a panic, he redoubled his efforts, but that only caused his muscles to seize up quicker as they reached their absolute limits.

His strikes slowed dramatically, then finally they stopped.

He heaved at the hammer but found he could no longer lift it.

It fell with a clang from numb and shaking fingers. Trembling all over, he felt he could no longer even stand. Chest heaving, he staggered as he tried to lift the hammer again and failed.

He dropped to his knees, and the crowd gasped.

Someone called out.

Someone started weeping.

A child wailed.

Soon a confused murmur rose to a rumble as everyone reacted to the awful sight before them.

Hearing the sounds of the crowd, the old man turned around to look at the people behind him and blinked as though seeing them for the first time.

Prisoner of War

Many older men were on their knees, praying and cursing, tears streaming down their faces, eyes looking to heaven in anguish. Younger men bristled and grimaced, furious at the injustice of it all, furious at their own useless tears. They were crying out for him to get up, crying out to him to stop in equal measure.

The women were simply begging for him to stop, burying their faces in their hands or the shoulders of the children they carried as they wept.

Older children who could stand on their own watched in incomprehension, not understanding the rising commotion. But sensing the despair that swept the adults, they burst into tears and added to the increasing clamor.

Even the ordinarily taciturn police officers were weeping openly.

The old man finished looking at the crowd and turned back at the wall.

Tears of despair filled his eyes and streamed down his dust-covered face. He looked at his bloodied hands and shaking thighs. He wasn't sure he could even remain kneeling upright anymore.

He prayed for strength.
He paused to listen.

"Still doing things the hard way, I see," came a calm voice in perfect German from behind him.

The old man jumped and turned around.

Against the glare of the midday sun stood a German Army Major in full military uniform, complete with overcoat and officers visor cap, looking down at him in disapproval.

"Do you have a better idea?" snapped the old man back.

"Yes," came the gentle reply.

"*Wir beginnen es.*"

Then the Major was gone.

The old man pondered the words. Then stiffened as understanding flooded his mind.

We start *it.*

Grasping the sledgehammer and using it as a support, the old man struggled to his feet inch by agonizing inch. Dimly, he was aware of the crowd's noise increasing in volume as uncertain calls for him to stop turned to desperate cries of encouragement.

Then, dragging the sledgehammer behind him and slinging it on his shoulder, he prepared for one last blow.

Prisoner of War

His life flashed through his mind. His youthful pride, the war, the humbling loss, salvation from certain death, and salvation from...something else.

He looked at the wall and spoke to it. "You will fall," he said simply.

"It won't be me to do it."

"It doesn't *have* to be me to do it."

Then he paused and looked at the wall again.

"But you *will* fall."

And with that, he bellowed a war cry and swung the sledgehammer with all his might.

A loud crack resounded. Different from the other ones.

Much louder and more profound.

Like the sound of a tank firing instead of a mere rifle.

In the same instant, a line appeared at the top of the wall and zigzagged down to where the old man had struck it.

The crowd was stunned into silence.

Then the silence was shattered as an earsplitting cry pierced the air.

The people stared in disbelief as Probationary Constable Simmons drew his baton and sprinted forward toward the wall, screaming as he ran. In seconds, he reached it and swung his weapon against the wall so hard that it shattered with a loud crack.

The sound was like a starter's pistol going off.

The crowd roared in response and surged forward as one.

Like an attacking army, they ripped through the police barricades like they weren't even there. The police officers, far from trying to stop the crowd, actually joined in. They all reached the wall quickly and started attacking it with anything they had.

Penknives, umbrellas, walking sticks, even broken remnants of the police barricades were used to attack any part of the wall each person could reach.

They crashed into the wall like an angry ocean. Each wave rolling forward to hit the barricade until penknives broke, umbrellas shattered, and hands bled, then melting back so a fresh wave of bodies could take their turn.

Someone picked up the sledgehammer, and someone else found the other tools. Soon, a steady thudding sound was heard as younger, stronger men found space to swing their hammers and strike the wall.

A DIY shop proprietor opened his shop and started handing out pickaxes, hammers, and drills to eager passers-by, who lined up to add to the assault.

A nearby construction crew quickly packed up their equipment and raced to the site. Soon, jackhammers and JCB diggers joined the fray, adding their destructive power to the growing onslaught against the wall.

A well-placed call to the construction crew's base mobilized yet more equipment, and soon a deep rumble that shook the ground heralded the arrival of bulldozers and cranes with wrecking balls.

Like the coming of tanks to a battle, the massive vehicles were cheered by the crowd as they closed in. The police hastily shifted people away so the heavy machinery had room to work.

A thunderous detonation sounded as the first wrecking ball struck the wall, and bits of mortar and debris flew from the impact point. Again and again, it hit the wall with increasing ferocity as the operator found his range.

Meanwhile, the initially oblivious crowd on the other side of the wall had heard the noises and finally understood. Loud cries broke out as they started attacking the wall from their side.

Soon, there was a steady cacophony of thumping, pounding, and grinding noises up and down the wall. Spaces unoccupied by vehicles and machines were quickly filled by a shouting mob, whose fury remained unsated, and battered the wall with whatever they had.

From where the old man had first struck the wall, a sudden cry of warning sounded, and people scrambled to get clear.

In an instant where time seemed to slow down, wrecking balls from both sides somehow managed to synchronize with each other.

Like graceful aerial acrobats about to perform their greatest stunt, the massive round bulks of iron swung lazily away from the wall and hung in space, suspended for an infinite moment.

Then, they swung back like opposing pendulums and smashed into the wall at precisely the same time.

Already weakened from the relentless assault, the wall could not withstand this final blow. It buckled, sagged, then collapsed on itself with a thunderous crash.

Prisoner of War

A mighty cheer arose from the crowd. The dust plume that ensued rose higher than the wall itself, and for long moments, no one could see anything or get near the broken barricade.

The people formed a large semi-circle around the breach and fell silent as the dust settled. Just in front of the wall, directly in front of the gap, stood the old man, standing tall in his uniform, unbowed by the destruction around him.

No one dared to ask how he got there. It seemed he had stood through the entire fall of the wall without moving.

He remained still as a statue.

Waiting.

A single figure appeared.

Silhouetted against the light that streamed through the gap, it started walking forward hesitantly, tentatively. It slowed as it navigated through a tricky patch of rubble, then resumed its original pace until it cleared the dust cloud, and sunlight shone on it to reveal its features.

It was a little boy.

No more than ten years old, he was blond and blue-eyed—a beautiful child by any measure. He walked forward a bit more, then balked at the apparition before him.

Shane Lee

Standing alone in front of the crowd was a tall, ancient soldier in full German Army garb. His steel-blue eyes met with the boy's, and he nodded slowly.

The boy swallowed hard, then bravely walked on toward the giant ahead of him.

The old man slowly knelt down and opened his arms in welcome.

Then he smiled, a *big* smile that covered his whole face from side to side. His eyes lit up like sapphires, and he opened his mouth and barked a laugh—a short "ha!"—that sounded more like a sneeze, followed by more until he was shouting with joy and laughter.

The little boy's face broke into a huge grin, and he ran forward toward this strange, joyful man and flung himself into his arms, almost pushing the old man over.

The people cheered with approval as they eagerly looked back toward the gap. They saw the boy's parents picking their way through the rubble. And behind them, another family, then a group of young men, then a group of school children helping their grandparents, and behind them, countless others pressing to get through.

The crowd surged forward to meet them with joyous shouts.

Prisoner of War

Long-lost loved ones hugged each other fiercely. Babies were picked up, cuddled, and lifted high into the air in triumph and celebration. Brothers held onto brothers; and sisters, to sisters. Old men dropped their walking sticks to embrace old friends. Children ran through the crowd, laughing with complete abandon, causing all sorts of trouble, but nobody minded.

Complete strangers met, greeted each other, and embraced.

For on that extraordinary day, no one was left alone, no one was a stranger.

The crowd swelled even more as people streamed through the gap from the other side till there was barely any place to stand. Spontaneous singing and dancing broke out as the mood turned decidedly festive. Beer bottles were found and opened, wine uncorked, and champagne sprayed onto onlookers who shrieked in delight.

In the midst of it all, the old man stood in the center of the swirling crowd, still holding the boy in his arms. Of all the people there, theirs was the strangest communion.

No words were exchanged. They simply looked into each other's eyes, and a wealth of understanding passed between them.

In the little boy, the old man saw his life begin anew—fresh, clean, innocent, full of hope. In the old man, the boy saw unimaginable sacrifice and loss, untold pain and suffering, so that he could have this chance to be free.

They said nothing in the middle of the noisy crowd, content to be silent.

The old man looked up in the sky, blinking as his eyes caught the light of the setting sun, and smiled to himself.

He knew it was time.

Closing his eyes, he drifted deep within himself, savoring the overwhelming sense of satisfaction that filled him.

Not for what he had accomplished, if he had accomplished anything at all.

Nor for his redemption—that was freely given and nothing he had earned.

But for the freedom the others now had. That what he had been blessed with so abundantly was finally available to those who never enjoyed it.

The exertions earlier had strained his failing body far beyond its limit.

Now, with the overflowing happiness bubbling around everywhere he looked, his heart literally burst with joy and then settled down to rest. The blood flow slowed until it was insufficient to sustain his legs, and he sagged and collapsed.

So thick was the surrounding crowd that for a moment, he remained standing, held up by the press of bodies around him. But the boy holding his hand sensed something amiss and looked up anxiously.

He cried out in alarm as the old man's knees buckled and gave way, and he slowly sank to the ground.

The boy rushed to kneel beside him, tears streaming down his face as he shook him and called him. Casting around desperately, he looked for any inspiration, any means to stir the old man to get up.

He looked more closely at the uniform and vaguely recognized it to be World War Two garb. Then, dimly recalling his country's checkered history, he shook the old man vigorously.

"*Heil Hitler?*" he cried, unwittingly uttering the near-blasphemy in his desperation to rouse the old man.

The old man's eyes actually opened at that, and he raised one eyebrow and stared at the boy.

"*Heil Hitler?*" repeated the old man incredulously.

"*Nein,*" he said wistfully as his eyes went distant.

"Screw Hitler," he growled softly in mock anger.
His heart's last few beats were soft, slow, and unhurried.
With his final breath, he looked straight into the blue eyes of the boy and whispered,
"*Heil Frieden.*"

Lightning Source UK Ltd.
Milton Keynes UK
UKHW012354231222
414383UK00006B/536